W9-BMU-208

THE POWER OF THE SERPENT

Luke was in another world.

As soon as the serpent band had been fitted onto his arm, he had felt a strange, warm sensation all through his body; then the room about him had disappeared, and he found himself soaring into the sky, faster than a bird of prey. Rising, rising, until he was amongst the stars and looking down upon all the islands. Then something in his vision changed, and he felt a chill.

From five of the islands a cold greyness began to leak into the atmosphere. The fog began to flow in different directions and appeared to be moving at random. Luke tried to stop it, to reach down and halt the evil plague but found himself powerless, remote. Then a pattern emerged and, in his skyborn aerie, Luke shivered.

The banks of fog were coalescing, moving now with an evident purpose. The gigantic spiral flowed slowly but implacably, always moving round, always inwards, until only a small circle remained clear within its serpentine coils. A small circle that would soon be overwhelmed.

At the center of the circle lay Starhill.

Bantam Spectra books by Jonathan Wylie
Ask your bookseller for the ones you have missed

The Servants of Ark Trilogy
Book One: THE FIRST NAMED
Book Two: THE CENTER OF THE CIRCLE

Servants of Ark

B O O K T W O

The Center of the Circle

J O N A T H A N
W Y L I E

BANTAM BOOKS
TORONTO · NEW YORK · LONDON · SYDNEY · AUCKLAND

THE CENTER OF THE CIRCLE
A Bantam Spectra Book / March 1988

All rights reserved.
Copyright © 1988 by Jonathan Wylie.
Cover art copyright © 1988 by Kevin Johnson.
No part of this book may be reproduced or transmitted
in any form or by any means, electronic or mechanical,
including photocopying, recording, or by any information
storage and retrieval system, without permission in writing from
the publisher.
For information address: Bantam Books.

ISBN 0-553-27056-7

Published in the United States

Bantam Books are published by Bantam Books, a division of
Bantam Doubleday Dell Publishing Group, Inc. Its trademark,
consisting of the words "Bantam Books" and the portrayal of
a rooster, is Registered in U.S. Patent and Trademark Office
and in other countries. Marca Registrada. Bantam Books,
666 Fifth Avenue, New York, New York 10103.

PRINTED IN THE UNITED STATES OF AMERICA

KR   0 9 8 7 6 5 4 3 2 1

to John . . .
the best man and the best friend

Prologue

*T*he dolphins thought it was very odd. They had always known that Csonka was not quite like the rest of them, but he had a useful knack of finding food and led their joyful games, so they followed him. However, this latest whim was quite beyond their comprehension. The floating boxes were angular, unnatural. They were not food. Yet the dolphins sensed that there was life in them and this made them strangely uneasy.

For two days now they had shepherded the wood and metal caskets, playing the tides and currents. It was madness, and they were all glad when, at last, they sensed that their task was nearly over. Csonka led them into a crescent bay of a tiny island. Here they left their strange cargo and watched as the waves drove them toward the lonely strand.

Their leader's voice called to them gleefully. He was obviously pleased. None of the others could fathom why. What was more, beneath his happy chatter, Csonka seemed—in some mysterious way—to be talking to someone who wasn't there. Someone perhaps who lived *out-water*. That was so ludicrous a thought that the dolphins soon dismissed it from their minds.

I've brought them!

The dolphin's high-pitched, singsong voice rang with self-satisfaction as it sounded in Ashula's mind.

I thank you, Csonka.

I hope they're what you wanted. They have a bad smell.

I am just a nosy old man, replied the wizard. *Thank you*

for indulging my curiosity. If only it were as simple as that, he added privately.

For you, anything. The dolphin's laugh was carefree but there was love in his voice. *Farewell, air-friend.*

Farewell. Speed fin and tail.

Ashula stood atop a small cliff. As he stared out to sea at the departing school of dolphins, there was a lump in his throat. *It may be the last time I call on your services, Csonka,* he thought. *After all these years.*

He was brought out of his reverie by a tugging at the hem of his cape. The wizard looked down at the small boy who stood beside him. He was some five years old but looked younger, and his sticklike limbs, watery green eyes, and pale complexion gave him an undernourished look.

"What is it, Kubiac?"

"It's cold."

Ashula cursed his own thoughtlessness. He always forgot how keenly his young apprentice felt everything in the world about him. The wizard's ancient bones were protected from the elements by his own unheeded skills, and now he took the boy's hands, letting a small measure of that power warm the delicate frame.

As Kubiac relaxed, the wizard's eyes returned to the sea and the two caskets which now waited on the shingle at the water's edge.

"Are those what we came for?"

"Yes. Can you get down to the beach and bring them up here?"

"Do I have to?"

"I don't think I—"

"But the sea is so cold. My feet will freeze."

Ashula directed a little more power to warm the boy's limbs.

"Go quickly," he said. "I'll warm you as we walk back and when we're home again we'll build a big fire."

Grumbling to himself about wizards who used poor boys when a simple spell would do, Kubiac set off and skittered spiderlike down the steep cliff path. He ran awkwardly across the shingle and timed his rush for the first box to be between waves. He reached it and tried to snatch it up but it was heavier than he expected and he staggered backward. Then the casket kicked in his hands as if it were alive and simultaneously a hoarse cry came from within.

Alarmed, Kubiac dropped the box and sat down involuntarily, just as the next wave surged in, soaking him from head to foot. Cold, wet, and scared, he scrambled up and lifted the now silent box. Anger—at Ashula, at the sea, at this stupid box—warmed him a little and he staggered to the foot of the cliff, then returned for the other. He retrieved that without mishap and carried each in turn to the top of the cliff. The exertion was so great that he grew hot beneath his salt, damp clothes. He waved away the offer of Ashula's hand and set off homeward carrying one of the caskets.

The icy wind soon made him regret his impetuosity and he was shivering uncontrollably when he plunged into the kitchen at Old Walls. Unceremoniously, he dumped the box on the floor and let the room's warmth seep into his body. Shortly afterward Ashula, with the other casket, and Mosi, the matronly cook, entered the kitchen. Both set about getting him out of his wet clothes and into a hot tub before the fire. It was gratifying that they should pay him such attention.

For the moment the caskets were forgotten.

———————————

Mireldi watched the wizard carefully. Ashula had been old when he was a boy, and that was fully sixty years ago! He seemed to have changed little. His wizard's eyes were still bright, an ageless blue. His silver-gray hair and beard were long but well kept. His skin was dark in contrast and the lines on his face were like tidemarks on the sand.

"Babies, you say?" Mireldi's voice shook slightly.

"Yes, your majesty."

"I wish you wouldn't call me that, Ashula. A fine king I am with fewer subjects than fingers."

"The habits of a lifetime are hard to break." Ashula spoke loudly, for both Mireldi and Reveza, his queen, who sat beside him, were partially deaf.

"Boys or girls?" asked the queen, a maternal gleam in her eye.

"Girls, my lady. Alike as twins, and of the same temper."

Both the tiny creatures had been red-faced and screaming ever since their caskets had been opened.

"Changelings?" said Mireldi, almost to himself.

"But how could they have survived? Strock is leagues from anywhere," said the queen.

"A shipwreck perhaps," replied Ashula. "They have remarkable powers of self-preservation. In any case, I feel they were meant to come here."

"Why?"

"I can't explain." *And even if I did you wouldn't believe me*, he added silently.

"Let's have a look at them then," said Mireldi.

Ashula went to the door and ushered in the cook, who carried the babies in the crook of each elbow. After she had overcome the shock of their unorthodox arrival and the unearthly beauty of their violet eyes, the cook had taken a shine to the girls. They were still squalling and she shushed them as she brought them forward.

The wrinkled faces of the babies were blotched with anger and their eyes stared accusingly, first at the wizard, then at the elderly couple. Both Mireldi and his wife drew a sharp breath.

"You see the likeness?" said Ashula, though their faces had already answered his question. Apart from the color of their eyes, both the girls looked remarkably like the king and queen's own daughter as a baby. She was long dead, drowned in an accident that scarred their memories still.

"We have no one to nurse them,"-said Reveza.

"Oh, we'll manage, ma'am," replied the cook. "The old cow produces more milk than we use these days. Shhh now, loves."

"You agree to keep them here then?" said Ashula.

They all eyed him curiously.

"Such tiny things wouldn't be a bother," said the cook. She smiled as the babies quieted down a little.

"We can't put them back to sea," said Reveza.

"It's not as if we don't have space for them." The king smiled, thinking of the dozens of empty rooms about them.

"This place could do with some young blood," said the cook. "Begging your pardons," she added, blushing.

"You're right there, Mosi," said Mireldi, laughing.

"They'll be like our own," whispered the queen.

Ashula sighed with relief.

Back in his own rooms, the wizard checked on Kubiac. The

boy had taken a chill and his forehead was hot, but he was sleeping peacefully enough. Ashula left him and went to his study.

Sitting at his desk, he took a parchment from an inconspicuous drawer and spread it out before him. His own neat handwriting looked back at him. Well he remembered copying out these words, long, long ago. The inscription in the stone had still been readable then, though he had had to scrape off age-old lichen to make out some of the letters. Now the stone itself was starting to crumble, eaten away by wind and rain. No one else would ever decipher the message at the tomb's door. But then no one else would need to.

How often had he pondered these enigmatic words? He glanced again at the top of the page. Now at last it began to make sense.

From the sea, peril.
From the sea, safety.

From the twain, one.
From the one, release.

But which one? he wondered. Receiving no answer, he read on.

Silver spiral, black as night,
Turning ever, ever still.
Circle's center at its edge,
Serpent's head upon its tail.

Evil's heir in chains set free
Shall chain the sun to break the link.
From ages past, the golden coil
Shall bring to life the quiet star.
Loving faith shall be the test
To stand within the whirlpool's eye.

PART ONE

Ark

Chapter 1

"*W*e're in sight of Starhill, my lord."

Pabalan glanced thankfully at the soldier who rode beside the royal carriage.

"The Stars be praised," Heald's king replied. "I'm being boiled alive in here."

He leaned out of the window and, looking forward, caught a glimpse of Starbright Tower. This was a slender column of smooth stone which rose from the center of Starhill Castle, which was itself at the center of the city. The tower gleamed in the fierce summer sunlight.

Pabalan turned back to his wife, who sat opposite him on the quilted seats.

"I can't think why you made me wear all this stuff, Adesina," he grumbled, running a finger around the inside of his ceremonial collar.

"Pabalan, you know perfectly well that you were the one who insisted on the outfit," the queen replied. "We will be there soon. And you do look splendid," she added guilefully. Her smile was echoed by that of the lady-in-waiting beside her, until she met the king's red-faced glare.

Pabalan grunted. "It's not every day we arrive at another royal court, I suppose," he said.

"Especially one where your daughter is queen."

"True," he replied quietly. "I still wish we didn't have to travel in this heat."

Pabalan leaned out of the window again.

"Can't we go any faster?" he yelled.

The visitors entered Starhill, the capital of the island of Ark, by the Sea Gate. It was one of five entrances equally spaced around the circular walls of the city and was so named because the road which led from it ran directly to Grayrock Harbor, Ark's main port. Pabalan's flagship, *The Ram*, had docked there the day before, after the five-day journey from Heald.

Once within the city they traveled along the straight road to the center, then circled to the left to the city square where the main gate of the castle stood. The huge wooden gates stood open and the party rode within, finally coming to a halt in a large courtyard. Before them stood the circular inner wall and within that Starbright Tower rose to dizzying heights.

As Pabalan and Adesina were alighting from the carriage and their escorts were dismounting, the gate in the inner wall opened and a young man ran nimbly down the steps toward them. He was simply dressed and of average build, but there was an aura of strength about him that was immediately apparent. His brown eyes were keen and his suntanned face spoke of glowing health.

How he's changed, thought Pabalan. *Two years ago he seemed just a boy*.

"Greetings, Pabalan. Welcome to Ark."

The young man's smile was warm and his grip was firm as he clasped the older man's hand.

"Greetings, Mark. It is good to be here."

Adesina joined them. "Hello, Mark."

"Welcome, Adesina." He kissed her on the cheek. "You're looking well. Kingship and fatherhood must suit you."

"In some ways," Mark replied, still smiling. "I am sorry I wasn't able to welcome you personally earlier. I hope the journey from Grayrock was pleasant."

"Fine," said Pabalan.

"Come and meet—" began Mark, but as he spoke, he became aware that his audience's attention was elsewhere.

Both Pabalan and Adesina were looking past him at the top of the stairs to the inner courtyard. Mark turned and laughed aloud.

On the top step stood a huge man dressed only in light-colored trousers. The sunlight reflected from his bald pate and the muscles of his massive shoulders. His hands held the feet of a small boy who was seated on his shoulders. Despite being far enough from the ground to cause vertigo in some adults, the child seemed quite at ease. In fact he made no effort to hold on to his mount but had, until that moment, been brandishing the curious combination of a small wooden sword and a miniature broom, one in each hand. He had also been yelling nonsense syllables, but when he saw the newcomers he fell silent, his arms still above his head. His face solemn, he stared intently at the people below him, as if weighing them up. The boy's eyes were a golden amber color, strangely beautiful, and their gaze was echoed by the dark brown eyes of the man who carried him.

Adesina saw an uncanny understanding flicker between those two pairs of eyes. Then the boy smiled.

"Your grandson has grown somewhat since you saw him last," said Mark. "Luke, come and say hello to your grandparents from Heald."

"That's Jani, isn't it?" said Pabalan quietly, as the big man came down the steps.

"Yes," replied Mark. "He's become a sort of guardian to Luke."

Jani lowered his charge to the ground, then took the toys from him. In his huge hands they looked like matchsticks.

Luke looked up at the new faces, a slight question in his eyes. Feeling distinctly self-conscious in front of so many people, Pabalan was not sure what he should do and was very grateful when Luke solemnly extended his hand. His tiny fingers curled round Pabalan's bulky forefinger and they shook hands, mimicking the earlier greeting with Mark. A murmur of amused approval rose from the watching members of the Healdean party and castle folk. Pabalan's face reddened slightly, but he could not help but smile as well.

Luke turned to Adesina, who squatted down and held out both hands. He took them and the queen felt the steady pressure of those remarkable eyes.

"Hello, young man. I see you have the manners of a prince already."

"He's not always so well-behaved," Mark said.

"I should hope not," replied Adesina. "That would be too good to be true."

"Meaning, I suppose, that no son of mine could possibly be well-mannered," said a new voice from the steps.

They looked up. Fontaine, princess of Heald, now queen of Ark, stood in the gateway, her green eyes sparkling with amusement. Her loose-fitting dress did nothing to hide the swelling beneath. Luke was soon to have a baby brother or sister.

"Mama," cried Luke, and set off toward her.

Fontaine started down the steps and Mark, among others, moved quickly to offer her assistance.

"I'm not *totally* incapable, you know," she said, good-naturedly waving him away. With Luke now holding her hand, she came up to her father.

"Hello," she said quietly. "It's good to see you."

Pabalan said nothing but hugged her gingerly before passing her on to Adesina.

"Hello, my love. How are you?"

"I'm fine, Mother. Just a bit slow on my feet these days."

"You look lovely. When . . . ?"

"About two months, I think. But if it's anything like this one"—she indicated Luke—"then it could be later. You are going to stay, aren't you?"

"Of course."

Mark noticed Pabalan's distaste at the turn of the conversation.

"You must be thirsty after the journey. Come and have a drink."

His father-in-law's face lit up.

As the royal family went their separate ways, the job of installing the newcomers in their accommodation proceeded with much bustle and chatter. Baggage was unloaded, horses led off to the stables, and introductions made.

Adesina's lady-in-waiting supervised the queen's personal luggage. A soldier in the livery of the Castle Guard approached her.

"At your service, ma'am. My name is Richard." He smiled.

She eyed him appreciatively.

"I'm Sophi. Can you show me where the queen's rooms will be?"

"Of course. Is all the unloading complete?"

"All but this," she said, reaching into the carriage and taking a small bag from beneath the seat.

"Let me carry that for you."

"No!" she replied quickly. "This is mine." Then she added more gently, "I can manage it. It's not heavy."

Richard looked at her quizzically, then smiled and said, "Let's go then."

They walked out of the courtyard, followed by several porters.

"I trust you had a pleasant journey."

"Yes, but it will be good to stay in one place for a while and not have the floor swaying up and down."

"Well, if there is anything I can do to make your stay here more comfortable, let me know."

Their eyes met.

"I will," Sophi replied. "Thank you."

They continued walking and the moment passed.

"Wasn't Moroski supposed to be coming with you?" asked Richard. "I haven't seen him."

"He'll be here tomorrow. He stayed in Grayrock on business of his own today. Don't ask me what."

"Wizards are a mysterious breed."

"Do you know him?"

"We met two years ago," said Richard, "but we had other things on our minds at the time. I didn't get to know him well."

"I don't think anyone knows him well, except possibly Adesina. He comes and goes as he pleases. Like that bird of his."

"Here are your quarters," said Richard, opening a door.

———

Some ten leagues to the east of Starhill, the subject of this conversation sat at a table outside a tavern overlooking the docks of Grayrock Harbor. Beyond the clutter of masts and rigging, hoists and signal poles, stretched the vast expanse of the harbor itself. Linked to the sea by a deep but narrow channel known as The Shoot, and protected by vast granite headlands, it was ideal for shipping. Grayrock was a thriving trading post with vessels departing to and arriving from other islands almost every day.

Moroski watched the activity about him but his thoughts

were elsewhere. He had hoped to meet an old friend that day—or at least receive a message from him—but he had been disappointed in both respects. There was a feeling of unease in his stomach that even the excellent ale he sipped slowly did nothing to quiet.

Thus, he found himself with nothing to do for the rest of the day. Even if he set out now it would be well after dusk by the time he reached Starhill, and he had no wish to ride over unfamiliar roads in the dark. Of course, he could have overcome that problem had he wished to, but wizards rarely chose to expend their hard-won power for such petty reasons.

So he whiled away the time in unaccustomed idleness. Nobody bothered him, not even the landlord who might ordinarily have been tempted to request such an unprofitable customer to move on. The reasons for this were twofold. Firstly, although he was not armed, Moroski gave the impression of being quite capable of looking after himself. Secondly, anybody who ventured too close came under the scrutiny of the wizard's companion. The falcon perched on the back of the chair next to her master. She was not hooded and the fierce eyes and wickedly curving beak were in full view.

Even the toughest of sailors gave her a wide berth.

Chapter 2

Fontaine and Adesina sat in the relative cool of the royal apartments. Mother and daughter had not seen each other since Luke's birth nearly two years earlier and they had a lot to talk about. Luke sat between them for a while but soon got bored and made periodic forays to other parts of the room, making considerable noise. However, nothing actually got broken, and Luke made no protest over his frequent tumbles.

"He's a hardy little individual, isn't he," said Adesina.

"Once he became mobile there was no point in trying to stop him. He never seems to mind a few bruises and Jani's almost always with him to make sure he doesn't do himself any serious harm."

"Jani was one of the outlaws who helped you, wasn't he?"

"Yes."

"He's very big."

"But incredibly gentle. Jani's been a very good friend to me." Fontaine smiled at the memories that flashed through her mind. "He dotes on Luke as well. The two of them have a kind of understanding, I think."

"I noticed."

"Even though Jani can't speak or hear—and Luke's vocabulary isn't very advanced yet—they seem to be able to communicate quite easily."

"He's not exactly the picture of a traditional nursemaid!"

"Luke doesn't need a nursemaid," said Fontaine, laughing, "and no one's going to threaten him with Jani around."

"I would like to get to know him better if I can," said Adesina. "I hardly saw him on my previous visits."

They were both silent for a while, thinking back to Fontaine's marriage to Mark and Luke's subsequent arrival. The fact that the two events had been separated by only six months had caused Pabalan some disquiet, but everyone else had accepted it readily enough, given the peculiar circumstances of the couple's courtship.

"For such an imposing figure, Jani can be quite inconspicuous," said Fontaine thoughtfully. "We take him for granted now, I suppose." After a moment, she added, "For so long he lived alone. Even though in the forest he was surrounded by other men, he was isolated from them and they ignored his humanity. Jani has a great capacity for love and when I came along he finally got the chance to show it. With Luke it's even more obvious."

"And soon Luke will have a brother."

"Mark's convinced it will be a girl."

"Men usually think that they will produce sons."

"I don't mind either way, but Mark seems certain. He knew Luke would be a boy." *So did I*, she added silently, *but that is too complicated to explain.*

"Perhaps all that magical training Ferragamo gave Mark has paid off," said Adesina. "He's made a seer of him."

Perhaps, thought Fontaine.

Aloud she said, "That or the moonberries!"

They laughed together.

"You're still eating them then?"

"Of course. Ferragamo insisted."

"You don't think it might . . ." Adesina's voice trailed off as she indicated her daughter's expanding girth.

"It didn't do Luke any harm, and I was eating a lot more of them when I was carrying him."

"That's true." The birth, Adesina remembered, had been remarkably easy for a first child, especially considering her daughter's slight build. "I'm just fussing like a proper grandmother should."

Their conversation was interrupted by a knock at the door. At Fontaine's invitation a woman came into the room. While not exactly pretty, there was a homely beauty about her that made her attractive to both men and women. Adesina recognized her immediately.

"Hello, Koria. I thought you must be away with Ferragamo."

"No, he's off on his own for once. Up in the mountains. It's good to see you again, Adesina."

The two women embraced briefly.

"We were just talking about the moonberries," said Fontaine. "Koria makes sure the kitchens use the right amounts," she added to her mother.

"The famous cake."

"Aye, well, it certainly made a difference in that business," said Koria. "And it's good to restore some of the old traditions."

"Especially when Ferragamo insists on it," teased Fontaine.

"As to that," replied Koria, smiling, "I can talk him out of most of his foolish ideas but I wouldn't even try about this. I know how important he thinks it is. Besides, it certainly tastes good."

"It does," confirmed Fontaine. "It's still a treat after two years."

"How often do you eat it?"

"About once a week. We pick a couple of berries and that makes enough for everyone in the castle. It must be about right as the tree seems to replace the fruit at that rate."

"We do much the same in Heald. You wouldn't think that six berries would go that far," said Adesina.

"Any more than that and we'd all run the risk of hopping around like lunatics," said Fontaine.

"The magic in them is very strong." Koria had a faintly disapproving tone in her voice. "I've seen some of the effects."

"Of course, I forgot. Ferragamo ate a whole berry once," said Adesina.

"It nearly killed him," said Koria, the memory painful in her brown eyes. "And he's a *wizard*."

"He was certainly very strange for a long time," added Fontaine. "And he's odd enough at the best of times." She grinned mischievously at Koria, who pretended to be mortally offended.

"Queen or no," she bridled, "I'll not have you insulting the love of my life." She paused. "However odd he is."

Their laughter was interrupted by a loud crash from the other side of the room. Luke had clambered onto a table, toppling a chair in the process, and was now busily sweeping the top with his miniature broom.

"Domesticated already, I see," said his grandmother.

"He's more enthusiastic than effective, I'm afraid," answered Fontaine. She stood slowly and went over to her son.

"Down from there, Luke. You're supposed to sweep the *floor.*" She scooped him up and deposited him below. As she straightened up she groaned.

"I feel so weak since I stopped training."

"Since you stopped *what?*" said Adesina.

"Training. With swords."

"Oh."

"Don't look so surprised. I started a long time ago. It helped me a lot after Luke was born and after that it became a habit, I suppose. It helps me stay lean and supple—as you can see," she added ruefully, running her hands over her swelling midriff.

A nearby room hosted another conversation. Pabalan had loosened his collar and was already on his fourth glass of iced wine. Mark, who knew himself well enough not to try and keep pace, sipped gently at his second. The first had disappeared quickly in a flurry of toasts to Luke's imminent second birthday, to the arrival of the new baby and so on. Mark could see that his father-in-law was embarrassed when talking about children. He came close to being contemptuous about "women's business," and so they passed on quickly to other topics.

Pabalan for his part was impressed by Mark's bearing, the new stature he carried so naturally. He was very different from the nervous and somewhat slight-looking young man he had last met. He was still young but, as Adesina had surmised, the responsibilities of family and of ruling the island had developed his character. The elder king found himself feeling more and more at ease with his junior counterpart.

They began to reminisce about the time when Mark had been forced into fighting to regain his kingdom from the evil sorceress, Amarino, who had been responsible for the deaths of his father and two elder brothers. To Pabalan's chagrin, his own part in the action had been restricted to a show of force at sea which diverted attention from the real struggle in Starhill. However, he enjoyed discussing those dramatic and violent events and wanted to know about the various soldiers he had met after their eventual victory.

"Shill is captain of the Castle Guard now. You'll meet him at dinner tonight."

"Good man, that," said Pabalan.

"He is," Mark agreed. "He's married to Anna now, of course. Bonet had wed too. There were quite a spate of weddings after that business with Amarino." Unconsciously Mark slipped into Pabalan's way of referring to the earlier conflict.

"Ansar's married as well," said Pabalan gruffly, referring to his son. "Rivera's a good girl. Maybe it will settle him down a bit. I've left Laurent with him on Heald in any case, just to make sure he doesn't do anything stupid while I'm away."

"He'll not lack for good advice then," said Mark, recalling his own dealings with the courtier's sharp intelligence. "And it is good to have a wife to rely on. They seem to see things so much more clearly. I'm sure you know what I mean."

"I do," said Pabalan gravely, "but it doesn't do to let *them* know that. Eh?" His gnarled face broke into a broad smile.

Quite right too! The agreement came silently and directly into Mark's mind. *Let them get their claws into you and you're lost.*

Longfur, Mark retorted mentally, *you know as well as I do that you are insufferably proud of your kittens. And you wouldn't have them without Penelope.*

True, came the response, *but one should preserve one's independence.*

Longfur sidled out from behind the chair and curled around Mark's feet. His black and white fur tended to stick out at odd angles but he carried himself with a cat's natural grace and the dignity of one whose abilities extended not only to looking at a king but talking to him as well.

Pabalan noticed the arrival.

"Confounded animals get everywhere," he said. "Mouser, is he?"

You can go off some people.

Be quiet, Longfur. I can't be expected to talk to both of you at once. Aloud, Mark said, "Oh, Longfur's one of the family. I couldn't have defeated Amarino without him."

"I remember," said Pabalan. "Your secret weapon, wasn't he? Must be a clever little blighter."

Can I bite him now or later?

You'll do nothing of the sort, replied Mark hurriedly, as he tried to stifle a laugh. *Can't you accept praise when you hear it?*

"Something go down the wrong way?" asked Pabalan as Mark tried to take a swallow of wine and nearly choked.

"No, no. It's all right."

Mollified, Longfur lay down and was soon purring in his sleep.

"What about that chap, what's his name, the outlaw fellow?"

"Jani?"

"No. I know him. The other one."

"Durc, you mean."

"That's the one. Mean-looking character, as I recall."

"He and Zunic grew tired of city life. After they'd helped us beat Amarino they became great friends with Hoban. You remember, the ambassador from Peven. He was on the fleet with you."

"Oh, yes."

"When Hoban returned to his home-isle he left a standing invitation for them to visit Peven as his guests. A few months ago they finally overcame their qualms about seasickness and set sail. I made them special emissaries of a sort. I've no idea when we'll see them again."

Some time later Mark suggested that they go to their separate quarters, as dinner would be served shortly.

"I'll send someone in the morning to tell Ferragamo you're here," said Mark as they went out.

"In Home, is he?" asked Pabalan, referring to the village in the south of the island.

"No, he's in the mountains, staying with Shalli."

"The mad hermit?"

"That's him," said Mark. *There's a lot more I could tell you about Shalli,* he thought, *but that will have to wait.*

Chapter 3

$\mathcal{A}$s always happened, the peace of the high mountains had flowed gently into Ferragamo's entire being. Since his first meeting with Shalli, the wizard had visited his remarkable cave on several occasions. He always went alone and brought nothing with him save his clothes, his horse, and his familiar, Owl. The hermit's retreat was the only place Ferragamo visited without Koria, with whom he shared everything else. He worried sometimes that she might resent his unwillingness to take her with him, but Koria had long since come to understand that Ferragamo and Shalli were brothers in spirit, communicating on planes she could not even begin to comprehend. She missed her dear wizard, but his absences lasted only a few days, and he always returned invigorated and so full of love for her that their time apart was soon forgotten.

Ferragamo could never quite explain why the time spent in the mountains had such a profound effect on him. It was not as if he were able to leave his worldly concerns behind him. Being free of other distractions, he spent a lot of his time pondering the problems and challenges his position in Starhill presented. He found the calmness of his surroundings enhanced his mental dexterity. There were other reasons of course. The beautiful landscape, the pure, cold air, the unexpected pleasures of the hermit's cave, and the quiet, undemanding friendship of Shalli himself all contributed to his relaxation.

Yet there was something more, something indefinable. Perhaps it stemmed from the fact that he and the hermit shared an experience that would have killed most men. Both of them

had, for their own reasons, risked both life and sanity in
trying to harness the ancient magical power of moonberries.
Perhaps it was their shared visions of what might be and what
should be; visions that were shared without words, without
conscious knowledge. Perhaps it was just their natural affinity.

Whatever it was, Ferragamo was grateful for it, and always
felt a wrench when the time came for him to reenter the
world.

Had there been anyone to see them, they would have presented an amusing spectacle. As was their habit on clear
days, the wizard and the hermit sat cross-legged on top of the
sheer cliff which protected one approach to the cave entrance. Both stared dreamily into the distance, but it would
have been impossible to tell whether they saw the glittering,
snow-decked panorama before them or whether they were in
worlds of their own.

Shalli was covered from head to foot in shapeless garments.
All were made from mountain-goat skins, making it difficult
to tell where one ended and another began. The natural
coloring of the skins gave him a piebald appearance. Ferragamo's clothes were more conventionally made but the coloring was even more eccentric. Greens dominated the color
scheme, matching his eyes, but there were flashes of blue
and red as well. He was bare-headed and his hair, kept
habitually very short, was pure white. Owl perched on his
leather-padded shoulder.

They were silent, and content to be so.

As he did so often, Ferragamo mentally reviewed the events
of the last few years and his plans for the immediate future.
The wizard knew that the defeat of Amarino was only the first
battle in a much larger conflict. He was convinced that the
island of Brogar, far to the west, was under the control of the
evil which had tried to invade Ark. Until that evil was eradi-
cated, it was only a matter of time until it began to reach out
once more. And, he believed, every month that went by
meant that the power they faced grew in strength and malig-
nancy. A shudder ran through the wizard's body as he remembered the first tentative attempt to investigate what was
happening on Brogar. That had taken place soon after Luke's
birth. Now the prince's second birthday celebrations were

approaching and Ferragamo's plans for the next attempt were only just coming to fruition. He hoped.

There was nothing more he could do now in any case. The wheels of wizardry turned at their own pace—slowly. Ferragamo smiled at the thought and moved on to more pleasant reminiscences. He recalled Mark's coronation and his marriage to Fontaine. The two events had, at Mark's insistence, been combined in one relatively simple ceremony. He had been persuaded to agree to a few of the normal trappings of such public occasions, but his unexpectedly mature bearing and unpretentious nature had made a deep impression on many. The people of Starhill, who were, after three months, still reeling from the horror of the fate from which they had so narrowly escaped, took the young king to their hearts. In the two years since then he had done nothing to change their minds, and Luke, in the way of royal babies, had enhanced the family's popularity.

Ferragamo sometimes missed the old Mark, the boy who had been the wizard's devoted pupil, intelligent but timid. Since the death of his mother, when Mark was still only an infant, he had been almost a son to Ferragamo and Koria— the son that they could never have. Now he had grown up and the wizard felt a father's loss.

You're a foolish old man, Ferragamo admonished himself. *He is a boy no longer; an inevitable and necessary fact. Just thank the stars he still listens to your advice!*

Owl shifted on his shoulder, then took to the air, swooping silently down toward the trail below their vantage point. Roused from his reverie, Ferragamo's thoughts turned to more mundane matters. He glanced at his companion and, still without speaking, they rose simultaneously and walked back toward the cave.

Even after repeated visits Ferragamo still marveled at Shalli's cave. Two years ago it had been a refuge first for the wizard and then for Mark and his company as they made their way toward Starhill and the confrontation with Amarino. Ferragamo's memories of that time were hazy but he recalled the others' amazement when presented with this unexpected haven. The party and their horses had walked up the grassy bank that led from the trail to the small plateau, green even when lower slopes were covered with snow. Shortly afterward, a raging blizzard had made all movement impossible.

Yet within the cave the entire party—over twenty men, one woman, and their horses—had been accommodated in comfort.

The branching cave system was magically lit from within the rock, needing only a word from Shalli to bring the stone chambers to life. A main tunnel led into the mountain, sloping slightly upward with many caverns of various sizes on either side. Even Ferragamo had not explored them all, but within their number were a "stable" where even the most nervous horses seemed at home, a "kitchen" which swallowed smoke and steam indifferently, a "bathroom" fed by a constant supply of hot water from a spring—there was a cold-water supply elsewhere—sleeping quarters, storerooms, and many more. Within, the air was humid and warm all year round.

It was no wonder that, despite several invitations to the court, Shalli had chosen to remain in his mountain home. As nobody, except those who had been in the original party, knew where the cave was, there was little chance of the hermit's chosen solitude being disturbed.

Long after he had come to take all the other wonders for granted, Ferragamo was still at a loss to explain the way in which Shalli's stores always seemed to be full. Even at the bleakest time of the year there would always be dried meat and vegetables, grain and nuts, salt and honey, even cheeses. The hermit, whose speech was so vague as to be almost unintelligible at the best of times, was particularly enigmatic about the matter, saying only that it came from "trading." Ferragamo never met any of the traders.

Owl solved part of the mystery for him when he reported that the mountain eagles were friends of the hermit and often left offerings—a rabbit or a salmon perhaps. That, and the obvious fact that the mountain goats also provided milk, cheese, and skins led the wizard to consider the possibilities of contributions from other animals. He knew, from personal experience, that squirrels could provide nuts, perhaps grain as well. The few bears that roamed the wilder parts of Ark might well be the bringers of honey. It all seemed highly unlikely, but no more so than many other facets of Shalli's life. Certainly the hermit has an uncanny affinity with all forms of wildlife, and seemed to converse with them all. Ferragamo, who had only ever been able to talk to Owl—

apart from one occasion—was not envious. The price Shalli had paid was a high one.

Though his communication with animals was remarkable, Shalli had great difficulty in his relationships with human beings. Many years ago, in fact centuries ago, his experiments with moonberries had, in the eyes of most men, driven him insane. Once he had been a wizard with a standing comparable to Ferragamo's own, but he had, perforce, become a wanderer, a vagabond lunatic. For years he crossed and recrossed Ark, taking every opportunity to espouse his theories. Any audience would do, whether it was a crowd in a marketplace or a lonely shepherd. His passionate oratory took the form of a call to action, a rousing harangue that moved many and amused some. The only problem was that his prophetic language was all but incomprehensible. Nobody could make head or tail of it. And when he ended with the habitual words which earned him his name, there were few who could take him seriously. Disillusioned, Shalli started to avoid the centers of population and became a recluse, appearing infrequently to berate startled groups of travelers with his fiery words.

And so he was lost from view, and the tale of the mad hermit whose speeches always ended "Shall I shut up now?" passed into the folklore of the island, a story to be told to disbelieving children, to make them laugh, and frighten them a little.

Chapter 4

"**H**e's not here then?"

"No. He's in the mountains with Shalli, but he'll be back soon. I sent Richard off this morning to tell him your company had arrived."

The late afternoon sun remained powerful, and within the courtyard the air was still and very warm. Mark and Moroski walked slowly from the stables, where the wizard had just left his horse, toward the food hall.

"Well, I have a lot to talk to him about," said Moroski, "but a few more days won't make any difference."

"The conclave?"

"What else?"

"How are the preparations going?"

"I wish I knew. Things seem to go well for a while, and then we are faced with some unexpected setback. There have been so many delays already, I'll believe it's going to happen when they're all here."

The two men entered the hall. Within the stone walls the air was refreshingly cool, despite the golden sunlight slanting down from the high windows. Tapestries and shields adorned the walls but the furniture within was functional and solid. They sat at the huge round table and Mark poured the traveler a mug of ale from the jug that had been placed there for them. The wizard took a long draft.

"Thank you. That's good," he said, wiping flecks of foam from his upper lip.

"Water for Atlanta?" asked Mark. The falcon had left the wizard's shoulder and was perched on the back of a chair.

"She'll find her own," replied Moroski complacently. "Besides, the heat doesn't affect her in the same way."

Mark glanced at the bird, taking pleasure in her fierce, streamlined form. He saw Atlanta's attention focus on something in a nearby doorway. Turning, he saw nothing at first but then a familiar "voice" made him lower his gaze.

It's quite safe, Mark heard Longfur say. *She won't hurt you. And besides, no son of mine should be afraid of a* bird.

Various scuffling noises came from the doorway. Moroski heard, and glanced round.

"Hello, Longfur," he said, and then added to Mark, "I see you're not the only one who has gained a family since I was here last."

Longfur walked into the room. Beside him, almost *underneath* him, was a small kitten.

"Longfur sends his greetings," said Mark, "and asks me to introduce his son Muscles."

The tiny bundle of fur came into view. He was a miniature version of his father, with the same green eyes and black and white fur. The only part of his mother's coloring he had inherited were four reddish-brown paws, which always made him appear as if he had been paddling in mud. He looked up at Atlanta, with fur bristling and his tail erect.

"He's the smallest of the litter, and the fiercest," said Mark, smiling. "The others are much better looking. They take after Penelope."

You obviously are no judge of catlike qualities, Longfur retorted in Mark's mind. *In due course Muscles will be as fine an example of feline virility as I am myself. Though I must admit that you are right about Penelope's beauty.*

The lady in question made her entrance, trailed by her other three offspring. She was a sleek and elegant tabby, mostly brown, with languid, almost yellow eyes.

I can't think what she sees in you, commented Mark silently.

She has better taste than some I could mention.

Just make sure she doesn't get her claws into you.

Very witty, came the sarcastic rejoinder. *Remind me not to ask your advice on family matters sometime.*

Mark laughed and Moroski looked around.

"Can we share the joke?" he asked, amusement twinkling in his dark eyes.

"Sorry," said Mark. "We were just comparing notes on our

respective families. Speaking of which, you've not met Luke yet, have you? He's quite a young man already."

That's a matter of opinion.

"I'll go and fetch him," Mark went on, ignoring the interruption. "You'll be all right here for a while?"

Moroski's smile broadened. "Oh, yes," he said, reaching for the ale jug. "Perfectly all right."

Longfur followed Mark out into the sunshine, leaving Muscles to face Atlanta's unnerving stare by himself. The kitten stood his ground for a few moments, then scuttled back to the security of his mother's side.

In the courtyard, Jani sat on the lower part of the steps which led up to the tree-yard within the inner wall. His expression was slightly gloomy, but he seemed pleased by Mark's approach.

What's wrong with Jani? Mark asked Longfur, having become used to the fact that his cat could communicate with the deaf-mute man. It was not, as Longfur had tried to explain, a two-way link like the one he shared with Mark, but feelings and a certain amount of intuitive information could pass between them. Even Longfur did not understand the process, but was content with the fact that it has occasionally proved useful, and was a pleasure for the permanently silent Jani.

He's all right, replied Longfur. *He's just a bit peeved that his position as princely playmate has been usurped.*

Jani glared at the cat, then grinned broadly and gestured up at the entrance to the tree-yard. This was Luke's favorite playground. The inner sanctum of the castle held the precious moonberry tree, the only one on Ark as there was only one on each of the islands. Beyond the tree was the base of Starbright Tower, or the Wizard's Tower as it was commonly known. Even though the upper levels were out of bounds to anyone unless accompanied by Ferragamo, the lower tower was full of fascinating things and many nooks and crannies which Luke found irresistible.

As Mark climbed the steps, some instinct made him move quietly. Standing in the shadows of the gateway at the top, he peered within. What he saw almost caused him to burst out laughing, but he stifled it and drew back into the shadows.

Within, flat on his back on the stone-flagged floor, Pabalan lay with an inane grin on his face. Astride his broad chest sat Luke, his hands curled in his grandfather's short, bristly beard. As Mark watched, Luke pulled on the hair with both hands, as if holding reins, and clicked his tongue.

"Clip-clop, Granna. Clip-clop!" he yelled.

Pabalan's eyes widened. He grimaced comically.

"Oooh! Aaah! That hurts," he exclaimed exaggeratedly. "All right. I'll be your horse, but you'll have to learn to treat your charger better than that."

Large hands lifted the boy to one side, then Pabalan maneuvered his considerable bulk until he was on all fours. Luke mounted his charger, his hands gripping tightly to its collar and yelling gibberish as Pabalan shuffled off round the yard.

"Charge!" shouted the king of Heald, his voice sounding slightly strangulated.

This is the man who doesn't really like children, who can hardly bring himself to speak about babies! thought Mark.

Grandparents are all the same, responded Longfur, who had climbed the steps as well.

All? You'll be one yourself before too long.

I was referring to human grandparents, naturally. They are shameless.

All the same, I think it would be better if we did not admit to being witnesses to this particular scene.

You may rely on my discretion, Longfur said pompously.

They tiptoed back down the steps and, with a shrug of resignation to Jani, Mark made his way back to the hall. Moroski had been joined in the meantime by Fontaine and Adesina. Penelope and the kittens were nowhere to be seen.

"Where's this son of yours then?" asked Moroski.

"He's rather involved in a game at the moment," replied Mark. "You'll meet him soon enough."

"Jani keeps him amused for hours," said Fontaine.

And not only Jani, was Longfur's parting comment as he went in search of his mate.

Some time later, Moroski stretched and said, "If you'll excuse me now, I'd like to go to my chamber to wash and change."

"Come and say hello to Luke first," said Fontaine. "They must have finished their game by now."

They went out into the courtyard. Jani was dozing in the

same place, but he roused himself as they approached, and stood up. He towered over them all, even the tall wizard.

"Is Luke inside?" said Mark loudly, hoping Pabalan would hear and be warned of their approach. Fontaine looked at him a little oddly. Jani, of course, remained silent.

All five climbed the steps and clustered in the doorway just in time to hear Pabalan say, "Give it to Grandpa. There's a good boy."

"He's not a *dog*, Father," said Fontaine, but her light-hearted laugh disappeared when Pabalan turned a worried face toward her.

"What's the matter?"

"He's picked one of the fruit from the tree," said Pabalan. "I couldn't stop him."

All eyes turned toward Luke's tightly clenched right fist.

"Don't let him—" began Mark.

Luke, wearing his uniquely solemn expression, looked at their worried faces. Suddenly, he smiled happily and put the moonberry in his mouth.

"No!" screamed Fontaine. "Stop him!"

Before anyone could move, Luke bit down hard and swallowed. His eyes opened wide in surprise, and flashed with golden fire. Then, still smiling, he sank to the floor, as if all his bones had suddenly turned to water.

Luke lay beneath the tree, as still as death.

Chapter 5

*F*or a few moments nobody moved, the silence more terrible than the anguished cry which had preceded it. Then everybody moved at once, clustering around the inert body. Luke's golden eyes were still open and they glowed unnaturally. Fontaine wanted to pick him up, hold him close, but she was afraid. The others felt similar reactions. There was power here, vast power which could so easily become uncontrollable.

Moroski gingerly lifted the boy's wrist. After a few moments he said, "His pulse is racing but it's strong. He's very hot." The wizard loosened Luke's collar. "I don't have any experience of this level of intake."

"Nobody does," said Mark. "Except Ferragamo." With a shudder, he remembered his first view of the white, emaciated wizard after Ferragamo had swallowed a moonberry.

"Oh, why did he have to do this when Ferragamo was away?" asked Fontaine plaintively. "It's almost as if it were deliberate."

"What can we do?" asked Mark, looking at Moroski.

Before the wizard could answer, Fontaine and Adesina gasped in horror. Luke's eyes had closed abruptly.

"He's not . . . ?" whispered Adesina.

"No. No," replied Moroski, who still held the prince's wrist.

Gently the wizard was moved aside. Jani reached down into the worried circle and lifted Luke effortlessly. His expression was calm. Cradling the prince, he turned and started to walk to the door.

"What are you doing? Where are you taking him?" shouted Fontaine, even though she knew Jani would not hear.

Hearing the hysteria in his wife's voice, Mark fought to control his own rising panic and took her in his arms.

"Jani's doing what we should have done if we'd been thinking straight," he said. "He's putting him to bed. Don't forget how well those two understand each other."

They rose to follow.

"Mark's right," said Moroski. "All we can do is watch over him. He hasn't come to any obvious harm yet."

"How do you know that?" said Adesina.

"I don't for certain, but maybe Ferragamo will. I'll send Atlanta to fetch him. She'll arrive before your messenger, Mark."

"Thank you."

They all followed Jani out and down the steps.

"I'm sorry," Pabalan said miserably.

Atlanta sped toward the Windchill Mountains, traveling southwest. She flew high so that the rays of the setting sun warmed her feathers long after the ground below was in shadow.

She had accepted, without demur, the tiny parchment that was attached to her leg, having served her master in this way many times before. When Moroski had told her she was to visit the hermit's cave, she was pleased; unlike the wizard, she had been there before, and had felt the strange awareness of the man called Shalli. She had even begun to talk to him, as she did with Moroski but no other. When she told her master this now, he replied, *This message is for Ferragamo. He cannot talk to you and, from what I hear, Shalli's way of speech is more than a little eccentric. This is too important to risk any misunderstanding.* Atlanta did not fully comprehend this, but accepted the wizard's decision without question.

Soon the sky darkened but the stars provided more than enough light for the falcon's matchless eyesight. On she soared, glorying in the tireless precision of her flight. The mountains rose before her. She recognized the winding trail which led to the hermit's valley and was soon sweeping down to the cave entrance. Within, it was pitch-black and even her sharp eyes could not guide her progress. She fluttered to a stop and called out.

Almost immediately, a faint glimmer grew within the rock about her and she flew on into the depths. Shalli came out of one of the caverns. He smiled, exchanging greetings and welcome with the falcon before gesturing to the cavern from which he had emerged. Atlanta flew in and alighted on a ledge. A pair of large eyes blinked slowly from a niche at the back of the chamber. Owl hooted softly and something stirred on the floor beneath the birds.

Shalli mumbled a word and the light within the cave brightened sharply, the different seams of rock glowing with individual radiance.

Ferragamo sat up, squinting and bleary-eyed from sleep.

"It can't be morning already," he grumbled, then caught sight of Atlanta and was instantly awake. He rose quickly and walked over to her.

"Atlanta?" The falcon shuffled on her perch and Ferragamo saw the message. Gently he undid the binding and scanned the writing.

"Oh, Stars," he whispered. "Well, old friend, it seems I shall have to leave earlier than I intended." He passed the note to Shalli, who glanced at it briefly. Ferragamo did not even know if he could still read.

"Luke is the son," said the hermit.

"That's right. Mark and Fontaine's son."

"Luke is the son!" Shalli waved the parchment.

Ferragamo appealed to Owl, who often seemed to understand Shalli quite well, but received no enlightenment.

"I'll set out at first light. The sooner I get back the better. I only hope I can help—quite what I'm supposed to do I don't know. Rely on instinct as usual," he muttered.

Shalli smiled suddenly and started to bounce a little on the balls of his feet. Ferragamo watched in disbelief as the bouncing became a sort of dance, until Shalli was whirling about the cave, limbs swinging wildly. All the time he shouted. From the jumble of words, only "the source, the source, at the center" were recognizable. The rocklight sparked and flashed, dimmed and whirled, making Ferragamo quite dizzy. He cowered back against a wall until the whirlwind subsided.

In the sudden calm, Shalli said, "Horse light. You go now. Horse light. Good riding," and hopped from the cavern.

Mystified, Ferragamo followed the hermit into the main cave. They turned toward the stable, but before reaching it,

Shalli disappeared into another cavern, emerging moments later with a small round pebble in his hand. He went into the stable and led Ferragamo's horse outside. Once beyond the cave's illumination the animal moved gingerly, testing its footing. They came to a halt.

Shalli moved close to the horse's head and the wizard caught tantalizing fragments of the mental conversation between the two. The horse bared its teeth, and in the darkness Ferragamo could just make out the shape of Shalli's hand as he placed the pebble beneath the horse's tongue.

"Horse light. Go now," said Shalli, looking very pleased with himself.

"I can't go in the darkness! We wouldn't get two leagues before one of us fell and broke a leg. I have to wait for daylight."

Owl's voice interrupted Ferragamo, informing him that, for the horse, it was already daylight, and would remain so as long as the pebble was in his mouth.

"And they say you can't teach an old wizard new tricks," said Ferragamo in astonishment.

"All wizards old," said the hermit in a rare moment of clarity, smiling broadly.

"I'm still not sure I believe this," said Ferragamo. But as Shalli had already saddled the horse he saw no alternative to mounting up. After a few moments the wizard felt more at ease. The horse was quite comfortable cantering across the small plateau and easily avoided obstacles Ferragamo could hardly see.

"All right, I believe it," he said, on returning to Shalli. "Farewell, my friend."

They clasped hands for a moment.

"Go to the source at the center," said Shalli. "Farewell."

Ferragamo set off, pondering the hermit's enigmatic words. *Always a puzzle*, he thought. *Will I ever know him properly?*

By the time dawn broke, Ferragamo had already completed the most difficult part of the journey back to Starhill. He reached the bottom of a steep path with zigzagged up a huge scree slope—a path which under normal conditions would have been lethal to both horse and rider except in good light—and knew that from then on the trail lay over the relatively gentle slopes of the foothills.

A few paces farther on, a tent was pitched beside the trail. As the wizard approached, Richard emerged from within and stared disbelievingly at the new arrival.

"Where did you spring from?" he asked. "I thought you were at the cave."

"I was. I've just ridden down."

"That horse of yours hasn't got wings, has it?" asked the soldier, rubbing his eyes.

"No," said the wizard with a laugh, and he explained briefly. Then the reason for his haste came back to him.

"Are you ready to ride? I'm in a hurry."

"Of course. What's the rush?"

Silently Ferragamo handed Richard the message. He read it quickly.

"I see," was all the soldier said, but his face had turned very pale. Quickly, Richard packed up his bivouac and the two set off at a good pace. Owl and Atlanta flew overhead.

"If Mark has any sense," said Richard, "he will have sent someone to meet us halfway with fresh horses."

"I'm sure he will have thought of it."

An hour before noon, Ferragamo's faith was justified, when a group of mounted soldiers came into view. The wizard and Richard swapped their mounts for the party's riderless horses and galloped onward. The day grew hot but neither suggested that they stop to rest.

Fontaine anxiously watched her son for any signs of a return to normality. She and Mark had watched over him all through the night. Jani had been in the room with them, but he kept so still it was difficult to tell whether the big man was slumbering or not.

To all intents and purposes, Luke had been asleep the whole time. His pulse had slowed a little but he still burned with a dry feverish heat, and he had thrown off all his bedclothes, preferring the cool night air. For part of the night he had lain tranquilly, but his eyes often moved rapidly beneath their lids, and his limbs twitched. Occasionally his dreams, if dreams they were, became more violent and his muscles spasmed. At those times, when his back arched and he cried out, Fontaine wanted desperately to wake him and comfort him, tell him the nightmare was over. She tried holding him as best she could, but he seemed impervious to her touch, as if she were not there. Yet he always quieted down after a while, returning to what seemed like natural rest.

Mark sat beside Fontaine at the foot of the bed, watching and waiting with her. They were both dazed through lack of sleep, but found enormous comfort in each other's presence.

"What's going on inside his head?" Fontaine wondered aloud.

"I don't think we'll ever know."

"He's quieter now, don't you think?" she asked hopefully.

Jani rose from his chair in the corner of the room. He stretched, then came over to the bed and peered at Luke. Apparently satisfied, he smiled briefly at the boy's parents and left the chamber.

"Jani doesn't seem unduly worried, does he?" said Mark.

"That's quite reassuring really, isn't it?" said Fontaine, hoping for agreement. "They've always understood each other, ever since Luke was tiny."

"I suppose so," said Mark, the doubt obvious in his voice, "but how he can sit there calmly during Luke's nightmares I don't know."

"Perhaps Longfur could tell us. Oh . . ."

Luke was dreaming again, but his movements were only slight.

A scuffling noise came from under the bed. As Mark stooped to take a look, a small black and white object hurtled out into the open, stopped abruptly, and turned back toward the bed. Muscles launched himself at the sheet and, claws extended, clambered up to the top. Once there he made a beeline for Luke, licking a twitching hand, and then snuggled up against the infant's side. Luke sighed, put his arm around the kitten, and lay still.

"Perhaps Muscles could!" said Mark. He and Fontaine looked at each other and laughed. It felt good.

Jani returned to the room. With him came Penelope's other three kittens. They, too, disappeared under the bed, but, unlike Muscles, they remained there. Jani sat down again and Penelope, whose arrival had been silent and unnoticed, curled at his feet. She looked curiously at the high window through which rays from the early morning sun were beginning to shine, then set her head between her paws. Mark followed her glance and nudged Fontaine.

"Luke has more visitors," he said.

On the broad stone sill beyond the windowpane stood perhaps a dozen small birds. A robin, sparrows, bluetits, a pair of wrens, and several of the tiny silvery finches known on Ark as tree fish bobbed and chattered. Their various songs had formed an unnoticed background to the morning for a while now, and as they watched, Mark and Fontaine saw that one of the birds would occasionally peck at the glass, as if demanding entry.

"Cats and birds," said Mark. "What next?"

"Grandmothers," replied Adesina from the doorway. "A wondrous species of animal. May I come in?"

"Of course."

"How is Luke?"

"Still asleep, or seems to be," said Fontaine.

"Goodness, you two look worn out," said Adesina after she had inspected her grandson. "Why don't you go and get some rest—and have something to eat. I'll wager you've not had a thing since lunchtime yesterday."

"I'm not hungry," said Fontaine wearily.

"You must eat, especially in your condition. You'll do Luke no good, nor the baby, if you collapse through lack of nourishment."

"She's right, love," said Mark.

"Jani and I can manage quite well," said Adesina. "I'll call you if there's any need."

"All right, all right. I'll do my nutritional duty, if only to stop you nagging."

They rose and, hand in hand, walked to the door. Fontaine paused to ask, "Where's Father?"

"Still asleep. He had quite a lot to drink last night," replied Adesina. "It's probably the best thing for him," she added resignedly.

"Oh, dear, poor Father. I shall have to go and talk to him."

"It wasn't his fault," said Mark.

"I know," said Adesina, "but try telling him that."

They found Moroski eating breakfast in the hall. He looked up as they came in, the obvious question in his eyes.

"No change," said Mark. "For better or worse."

"I'm glad to see someone has an appetite," said Fontaine, eyeing the wizard's plate.

"Even wizards have to eat," Moroski replied, somewhat shamefacedly.

"So do pregnant ladies," said Fontaine, "as I am constantly being told."

They sat down at the table but it was not long before food took second place to discussion.

"What I don't understand," said Mark, "is that when Ferragamo swallowed a berry it had all sorts of drastic effects. His hair turned white, he grew thin and weak. He talked nonsense. There was magic leaking everywhere, causing all sorts of problems. None of that has happened with Luke."

"Perhaps Luke can control it," said Moroski.

"But he's only a little boy!" exclaimed Fontaine. "And he's no wizard."

"No, but he is a Servant," said Mark quietly.

"So are you," replied his wife. "Would you eat a whole moonberry?"

"My time is past," said Mark, sounding part rueful, part relieved.

Moroski raised his eyebrows. "I know the old stories," he said, "but this is new to me."

"Didn't Ferragamo ever talk to you about it?" asked Mark.

The wizard shook his head.

"I wonder why," said Mark thoughtfully. After a few moments, he went on. "It seems there is some sort of link between me and one of the Servants in the War of the Wizards, my long-ago namesake. I used to have dreams . . ."

Mark's voice trailed off.

"I believe it's the same with Luke," he added after a while, "although none of the original Servants was called Luke."

"I think you chose the name deliberately because of that," said Fontaine, half jokingly.

Mark avoided her eyes.

"I wouldn't want him to have to go through some of the things I did."

"That might be his destiny," said Moroski. "It wasn't just luck that brought you to face Amarino."

"There are no prophecies about *Luke*," said Mark.

"That we know of."

"I don't know how you two can sit here babbling on about prophecies and destiny when Luke is lying there in that state," said Fontaine. "Isn't there *anything* we can do?"

"Not that I can think of," said Moroski. "I've been up most of the night going through Ferragamo's library to no avail. All the old references to moonberries assume that they can be eaten like grapes and all the modern ones say they're akin to poison. There's nothing in between. We'll just have to hope Luke can control it."

"But how can he if Ferragamo couldn't?" Fontaine said desperately. "Even if he *has* any special abilities, he's so much smaller that any concentration must be much bigger."

"Don't forget he practically lived on moonberry cake in the womb," said Moroski. "Perhaps he built up an ability to deal with the power right from his conception. The only other possibility is that the berries are losing their potency. *That* could have serious consequences for us all."

While the wizard continued this discussion with Fontaine, each of them trying desperately to reassure the other, Mark felt a familiar presence twine around his legs.

Any chance of some fish? Or have you gluttons stuffed the lot?

Don't you ever think of anything else but your stomach, Longfur?

Well, I like that! came the retort. *Here I am bringing the resources of my whole family to aid you and you begrudge me a little food.*

Mark passed down some fish.

What have you been doing? he asked.

Talking to Jani, Longfur replied.

Talking?

Well, the next best thing. He's quite happy about Luke, you know.

We'd noticed that.

He seems to think it's just a natural process. But then I'm not sure he really understands what's going on.

I wish you hadn't told me that last bit, said Mark.

And apart from that, my family is aiding with Luke's recovery, went on the cat, munching happily.

I don't see that they can do him any harm, replied Mark. *And he does seem to get along with Muscles.*

Like you and me, replied Longfur smugly.

Mark smiled, then the implication sank in. *You mean . . .*
Yes.
Fontaine was speaking.
"What?" asked Mark, confusedly.
"Where had you gone?"
"Just thinking."
"I was asking how soon you think Ferragamo can get here?"
"Well, if he left at first light, with the relay horses he could
be here late this evening, if we're lucky. They should be all
right doing the last stretch in darkness."

In fact, to everyone's amazement, it was only mid-afternoon
when the wizard arrived. He wasted no time in going to
Luke's room. As he entered, Fontaine rose from her bedside
vigil.
"I'm so glad you're here!" she cried.
"That's the trouble with wizards. They're never around
when you want them," he replied.
Ferragamo approached the bed. Luke appeared to be sleeping peacefully, with Muscles still cuddled against his side.
The wizard stood silently for a few moments, and was about
to speak when Luke suddenly sat up. His eyes opened wide.
They sparkled with their own color; the unnatural glow had
gone.
Muscles meowed loudly at being disturbed.
"Hello, Uncle Ferragamo," Luke enunciated perfectly. "I'm
glad you've come back. There are some things I wish to
discuss with you."

Chapter 6

$\mathcal{N}$obody realized it at the time, but Luke's first adult sentence marked the beginning of his lifelong devotion to magic—and Ferragamo. Like his father before him, he was to spend hours in the wizard's company listening, questioning, and learning. But whereas Mark had been dreamy and inclined to lose the gist of an argument, Luke would be precise and intuitive, often surprising Ferragamo by being one step ahead of his instruction. This was, of course, when Luke was in his "adult" phase, which would alternate, since swallowing the moonberry, with times when he acted like the little boy he was. In those periods he played, fell over, broke things, and cried for his mother. His speech returned to the unformed prattle of infancy until his natural growth caught up with his magical development.

It was to be extremely disconcerting for those around him, who could never be sure if Luke would demand that they become a horse for him to ride, or launch into a learned discussion of the theory of magical distortion of time. Only Jani would be perfectly at ease with his young companion's diverse personalities and be able to predict and cope with the sometimes very sudden switches from one to the other. Everyone else would be constantly taken by surprise and take a very long time to get used to the idea. Ferragamo would come to believe that even Luke himself found it frustrating, with neither of his selves being quite sure which was real.

As he grew older the difference between the two phases would become less and less marked, but by the time the two Lukes were practically indistinguishable, there were other problems with which he was struggling, other facets of his character he had to fight to reconcile.

All that lay in the future. For now, his family was over-joyed just to have him conscious again, and very much alive. When Ferragamo examined Luke, he could find nothing wrong with him. There would be plenty of time to worry about the long-term effects, if any, of his adventure. However strange he might seem to be, Luke was still their child, and the preparations for his second birthday celebrations would go on with increased vigor. The day ended happily, and Ferragamo finally took his chance to seek out Koria and renew their partnership in a night which owed nothing to wizardry and everything to love.

You can hear me, can't you?

Of course I can hear you. What did you expect?

This is all rather new to me. I feel different. Will you by my friend?

If you like.

A few moments passed in silence.

I've got to go now. To find my mam. I want some milk. She doesn't like you. You pulled her tail once.

Tell her I'm sorry. I won't do it again.

All right.

Needlelike claws extended from four mud-brown paws. There was a twitching of the bedclothes, the Luke was left alone. He turned over and went back to sleep.

The next morning, Ferragamo woke late, momentarily dis-oriented by his surroundings. Why was the rock above him not glimmering with its own light? Where was Shalli, who was always awake before him? Then the softness of the bed and the room in which it stood became familiar and he reached out to embrace the woman who lay at his side. She way always the best thing about coming home.

Some time later he and Moroski checked on Luke's prog-ress and, finding nothing amiss, retired to discuss their own plans. Inevitably they ended up amid the eccentric paraphernalia of one of the upper rooms of Starbright Tower. There they were sure not to be disturbed, and the chaotic surroundings made both wizards feel very much at home.

They discussed Luke briefly, but soon decided that they

could only watch and wait. Both wizards were mystified at how the boy could have come through such an ordeal apparently unscathed, but they had seen so many remarkable events in their long lives that they were soon able to turn to the other matter which occupied their thoughts.

"It looks as though we're all set. *Finally*," said Ferragamo.

"I hope so," replied Moroski doubtfully.

"That sounds ominous. Tell me the worst."

"There should have been a message from Iolo waiting for me when we arrived. I stayed an extra day in Grayrock but there was no sign of any arrivals from Rek."

"He *will* come, won't he?"

"I think so, but he's a stickler for protocol and he's never actually confirmed that he will. I was hoping the letter would make it certain."

"And if Iolo doesn't come, neither will Geralti," said Ferragamo in exasperation. "How can they be so shortsighted?"

"Those two have always been close. Some of the islanders even believe them to be brothers."

Ferragamo paced the room impatiently.

"Don't they know what's at stake here?" he exclaimed. "Just because their islands are big and strong do they think they can stand alone? Let *them* sail for Brogar. See what *I've* seen. They wouldn't worry about protocol then!"

"You don't have to convince me," said Moroski gently.

Ferragamo looked taken aback, then ashamed.

"I'm sorry, my friend," he said, "but I confess this whole business is fraying my nerves. If it weren't for you, I think I would have done something very foolish by now."

"I doubt that," replied Moroski. "Koria has more common sense than the two of us together—and you still heed *her* words, I'll wager."

A smile crept over Ferragamo's face.

"I do," he said simple, then added, "But she's no more a politician than I."

"And I am?" Moroski grinned.

Ferragamo began a stuttering explanation, then gave up and laughed.

"If you like," he said. "In this game we need all the skills we can muster."

"I'll take that as a compliment," Moroski replied, still smiling.

"It was meant to be," said the other gravely. "Now back to specifics."

Ferragamo sat down again and began counting on his fingers.

"Rek and Tirek we've talked about already. We'll just have to wait and see about them. Saronno's coming from Strallen, of course."

"And Xyda from Peven."

"Thank the stars we don't have to worry about convincing those two," said Ferragamo. "What about the southern isles?"

"Cai from Arlon is a friend of mine," said Moroski. "He'll definitely be here, and with a bit of luck so will Drogo, though he's been muttering about the journey. Cai's visited Lugg and I think he convinced the old grumbler, but he's so ancient he's practically fossilized."

"If he's not up to a simple sea voyage," said Ferragamo cruelly, "perhaps it's time he named a successor. We might have got something done long ago if it weren't for these old dodderers."

Neither of them found anything at all odd about the fact that this pronouncement came from a man who was himself well over two hundred years old.

"There may be some others from the minor islands in the south but I don't know about them," added Moroski.

"That leaves the northern group, Dawn, Set, and the smaller isles."

"Briodi said he'd come. In fact he should already be on his way. I hope Faramondi will be with him, but we've had no reply at all from Set."

"They'll come via Rek, won't they?" mused Ferragamo. "If Iolo is being stupid I hope they don't let him influence them."

"Briodi's got more sense than that. Perhaps it could work the other way."

"It takes two years for a man of sense to agree to a conclave a child of three could see is necessary?" said Ferragamo caustically.

"That's not entirely fair," replied his friend.

"Where does it say I have to be fair?"

By now they were both smiling again but Moroski went on to make his point anyway.

"You called for this conclave considerably less than two years ago," he said, "and unlike them you have direct experience of what we're up against. You mustn't be too surprised that the others take some convincing. We didn't want to believe it for a long time, did we?"

"Huh," was all the response Ferragamo gave before he rallied and continued the argument.

"But even if what happened here doesn't count for anything, what about Brogar? How do they account for that?"

"You're the only one who's seen it—"

"And Mark. And an entire ship's crew. Don't they count for anything?"

"Not to wizards."

"Pah!"

"Besides, it could have a number of natural explanations."

"Name one."

"I can't, but people will always try to explain away something they don't like."

Moroski held up his hands to forestall his companion's retort.

"You don't have to convince *me*," he repeated.

Ferragamo shrugged and smiled in apology. They were silent for a while, both thinking of the abortive voyage to Brogar that Ferragamo and Mark had undertaken a year and a half ago. The horror of it was still very much alive in Ferragamo's mind, and even Moroski, whose only knowledge had been gained at second hand, shuddered as he recalled the descriptions the travelers had given.

They had sailed from Grayrock on a chill, gray day in late autumn. Rounding the northern reaches of Ark, they had set a course almost due west. Battling against the prevailing winds, they had made slow progress, and it was not until the morning of the tenth day at sea that the lookout shouted from the crow's nest that their goal was in sight. Shortly afterward, however, he reported that he could no longer see Brogar. This mystified the captain as visibility was good and they were moving ever closer to the island. He sent another man aloft, but on returning to the deck, the seaman confirmed the lookout's sighting, or rather lack of it.

"The island should easily be in range now," said the puzzled captain, "unless my navigation is hopelessly wrong." His tone implied that he thought this unlikely.

"There's an odd cloud formation west of us, Captain," said the sailor. "But it's too small to hide a whole island."

As he spoke, the lookout shouted again, and this time they

all saw it. The angular shape of Brogar appeared to the west, far closer than anyone had expected. From a distance, islands appear gray. Brogar was black. Even at this range it had a forbidding look. Ferragamo, who had been experiencing a sense of unease all day, suddenly felt very cold. Then, as they watched, the island simply disappeared. There were shouts of shock and disbelief but no one could deny the evidence of their own eyes.

One moment the island has been there, then there had been a flicker, as brief as a flash of lightning, and it was gone. In its place was a column of water vapor like the spray from a large waterfall. In its midst was the incongruous beauty of a rainbow.

For a moment the island reappeared, closer than ever, but the sickening flicker was repeated and the water was seen again. This time, however, the column was twisted, its vapors writhing as if in agony. The rainbow within it was warped as well. No longer a smooth arch of natural color, it was bent and knotted, an abomination to all who beheld it.

Into the silence of the terrified watchers came the sound of laughter, seeming at once both impossibly distant and horribly close. There was no mirth in the sound, and several men fell to their knees, their hands pressed over their ears in a vain attempt to escape its malice.

At last the laughter faded, to be replaced by another sound. To the seamen it was even worse, a noise from their worst nightmares.

Even if it had not been connected to the appalling spectacle presented before them, the terrible thundering roar of the whirlpool was unmistakable. Though they were still some distance away, the scale of it defied the imagination. Foamwhite, the waves crashed around a gaping maw in the sea, whence both the roaring and the column of spume rose.

Some of the sailors panicked and there was chaos as several uncoordinated attempts to turn the ship about failed. Eventually the captain and Ferragamo restored order and the maneuver was completed.

No crew was ever more glad to be running before a strong and constant wind.

Even safe within the walls of Starhill, Ferragamo remembered the terrible groaning of the tortured sea with something close to dread. Breaking the long silence, he said, "Even if I could have persuaded the crew to sail any closer we would have accomplished nothing. There is a power there that dwarfs us all."

"Perhaps not, if we act in unison," replied Moroski quickly. The faraway look faded from Ferragamo's face and his voice lost the awestruck tone that had disturbed his companion.

"That's a big if," he said, "given our progress to date."

"It won't be long now."

"For which small mercy I am very grateful. I've never been very good at waiting."

"In that case, may I suggest we occupy ourselves in a more obviously useful concern for now?"

"What's that?"

Moroski smiled. "Planning Luke's birthday celebrations," he said. "What else?"

Luke's room was crowded. His parents and Jani had again stayed with him through the night, though this time they had been able to get a little sleep themselves. Luke had awakened soon after dawn, and had been visited first by the two wizards and then by his grandparents and Koria. All but the wizards were still there at mid-morning.

Luke was still in bed. He had protested vigorously at the enforced rest, but had been told firmly that he was to stay where he was. Lapsing into a sullen silence, he sat there quietly, trying to make sense of the events of the last two days. His thoughts were confused, so he listened to the conversations about him, hoping for some comfort and explanation.

"But what happened after that?" Adesina was asking.

"Not a lot," replied Mark. "We were all so taken aback at his waking up and talking perfectly that we didn't really react at all."

"Ferragamo recovered first," added Fontaine. "He said, 'What is it you want to talk about, Luke?' as calm as you please."

"And?"

"Luke muttered something that we couldn't catch," said Mark, "and the next moment he was crying for his mother."

"He seemed to be back to normal then," said Fontaine. "After I gave him a cuddle, Ferragamo had a look at him, and then he went to sleep."

"Well, he looks all right now," said Koria. "He must be over the worst."

"Judging by the noise he was making a short while ago," said Pabalan, "it hasn't done his lungs any harm!" The jocularity in the king's voice sounded forced. He had said little during his visit, and glancing at him now, Fontaine saw the pain in his eyes and determined to speak to him alone as soon as possible.

Koria noticed the exchange and said quickly, "That's true. If we don't let him get up soon I won't answer for the consequences."

"Ferragamo didn't say he had to stay in bed," added Mark. "Perhaps—"

"What about the long-term effects of all this?" said Adesina suddenly. "Ferragamo didn't mention them, did he?"

"I don't think he can tell us anything about them," said Fontaine. "Nobody can."

"Perhaps Luke will," said Mark quietly.

They all looked at the young prince. Golden eyes stared back inquiringly, then were diverted by a sudden disturbance beneath the bedclothes. The adults laughed as a small furry head appeared at Luke's side.

What are they laughing at?

I don't know.

They seem to be fussing over you an awful lot. Can't you get up and play?

They think I'm ill.

Then tell them you're not.

I don't have the words.

Why? You have with me. And you had words for them yesterday.

I don't know.

You humans don't know a lot, do you?

Sometimes I know lots of things . . .

Tell me some.

. . . but not now.

Muscles struggled out onto the pillow, stretched and looked about him.

Well, at least I seem to have got them moving, he said silently.

"Come on, Luke," said Fontaine. "You can get up now. Your playmate seems a bit impatient!"

Chapter 7

A month later the wizards began arriving for the conclave. Luke's birthday had come and gone; the celebrations had encompassed the whole of the castle community—and been used as the excuse for considerable revelry throughout the city.

Despite his preoccupation with other matters, Ferragamo had, with Moroski, played a full role in making Luke's day special. The diversion had been good for Ark's wizard, allowing him to use his magical talents toward lighthearted ends. That was the only break in the monotony of waiting, however, and once it was over the time had passed with intolerable slowness for Ferragamo. Koria was worried. The wizard was still as tender and loving to her as ever but she saw the strain beneath the façade he presented to everyone else. Even during the time of Ark's direst peril he had been able to conserve an inner strength, allowing him to remain in control. Now, with the island's fate in the hands of so many others as well as his own, Ferragamo appeared nervous, full of foreboding, near to breaking point. Even Koria could not always calm his agitation and several people felt the sharp edge of his tongue. She almost suggested that he return to Shalli for a while, but refrained, knowing that to Ferragamo this would be admitting defeat. Besides, she knew he would not go while Luke still showed the slightest aftereffects of his escapade.

The wizard's mood began to affect the whole castle, and knowing this, Ferragamo kept more and more to himself, leaving Koria and Moroski to organize accommodation for the expected visitors and their familiars.

Mark felt Ferragamo's self-imposed isolation most keenly. He, too, was anxious about the conclave, knowing that so much depended on its outcome. The wizard's advice had always been Mark's mainstay, even before the prince reclaimed Ark's throne, and now that it was withdrawn he began to feel less sure of his own authority. He was also finding his personal concerns a strain at this time. Luke's health appeared perfectly good but there was no doubting that the little boy was *odd*. Even in this short time his variable mental phases had become obvious. Then, of course, Mark was concerned about Fontaine. From her point of view, Ferragamo's withdrawal was probably beneficial. A fraught and emotional atmosphere was not to be recommended for an expectant mother in the last weeks of her pregnancy, and Mark was glad that Adesina was staying with them. Despite their limited acquaintance he had come to love his elegant mother-in-law and to appreciate her calming influence.

Her husband was another matter, so different in character from Mark that they found talking difficult. Pabalan was a proud and honorable man but aware of his own limitations. Though he clearly doted on Luke, he found it difficult to display his emotions in public, and since the incident with the moonberry, he was chary of being alone with his grandson. He became frustrated with his confinement within Starhill and cultivated friendships with several of the Castle Guard. Shill took him hunting on several occasions, much to Pabalan's delight and everyone else's relief.

Mark's tense state was exacerbated by the fact that Longfur, his usual confidant, had family matters of his own to attend to, and thus spent less time with his human companion. It was a great relief to all when news came from Grayrock that two ships had docked, within hours of each other, and that each carried a wizard and his companions. Ferragamo's delight subsided somewhat when he learned that the arrivals were Saronno and Xyda, both of whom he had been sure of, but he was still all smiles when, the next day, they arrived at Starhill.

Mark, Ferragamo, and Moroski led the welcome party as the coaches pulled to a halt in the castle courtyard. Amid the immediate bustle, Mark had eyes only for the two wizards. Moroski had warned him what to expect but their appearance was still startling.

Saronno's hair was straight and black, his skin a dry, unhealthy gray. He was dressed entirely in midnight-blue and his cape swirled about him like a shadow. In his left hand he carried a staff. It was featureless, unmarked by carving or rune, and as gray as the fingers that held it. The wizard stooped slightly. He looked old, in spite of his dark hair, and was probably ancient.

Mark took all this in at a glance but his eyes returned in fascination to the most obvious feature of the wizard's appearance. Twined around his right arm, with its head on his shoulder, was a snake, slim and beautiful. Its scales glittered jewellike, the various shades of blue and green shining in contrast to the wizard's somber apparel.

When Mark took Saronno's hand in greeting, he felt the tip of the familiar's tail as a sixth finger to the wizard's grasp, but he did not flinch. The snake's skin was smooth and dry. His words of welcome said, Mark turned to the other visitor.

Xyda was very tall with blue eyes, fair hair, and a pale but youthful complexion. He was dressed simply in brown leather and wool. The impression was of a strong young woodsman but this was betrayed by the large silver-gray wolf at his side.

Mark extended his hand. "Greetings, Xyda. Welcome to Starhill."

"Thank you, my lord. It's pronounced 'See-da,' by the way." The deep, resonant voice held no trace of resentment.

"My apologies. I still have much to learn."

"You are young," Xyda said amiably, but Mark caught the faint note of condescension in his words.

"Hoban sends his greetings," the wizard went on, "and asks me to pass on the message that Durc and Zunic have arrived safely on Peven. 'We'll make sailors of those reprobates yet' were his exact words."

This time the supercilious tone was obvious, and Mark was glad when Ferragamo and Moroski took over the role of host and began to plan the accommodation and dietary arrangements for their unusual guests.

Some time later, alone with Fontaine, Mark exclaimed, "Phew! They're a cold pair of fish."

"Not all wizards are like the ones we've known," his queen replied.

"No wonder Ferragamo is worried, if those two are the ones he's most confident about," Mark added, his eyebrows raised.

"You'll get used to them soon enough. At least they're here."

Only two days remained before the date specified for the conclave when the next arrivals were announced. The ship from Arlon had arrived in the early morning. On board were Cai, the wizard from that island, and Drogo, the wizard from the neighboring isle of Lugg, with their respective parties.

Cai rode immediately for Starhill. He was keen to renew his friendship with Moroski and knew that his senior traveling companion would not be ready to move on from Grayrock that day—and possibly not the next. Drogo was centuries old and no longer knew the meaning of the word "haste."

Cai's entrance into Starhill caused a stir among the city's inhabitants. "Quite a buzz," as Fontaine put it to general groans, later in the evening. The reason for this was the wizard's unusual retinue. His baggage and human companions had been left behind in Grayrock to follow at a more leisurely pace but as he galloped toward the city gates he was followed by a small black cloud.

As he slowed to enter the Sea Gate, this cloud resolved itself into a swarm of bees. They gathered into a tightly packed mass, just above and behind the wizard's head, and stayed there, causing considerable comment and not a little alarm, all the way to the castle. The noise they made was remarkably loud and quite fearsome. As a consequence few people paid much attention to the wizard himself. Cai was dark-skinned, of slight build with a look of almost boyish youthfulness, and was dressed in the light clothes of his southern home-isle. His long brown hair flowed out behind him as he rode, and his green eyes glinted mischievously at the consternation his bees provoked.

He was the only wizard whose familiar consisted not of one animal but of a group which made up a single entity. Cai had never been able to give a satisfactory explanation of the nature of his link with the swarm, even to the other wizards. He knew that no single insect, not even the ever-present queen bee, was capable of sustaining the link with his mind. Yet the link was there and somehow it was with the whole swarm at once, as if each bee's awareness was a part of a single mind. The wizard had long ceased to question the nature of the relationship and accepted it as fact.

Cai's unexpected arrival at the castle caused an uproar. Recent events had accustomed the inhabitants to wizardly presence, but this newest phenomenon was beyond them. Horses panicked, children ran to hide, and most of the adults were distinctly wary. Only Moroski, who had met the swarm before, was unperturbed. He strode out to meet his friend as the latter dismounted.

"Hello, Cai. Still causing trouble, I see!"

"Can I help it if people don't understand me and my friends?" Cai spread his hands and smiled innocently. The wizards embraced warmly.

"Can't you even quiet them down a bit?" asked Moroski.

"Only when they land," Cai replied. "Show me my room and I'll put them to bed. Put you all out of your misery." He grinned.

A short while later the two wizards sat in Cai's room. The bees rested silently on a large wall hanging, their movements adding changing patterns to the tapestry's own. Mark, who had missed Cai's arrival, had visited him briefly to show welcome, and now Cai and Moroski were using the hour or so before dinner to exchange news.

"I had to go to Lugg to collect him," said Cai. "It was the only way I could get the old sluggard to agree to come."

"Drogo is old and set in his ways, Cai, but he's a long way from being powerless—and he has immense knowledge. We need him."

"All right. Point taken. I'll only be rude about the old fossil when he can't hear me," Cai said, laughing.

"Better still, don't be rude about him at all."

"*You* haven't had to put up with him on an interminable sea voyage. It was an effort to restrain my bees from stinging him into unconsciousness!"

"Where is he now?"

"In Grayrock. Probably asleep. I think he's starting to hibernate like that hedgehog of his."

"Hedgehog?"

"Yes, didn't you know? That's his latest familiar. The eagle finally dropped dead, of boredom probably, and he decided to choose something closer to his own nature. Got it about right too. Slow and prickly."

"I'll have to tell Koria. I don't think what we've provided is going to be suitable," said Moroski.

"There'll be no pleasing him, however hard you try," warned Cai. He evidently spoke from bitter experience. "You've got a bit of time anyway. At the earliest he'll arrive tomorrow evening. More likely the next day."

"That's cutting it a bit fine. The day after that is the conclave."

"Don't hold your breath," said Cai.

———————————

Dinner that night, with five wizards around the circular table, was a strained and tense affair. Mark, as host, tried to keep the atmosphere light and succeeded for a while as, by an unspoken agreement, conversation was limited to unimportant matters. Serious discussion would wait until the conclave. However, it was not long before Mark became aware of undercurrents within the flow of conversation. Xyda and Saronno treated Cai with barely concealed contempt, and the youthful wizard did little to help his own cause with his jests and murmured asides. Moroski tried to pour oil on troubled waters but Ferragamo spent the latter part of the meal in stony silence. Koria watched him seethe inwardly and fervently hoped that the explosion would come later, after the dinner party had split up.

Everyone was relieved when the evening came to an end. At the wizards' own suggestion, it was arranged that meals from now on would be taken in the privacy of their own chambers, superficially to facilitate the tending required by their familiars, but leaving no one in any doubt as to the real reason.

Koria quickly steered Ferragamo away from the hall and to their apartments. Once the door was closed, she said, "If you're going to break anything, let me look at it first. It might be something I like."

The wizard looked nonplussed for a moment, then the muscles in his face and neck relaxed visibly. His white hair became less spiky and he managed a smile.

"But that would take away the grandeur of the gesture!" he said. "If I want to smash something to show what a foul temper I'm in, I don't want to have to consider it first."

They found themselves in each other's arms.

"Have I told you how good you are for me?" he whispered.

"Not enough," she replied.

After a few moments' silence, he said, "It wasn't the best of starts, though, was it? There's only half of us here and we're already bickering like spoiled children. With only two days to go there's *still* no word from the northern isles. If they don't come now, I'll never get them all together."

"There's time yet. Let's cross the bridges when we come to them, not before. Between the six of you there's enough sense to sort this out, even if magic has addled your brains somewhat."

"I wish I had your faith. I know wizards."

"I know you."

After another silent interlude, Ferragamo said, "How do you do it? I feel so much better now."

"All part of the service," Koria replied. "My fees are very reasonable too. Is there anything else I can do for you?"

"Yes," he said. "Come to bed."

Cai's prediction proved accurate. Drogo did not appear the next day, nor the morning after that. It was well after noon when the wizard's carriage drove slowly into the castle courtyard. Mark, Ferragamo, and Moroski were waiting to meet him, but although the carriage door was flung open the moment it came to a halt, nobody emerged from the darkened interior. Mark peered into the gloom and was about to step inside to offer his assistance when a girl of perhaps fourteen summers jumped down and almost collided with him. She was pretty, with clear blue eyes and straight blond hair, cut quite short.

"Oh, I'm sorry," she said.

"That's all right," Mark replied. "I'm Mark. Is Drogo here?"

"Yes, my lord," the girl said. "He'll be out in a moment. He's just composing himself." Mark glanced back at Ferragamo, who shrugged. The girl leaned into the carriage and lifted out a wicker cage. Within its widely spaced bars was a sleepy-looking hedgehog.

"This is Yevtu, Drogo's familiar, and I am Yve, his apprentice."

A *female* apprentice? Mark was saved from having to reply to this surprising statement by a loud voice from inside the carriage.

"Stop this chattering and let me out. Is an old man to be left to suffocate in the dark?"

Mark and Yve drew back and Drogo appeared in the doorway. He was brown and wrinkled like a dried fruit, and almost bald. His back was bent in a permanent curve and he carried a walking stick of gnarled wood. The clothes that covered him were ragged and predominantly black. Yet the overall impression was not of aged weakness but rather that of obstinate strength. The wizard's eyes were almost colorless, but they were as bright as stars, and he glared defiantly at all about him as if daring them to judge by appearances. Drogo was obviously quite ancient but, as Moroski had remarked, a long way from being powerless.

"The steps, girl!" he snapped in a voice that had lost its earlier wheedling tone.

Yve quickly pulled down the carriage footplate and her master tottered down, making great play of his supposed instability, this effect being somewhat spoiled by the fact that his feet never actually touched the steps, staying a finger's width above them. Though few people noticed it, Drogo floated down, grumbling the whole time about his poor bones.

"Greetings, Wizard Drogo!" said Mark.

The old man ignored him completely, turning away to shout at his servants who were unloading the carriage. Although all was going smoothly, he berated them as lazy and incompetent, threatening dire punishments if anything should be broken. Mark could only look on in astonishment.

Finally Drogo, who still floated slightly above the ground, turned back to Mark and said, "It's *Master* Wizard actually. Where are my quarters?"

Moroski stepped into the breach and led the old wizard away. With a brief smile of apology, Yve set off after them, still carrying the cage and its inhabitant. Mark was speechless.

"And you thought it couldn't get any worse!" said a voice behind him. Cai had appeared from nowhere and now stood with Mark and Ferragamo watching the retreating wizard. "I did try to warn you," he added.

Later, Mark learned that although Drogo had left Grayrock the day before, his progress had been so slow that by dusk the journey had been only half completed. There being no first-class hostelry on the road, Drogo had simply picked the most prosperous-looking farmstead in the vicinity and foisted himself upon the bewildered owner. He had received food and lodgings for himself and his servants, and stabling for the horses. In the morning he left without thanks or offer of reparation, even criticizing the hardness of his bed—the farmer's own—and the mediocrity of the breakfast fare.

On hearing this, Mark immediately arranged for a messenger to ride to the farm with payment, and a note of thanks and apology from the king. When the rider arrived, his offer of money was refused. The farmer said that the laws of hospitality, whether abused or not, were to be respected. However, he did beg Mark to ensure, if possible, that alternative arrangements be made, should Drogo require future accommodation on that route.

The next day dawned with the city shrouded in a cold, gray mist. The weather matched Ferragamo's mood entirely. This was supposed to be the morning when the conclave began, but there was still no message from the wizards of the north. He sent a rider to Grayrock to seek for news—even though he knew that if there had been any sightings, they would have been reported immediately—and sent messages to his five fellow wizards suggesting they delay the start of the conclave until the rider returned. He received cheerful agreement from Cai and Moroski, curt and formal replies from Saronno and Xyda, and no response at all from Drogo.

The messenger returned by nightfall with the depressing but not unexpected news that there was no sign of a ship from Rek or any of the other northern isles. Ferragamo reluctantly agreed that the conclave would begin the next morning.

"The greatest threat we have faced for thousands of years," he said bitterly, "and only six of the ten supposed guardians of the islands deign to turn up."

"Six of the eleven, you mean," said Moroski grimly.

"The eleventh can't be counted as a wizard anymore," Ferragamo replied, equally stern. "And I'm very glad he *isn't* here—he'd see what feeble opposition he faces!"

Earlier in the day Yve had finally escaped from the incessant demands of her master and had been able to explore her fascinating new surroundings. She respected and even loved the crotchety wizard, not least because he had been willing to take the unheard-of step of making a girl his apprentice. However, she knew the effect his rudeness had on others, and could, from experience, deflect the worst of his temper. This meant that she bore the brunt of his moodiness herself, and so it was a relief to have some time on her own.

She walked the castle battlements, explored the stables and warrenlike servants quarters and kitchens, and peeked into the central courtyard where the moonberry tree grew. It was here that she first encountered Luke.

The little boy sat on the floor, engrossed in the inspection of one for the cracks between the paving stones. Beside him a black and white kitten with mud-colored paws was cleaning itself. Yve was charmed by the scene and felt a momentary quiver of doubt about her chosen profession and the child-lessness that it entailed. This passed in a moment, however, and was replaced by a quite different tremor as another character was added to the tableau framed in the inner court-yard door.

Jani's appearance often caused such reactions but, in truth, he was the gentlest of men, despite his size and strength. Luke turned and looked up at his guardian.

"Jay-nee," he said delightedly, and pointed to the crevice he had been studying. Jani squatted down to inspect Luke's discovery. As he did so, both of them became aware of Yve's presence. Even the kitten looked up at her.

She felt embarrassed under the triple scrutiny, as if she had been caught spying, and was about to move away when Luke shouted and beckoned with both arms. Yve hesitated until Jani also motioned for her to enter. She climbed the last steps and went in. Jani rose slowly, towering over his charge who scrambled to his feet and held out his arms to Yve.

"Cuggle!" he cried.

Yve glanced at Jani, who smiled encouragingly.

"My goodness, you are a weight!" she said as she lifted Luke into her arms. "Is this Prince Luke?" she asked.

Jani gave no sign of hearing her question but the child said, "Lu, Lu," before stoppering his mouth with his thumb. His eyes closed and he fell asleep immediately.

Now what do I do? thought Yve. Aloud she said, "Should we put him to bed?"

Again there was no response from the big man. Yve began to be a little frightened. She tried again.

"Is your name Jani?"

He had been watching her lips closely and now he nodded hesitantly. Then his attention switched abruptly to Luke. The boy wriggled in Yve's arms and his eyes opened. She found herself looking into their golden depths.

"Who are you?" asked Luke clearly.

Yve was so surprised that she nearly dropped him. Hastily, she set him down on the floor whence he stared intently up at her.

"My name is Yve," she said. "I'm Master Wizard Drogo's apprentice."

The golden eyes widened slightly. "There haven't been any lady wizards before, have there?"

"Only one. A very long time ago . . . You can talk very well."

"Sometimes," replied the child enigmatically. "I'm Luke and this is Jani. He's deaf and dumb but we understand each other very well. Would you like me to show you the wizard's tower?"

"Yes, please."

Luke held up his hand for her to hold and they set off across the tree-yard. Jani and the kitten followed silently.

The next dawn brought Ferragamo better news. Another rider had reached Starhill and reported that a ship from Rek had docked in Grayrock Harbor during the night. The wizard on board would be making his way to the city as quickly as possible.

"Wizard?" said Ferragamo. "Only one?"

"I only know of one for certain," replied the messenger. "There may have been others, sir, but I set off in haste, as you requested."

"Of course. Thank you."

The rider left to get some much needed rest. Koria came into the room, rubbing the sleep from her eyes.

"They're coming then," she said.

"One of them is, at least. That's better than none but it should have been four!"

Shortly afterward Ferragamo received another message,

this time from Drogo. The master wizard's note inquired testily when the conclave would begin—as he has preparations to make—and implied that it had better be today.

"He wants me to hurry up so he can keep me waiting," said Ferragamo, after he had dispatched notes to all the wizards suggesting noon as the time for their gathering. "I only hope Iolo, or whoever it is, can get here in time."

In fact, even though a watch was kept on the Sea Road until the last minute, no wizards were observed approaching during the morning, and Ferragamo resigned himself to starting the conclave without any of his northern colleagues.

The site chosen for the conclave was the Wizards' Hall, a sparsely furnished, circular room near the top of Starbright Tower. A round wooden table stood at its center, with twelve high-backed chairs set about it. The floor was bare stone, as were the walls. There were five large windows and between these were five empty braziers with miniature chimneys above them to carry away smoke from any torches. The walls were otherwise undecorated, except for several strangely shaped niches which looked as if they had been designed to hold statues, but now stood empty. The only entrance to the room was a heavy iron door, approached from the spiral staircase that rose within the walls of the tower. The door had not been opened in decades.

Mark, the wizards, and their familiars gathered in the tree-yard. All were dressed in their usual manner except Drogo who, though arriving last, as expected, was surprisingly not late. He had changed his black rags for a fantastic and voluminous hooded black robe patterned with a variety of arcane symbols picked out in gold and red.

He tottered into the courtyard and scanned the company with his gimlet eyes. His expression showed that he did not think much of what he saw.

"So much for observing the formalities," he announced. "And you call yourselves wizards." His tone made it a term of contempt. Before anyone could reply, Drogo went on, "Let the conclave begin. As the senior mage here I will lead our entry."

So saying, he swept past the other wizards and, abandoning all pretense of immobility, began to ascend the staircase, floating smoothly above the steps. Behind him, also in mid-air, but curled up and apparently fast asleep, flew the hedgehog. It looked quite absurd but only Cai was forced to stifle a laugh.

As the others followed in more conventional fashion, Cai whispered to Moroski, "Now we know why he didn't keep us waiting. A grand exhibition like this would have been wasted if we were all upstairs already!"

Ferragamo and Mark brought up the rear. Both of their minds held premonitions of disaster, but it was too late to turn back now. Owl rode on the wizard's shoulder and Longfur padded silently at Mark's heels. No one noticed a blond girl and a small boy slip into the now-deserted tree-yard and, after a discreet pause, begin to tiptoe up the spiral stairs.

As the wizards entered the hall, each familiar moved, in its own fashion, to one of the niches around the walls, their actions prompted by some ancient instinct. Curiously, though the makeup of this conclave could not have been known when the tower was built, each animal found a suitably sized refuge. Even Cai's queen bee, the only one of his swarm he had chosen to bring, flew unhesitatingly to a tiny hole high in the wall. Like the others, she settled and became quite still.

The wizards each selected a chair and sat down without ceremony. Mark, who had been briefed earlier by Ferragamo, stood behind the wizard of Ark's chair. The iron door clanged shut.

After a moment's silence, Ferragamo began to speak.

"The reasons for calling this conclave must—"

"Wait!" commanded Drogo. He threw back his hood and glared about him. "Have you *all* forgotten *everything*?" he demanded angrily. "Youth's inexperience"—he waved a hand vaguely in Cai's direction—"I can understand, but for the rest of you it is inexcusable."

Drogo looked directly at Mark.

"There is one present who is not of our company," he declared. A gnarled finger pointed. "He must leave!"

"Mark is here, at my request, for several reasons," said Ferragamo. "Firstly, he is our host. This is his castle by ancient right. Secondly, he can bear witness to the matters we are here to discuss. His evidence in unique and cannot be replaced by second-hand accounts. Lastly, he is a Servant and claims the rights of such."

Moroski mentally applauded his friend's calm rationality. Ferragamo paused to let the import of his last statement sink in, and then said, "I say let him stay."

"You have proof?" Xyda's voice held a note of skepticism.

"Hear him. Decide for yourselves."

"That still does not make him a wizard," said Saronno. "Conclave rules—"

"*Rules?* There hasn't been a conclave for over two hundred years! Doesn't that make this a special case?"

"There is no precedent—" persisted Saronno.

"Yes there is," interjected Moroski. "In the time of the first Servants, many of their number attended conclaves."

"I see you have turned scholar," said Xyda sarcastically.

"But that was in the time of the War," added Saronno loudly. "Surely you're not suggesting—"

"Has he a familiar?" asked Drogo suddenly, in a voice which silenced the hubbub about him.

Don't speak, said a voice in Mark's mind. *They haven't accepted you yet. I can sort this out.*

Longfur, who until now had sat unnoticed at Mark's feet, leapt from the floor to the arm of Ferragamo's chair and thence onto the table. Tail erect and fur bristling, he glowered at the wizards round the table.

"Bravo!" exclaimed Cai and was rewarded by a painful kick on his ankle from the neighboring chair where Moroski sat, stone-faced. Cai wisely refrained from clapping.

Drogo stared across the table at Longfur, then mumbled a few words in a low voice. The cat hissed in response and Mark started to move, but was halted by Longfur's silent message. *I'm all right. It sounds quite simple.*

What sounds quite simple?

Watch.

"Let the cat take its place," said Drogo.

Longfur jumped from the table, made his way to a niche, previously unnoticed, and climbed in. He curled up, settling his chin on his forepaws.

I'll just take a short nap. Try not to mess things up while I'm asleep. Longfur closed his eyes, apparently quite at ease, and became still.

Mark turned back to face Drogo as the ancient wizard spoke again.

"You agree to the seals being set?"

"Yes," said Ferragamo.

Mark nodded, his face bleak, knowing intuitively what Longfur risked for his sake.

"If you and the cat are not what Ferragamo claims you to be," said Drogo, "the transformation will not take place. And the animal will die."

Drogo paused theatrically and Mark heard his own heart thumping. *Let him be all right,* he pleaded silently.

I never knew you cared. Don't wo—

Longfur's thoughts were cut off abruptly as Drogo spoke again. The words he declaimed made no sense to Mark but they had a cold, closed ring to them. As the last syllable died away into silence, everyone looked at the animals ranged about the room. As Mark watched, their stillness became the stillness of stone. Slowly the animals turned to life-size statues of themselves, complete in every detail. Each fur, feather, and scale, each now-sightless eye, became the light, lifeless color of the walls about them.

All the wizards' eyes now focused on Longfur. He, too, was changing but, unlike the others, it was not a smooth, continuous transformation. Different parts of him seemed to change at different rates and the whole process flickered, reversing itself momentarily, as if unsure of its own progress.

No, no, no! thought Mark desperately. *It's not working!*

Don't . . . fight . . . it. Longfur's voice sounded faint, in pain. *Help . . . me.*

Mark shut his eyes, unable to watch anymore, willing himself to relax, accept. When he opened them again he saw a stone cat curled within the niche. Quickly he looked at Ferragamo and received a weary, reassuring smile.

"The transformation is complete. The seals are in place," announced Drogo. "The conclave may begin."

Chapter 8

Centuries before, long after the unity imposed by the War of the Wizards had begun to decline, there had been several unfortunate incidents at wizards' conclaves. Many of these had involved familiars, who had been used, according to their various capabilities, to threaten, annoy, or spy upon other wizards or their animals. On one notorious occasion a familiar had actually been *eaten* by another, with disastrous results for both their masters and the conclave as a whole.

The increasingly competitive community of wizardry had recognized the danger of such incidents and an agreement had been reached. The niches in the Wizards' Hall were a legacy of that ancient covenant. By immobilizing all the familiars present, the wizards achieved a double benefit. Firstly, any antagonistic use of the animals was made impossible, and secondly, they gained additional privacy. Some discussions were so sensitive that they could not be shared.

Mark knew nothing of this and felt a certain resentment toward Ferragamo for not telling him what was involved. He and Longfur had been through so much together that Mark no longer thought of the cat as an animal but as a person. It was a measure of their mutual respect that Longfur privately regarded the young king as an honorary cat.

Ferragamo's voice brought Mark back to the present.

"Sit down, Mark. You've earned your place among us."

With a last glance over his shoulder at Longfur, Mark took the seat between his mentor and Cai.

Ferragamo then related his reasons for calling the conclave. He had spent a great deal of time mentally rehearsing this, knowing that what he would say must have the greatest import. Even his sleep had been invaded and he had awoken on more than one occasion soaked with sweat, finding himself, in his dreams, at a loss for words.

He was relieved now that the other wizards seemed prepared to give him a fair hearing. There were no interruptions as he told them of how Ark had nearly succumbed two years ago. He called upon Mark, and occasionally Moroski, to add their testimony where relevant and laid particular stress on the nature of the magic which had been used against them.

"The evil was so great I did not recognize it for a long time," he said. "Amarino was siphoning power directly from the minds of the people of Starhill, reducing them to mindless beings and eventually sentencing them to a living death. If we had not acted when we did, the whole island would eventually have been used to feed her greed for power."

"*Directly* from their minds, you say?" asked Xyda.

"That can't be done," exclaimed Saronno. "It's impossible!"

"Not impossible," said Moroski, "just extremely difficult. We all believed that the technique had been lost eons ago, but it has been revived."

"What *proof* of that can you offer?" asked Drogo. "All we have heard so far is hearsay, a petty conflict of no consequence."

"*Petty!* Haven't you been listening?" shouted Cai. He was about to continue but was restrained by Moroski's hand on his arm.

"The proof was all too obvious," ventured Mark. "We saw it with our own eyes."

"That is not *proof*, young man," said Drogo. "There could by any number of explanations for what you think you saw."

"Are you implying that I have not been telling the truth?" said Mark angrily.

"I was merely pointing out the possibility that you may have been deluded. You admit yourself that Amarino could influence appearances. Is it not possible that the manifestations of evil that you saw were more of her illusions?"

"Talk to anyone who was incarcerated in the dungeons," snapped Mark. "Ask *them* if it was an illusion."

Xyda said, "We will talk to whoever we please, *if* it proves necessary. It is not for you to tell us our business."

Mark lapsed into a sullen silence and Ferragamo took up the argument.

"Surely the proof lies in the fact that the magic we faced was counteracted by the moonberries, could only be defeated with their use. We know they were specifically created to prevent the spread of just such an evil."

"We've all heard those *myths*," said Saronno. "You cannot believe everything you read in storybooks."

"I'll not deny that moonberries are powerful," added Xyda, "but any wizard worth his staff could turn that power to his advantage, whatever enemy he faced."

"But the berries were effective in protecting even those with no magical ability or training," said Moroski.

"That's still not proof," said Saronno.

"All right, all right," said Ferragamo, the first cracks in his composure beginning to show. "Let's leave that and move on—"

He was interrupted by an eerie howling and the dull thunder of a fist being pounded on the far side of the iron door. There was also a small scrabbling noise, soon silenced, from above, but no one paid that any attention.

"At last," said Ferragamo. "Would you release the seals, please."

Drogo did so and the door swung open. At the same time the animals returned to their natural state, though none of them moved. Mark looked round quickly and was glad to see Longfur back to his normal coloring, apparently unharmed. He turned back to the door to see the newest arrival.

The wizard who entered was a big burly man, with fiery red hair and beard. Freckles marked his pale skin and his large hands were calloused. He was dressed in the sealskins and furs of a northern sailor. Beside him strode a huge hound, its bristly coat a varied gray, except for its head and pointed ears, which were red, matching its master's curls.

Ferragamo rose. "Greetings, Briodi. You are indeed welcome."

The wizard from the isle of Dawn inclined his head.

"I came as soon as I could," he said. "I hope I am not too late."

"Are the others with you?"

"No, Ferragamo. I come alone."

"Then we are seven. We shall continue," said Drogo portentously. As if by a secret signal the hound immediately lay down in a niche that had mysteriously appeared where none had been before. Drogo spoke and the door clanged shut again. Mark looked round at Longfur but this time the transformation progressed smoothly. Surrounded by the stone replicas of their familiars, the wizards resumed the conclave.

Briodi greeted his colleagues, then sat in the vacant seat between Xyda and Saronno.

"I beg leave to explain my tardy arrival," he said.

"Granted," replied Drogo.

"I set sail a month ago, making first for Set. I thought to join with Faramondi and offer him passage on my vessel. At first he was not to be found, the court all but deserted. I wasted some days in tracking him down and when I did so it was to no avail. He was no interested in the conclave, holding it to be of little importance."

Ferragamo groaned.

"However much I pressed him," Briodi went on, "he would not be moved, and in the end I was forced to sail without him. I got to Tirek in good time but when Geralti learned of my intentions he flatly refused to see me. I'm afraid I lost my temper a little, even broke a few heads, but it was no use. All I could get out of his lackeys was a message to go and talk to Iolo, his brother as he calls him."

"Extraordinary behavior," said Saronno.

"Go on," prompted Xyda.

"Having little choice, I sailed for Rek. That was a tedious journey. The Tirek Straits are dangerous when the autumn winds begin to blow, so I had to go all the way around the south of the island."

"Get on with it," said Drogo irritably. "Your navigational problems don't concern us."

Briodi was unperturbed by the interruption and continued evenly.

"Iolo was already in high dudgeon when I arrived. I think he'd had some message from Geralti although he would not admit it. In any case, when I approached him to see if he was going to accompany me to the conclave, I met with a torrent of abuse. I restrained myself admirably." Briodi grinned. "I'd made enough enemies already."

"Stars!" said Ferragamo. "What a sorry tale."

"I couldn't make much sense of what Iolo was saying," added Briodi, "but he did give me this letter."

He took a sealed parchment from his jerkin and slid it

across the table. The others waited in silence while Ferragamo read its contents. Mark and Moroski watched him anxiously, recognizing the signs of their friend's fiery temper.

"May I?" asked Drogo as Ferragamo finished reading. Wordlessly, Ferragamo handed the parchment to Mark, who rose and walked around to Drogo's seat.

The master wizard scanned the missive, then said, "As this concerns us all, I will read the relevant portions," and he went on to quote Iolo's objections to the conclave which, when stripped of their rhetoric, boiled down to three main points. These were that what had reportedly happened on Ark was an internal affair of no consequence outside that island; that the isolation of Brogar was a self-imposed political separation and as such should be dealt with by kings and diplomats, not by wizards; and, judging by the length of the diatribe on the subject, his most important objection was the lack of attention paid to matters of protocol in calling the conclave. Iolo protested strongly at the "arbitrary" choice of venue, claiming that Rek as the larger island had more right to the honor of hosting the first conclave for two centuries. The letter also stated that Iolo spoke for Geralti as well as himself.

"He has a point about the choice of venue," said Xyda. "Though Peven is bigger than either Rek or Ark."

"Mere size has nothing to do with it," said Drogo testily. "To my mind, seniority of wizardry should have been the deciding factor."

"For goodness sake," said Ferragamo. "We're here because *I* called for the conclave. *This* is where the event we're talking about happened and *Ark* is the nearest island to Brogar. Isn't that enough?" His exasperation at the latest turn of events was obvious. Things had been going badly enough as it was, but the letter from Iolo and the indifference of the other two absentees was disastrous.

Moroski came to his rescue.

"We should get back to the main discussion," he said. "Briodi, we've already talked about what happened here on Ark two years ago. You should have some idea of that from Ferragamo's letters, but I'll recap on what was said later if you wish. When you arrived," he went on, "Ferragamo was about to tell us about Brogar. With your permission, we should now allow him to proceed."

"As you wish," said Briodi.

"Granted," said Drogo unnecessarily.

Everyone turned to Ferragamo, who roused himself, making yet another effort to convince them of the seriousness of the situation. He told them of the horrific trip to Brogar, again calling on Mark to corroborate his evidence and add details of his own. Both men found it a formidable task to remain coherent, jumbling their words in an effort to stress the importance of what they had to say, and often talking over each other. Their confusion grew worse when it became clear that the terror they had experienced was not being re-created by their account. They were finally cut short by Xyda.

"How much longer do we have to listen to this nonsense?" he asked.

"We've heard quite enough," said Saronno.

"Forget the manner of the telling," said Cai vehemently. "It's the content of the tale that matters."

"We are quite capable of discerning the content, such as it is, for ourselves, young man," said Drogo.

Cai muttered something under his breath.

"What?" snapped Drogo.

"Nothing." Cai flashed back.

"Your manners leave something to be desired," said Xyda. "Remember where you are."

"Cai is the only one who *does* remember where he is," said Ferragamo loudly. Ignoring warning looks from Moroski he ploughed on. "This conclave was *supposed* to discuss the most dangerous threat the islands have faced in an age."

"You say," interjected Saronno.

Ferragamo ignored him.

"Something so massive, so *evil*—and I don't use the word lightly—that it could destroy our whole world. And yet you're bickering about *manners* and *protocol!*" He spat the words out as if they tasted foul.

The color had risen in Saronno's gray face as the implications of Ferragamo's words sank in.

"Do you seriously expect me to believe," he said, "that we are on the brink of a second War of the Wizards?"

"YES!" roared Ferragamo. "That's *exactly* what I expect you to believe!" He had risen to his feet, and banged his fist on the table. In the tense silence that followed, Mark fancied he heard voices above him, but dismissed the thought as absurd.

Eventually Drogo spoke in a voice that was dangerously quiet.

"If what you say is true—"

"But that's ridiculous," put in Saronno.

"—what do you propose we do about it?" concluded Drogo calmly.

It's now or never, thought Mark. *This is your last chance.*

Ferragamo knew it. The effort to stay calm showed in his face. He remained standing. At last he spoke.

"I believe that what happened here was just one small flexing of the power now ruling Brogar. That power is awesomely strong, and can only grow with time. Already it dwarfs the strength of any one of us. Only by acting in unison do we have a chance to defeat it. If we do not, then as sure as I am standing here, a time will come when nothing will be able to stand in its way. It will sweep us all aside like a horse's tail brushing away troublesome insects. That's all we will be by comparison—insects! We must act and act *now*, before it is too late. We must invoke the Rite of Yzalba!"

There was a stunned silence. Mark, who had no idea what Ferragamo was suggesting, noticed that even Cai had blanched.

"Are you mad?" exclaimed Saronno in astonishment.

"We're as like to destroy the world as save it that way," said Xyda.

"Is it really the only way?" asked Cai quietly.

"Yes," replied Ferragamo shortly. Exhausted, he resumed his seat.

"You know what it entails?" asked Drogo.

"Of course."

"Then you are indeed mad. To risk all on such a gamble with such flimsy evidence."

Before Mark and Moroski could move to restrain him, Ferragamo had risen again, his chair crashing to the ground behind him. Leaning over the table, he screamed at Drogo.

"Evidence? You wouldn't recognize evidence if it was stuffed up your nostrils. What do you think we've been talking about for these last hours? If you refuse the Rite now, we are lost. We will all rot in thrall to this evil. And *you* will deserve it!"

By this time both Mark and Moroski were at the wizard's side. Between them they eased him back into his chair,

which Mark had righted. Ferragamo slumped, covering his
face with his hands. His two friends sat down again on either
side of him.

Drogo spoke again in a cold, quiet voice.

"Our colleague seems to have lost control of himself," he
said. Mark heard the pity in his voice and hated him for it.
"In the circumstances I suggest we settle this in the only
manner possible; a vote. Ferragamo proposes that we invoke
the Rite of Yzalba against the supposed power in Brogar."

He fixed the youngest wizard with steely eyes.

"Cai, are you for or against?"

Cai felt the eyes of all his peers upon him and swallowed.

"For," he said softly.

"Moroski?"

"For." The reply was quick and firm.

"Xyda?"

"Against. It would be—"

"Enough! Briodi?"

The big man hesitated, the pain of his indecision showing
in his eyes.

"I don't . . ." he began. "I can't. I abstain."

Xyda was about to remonstrate with Briodi but Drogo
silenced him with a look and continued.

"Saronno?"

"Against. Most definitely."

"I, too, am against," said Drogo, "which makes it three
apiece."

"Don't I get a vote?" asked Mark.

"You do not," replied Drogo firmly. "Even if it were not
clear that our absent colleagues would have voted against, my
vote as senior mage would decide the issue. The proposal is
rejected. That is the end of the matter."

"No!" exclaimed Moroski. "Don't you see what you're doing?
Briodi, will you not reconsider?"

"The vote is concluded," said Drogo.

Now Mark rose to his feet. "This isn't good enough—" he
began, but stopped as attention turned from him to the iron
door. This door, which had been sealed shut by an unbreakable spell, and which could not be opened from the outside
until the conclave was over . . . this door was slowly opening,
apparently of its own volition.

Luke walked into the hall.

Everyone was on their feet now.

"How did he—"

"This is outrageous!"

Mark hurried to his son, lifted him up, and was about to take him outside when Luke spoke. The authority in his voice froze everyone in the room.

"There are very good reasons why you should reconsider your vote," he said. "Let me stay a while and I will explain."

Mark felt a surge of hope. He could see that the wizards were intrigued. Any two-year-old who could speak clearly and authoritatively, defy a powerful sealing spell, and enter a hostile conclave was clearly a curiosity that had not encountered before. He would get a hearing at least. As Mark carried Luke to the table, the door closed itself.

Mark deposited his son on the empty chair between Ferragamo and Xyda and stood behind it himself. The others resumed their seats.

Luke looked across the table.

"Master Wizard Drogo," he said, "have you considered the precedents? The company assembled here . . ."

Luke's voice faltered, and he looked round at his father. Mark saw the bewilderment in the boy's eyes and his heart fell into his stomach.

Not now, Luke. Not NOW! he thought desperately.

"Dada," said Luke, stretching up his arms. "Dada. Cuggle."

Mark lifted his son into his arms and held him tight. With tears in his eyes he looked at Ferragamo and saw his last hope drain away.

Chapter 9

Starhill Castle was a wretched place after the disastrous conclave. Drogo left that night, outraged both by the insults he had received and by the questioning of his authority. His sudden departure caused little surprise and nobody attempted the obviously hopeless task of persuading him to stay.

As Drogo's apprentice, Yve naturally left with him. She was still shaken from her experiences that afternoon and was glad of the activity which allowed her to forget, for a while at least, the terrible things she had overheard. She and Luke had climbed the tower stairs after the wizards and made their way to the topmost room, two floors above the hall where the conclave was being held. Luke had recently discovered that some broken stonework had opened a hole into one of the small chimneys that served the tower. By listening at the opening he could hear, through some strange acoustical anomaly, what was being said almost anywhere in the tower, including, as it turned out, the Wizards' Hall.

Yve had been terrified at what they had heard and appalled by the vehemence of the arguments among the wizards. She found herself desperately hoping that Ferragamo would win over the conclave and cursed her master for his intransigence when it became clear that all was not going well.

When Luke announced suddenly that he must go and talk to them, Yve was assailed by fresh fears. The consequences of discovery and the punishment she would receive for indulging her curiosity in such a way were too terrible to contemplate. She was also terrified for Luke's sake and tried to stop him, but he slipped away easily and she dared not call out too loudly. For a few moments she was rooted to the spot, the angry words from below continuing to hold her.

Finally she gathered her courage and ran after Luke, slipping once or twice on the old stone. She rounded the last curve only to see Luke push open the hall door and step inside. Aghast, she waited for a moment, then her nerve broke and she fled down the stairs. By the time she reached the base she was giddy, but pelted across the deserted tree-yard and raced to Drogo's quarters, where she hid, trembling and sick, and tried to regain her composure.

Shortly afterward the wizard arrived and announced that they were leaving immediately, that Ark was an island of madmen and he hoped never to set foot on it again. Yve set about her tasks and roused the other servants but still found time to slip away and seek out Luke. She found him with Fontaine in the royal apartments, and was relieved to see the little boy apparently none the worse for his exploit.

"Hello," said Fontaine. "You're Yve, aren't you?"

Yve curtseyed awkwardly.

"Yes, my lady. I . . . I just came to say goodbye to Luke."

Fontaine gave her a curious look but asked no more. Luke toddled over to Yve, and smiled as she picked him up.

"You've gotten to know each other well in such a short time," said Fontaine.

"He's a remarkable little boy," replied Yve.

"I know," said the queen fondly. "Too remarkable sometimes."

Yve looked up sharply but Fontaine's smile held no secrets. "And now you've got to go."

"Yes," said Yve sadly.

"Perhaps you can come back sometime."

"I hope so."

Quietly, not knowing whether Luke understood her or not, Yve added, "I *will* come back. I have to. Goodbye, Luke, for now."

She handed the boy back to his mother.

"Goodbye, then. Thank you, my lady."

"Goodbye, Yve."

Luke waved a small hand in farewell.

After the conclave had broken up, Ferragamo had stormed off to his private apartments, deaf to all about him. Moroski did not attempt to calm him down, knowing that Koria would stand a better chance than anyone of soothing her lover. Even Owl kept his distance that night, preferring to roost alone in the tower.

As the evening drew in the wizard found himself sitting beside Koria in their bedchamber, drinking a potion she had brewed for him. He suspected that it contained something to take the edge off his temper and perhaps make him sleep. He didn't care. He doubted if anything would help him sleep that night.

Inhaling the bitter fumes, his thoughts returned to the conclave and he grimaced. Koria watched him, and tried again to coax him into talking about it. So far the wizard had maintained a stubborn silence, but she knew that inside he was boiling up and needed to let off some steam. She only hoped it would not scald her.

"It can't be *that* bad. You can try again later," she said tentatively.

"And what would you know about it!" he snapped; then, seeing the stricken look on her face, he put his free arm around her rigid shoulders and added, "I'm sorry my love. You, of all people, do not deserve my bile."

He felt her muscles relax in his embrace. Koria knew now that he would begin to talk without prompting. She merely had to wait and the healing process would start.

"It went wrong right from the beginning," Ferragamo said quietly. "Perhaps I should not have insisted that Mark be there. That gave them the chance to argue about side issues. It was a mistake, I think, and for all the use he was, Mark may as well not have been there."

Koria was shocked by the wizard's tone. The bitterness she detected was not at all to her liking.

"It took *two years* to set up this conclave," Ferragamo went on. "The next one will probably take six! Then I expect only half of them will turn up. What a mess I've made of things."

Staring into space, he added, "As a diplomat I make a pretty good warthog."

He laughed without humor, then began coughing.

"What is this stuff?" he asked, sniffing his drink suspiciously.

"Eye of newt and horn of toad," she replied.

"I wouldn't put it past you."

"Just drink it."

"What, so you can have your wicked way with me?" he said, desperately trying to lighten his own mood.

"Of course," she replied, relieved, and began unfastening his shirt.

Xyda and Saronno left the following morning. Although Mark and Moroski saw them off, there was no cordiality in the parting.

They were potentially our most powerful allies, thought Mark. *Now it will be twice as hard to enlist any help from their islands*. Not for the first time he silently cursed the memory of the conclave and Ferragamo's outbursts which had completed the fiasco.

For Mark, the only positive note from the aftermath of the whole episode was that Longfur had emerged unscathed. In fact the cat was quite enjoying this further proof of his special nature.

Nothing to it, had been his casual response to Mark's first anxious inquiry. *How did it go?*

Don't ask.

Why is Luke here?

Longfur, I don't want to talk now. Let's just get out of here.

Sorry, I'm sure, came the aggrieved reply. *Of course it was silly of me to expect a sensible answer. I only made the whole thing possible. That's all.*

Longfur had stalked out of the hall and down the stairs. Some time later Mark had sought him out, apologized, and explained what had happened as best he could.

Muscles should have been there, Longfur said on hearing of Luke's failure. *That would have tipped the balance.*

You cats don't lack confidence, do you? said Mark, smiling for the first time in hours.

We generally make a much better job of things than you humans, came the smug reply.

I can't argue with that, said Mark glumly.

See what comes of turning us to statues?

What was it like? asked Mark curiously.

It was a bit sticky at first, replied Longfur. *I started feeling . . . sort of gritty. Like not having enough sleep and finding*

*your breakfast milk has gone off. After that it was just like
going to sleep. I had some interesting dreams.*
    What about?
    The picture which Longfur painted was clear and colorful.
For Mark it had the stamp of reality. The dream had been
eerie and frightening but ended on a comfortable note.
    In it, Longfur was curled up in long grass, basking in the
warm sun. All was quiet and peaceful, the only sound that of
birdsong.
    Suddenly he found himself on board a ship which was
tossing in a stormy sea. About him, all was chaos, and he
knew that those he loved, though not specified personally,
were in danger of being swept overboard. The ship was
nearing a whirlpool, yet he knew that this was not the voyage
made by Mark to Brogar. As the seemingly inevitable catas-
trophe drew nearer, Longfur looked around desperately but
could not see a familiar face. Just as the ship lurched and
began its final descent, he looked down and noted the curious
fact that his paws had turned brown. The ship groaned as it
began to break up . . .
    . . . and I found myself being driven in a carriage!
    Just like that? queried Mark, forgetting the quicksilver
nature of dream scene-changes.
    *Yes. Penelope was with me. We were on the way to the
fishmongers.*
    What for?
    To buy some fish for the family, of course.
    But that's ridiculous!
    Yes, agreed Longfur. *Penelope hates shopping.*

The next to leave was Briodi. He had stayed an extra day
but was clearly embarrassed by the situation and apologetic
about his late arrival and ineffectual contribution. He con-
fessed himself to be a simple man, unsuited to the profession
into which he had been pressed, and this was borne out by
the fact that he was obviously more at ease with the castle's
artisans than with any of the wizards. His yearning to be back
in his remote northern home-isle was painfully obvious and
nobody was surprised when he made his farewell.
    Cai lingered a few days more. When he was not with one
of the maidens of the castle, who found him much to their

liking, he spent a lot of his time with Moroski. Their relationship was overshadowed by recent events, however, and their earlier, easy comradeship never fully returned. Even so, Cai's optimistic nature soon reasserted itself. He was secretly glad that Ferragamo's drastic proposal had been refused, preferring to let the future of the world take care of itself and hope for the best. The result of the vote absolved him of a frightening responsibility, and, he reassured himself, it was possible that Ferragamo could be wrong. He kept these thoughts to himself and resolved to enjoy his stay in Starhill as much as he could. That he succeeded in doing so was a tribute both to his own sunny personality and to the female population of Starhill.

Moroski could not help but smile when he met Cai at the castle gates one evening, bidding a fond farewell to one of his acquaintances.

"You are a disgrace to our profession," he said jovially as the younger wizard came toward him.

"You're only young once," Cai replied. "Well, *they* are. I'm working on it."

"I suppose you'll grow up one day."

"Not if I can help it. Besides, where's the harm in enjoying life? Just because I'm a wizard it doesn't mean I'm made of wood."

"Neither are the girls who seem to find you so devastatingly attractive—"

"With good cause," put in Cai with a smirk.

"Don't you have any feelings for them?"

"Of course," said Cai, looking hurt. "And they don't seem to object to my attentions." He paused and smiled again. "It's not as if I'm going to leave a trail of bastards behind me."

"You have some advantages, I'll admit," Moroski said, laughing. "Are you hungry?"

"Starved!"

"You mean to tell me you didn't even buy the poor girl dinner?"

Arm in arm, they walked to the food hall, where they found Mark, alone, among the remnants of a meal. He had a glass of wine in his hand. He looked blearily at them, and Moroski realized that, unusually, Mark was on his way to becoming drunk.

"Just the people I want to see," said the young king. "I want to talk to you."

"At your service, my lord," answered Cai, bowing low. "If I could just fill a plate at the same time?"

"You're in a good mood," said Mark, slightly disbelievingly. "Help yourselves. Have some wine. It's rather good."

The two wizards sat down and he poured the extra glasses as they served themselves.

"What was it you wanted to talk about?" asked Cai, through a mouthful of food. Mark didn't answer at once. He took another swig of wine and refilled his glass.

"I don't seem to be able to talk to Ferragamo anymore," he mused, as if talking to himself. The wizards exchanged glances. "What is this Rite of Yzalba?" he asked abruptly.

Cai lost his appetite. He set down his knife and looked at Moroski, who said, "It's difficult to explain."

"We have all night," replied the king expansively, "unless you have other commitments?" He looked at Cai with raised eyebrows.

Moroski said, "You know the human mind is the prime source of energy we know as magic?"

"Of course."

"And that this power can be added to from outside sources—"

"Yes, yes," said Mark impatiently.

"Well, the most powerful source of all is the world-mind."

Mark's memory conjured up an earlier time, long ago, and Ferragamo's voice saying, *There are many sources of magical power. Look about you. There is potential in everything. The world has a mind, of a sort, just as you do. You know that some places, the old places especially, have a strange and powerful atmosphere. That is the legacy of magical history, and the reserves to be tapped are vast, unknowable—*

"The Rite of Yzalba enables a group of wizards to harness the power of the world-mind," said Moroski, "in a direct link."

"If it works," added Cai softly.

"It scares you," said Mark.

"Yes," said Moroski. "Unleashed, the power could be so great that even all the wizards acting in unison would not be able to control it."

"It would become wild, run amok," said Cai.

"And could destroy the world completely," concluded Moroski.

Mark pondered this for a while.

"So that's why the conclave was so important!"

"Yes. Two or three of us would stand no chance. We'd be swallowed up like minnows by a shark."

"Has the Rite ever been used before?"

"Only once," replied Moroski.

"In the War of the Wizards," Mark finished for him. "It all keeps coming back to that." He swallowed more wine and his eyes took on a glazed look.

"It worked then?"

"Yes," said Moroski. "Just."

Chapter 10

In the days that followed only Koria saw much of Ferragamo. He became a semirecluse, spending his time alone in the tower library, searching in vain for an alternative to the Rite of Yzalba. Each time he ended up brooding on the failure of the conclave and on the dreadful necessity of trying again. Miserable thoughts trickled round his brain like acid, eating away at his self-confidence and leaving him permanently exhausted.

Cai left, knowing that any further delay risked a rough passage as autumn slid slowly into winter. Most inhabitants of the castle were sorry to see him go and missed his lively presence, but Ferragamo hardly noticed his departure. Two weeks later, however, an arrival at Starhill roused the wizard from his self-imposed stupor.

Fontaine gave birth to her second child during the gray time shortly before dawn; the wolfing hour, the old maidservant called it. The delivery was an easy one and Adesina, who was acting as midwife, had no need to call upon the healing skills of Ferragamo. Nevertheless, the wizard was second only to Mark in visiting the baby, and for a short time at least, the two men were once again at ease with each other, united by a common tenderness.

The baby girl was named Beca, and from the first was a lively and demanding child. She basked in the attention she received, giving those around her a foretaste of the effect she would have in later life, when her golden curls and huge blue eyes would captivate all who saw her.

Fontaine was up and about soon after the birth, and it very quickly became clear that she had no intention of heeding her mother's advice to rest. She began talking of resuming her sword training and had to be restrained from making for the practice yard. Her rapid return to robust health hastened the departure of the party from Heald. Pabalan had been kicking his heels for some time, and now that his granddaughter had safely arrived, he was anxious to return to his own home. The periodic letters which had arrived from Ansar and Laurent told a satisfactory tale, but Pabalan preferred to trust his own eyes more than the written word.

Adesina reluctantly agreed that it was time to go and began to make arrangements for their departure. Moroski, too, began to gather his few possessions in readiness for his return to Heald. He visited Ferragamo and they talked for several hours, in itself something of a breakthrough. Moroski promised that he would strive to begin the slow process of organizing another conclave. It was all he could do.

Not all of the Healdean party wanted to return to their home-isle. As Mark and Fontaine sat talking with her parents the day before their departure, they received a surprise visit.

After they had made their formal greetings, Richard and Sophi stood before them in an embarrassed silence.

"Sit down, you two," said Mark. Though he had already guessed the purpose of their visit, he added, "What can we do for you?"

"My lord," began Richard, "my suit is to you but—"

"First I must ask something of my mistress," finished Sophi. She turned to Adesina. "My lady, I wish to be released from my service to you, so that I may remain on Ark."

"No release is necessary, Sophi. You are free to choose your own course," replied Adesina. "Ever since you came to me from Rehan's household you have proved worthy of anyone's regard. I shall be sorry to lose you," she added, smiling.

"Thank you, my lady."

"Then, my lords, with your permission, I would like to wed Sophi," said Richard, taking her hand as he spoke.

Pabalan, who knew Richard well by now, said gravely, "What do you say, Mark? Is he a suitable match for this flower of Heald?"

Equally grave, but with a twinkle in his eye, Mark replied, "There is no finer soldier, no finer man in all Ark."

Color crept into Richard's face.

Fontaine could contain herself no longer, and leapt to her feet.

"Ignore these pompous kings," she said fondly. "We're all delighted!"

She embraced both Richard and Sophi in turn. For a while all was smiles and congratulations. Wine was produced and toasts drunk.

The exchange of vows took place, at the couple's own request, that very evening. The marriage came as no surprise to the more observant inhabitants of Starhill Castle. The castle guard and the former lady-in-waiting had spent too much time in each other's company for it not to have been noticed. Most of those present at the ceremony, whether from Ark or Heald, felt that Richard and Sophi were perfect for each other.

One notable absentee from the wedding and the subsequent, hastily arranged banquet was Ferragamo. Koria had tried to persuade him to attend, but he was in such a morbid mood that she gave up the attempt. *Like that*, she thought, *he will only upset people and spoil their gaiety. It's good to have a reason to celebrate for a change.*

The festivities ceased around midnight. They would have gone on longer, but many of the revelers had to be up early to begin their journey back to Heald. The newlyweds retired to their temporary accommodation in Sophi's room, this being more suitable, in terms of both privacy and comfort, then Richard's quarters.

Sophi removed her gown and folded it carefully. As she was putting it away in the chest, Richard slid his arms around her from behind and nuzzled her neck. His glance fell upon a soft leather pouch in the drawer.

"What's that?" he asked, pointing.

Sophi stiffened slightly within his arms.

"Oh, nothing," she said. "Besides, a woman has to have *some* secrets."

She wriggled around within his embrace and kissed him. Very soon, Richard forgot all about the contents of the drawer.

Mark felt slightly dizzy as he left the food hall, and blamed this on the heat within the hall and the large meal he had eaten. Deciding to get some fresh air, he walked into the courtyard. The night sky was clear, and the castle bathed in silvery moonlight. It was cold, the first frosts of the year rapidly approaching.

Mark inhaled deeply, hoping to clear his head, but it remained obstinately fogged. He raised his head to look at the myriad stars, but they refused to stay still, swaying and whirling so that he was forced to look down again. He was about to go inside and rejoin his queen, when a familiar figure appeared in the doorway of the inner courtyard.

The stared at each other in silence for a while.

"Where've you been hiding yourself?" asked Mark eventually.

"I wasn't aware that I had been hiding," replied Ferragaino, his face a white mask.

"We haven't seen much of you since—"

"Since when?" said the wizard in a voice as cold as the night.

"Since your brilliant performance at the conclave," retorted Mark. He felt his pent-up resentment break loose in a flood. "You wizards are all the same," he went on recklessly. "You act as if no one else could possibly contribute anything useful and then, when you get together, what happens? You behave like spoiled children and can't even talk civilly to one another! As a consequence, *nothing* gets done."

"I tried, Mark, but I don't make a very good diplomat," said Ferragamo miserably.

"You can say that again!"

"You weren't exactly a big help yourself," retorted the wizard, anger rising in his voice.

"Oh, so it's my fault now. *I* didn't start insulting people. *I* didn't act like a madman. I'm not surprised you lost the vote."

"That's not fair, Mark. I—"

"Don't patronize me!" Mark was shouting now. "I'm no longer the little boy you used to lecture!"

"More's the pity. You used to listen to reason then."

"You call what wizards talk reason?"

"You're drunk," said Ferragamo, unable to keep the disgust out of his voice. "Why don't we talk in the morning?"

"What's wrong with now?" Mark yelled, but as the words came out the ground lurched under his feet, and he staggered. When he looked back at the doorway, Ferragamo had disappeared. At the same time he became aware of someone else watching him. Turning slowly he looked into Fontaine's frightened eyes. Beside her stood Koria, her face anguished.

"Where'd he go?" he mumbled.

"Not now, love," said his wife gently. "Come inside. We'll go to bed." She came to his side and took his arm.

"It's cold," he said, inconsequentially.

Koria fled.

The next morning Mark woke late, and alone, with a severe headache, and lay wondering how the day could get any worse. A moment later he found out.

I hope you're proud of yourself, admonished Longfur. *A fine example you set*, Your Majesty.

Go away, Longfur. Mark winced at the sound of his own thoughts and hid his head under the pillow. He could not escape.

I just thought I'd better let you know that unless you get up immediately, you will miss the departure of your in-laws.

"Oh, no," groaned Mark aloud. *Is it that late?*

They're packed and ready to go, came the reply. *Though looking the way you do I don't suppose they really want to see you anyway.*

You heartless . . . Mark sat up and flung a pillow at his tormentor, then regretted his sudden movement.

Missed! came Longfur's parting comment. *You have to get up earlier than that to catch me.*

Gingerly Mark rose and dressed. Even if his face didn't look green, it felt it. He made his way slowly out to the courtyard, where carriages were waiting.

"There you are," exclaimed Adesina. "We're just off. Are you feeling better?"

Mark began to nod, then changed his mind and said, "Yes. Sorry I'm late." Adesina pecked him on the cheek and gave him a slightly worried smile. Pabalan's grin, as he approached, was much broader.

"That's all right," he said, much too loudly for Mark's liking. "I know just how it is."

For one horrible moment Mark thought Pabalan was going to slap him on the back, but he was saved by the emergence of Fontaine and Luke from one of the carriages.

"Luke says your carriage is now ready," announced Fontaine, avoiding Mark's gaze.

"On our way then," boomed Pabalan, lifting his grandson up above his head. "I won't be able to do that next time I see you, I'll wager."

Adesina hugged her daughter, and then, with a rattle of harness and many shouts of farewell, the visitors took their leave.

Mark and Fontaine stood in silence till they were out of sight. Luke began to cry, and his mother scooped him up.

"He'll miss them," said Mark.

"Yes," replied Fontaine, "so will I. And not only them."

"What do you mean?" asked Mark, puzzled.

"Ferragamo's gone too," she replied.

Chapter 11

It took Ferragamo and Koria four days to arrive at their destination, the remote fishing village of Home in the far south of the island. After their initial flight from Starhill, they rode at a more leisurely pace, but it was some time since either of them had spent so long in the saddle, and they were glad to reach their journey's end.

Ferragamo had kept a cottage in Home for many years, using it as a retreat, a place to relax in simple comfort, away from the bustle and tensions of the city. Only once before had he been in such need of this haven.

They reached the cottage in the early evening, and because it was on the outskirts of the village, close to the northern trail, they were able to settle in unnoticed. The woodstove in the kitchen soon warmed the whole house, and Koria quickly produced a delicious meal. As the gloom of the rainy autumn night drew in about the snug cottage, they sat together on the quilted settle and felt very much at home.

"This is good," said Ferragamo. Koria was not sure whether he mean their closeness, being where they were, or just the last of their wine, and did not really care.

"We'll have to go back eventually," the wizard said.

"But not for a while."

"I still love him," he went on.

"I know."

"I suppose I should just accept that he's king of Ark. He may not want an old fogey like me interfering."

"That's the trouble with children we love," said Koria wistfully. "They grow up."

"Mmm."

"Besides, you're exaggerating. Ather was a lot older than Mark and he still wanted you to *interfere*. You're both upset at the moment, but it'll soon blow over."

As she spoke, Koria desperately hoped that her words were true and not just the product of wishful thinking. The scene that she and Fontaine had witnessed in Starhill was still fresh in her mind; it had shaken even her considerable composure to its foundations. When Ferragamo had vanished before her eyes she had had to face just how deeply he was troubled. Leaving Fontaine to take care of Mark, Koria had rushed to their apartment, running as she had never done before.

Arriving breathless and sweating, she found her love sitting on the edge of the bed, shaking violently, his face nearly as white as his hair. His expression was emotionless and his eyes stared blankly but she knew that, within, he was in turmoil.

Kneeling before him, she took his cold hands in her own, automatically setting about rubbing some warmth back into them. Slowly, the shaking subsided and Ferragamo's eyes came back into focus, but he remained deathly pale.

"What sort of w-wizard am I?" he whispered wretchedly. "To use magic like that? To run away?"

Koria did not reply. She watched his face but he still would not meet her eyes.

"I've never done that before," he said. "In all these years! And to Mark of all people."

"It's over now. Mark is all right."

"Is he? Will he ever trust me again?" Ferragamo at last looked at Koria, and she saw the pain in his eyes.

"Of course he will. Relax now, my love."

"How can I relax?" he asked. "I've been so stupid. I can't seem to do anything right. And now this."

"What happened at the conclave wasn't your fault. You did everything you could," she said, knowing how lame her words must sound.

"But my best effort wasn't good enough," he answered bitterly. "By a long way. I can't go into the tower now without reliving that nightmare."

"Then let's go away," said Koria, "and spend some time at Home. It'll do us both good."

She waited, watching him hopefully.

At last he said, "All right, we'll go. It's time to put all this business into perspective."

Koria smiled. "We'll leave first thing in the morning."

"We'll leave now," he replied firmly. "This very moment."

She started to protest, then thought better of it and said, "I'll get some things packed."

"Don't bother," he said. "Just change into something more suitable for riding. We can supply the rest as we go."

Koria didn't argue. It was good to see Ferragamo in such a decisive mood.

Her gown replaced with traveling clothes, Koria walked with the wizard to the stables. Shalli's horse-light proved its worth again as Ferragamo's mount accepted the pebble without alarm. Koria's horse followed in his wake as they left the castle, passed through Field Gate, and rode out into the starlit night.

When Pabalan, Adesina, and Moroski came to bid them farewell the next morning, they found the apartment empty. By then Ferragamo and Koria were many leagues to the south.

Life in Starhill Castle gradually took on a more normal aspect. After the hectic pace of recent events, the departures made it seem very quiet, and many found it difficult to return to their everyday business. Fontaine was fully occupied with Beca and with Luke, who was dejected, moping over the loss of his grandparents and, to Mark's slight chagrin, Ferragamo. Time weighed heavily on the young king's hands. After the shock of the wizard's disappearance, Mark had become melancholy, blaming himself for the argument. He felt queasy when he recalled how it had ended and vowed never to drink more than a glass of wine again. Like all such oaths it was soon broken, but, for a few days, he drank only water.

He realized where the wizard and Koria were going but decided against dispatching anyone after them or sending a message to Home. Like Koria, Mark recognized that a separation would probably benefit both of them. It would clear the air, and he wanted Ferragamo to choose his own time to return. He still felt a degree of resentment toward the wizards, feeling that they had treated him with less than respect. It also rankled that Ferragamo had not told him either about the "sealing" and Longfur's role in that, or about the Rite of Yzalba, which had proved to be the crux of the matter.

However, Fontaine and Longfur did their best to soothe his ruffled feathers and eventually his resentment faded.

Fontaine took up her unusual regimen of exercise again and on many occasions Mark was her sparring partner, always fighting with his ancient sword. This had an ugly black stain running almost the full length of the blade, a reminder of an earlier, more serious combat, and he had made no effort to clean it off. Luke frequently came to watch, finding the whole spectacle highly amusing.

Luke remained an enigma. In his adult phase he laid claim to memories and manners so far in advance of his years that it was hard for even those closest to him to accept. Yet there were great gaps in his knowledge which only experience could bring. It was obvious that he found Ferragamo's absence frustrating, the wizard being the only person who might have been able to replace experience with explanation in such a way as to reconcile the boy's disparate feelings.

Beca had no such problems. Her needs were more than adequately catered for. Like everyone else, her brother doted upon her, and was minutely inquisitive about her small life.

Luke never mentioned the conclave or what had happened there. Nobody knew whether this was because he was deliberately avoiding the subject or because he had forgotten it entirely, and they dared not ask him.

Time passed. Ferragamo and Koria settled into a comfortable pattern of life. The villagers soon knew that the Visitor, as they called Ferragamo, was at the cottage, but natural courtesy kept them from being too inquisitive. For some time the only callers were the bolder children, drawn by the reputation—and the smells—of Koria's cooking.

The couple went for long walks, tended the small garden, told each other tales, and eventually renewed old acquaintances in the village. They went out fishing in the local boats, drank at The Mermaid a few times, listened to local gossip, and caught up on the news of the village.

They were very much at ease in their simple surroundings, but after a month had passed, Koria began to notice the telltale signs of Ferragamo's restlessness, and knew that the time was coming when they would have to return to the city. She waited for Ferragamo to raise the matter, savoring the last few days of freedom, but when he did speak of leaving, Koria was in for a surprise.

"I've been thinking," he said. "I want to go and see Shalli."

Koria felt mixed emotions about this proposal, knowing that he always went alone, and was taken aback when Ferragamo added, "Come with me."

"You're sure?" she asked, unable to hide her delight.

"Quite sure. It will be cold in the mountains but once we get to the cave that won't be a problem. Will you come?"

"Oh, yes!" she replied, hugging him. "It's a lovely idea. Of course I'll come."

Two days later they set off, their horses laden with farewell gifts from the villagers. Again they traveled without haste, staying the first night at Stane, then riding through the great forest to Ashwicken. Their journey brought a flood of memories to Ferragamo, as he relived in part the fateful expedition of two years before. Then, the forest had been inhabited by two warring bands of outlaws, but most had been killed and the rest scattered over the island. Three of them, Durc, Zunic, and Jani, had become a loyal part of life in Starhill.

The next day they rode on, passing a place that Ferragamo knew only too well, where the seasons were always out of step, and stayed the night at a lonely coaching inn in the Iron River Valley. From there they followed the river upstream into the Windchill Mountains. Koria had never been in the mountains so late in the year and was awed by the somber majesty of the scenery. The higher peaks were hidden in cloud and several times the travelers were themselves shrouded in mist. It was cold, as the wizard had predicted, and their horses were soon treading carefully through the snow. Ferragamo had no difficulty in picking out their route, though to Koria it seemed invisible, and by late afternoon they were in sight of their goal.

Shalli accepted their arrival as if he had been expecting them. *Perhaps he had*, thought Ferragamo.

The hermit and Koria liked each other immediately. Although they were worlds apart, almost opposites in outlook and abilities, their personalities were somehow a perfect match. Ferragamo watched delightedly as Shalli showed Koria the secrets of his dwelling and she exclaimed at each new wonder.

"It's even more amazing than you told me," she said to the

wizard after completing her tour of inspection. "No wonder you like it here so much."

That evening she and Ferragamo took a hot bath together in the huge natural tub, soaking away the last vestiges of travel weariness.

"This is fun," said Koria. "We could do with a bath like this in Starhill." She immediately regretted mentioning the city, but Ferragamo smiled.

"We'll have one built," he said. "This could become a habit."

They stayed with Shalli for six days, and in that time Koria began to appreciate the serenity of this mountain home. At first, she felt excluded and restless when the hermit and Ferragamo meditated, but soon decided to join them. She could not hope to take part in their rarified communication but she worked out her own set of mental exercises, sitting quietly, and letting her mind slip deeper and deeper into the peace of her surroundings.

By the end of their visit Koria even understood a fair proportion of what the hermit said. Shalli's speech was as enigmatic as had been reported, but after a while she found it began to make sense, and wondered if it was Shalli who spoke properly and the rest of humanity that spouted gibberish. She was aware, too, although she never actually saw them, of the animals that came and went. She loved the place and its eccentric inhabitant and was sad when Ferragamo announced that they must leave soon. Starhill was beckoning.

As they were saddling their horses and wondering if the light, early morning snow would become more serious, Shalli came to them, his expression beatific. Reaching out, he took one of each of their hands and clasped them together within his own.

"Beyond the line," the hermit said. "All change. No change." He was smiling, but Koria saw a sadness in his eyes. A momentary chill, deep within her, gave way to a great, glowing warmth and, inexplicably, she felt a lump in her throat. Tears started to well up but she held them back, feeling ridiculous, until she saw them running down Ferragamo's cheeks.

Shalli, still smiling, turned away and made his way back into the depths of the cave.

"Farewell, old friend," whispered the wizard. Then he

helped Koria mount and swung himself into the saddle. They rode out into the cold morning.

After a while Koria found her voice and asked, "What did he mean?"

"Your guess is as good as mine," he replied. And though his tone implied more than his words, he would say no more.

Koria was to meet Shalli on several occasions in the future, but he never repeated those peculiar words and, in the end, they became just one more of his mysterious sayings.

Chapter 12

Ferragamo and Koria were welcomed back to Starhill with quiet relief. The castle had not felt right without them.

The wizard and Mark greeted each other politely, and it was not long before they were once again quite cordial. They knew, however, that their relationship would never be the same. A cord had been severed and, no matter how many knots they tied, the ends could not be rejoined.

Life went on. Years passed. No great disasters befell Ark, or any of the other islands, and Ferragamo began to wonder if his terrible premonition had been the misguided vision of a cranky fool. Everyone else slowly forgot about the whole episode. Moroski occasionally mentioned another conclave in his letters but, eventually, his remarks became less urgent. In a time of peace and general prosperity it proved difficult to believe in a remote evil, still harder to rouse anyone to action against it.

Brogar remained isolated. No ship ever went near the island and the story spread that it had been destroyed by some huge natural disaster—an earthquake or volcanic eruption.

Trade with all the other islands was thriving. Durc and Zunic returned from Peven with a newly acquired taste for travel and, as a consequence, were forever setting off on voyages to distant parts. Mark and Ferragamo made use of the reformed outlaws' new way of life by making them unofficial ambassadors and gatherers of information. They proved particularly adept at their new trade and spread their network of business and social contacts far and wide. They always returned with new treasures as gifts, especially for Luke and Beca, and—even more exciting in the children's eyes—brought back a fresh supply of stories; travelers' tales, adventures and romances, yarns concocted from myth and legend and the gossip of the world. The children listened avidly, and even though Luke knew that the tales were occasionally embroidered—just a little—they still made him long for the time when he could set off on adventures of his own.

In the meantime, he found more than adequate compensation in the company of Ferragamo and his magical tuition. In this, he had unknowingly taken the place of his father, now an older, more worldly man, concerned with statesmanship rather than with magic.

At first the wizard found it difficult to talk seriously to the infant prodigy, and hard to reconcile the boy's mental capacity with his physical development. Soon, though, Ferragamo learned to trust Luke with more and more information about the theory of wizardry. The boy absorbed it all and, even after extended periods in his infant phase, still retained the words and ideas when he became an "adult" again. He constantly surprised Ferragamo with his ability to grasp a theory and his intuitive understanding of the nature and interaction between magic and the normal world. The trouble started when Luke tried to put the theory into practice.

Luke had power. Both of them knew that; he had shown it on two notable occasions. What he did not have was control of that power. He could not remember how he had used it, either in absorbing the moonberry's potency or in entering the sealed conclave, and no amount of theoretical discussion with Ferragamo could enable him to channel it successfully now. On the few occasions when he *had* tried, the spells had rapidly got out of hand. The simple act of remotely lighting a candle had resulted not only in the candle melting instantly into a pool of wax but also in the table beneath it bursting into flames. Only Ferragamo's prompt action had saved the entire contents of the room from going up in smoke.

Similarly, when he had tried a searching spell to find a special marble, secreted somewhere in the castle by Owl, the flying sensation Luke experienced, as his mind reached out, was so sudden and so violent that he had thrown himself out of his chair and had been quite sick.

Muscles, who had rapidly grown into a strong, agile cat, was almost always present at Ferragamo's magical lessons.

Like Luke, he learned rapidly, and one of the first things he understood was to hide when Luke tried a spell.

After one particularly harrowing experience, the cat said, *I do wish you wouldn't shout so. It hurts my head.*

I wasn't shouting, replied Luke, mystified.

What! As soon as you started on that spell it was as if your head exploded, said Muscles. *Words and thoughts and things were shooting off in all directions, all so loud you couldn't tell what they were. It hurt!* he ended aggrievedly.

I'm sorry, said Luke, remembering only that he had whispered a few syllables and the spell had taken on a life of its own, quite beyond his awareness. It was very frustrating.

Ferragamo, while not affected directly as Muscles was, was also shaken by Luke's unpredictable attempts and tried, without success, to find some enchantments where the results did not include fire, illness, or random rearrangement of his furniture.

"Perhaps we had better try this outside," he had said on one occasion. The first nail that Luke had attempted to drive into a block of wood from the opposite side of the room, had gone through the wood *and* the table on which it stood, before disappearing into the stone floor. Moments later, now distinctly bent, the nail reappeared from another part of the floor and buried itself in the wall not far from Owl's perch. When they finally dug it out of the masonry the nail was a finger's width shorter than it had been.

In a forlorn attempt to solve the riddle of his unruly talent, Luke turned to books, and rapidly taught himself to read and write, enlisting the help of Ferragamo or Fontaine when necessary. Though he did not find anything to help him in the way he desired, Luke did discover a whole new world of words, devouring almost the entire contents of Ferragamo's library and searching out books from any other available source. As a consequence he became a theoretical expert—without any mature understanding—on such diverse subjects as animal husbandry, land ownership records, and the use of herbs in treating various internal disorders.

Some of the wizard's books were forbidden to him. The boy respected this, knowing the havoc he could wreak with his simple spells, but he regarded one volume with fascination. Ferragamo had brought it back with him from one of his periodic trips to Home. Mark had seen it, and before Luke could get a proper look, his father had snatched the book away. This led to an argument between Mark and Ferragamo.

"They're only stories!" the wizard had said at one point.

"How can you say that, after what happened?" replied Mark. "I know better."

Now the large, leather-bound book sat on a high shelf well out of Luke's reach. He could read the title, *Sages of the Servants*, but that was all. It sounded familiar, but in a way he could not place. He resolved to read the sagas as soon as he got an opportunity, whatever his father might think. How could stories hurt him?

His chance came one afternoon when Ferragamo was called away to tend to someone who was ill. Although Luke knew a good deal about the theories of magical healing, this was one branch of wizardry which, for obvious reasons, he had been forbidden to practice. Luke and Muscles had been playing with a long ball of twine, winding it around the legs of various pieces of furniture and each other to produce interesting patterns.

Left unsupervised, Luke immediately hit upon a plan.

I bet you can't climb to the top of those shelves, he said, knowing full well that Muscles, like his father before him, would not be able to resist such a challenge.

Of course I can, came the reply and the cat immediately hurtled across the room, sped over a chair, scrambled up the tapestry behind it, and, with contemptuous ease, leapt from there onto the uppermost shelf. He then stalked along it, looking smug.

Catch! cried Luke, and tossed up the partially unraveled ball of twine. Muscles snagged it with one paw.

Now thread the twine around the back of that big book there, went on Luke excitedly.

Why?

So that I can climb up too!

Don't be silly. It will never hold your weight.

It's an experiment, Muscles!

Oh, no! I've seen the results of your experiments.

Please.

All right then.

Muscles maneuvered the ball of twine around the book and dropped it down the other side to Luke, who pulled gently. The book moved slightly.

Look out, said Muscles, and then realized what Luke was up to. *You want to pull it down! You sneak.*

We were playing. It was an accident. Where's the harm in that? asked Luke innocently.

Just be careful the accident doesn't land on your head, said Muscles as the book moved nearer to the edge.

It landed with a loud thump on the desk below, and was closely followed by a curious cat.

I suppose you're going to have your head stuck in there for hours now, said Muscles as Luke inspected the book for damage.

The cat's prediction proved correct. Bored, he wandered off, leaving Luke lost in the ancient world of the Servants. The stories were wonderful, many of them dark and grim, telling of an ancient conflict between an evil sorcerer and the wizards who opposed him and specifically of the deeds of a group of heroes who aided the wizards and named themselves the Servants in honor of the cause they followed. Luke was enthralled and read the book from cover to cover, missing his tea in the process.

From that day on the stories stayed in his mind. He could picture many of the scenes and recite long passages from some of them. Curiously, although he never felt the need to reread them, the stories did not fade from his memory. Instead, as Luke grew older, his recollections grew more vivid.

Others were growing up or growing older, except Ferragamo, of course, who was hardly marked by the passage of time.

Beca developed first into a golden-haired toddler with a mischievous smile that no one could resist, then into a very pretty young girl, who knew she could wind anybody around her little finger—and frequently did. Her victims rarely minded and Fontaine ensured that she did not become spoiled. She shared her brother's interest in animals but not his passion for magic.

When Beca was just over a year old, Richard and Sophi's daughter, Alena, was born. The two girls grew up together and became firm friends. Alena was small and dark, and somewhat in awe of her dazzling companion. But Beca was fiercely protective of Alena, and their mutual trust grew to the point where Alena felt confident enough to show Beca her greatest, most secret treasure.

Alena opened the drawer of the cabinet in her bedroom and took out a soft leather bag.

"Promise you won't tell anyone?" she whispered.

"I promise," replied Beca equally softly.

Alena reached within and took out a smooth sphere of milky white glass, about the size of a large orange.

Beca stared at it. "What is it?" she asked.

"I don't know," said Alena slowly. "But it's magic. Sometimes I see pictures in it." She looked at her friend, expecting her to be impressed, but instead Beca looked doubtful.

"Do you want to hold it?" asked Alena.

"No, I don't think so," replied Beca. "It's your special thing. I might spoil it."

"There! Look!" exclaimed Alena.

The milky color of the glass seemed to waver as if about to clear but then clouded over again and was still.

"Did you see it?" asked Alena excitedly. "Isn't it wonderful?"

Beca did not agree, thinking it strange and a little frightening. Still, she did not want to upset her friend and so she nodded.

"I'd better put it away now," said Alena, sounding slightly disappointed. "It's a secret," she added by way of explanation. "You mustn't tell."

Longfur, too, grew older. He became a grandfather, then a great-grandfather, and soon lost track of all his offspring. He retained a special relationship with Muscles, who resembled him in many ways, and of course with Mark. Together the king and his cat discussed all manner of subjects from affairs of state, management of the castle—*it is essential to have enough fish at all times*—and the irresponsible nature of young people today, to the news that Ansar and his wife, Rivera, now had a daughter named Gemma, and much, much more.

Together they passed beyond the age when childish dreams could alter their lives and entered the adult world, which is at the same time both more simple and more complex.

Both knew that if another great challenge were to present itself, it would be the younger generations who would step forward to meet it.

Chapter 13

*L*uke's sixteenth birthday was only a few days away. The difference between his "adult" and "normal" phases was now so negligible that he hardly noticed it; everyone found him a lot easier to live with.

After more than a decade of peace, only Ferragamo still worried about the reappearance of Amarino's evil magic. His attempts to organize another conclave had failed. Nobody, least of all his fellow wizards, took his ideas seriously, and he began to hope that all would remain tranquil, at least for Koria's lifetime—which was as far ahead as he was prepared to look.

The wizard's appearance had hardly changed since Luke's birth, but time had marked Koria a little more, if not unkindly. Though a few gray hairs now appeared among the black, she was still slim and had the energy of many half her age. The physical attraction between them had not waned, and they returned each other's love as deeply as ever.

That summer was the hottest anyone could remember. The small river that ran to the north of Starhill flowed sluggishly and the irrigation systems in the fields were put to full use. It became Luke's habit to go swimming in the afternoons. He and Jani, who had remained his close friend and guardian long after any need for physical protection had gone, walked out of the city through Star Gate and made for the largest of the irrigation reservoirs, which provided a splendid swimming pool.

Beca often tried to accompany them but Luke usually refused her. She could not swim very well, and he did not want to be responsible for her safety. "Besides," he would say, "it's not proper. You're a princess."

"And you're a prince," she would retort.

"That's different."

Beca was not used to having her wishes denied, and persisted, petitioning her parents, Ferragamo, and even Jani until, inevitably, she got her own way.

"Oh, good," she rejoiced. "Alena can come, too, and keep me company."

Luke groaned, but submitted with good grace. Mark made them take a carriage to the edge of the fields, which robbed Luke of his enjoyable walk through the noisy, odorous streets and the emergence into the greenery beyond Star Gate. He accepted it philosophically, reasoning that at least he would not get too hot on the way back, something that always made him want to swim again.

The two girls were in high spirits. As soon as the carriage pulled up, they ordered Luke out so that they could change into their swimming costumes. Jani climbed down from the driver's seat and waited patiently, but Luke soon grew tired of biding his time this way and set off for the pool. After a moment's hesitation, Jani followed. At the waterside they stripped down to their costumes and dived in.

Shortly afterward, amid much giggling, Beca and Alena arrived, swathed in large towels.

"You might have waited for us," reprimanded Beca. "You're no gentlemen!"

"You shouldn't have taken so long," replied her brother.

"Did you know there's water escaping from the cracks in the bank?" Alena asked nervously.

"It doesn't matter," said Luke. "Some water always gets away. Come on in."

The girls now suffered an attack of shyness which Luke found quite ridiculous. As if anyone would be interested in looking at them! They slowly unwrapped their towels then hesitated at the water's edge, testing the temperature with delicate toes. Only Luke's threat to throw them in persuaded the maidens to jump in. They did so together, making a tremendous splash.

Once wet, they lost all inhibitions and played and shouted, leapt and pushed, until Luke was quite exhausted and told them to be quiet. Surprisingly, they obeyed, and he floated peacefully, looking up at the sky. In the sudden stillness, Luke became aware of voices from the other side of the bank.

"Open the sluice gate, Rob," a man said.

That's wrong, thought Luke, *they shouldn't do that until after sunset*. Then the implication sank in. He was about to shout to the men to wait when he was unceremoniously ducked by Beca and Alena who had surreptitiously sneaked up on him. He fought to the surface, spluttering and coughing, and heard, over the girls' laughter, the gurgle of flowing water. Unable to speak properly he waved frantically to them to get out, but they only thought he was reacting to their prank and giggled even more furiously.

Suddenly, Luke felt the tug of the current on his feet and Beca gave a little scream, cut short as she was dragged below the surface of the water as if by an unseen hand. Jani, by now aware of the danger, swam strongly toward them and shoved the bewildered Alena to the bank before returning for Beca. Luke recovered his breath and dived beneath the water. This was now churning with mud, making it difficult to see, but he felt the pull of the sluice and went with it. Beca and Jani were both before him, struggling to get to the surface, and Luke saw that Beca's ankle was caught by some reeds. He scrabbled frantically to free her, and soon felt his sister and Jani pull away upward. However, he was now entangled himself. His lungs were bursting and he was close to panic when he pulled free and thrust upward. Jani's strong hands lifted him to the safety of the bank. The girls were wrapping themselves in towels, crying piteously.

Jani shut the sluice gate; the men who had opened it were nowhere to be seen.

That night Luke had a nightmare. He knew he was dreaming but everything seemed oddly familiar, and he found himself anticipating events with uncanny accuracy. Unlike most dreams this one had an only too logical structure, but the knowledge did nothing to stem his terror.

He was at sea in a small boat, racing against time to rescue somebody that he loved. Yet his boat was tethered with fronds of seaweed so that it could not move. He slashed away at these bonds, only to find when finally free that the boat was swept away by a fearsome current. Almost out of control, he had to navigate his flimsy craft through a rocky strait dominated by a terrible whirlpool. He had only one chance, but the thought of this horrified him. Turning the tiller, he edged the bows around until they pointed directly *toward* the roaring chasm at the eye of the whirlpool . . .

Asleep in the next chamber, Beca's rest was also troubled. Pictures of frightening clarity appeared momentarily: a boat tossed by a raging sea; a boy fighting for survival; an immense whirlpool.

She woke and heard Luke screaming.

Running to his room, she found him sitting bolt upright in bed, eyes wide open and his hands grasping at nothing around his neck. For a moment she was too scared to approach him, then he yelled frantically and she overcame her fear. She shook him awake, and by the time Mark and Fontaine arrived she was holding him like a baby, gently rocking him back and forth, murmuring softly.

Beca knew that she had somehow shared a small part of Luke's nightmare, and was convinced that the accident earlier in the day, for which she felt partly responsible, had prompted it. This doubled her feelings of guilt, and she spent much of the next few days dogging Luke's footsteps, taking every opportunity to let him know she was sorry and that she cared.

Nobody went swimming for the rest of the summer.

Fontaine and Koria tended to agree with Beca's interpretation of the dream, but Mark remembered a dream of his own and was not so sure. He asked Ferragamo's opinion, but the wizard refused to be drawn. Mark privately resolved to keep Luke on dry land, just in case the dream proved to be as prophetic as his had been.

On hearing this, Fontaine remarked, "That could be a bit difficult, you know. We do live on an *island!*"

Alena had also been unable to sleep that night, mixed feelings of guilt and pleasure surrounding her memories of the afternoon. She felt hot and confused, unable to relax.

Throwing off her bedclothes, she rose and went over to the window, gazing at the stars. Then she turned and, suddenly purposeful, went to the cabinet and removed the leather bag containing her secret treasure. Sitting cross-legged on the floor, she took out the sphere. Almost immediately the surface rippled, and within the glass a man's face appeared, gnarled and ugly, covered with an unruly black beard. His eyes were malevolent and almost colorless.

"I've been waiting for you," said the vision. "But I see by your face that you have failed. That is not very wise, is it, my chick?" He smiled, displaying discolored, broken teeth.

Alena tried to speak, but was cut off by a brusque gesture.

"No words!" the vision said. "Put the glass down."

Silently, she obeyed.

A wisp of something like smoke drifted up from the sphere, grew and took shape until the lifesize image of the man in the glass stood before her. Alena looked on openmouthed. This had never happened before.

"We meet at last!" said the man with a laugh, holding out his hand for her to shake. Alena stretched up obediently, but when she tried to grasp his hand, her fingers slipped through his as if through water and she realized that the man was not real, not solid.

"Not yet!" he said, and laughed again at her discomfort. She could see right through him!

"I will return," he said. "For now, put the glass away."

The awful vision disappeared and the sphere was an innocent white again. Alena carefully returned it to its hiding place, then got into bed.

She fell asleep immediately.

A few days later, after the celebrations for Luke's birthday, strange rumors started arriving from the outlying islands. Freak weather conditions were reported. Icebergs had been seen, and dense banks of fog.

"Icebergs in midsummer?" asked Mark incredulously.

"That's what they're saying," said Shill, captain of the Castle Guard. "I didn't believe it, either, but the same story's come from several sources now. And not all of them drunk!"

More disturbing still were reports of "gray ships" raiding lonely ports and attacking trading vessels.

"We haven't had trouble with pirates for decades," said Mark. "Why now?"

"Some are saying they aren't pirates," Shill said.

"What then?"

"Ghost ships," replied Shill, straight-faced.

Not long after these early reports, news came in of a ship that had set out for Peven from Grayrock Harbor only to meet an incredible bank of fog a hundred leagues from land. It stretched north and south as far as they could see and appeared quite impenetrable. The cloud seemed to be moving northward, possibly edging to the west, the directions making no sense at all given the wind conditions.

Several crewmen claimed to have seen strange gray shapes moving within the fog, but nobody was keen to go in to find out which of the most popular theories was correct—pirate ships or icebergs. Faced with an almost certain mutiny if he tried to sail on, the captain ordered his ship around and headed back to Ark.

Shortly, more vessels returned with similar tales. The shipping world was close to panic.

After listening to the latest reports, Fontaine looked at Mark and said, "Durc and Zunic are out there somewhere, beyond that fog."

"I know," said Mark. "They should have been back two months ago."

"Their trips do have a habit of being extended, but . . ." Fontaine's voice trailed off.

"This time I wish they'd get back," completed Mark.

"Perhaps they can't," added his queen.

Ferragamo disappeared. After a desperate search, Koria found him, two days later, closeted in an upper room of Starbright Tower. He had not eaten in all that time and his already thin face was gaunt when he turned to look at her. What shocked her even more was the utter dread she saw in his eyes.

He opened his mouth to speak, but no sound came out. She knelt before him.

"What . . . ?" she began.

"I've seen it," he croaked. "I can *feel* it."

He coughed painfully.

"I was right all the time," he yelled hoarsely, making Koria flinch. "And now it's too late!"

He faced her again and his voice fell to a hollow, agonized whisper.

"It's coming."

PART TWO

Strock

Chapter 14

"*B*ut Strock is so small!" exclaimed Julia. "There must be more to the world than just this island."

"Of course there is," Ashula replied wearily.

"I can walk around it in a day," the girl went on, "and I've seen it *all* before, so many times. I want to see something *new!*"

"You will, in time. For now, please come with me. Your parents are waiting for you."

"They're not my parents, though, are they?"

"That, young lady, is a very unkind thing to say," said the wizard sternly, anger flashing in his bright blue eyes.

"I'm sorry," replied Julia. "I didn't mean it like that. I just meant they're not my *real* parents."

"They adopted you, it's true," snapped Ashula, "but that doesn't make them any less real. Now come on."

The wizard's expression told its own story. Julia rejected the idea of making his anger subside and delaying their departure a little longer. She had always instinctively shied away from employing her own special talent where Ashula was concerned, and, never having been guided in its use, had learned to trust her intuition.

"All right. I suppose I'd better put this on."

She indicated the soft blue gown which lay on her bed. It contrasted sharply with her usual attire which was sturdy and practical; leather breeches and a soft shirt were topped with a thick fisherman's sweater, protection against the winter cold.

"It *is* your name day," said Ashula. "I'll wait outside."

No escape then, thought Julia as the door closed. Reluctantly, she began to change. She had to admit that the dress was beautiful, and it fitted her slender form perfectly. She wished suddenly, with a great surge of longing, that there was someone else of her own age on the island. Kubiac didn't count. It was so tedious, having no one but old people around her. If only her sister . . .

Ashula knocked impatiently at her door.

"All right," she said loudly, fastening the last of the dress's buttons. She shivered and hoped that the hall would be warm. As she opened the door and stepped out into the corridor, Ashula looked at her appraisingly.

"Lovely," he said shortly and led her quickly away. Julia matched the wizard's pace easily, for Ashula shuffled rather than walked. She suspected that he did it deliberately, to remind her, unnecessarily, how ancient he was.

The material of her gown whispered softly about her legs as Julia walked down the cold, dingy passageway which turned and twisted chaotically, passing many doorways. She regretted once more her impulsive decision to choose a room in the deserted west wing of Old Walls. As soon as she had been old enough to want a space of her own she had moved in, deciding on the chamber because of its window overlooking the sea, and for its distance from the other inhabited rooms in the decaying settlement.

The name Old Walls applied both to the village and to the sprawling building at its center, in which she lived. None of the other houses was occupied; most were now uninhabitable. Even in her own home, only one room in ten was in use. The doors she and Ashula passed on their way to the hall hid dusty, barren chambers. As a child she had played in this apparently endless maze, finding it fascinating and sometimes frightening. Now it simply bored her.

Sixteen years, she thought suddenly. *I've been here sixteen years! And Ashula's been here for hundreds!*

It was an appalling thought.

They entered the hall and Julia was glad to see the roaring blaze in the huge stone fireplace and feel its warmth through her thin dress. Although every inhabitant of Old Walls was there to greet her, the room was still far from crowded. She saw that the place of honor at the head of the table had been left free for her, and feeling a little self-conscious, she walked over to the high-backed chair, as Ashula went to his habitual place at the far end.

On either side of Julia sat her "parents," Mireldi and Reveza, king and queen of Strock. They refused to use their titles, believing them unnecessary and ridiculous. They were both over eighty years old and their sight and hearing were failing fast. They seemed unaware of Julia's entrance until she sat down, but then both smiled and said, "Happy name day, daughter."

"Thank you," Julia replied, feeling the strength of the old peoples' love. She leaned over and kissed each of them in turn.

The others around the table had risen to their feet as Julia came in, and she now motioned them to resume their seats. Next to Reveza sat Blackwood, a solidly built man whose weather-beaten face and callused hands told of an outdoor life. He it was who fought the lonely, losing battle to keep Old Walls from falling into decay. He also kept the house supplied with firewood, peat, and fish and, with the help of the two farmhands, with milk, grain, and vegetables. He was a man of simple habits and few words. Opposite him sat his wife, Mosi, who was cook, housekeeper, and nursemaid all rolled into one. She had grown a little rounder with each of her fifty or so years, and her ruddy face beamed in the firelight as she added her greeting to the others'.

Next to her sat Kubiac. He was easily the youngest person in the room except for Julia. In fact he was some five years older than her but still had the look of an adolescent. Since being orphaned as an infant, he had been small and pale, and the years as Ashula's apprentice had done little to fill out his sticklike limbs or spindly frame. He was the only playmate Julia had ever known, and doted on her still, like a brother or, as Julia thought rather unkindly, like a loyal dog. His green eyes, which always seemed on the edge of tears, regarded her with devotion as he added his own congratulations.

"Happy n-name day, Julia," he stuttered.

She smiled and thanked him, thinking all the while that it was only her name day, not her *birthday*. Nobody knew when that was. Still, it was nice of them to make a fuss on the anniversary of her arrival. There was certainly a fine spread on the table before them; Mosi had seen to that. Plates were passed around and wine poured out. The evening drew in and the fire sent shadows flickering over the wall coverings, tapestries which had once been detailed and richly colored but were now faded and worn. Blackwood lit the oil lamps and the meal continued, with Mosi or Kubiac occasionally fetching more from the kitchen or cellar.

Inevitably, there came a point in the evening when the conversation turned to that strange day, sixteen years ago, when Julia had arrived on the island. She had heard many times how she had been washed ashore in a casket, miraculously saved from what everyone assumed had been a shipwreck. She knew that the dolphins that she loved so much, and that Ashula regarded as his friends, had been involved in her rescue. They had brought her safely to the island and she had been adopted by the elderly, childless couple who now sat beside her.

After her ordeal at sea, she had been unwell for a time, fevers racking her tiny body. She had survived, and grown strong and healthy, until she could now outrun and outswim anyone on Strock—though that was not an enormous achievement. At the same time she had developed into a pretty girl, now on the brink of womanhood. Her lovely violet eyes were set against skin that was naturally pale but almost permanently tanned, and black hair which, even from childhood, had a few strands of white or silver within the raven sheen.

Mosi was handing around slices of her special cake, the traditional recipe that she made for all occasions of note. It contained a little of the juice of the fruit from the little tree in the courtyard. Ashula used a long and complicated name for the fruit, but Mosi simply called them moonberries. Julia had been warned never to take these fruit as they were too strong to eat whole, but the flavor they gave the cake was delicious. In the past, though Julia could not resist it, she had suffered from indigestion and dizziness every time she ate Mosi's delicacy. She had now grown accustomed to it, though, and bit into her slice gladly.

Reveza watched her eating and smiled fondly, a faraway look in her eyes.

"You never used to like moonberries, did you, dear?" mused the old woman, almost as though talking to herself. Julia was about to reply but Reveza went on without waiting for an answer.

"We thought you were going to die," she said quietly.

Julia saw Ashula glance up quickly and flash Reveza a warning look, but the queen either did not notice or chose to ignore him. Julia was intrigued.

"The first time you had some of the cordial, you made such a fuss . . ." The old woman's smile faded as if remembering something else, something unpleasant. Ashula cleared his throat and Reveza looked around at him.

"There, you don't want to listen to a silly old woman like me talking of those things, do you?" she said.

"What did you mean—" began Julia, but Ashula interrupted her.

"A toast!" he cried, raising his glass. "To Julia, the life of this island." The wizard's ageless eyes watched her over the rim as he drank. She accepted their mute plea and did not try to reopen the conversation.

After they had drunk, Mireldi said, "Ashula has it right, my dear. You *are* the life of this island. Before you came I often wondered why we were still alive."

"Oh, father!" she exclaimed, her shock visible in her eyes.

"No, it's true," he went on, his voice now slightly slurred. "Strock was dying and we all knew it. You gave us a new purpose. If it weren't for you, this island would be the home of ghosts by now." He subsided into his chair, looking very tired, and Julia felt a lump in her throat.

"How can you say that?" she said, indicating the others around the table with her hand.

"We would all have left," he replied. "One way or another." His voice held an infinite sadness and Julia knew somehow that her father spoke the truth.

Soon after that the meal ended and they went their different ways. Julia kissed the others goodnight, and took one of the lamps to light her way back along the now darkened passageways. When Kubiac offered to see her to her room, she agreed, not because she felt in any need of company, but because he was always so pleased to make himself useful to her.

Once they were out of earshot, Kubiac said, "You looked l-lovely tonight, Julia. The b-blue of your dress suits you p-perfectly. I'm glad you decided to wear it." His words came out all in a rush and he ended slightly breathless. Julia had the feeling that he had prepared what for him was quite a long speech in advance, and had only now found the courage to get it out.

"Thank you," she replied. "I'm glad you like it. You look very smart too."

"D-do you really think so?" he asked anxiously.

"Yes. It's nice to have the excuse to dress up now and then, isn't it?"

They walked on in silence for a few moments, listening to their footsteps echo down the empty side passages.

"Did you like the flowers?" asked Kubiac hopefully.

Julia, who had only been vaguely aware of the arrangements on the table, said, "They were lovely."

"I did them," he replied. "F-for you."

"For me? How lovely of you." Julia was touched. She wished now that she had brought one of the vases with her for her room. The delicate winter blooms might not last until tomorrow.

They reached the door to her chamber and Julia paused as if in thought. Kubiac stood silently, obviously unsure of what to do.

"Kubiac, can you tell me something?" she said after a while. "When I arrived here, as a baby, I mean, and I was ill, did that have anything to do with the moonberries?"

She waited expectantly but the question obviously confused her companion. When he eventually did manage to answer, he was not very helpful.

"I d-don't know," he said. "I was ill at the same t-time. Perhaps you should talk to Ashula."

Julia looked at him for a moment and made up her mind. "I think I will," she said. "Goodnight, Kubiac. Thank you for acting as my escort—and for the flowers."

She kissed him briefly on the cheek and, by the lamplight, saw the color rise in his face. Part of her despised him for his foolishness, but she loved him for it too.

Alone in her room, Julia quickly took refuge in the warmth of her bed, but then found that she could not sleep. She stared at the ceiling, listening to the distant crash of the waves breaking on the beach, her thoughts going around in circles. She wished Ashula was there to answer her questions.

When, a short while later, there was a gentle knock at her door, Julia was not unduly surprised

"Come in," she called immediately.

The wizard entered and she sat up in bed, pulling the blankets around her. Ashula carried a lamp, but it was burning low and it was difficult to see the expression on his face.

"Kubiac said you wanted to talk to me," he said as he lowered himself slowly into a chair.

"I didn't mean tonight!" she replied. "But now you're here
. . . I couldn't sleep."

"Neither could I."

"It's what Mother said about the moonberries. I can't get it
out of my mind."

Ashula sighed. "I think you're old enough now to know the
truth about your arrival here. Most of it you already know,
but there are *some* details we thought it better to keep
secret." The wizard's voice was grave. "Don't think too badly
of us. We did what we thought was best."

Julia was silent. As Ashula began his story, his memories of
that fateful day came flooding back.

"This place could do with some young blood," said the cook.
"Begging your pardons," she added, blushing.

"You're right there, Mosi," said Mireldi, laughing.

"They'll be like our own," whispered the queen.

Ashula sighed with relief.

"Then we'll provide a room for them," he said, "and I will
prepare for the ceremony of adoption."

"I'll have to look for some things for them," said Mosi.

"May I hold one of them?" asked Reveza softly.

"Of course, ma'am," Mosi replied, allowing the old queen
to take one of the infants.

"It's like a miracle," said Reveza, looking down at the
child, who, though quiet, still appeared red-faced and angry.
"To have the chance of a family again, against all hope, after
all these years."

She glanced up at her husband, who was watching her
fondly, then at Ashula. "You do think this is right, don't
you?" she asked anxiously.

"I do," the wizard reassured her.

As one, the babies began to howl. Above the tumult Mosi
declared that they must be hungry again, took charge of them
both, and hurried away to the kitchen.

"When do you want to hold the ceremony?" asked Ashula.

"This evening," replied Mireldi. "If that is possible."

"Can everything be ready in time?" asked Reveza.

"Oh, yes," said the wizard. "It's quite simple, but there are
a few conventions I should like to observe."

"What was that?" asked Mireldi, cupping a hand to his ear.

Ashula repeated his statement in a louder voice.

"We'll leave it to you," said the king.

"At dinner then," said Ashula and left the royal couple alone. As he went out they were holding hands and looking into each other's eyes like young lovers. The wizard smiled as he went to check on Kubiac. The boy had taken a chill after getting soaked in the sea, and had been put to bed. Finding the apprentice asleep, Ashula went to his study where he pondered for a while on the significance of the inscription that he had copied from the tomb at the island's center. He had known from the moment of the girls' arrival that the enigmatic verse concerned their fate, but was no nearer understanding the meaning than he had been over two hundred years ago.

Perhaps I will find out tonight, he thought, then got out his books to check the correct procedure for the adoption ceremony.

Mosi was kept very busy that afternoon. Apart from feeding and cleaning the babies, she organized Blackwood and the men from the farm who had come in to see the mysterious new arrivals. Between them they found one cot, manufactured another, and secured bedclothes for both. Towels were converted into clothing, and various items set aside for the girls' feeding. Mosi also found time to bake a special cake—using one of the moonberries from the tree—knowing that the meal this evening was to be a unique occasion. She also made, at Ashula's request, a small amount of cordial from the juice of the berry, sweetening it with a little honey.

That evening, everyone on the island, except Kubiac who was still abed, gathered in the hall. The king and queen had been joined by Ashula, Blackwood, and Martin and Tam from the farm. Even the two fishermen's widows, who lived in the last of the village cottages, were there when Mosi proudly carried in the two small guests of honor.

The excitement of the unexpected celebration—and the prospect of the food and wine that went with it—had put everybody, except Ashula, into a merry mood. The wizard was outwardly calm, almost solemn. He knew that what was happening here concerned more than the fates of two baby girls. All went well for a while. Mireldi and Reveza repeated the formal phrases that Ashula said were necessary, and the others present were called upon to witness their words.

"All that remains now," said Ashula, "is to name the girls and for them to take the initiation water. They will then be part of the family and we can start our meal." He grinned at Tam, whose eyes had been straying to the piled plates and bottles.

Mireldi brought the first of the babies to Ashula.

"You take this child as your daughter?"

"I do," replied the old king firmly, "and I name her Julia."

Ashula picked up the ceremonial cup which held the moonberry cordial that was known as the initiation water. Dipping his fingers in the liquid, he dabbed a little onto her forehead, over her heart, and on both palms. Julia, who had until now been relatively calm, immediately began to cry, but quieted down long enough for the cup to be held to her lips. She drank a little, then sputtered and, red-faced, continued her yelling. There were smiles as Mireldi tried unsuccessfully to quieten his young charge.

Then Reveza came forward. The formula was repeated, and Julia's sister named Bela, but as Ashula touched her with the liquid she began to struggle and cry, and the queen had difficulty holding her. Mosi had taken Julia from Mireldi, and was becoming worried about her. There was something wrong with the child. Ashula, despairing of Bela ever becoming quiet, chose his moment and tipped some cordial into the baby's open mouth. Bela immediately choked, swallowed, and began to scream. She flailed out, almost causing Reveza to lose her hold, and making the wizard spill more of the liquid. It splashed her arm and legs as well as the queen's dress.

Mosi's anxious voice now rose over the bedlam the two girls were creating.

"Help us," she cried. "She's having a fit!"

Julia's skin was covered with livid blotches, she was shaking convulsively, and her eyes had rolled upward so that only the whites showed. She screamed piercingly and then became ominously quiet, causing Mosi, and all who watched, the deepest dread.

Bela was faring even worse. Where the liquid had been spilled, her skin was already red and blistered, her limbs twitched violently and her breathing rasped painfully between screams.

"What's happening?" asked the bewildered Reveza.

Ashula took Bela from her and beckoned Mosi to follow him with Julia. "To my study, quickly."

They hurried out, followed by most of the others. In his study the wizard called upon his considerable healing skills. Salves were applied and potions brewed, but when Ashula tried to use his own special powers he recoiled in horror. The touch-skill, which came so naturally to him when he wished to warm Kubiac or still a fever, failed him utterly when he tried to reach Bela. His mind roiled in confusion.

Both girls were now quiet but they were still suffering from convulsions and their eyes were sightless. Ugly weals had appeared at head, heart, and hands, and in Bela's case, on her limbs as well. Their breathing and heartbeats were racing dangerously.

Ashula admitted the obvious truth. This was something outside the limits of his skill, an allergic reaction so powerful that it amounted to poisoning. That in itself would not have been beyond his understanding, but there was something more in this case. He felt profoundly disturbed.

"There's nothing we can do," he said quietly. "Mosi and I will watch over them, and we'll let you know if there's any news."

Silently the others dispersed, their meal forgotten.

Some hours later Ashula emerged from the study to find a weary-looking Mireldi waiting outside. The sounds of Mosi's gentle sobbing followed the wizard out and the king immediately feared the worst.

Ashula's face was drawn. His eyes reflected the sorrow of his thoughts. *From the twain, one. From the one, release,* he thought. *At least now I know which one.*

Seeing the question in Mireldi's eyes, he said aloud, "Julia seems to be recovering, though I suspect it will take her a long time."

The old king closed his eyes as he sensed what was coming next. Ashula cleared his throat.

"Bela's dead," he said.

Chapter 15

"You knew, didn't you?" Although Julia spoke softly, there was accusation in her voice. Much of Ashula's tale had been familiar to her, but the crucial role played by the moonberry cordial was new. As the wizard's story came to an end, several questions rose to the surface of her mind.

"I knew *something* would happen," replied Ashula. "The power of the moonberries is very strong . . . but I did not expect so violent a reaction."

"You saw what was happening to me, yet you still gave the cordial to my sister, and it killed her!" Ashula winced at the anger in Julia's voice and heard the words she did not speak. *You killed my sister*.

"Bela killed herself," he said so quietly that Julia had to strain to hear him.

"How can you say that?" she retorted. "A tiny baby?"

Ashula's head came up and he met her angry stare.

"Because it's true!" he said, his voice suddenly strong again. "She would not compromise. She kept fighting and fighting until her poor little battleground of a body couldn't take it anymore."

Julia heard the agonized conviction in the wizard's words and held back her harsh response. After a few moments Ashula spoke again.

"I did everything I could for her, but it was no use."

"And me?" asked Julia. "Did I compromise?"

"In the end," he replied slowly, watching her closely, "you did."

"And if I hadn't, I'd have died too?"

"Yes."

"This is insane!" Julia shrieked. "Everyone on Strock eats the moonberries all the time. So do I now. How would they have killed me *then?*"

"That's a long story."

"I've got all night," she replied bitterly, and then, unable to wait for Ashula to continue, burst out, "How have you all kept this secret for so long?" She was aghast to learn that everyone she knew, and found so easy to manipulate, who would do almost anything for her, should have combined in a conspiracy of silence.

"Some things are easier *not* to talk about," replied Ashula sympathetically. He could almost see the painful reassessment of her life going on behind her lovely violet eyes.

"Julia, how much do you know about moonberries?" he asked after a while.

"Only what you and Kubiac kept telling me," she replied thoughtfully. "That they were dangerous if you ate too much."

"So they are," agreed the wizard and he went on to tell her of the creation of the moonberry trees, long ages ago. The great wizard who had brought them into being had done so following the War of the Wizards, a magical conflict on an unimaginable scale. By a skill now lost to the world, he had implanted in the seeds of the tree all the tenets of magic that wizardry held dear. He hoped by this to ensure the survival of true magic long beyond his own lifespan and so protect the world against the perversion of magic that had caused the war. A single tree had been planted on all the islands and a guardian appointed for each. These men became the islands' first kings, though they were not known by that term then, and their descendants tended the trees still.

Julia was so engrossed in Ashula's tale that the implication of his words only sank in as his explanation ended. When it did, it hit her like a thunderbolt. Her eyes went wide.

"But if . . . the berries are true magic . . . then what happened . . ."

She stared at Ashula.

"Am I *still* evil?" she asked then, her quiet voice belying the horror beneath the words.

"Of course not!" said the wizard, trying to sound as reassuring as possible. "Don't even think that."

"Why not? That's what killed Bela, and nearly killed me,

isn't it?" She fixed Ashula with her gaze and repeated loudly, "*Isn't it?*"

"Julia, you and Bela had been *used*," said the wizard, keeping his voice as calm as he could. "You know your arrival here was—to say the least—unorthodox. Given that you had survived a shipwreck, the time at sea would have killed any ordinary baby. There was no sustenance in your caskets, yet when you arrived, you were both perfectly healthy with powers beyond your age. Where they came from we still do not know."

"So you tested us."

"It was the only way. As you know, no one could live on Strock and not eat moonberries—it would be unthinkable. Everyone here was practically weaned on their juices. And if you were to be adopted, there was no choice but to hold the initiation ceremony."

"We certainly gave you a show, didn't we!" said Julia, a variety of emotions showing in her face. "No wonder you didn't want to talk about it."

Ashula waited, letting Julia organize her chaotic thoughts.

"Is it gone now?" she whispered eventually. "The . . . evil power."

"Sixteen years is a long time," Ashula said, smiling. "You're one of us now."

"Don't patronize me," she snapped. "Answer the question."

"I *did*," he replied firmly. "Nobody could live here with us for so long, living the way we do, and retain any evil influence." Ashula only hoped that the truth was as simple as that.

"You mean *eating* the way we do," said Julia.

"That too."

"But?"

"What do you mean?" said the wizard.

"With you there's always a but," said Julia. "I'm still waiting for it."

"All right," conceded Ashula, knowing he was cornered. "Do you think yourself an ordinary girl?"

Julia laughed, somewhat taken aback, and exclaimed, "Of course not!" Then she saw that the wizard was serious and quieted down. "How would I know?" she asked resignedly. "I have no one to compare myself with."

"True enough," he replied, "but I know more about you than you realize."

She looked at him expectantly, a small worried frown creasing her face.

"You dream," said Ashula baldly.

"Everyone dreams!" she responded, but averted her eyes.

"But yours mean more than most. And they frighten you sometimes," stated the wizard.

"How do you know?" she conceded in a whisper.

"I have ears even if others here do not," he replied, smiling. "Even as a child you were often quite voluble in your sleep. I rarely understood anything you said, but it didn't take much intelligence to know how you were feeling. I have a certain talent of my own in that direction," he concluded significantly.

Julia looked at him sharply.

"You know?" she asked, disbelievingly.

"That you often know instinctively what someone is feeling? That you sometimes nudge their thoughts in the direction you would like them to take? Oh, yes. Did you really think you could hide that from someone who has lived as long as I have?"

He smiled encouragingly but, again, Julia could not meet his eyes. She sank deeper into the bedclothes.

"I feel so ashamed," she murmured at last.

"Don't. You have a talent. All you have to do is make sure you do not abuse it. So far I see no evidence of that."

Julia looked up, new hope brimming in her eyes.

"Then you think . . . ?"

"Yes. Julia, there is nothing evil in you. You are *good*, and at some time in your life you will get the chance to prove it." *Please let it be true. Make it true*, he pleaded silently.

"When? How?" asked Julia, who was both intrigued and daunted by his words. The wizard refused to be drawn, however, and another thought occurred to her.

"You knew we were coming, Bela and me. You were expecting us!"

It was Ashula's turn to be taken aback. He considered for a moment and then said, "We may be isolated here on Strock, but there are certain events in the world that cannot be hidden if you know how to look for them. You were part of such an event."

"Me?"

"Yes. Your arrival here was not entirely an accident. I had a little help locating you."

"The dolphins?" exclaimed Julia in delight.

Ashula nodded, smiling at her quickness.

"You love them as much as I do, don't you?" she said. "I almost think you talk to them."

"I do," he replied, "to one of them at least."

Julia gasped.

"All wizards have a companion from the animal world," he went on. "A familiar. Mine is just a little more unusual than most."

"But that's wonderful!" she exclaimed. "How do you do it?"

"Enough. Enough!" the wizard held up his hands as if in self-defense. "You have heard more than enough for one night. If we go on like this, it'll be dawn before we know it, and I need my sleep even if you don't."

He rose and went to the door, forestalling any attempt to detain him. There he paused.

"We'll talk again tomorrow. Goodnight, Julia."

"Thank you," she replied softly. "Thank you for trusting me enough to tell me."

"It was time," he said simply. "Sleep well."

"Goodnight," she said, as the door closed.

As the wizard's footsteps receded, she snuggled down into her bed and added once more, this time in a whisper, "Thank you."

No dreams disturbed her sleep that night.

Chapter 16

The tower was Julia's favorite place on Strock. Standing at the end of a rocky spit of land on the opposite side of the island to Old Walls, the tower appeared to most people to be a ruin, like almost all the buildings on the island. Julia knew better. She saw that its irregular shape and ridged yet seamless surface were an intrinsic part of the tower's design. Her private theory was that it was the trunk of a huge tree that had once stood at this spot. In time it had turned to stone, with the twisting stairway that commanded its full height now exposed from openings where once the tree's branches had been.

From the top, many times her own height, Julia could see almost all of the eastern side of the island. When the weather was clear, she could glimpse both Old Walls and, directly beyond the mound at the center of the isle, the stone circle which she found curious mainly because it appeared to be a completely useless construction. When the sea was wild, the tower made a spectacular vantage point as the waves raged about it on three sides.

Julia always felt a reassuring calm there and somehow knew that it was a very ancient place, one which events beyond her imagining had touched.

Kubiac had often accompanied Julia on her explorations and had pointed out to her the island's most curious feature. An earthwork, known as "the snake," ran from the tower, circling the isle, and curving ever inward until it reached the mound at its center. It was obviously man-made, and Julia had marveled at the colossal effort which must have gone into its construction. Even though she knew that Strock had once been home for many more people than it was now, Julia could not understand the reason behind the making of the snake. Ashula had not been able to enlighten her, although he had told her that the mound at the center was a barrow. Whoever had been buried there—all those ages ago—had presumably been very important if the snake was part of his memorial.

Julia and Kubiac had once walked the entire length of the earthwork, from the tower to the mound; it had taken them all day and they returned to Old Walls exhausted. An interesting idea had become a tedious exertion, and only the stubborn streak in Julia's character made her complete the pointless exercise. Now whenever she visited the tower she walked straight across the isle, climbing over the snake several times. This she had done on the morning after her name-day celebrations and late-night conversation with Ashula.

The wizard had promised that they would talk again, but Julia found that she had quite enough to think about, and when the day dawned clear, the lure of the tower drew her to it. Though the winter sun was pale and watery, and its rays held little warmth, it was still strong enough to dazzle her. She walked briskly, glad of her warm clothing.

An hour after sunrise, she was sitting in the open at the top of the tower, watching the sea. Cold breezes occasionally ruffled her hair but Julia hardly noticed. Her thoughts were racing as she recalled events from her life and saw them anew in the light of her recently acquired knowledge.

When younger, she had tried to talk about her dreams, but had been unable to make anyone take an interest. Mosi and her parents regarded her tales as part of the nonsensical babblings of childhood and even Ashula did not seem to pay much attention. In fact, the wizard often appeared to actively dislike her mentioning the dreams, and she had in time learned to hold her tongue. For years now they had been her secret, bringing with them a mixture of joy and unhappiness. She had hidden both from those about her and, until last night, had been sure that her infant chatter was forgotten.

The most vivid of her dreams, and the most painful, were those concerning Bela. She had always known it was her sister because the other girl looked so very much like herself;

yet the girl in the dream was always *outside* her, beyond her reach. The dreams were distressing because, on each occasion, Bela was in a terrible predicament, calling for help. Julia was always forced to look on helplessly as her sister drowned, or was engulfed by flames or fell from a high place. However hard she tried, there was nothing Julia could ever do to save her sister, and she awoke several times with her pillow wet with tears of grief and frustration.

Julia had always assumed that these dreams were a reaction to the knowledge of her sister's early death and her own lack of a playmate. Knowing how Bela had really died now gave the images a more sinister twist, but their meaning was still beyond her.

However, not all her dreams were unpleasant. One in particular was far easier to recall. With minor variations, this dream had recurred several times, starting with a blinding flash of light which resolved into the multifaceted reflection of the sun from the golden cloak of a tall, blond man. He always appeared with his back to her, his arms stretched up to the sky, as if in supplication. Each time, Julia moved toward him as he stood in one of the special places on Strock—the tower, the barrow, or the stone circle. She seemed to be floating and a great warmth filled her as she drew closer. Though she never succeeded in reaching the man and at no time saw his face, she woke from these dreams feeling happy, with a disconcerting flutter of excitement. She used to fantasize that this would be the man who would come to Strock and carry her away to be his bride and share his adventures.

Although Julia smiled to herself at these girlish ideas, a tiny glimmer of hopeful longing still existed deep within her. Once more she cursed her tiny, enclosed world and wondered what lay beyond its shores. Her imagination could not make the leap, however, and she returned to the easier contemplation of her dreams.

One in particular had frightened her badly. Fortunately it had only occurred once, but though it had been perhaps four years ago, Julia knew she would never be rid of the memory of that nightmare. Now it seemed that she must recall its terrors once again. She would have given much to erase it from her mind, but she knew that until she thought it through she would have no peace.

As the dream began Julia was standing alone in a desolate and barren landscape; she was naked and the air was damp and cold. The view was the same in every direction; wet black rock with a few patches of stunted grass and pools of stagnant water. In the distance everything was obscured by a gray mist. As Julia watched, the fog began to thicken, almost to take shape. Then it began to draw in toward her. She wanted to run away, to escape the creeping menace, but could not. The roiling banks of mist were all around her.

In despair, she crouched down, hugging herself as she was enveloped by the cold, clammy fog. Though her eyes were still open, Julia could see nothing. She trembled, trying to make herself as inconspicuous as possible. Then a voice spoke to her in a tone that made her shiver even more. She could not recall what had been said, but remembered screaming when the fog drew back abruptly and a man appeared before her. He was immensely tall, his bulk shrouded in a long black cape. His bearded face was ugly, and his eyes, which held her gaze against her will, were cold and colorless.

He spoke again and Julia replied. At her words he frowned, then threw back his head and laughed. Julia cowered before him, dread rising within her. The man vanished, but that brought no relief, for the fog now closed in again. This time it appeared more like living smoke, choking her and stinging her eyes. She could not breathe. Clawing at her throat she found that, although she wore no clothes, her pendants were still about her neck. They, too, were strangling her and she tore them off and flung them away. Immediately, the scene shifted and she found herself in the sea, struggling to keep afloat, gasping for air. A dolphin appeared with the pendants held in its mouth, and they were somehow fastened back around her neck. Julia gave up the struggle and sank.

She had woken, bathed in icy sweat, her fingers clutching at the twin chains. The pendants had marked her skin, as if they had been red-hot, but Julia was shivering with the cold.

The memory made her tremble as she sat at the top of the tower. Her hands had gone involuntarily to her neck, and her fingers were now entwined in the slender silver chains that lay there still. She tugged at them experimentally but only succeeded in hurting her neck. She knew they would remain as unbreakable as ever, and it had been some years since she could remove them by lifting them over her head. Like it or not, she was stuck with them.

Julia considered the pendants. The chains were now too tight for her to see them without a mirror but she recalled what they looked like. Each was a circle of black glass with a tiny hole near the edge for the chain to pass through. She had often thought that there was a lighter-colored pattern hidden within the black but had never been able to make it out properly.

She knew that both she and Bela had worn a pendant when they arrived on Strock, and that on her sister's death she had inherited the second. They now lay cool and smooth against her skin, but—after Ashula's revelations—she began to doubt their innocence.

They're part of it, she thought. *Part of what I was.*

Shivering, Julia deliberately moved her fingers away from the pendants. Their role in her nightmare confused her. They had hurt her—both in the dream and on waking—yet a dolphin had returned them to her. She loved the dolphins and could not believe them capable of harming her. Perhaps the dolphin in the dream had really been something else. She hoped not, for in other circumstances those lovely creatures of the sea had provided her with many moments of wonder and happiness.

When Julia had learned to swim, she discovered that a school of dolphins often came in quite close to the shore. After a while they allowed her to join in their games, and nothing could surpass the exhilaration of those times. One of the dolphins had even allowed Julia to ride upon his back. She had gone far out to sea that summer's day, unwittingly causing Kubiac a great deal of worry as he watched from the shore.

In Julia's dreams, too, the dolphins were usually synonymous with joy. The nicest dream she had ever had was one in which she *became* a dolphin, and dived and leapt, listening to the laughing voices of her companions. The memory made her smile now as she returned to thoughts of the present.

As she reflected on Ashula's other disclosures—that he knew of her abilities to interpret and even influence people's moods—she decided that it had come as no real surprise. Julia had instinctively avoided using her talent on the wizard, and now she knew why. Reserving her efforts for easier targets, especially her parents, had come naturally. Was that wrong? It had never felt so, though she admitted that, on occasion, it had been very useful for getting her own way. She resolved to heed Ashula's words and try not to abuse her ability.

As she sat there, Julia was once more seized by a great restlessness. The island was so small and the world, she was sure, was so large. Why was she imprisoned here? What had Ashula meant when he said she would get the chance to prove that she was good? How could she be anything else on Strock?

She rose, descended the steps to the ground, and ran off along the top of the snake as fast as she could. She was soon breathing so hard that she could not even hear the crash of the sea to either side of her. Reaching the end of the spit, she turned right, coming down the bank of the snake, and set off at a trot across the island toward Old Walls. There was a great deal she wanted to talk about but another matter was now demanding urgent attention. Her stomach, lacking breakfast, was sending out distress signals.

Julia was still jogging when she reached the peat field. Blackwood was there, hard at work with his long-bladed cutter. There were few trees on Strock and wood was always at a premium, so peat formed their main fuel.

Blackwood looked up from his trench as Julia approached.

"You're in a hurry," he observed.

"I'm hungry." She came to a halt, breathing hard, and added, "There's no other reason to hurry on this island, is there?"

"Maybe not. Some folks'd count that an advantage," he replied, watching her closely.

"Oh, Blackwood, didn't you ever want to see the world? Is everyone on Strock *born* old?"

Blackwood did not take offense, but laughed, white teeth shining within his dark face. "Are we all so boring then?"

"I didn't mean it like that." Julia looked contrite. "But there must be more to life than this." Her arms swept around, indicating the land about them.

"Aye. There's the farm." He was teasing her now. "And the ruin down by south beach. And a lot of sea."

"And the fish in it?" she retorted, smiling in spite of herself.

"That too."

"You're hopeless!" Julia exclaimed. "Don't you understand?"

"You're young," Blackwood replied, as if this explained everything. "You'll get your chance if you want it bad enough."

"Everyone keeps telling me that, but I don't think it'll ever happen. Nothing ever happens here!"

So saying, Julia sped off. As she climbed over the last loop of the snake, Blackwood called after her. "Come to the farm this afternoon. Tam has something to show you." He was not sure whether the girl heard but she waved as she disappeared from sight. Blackwood watched the empty skyline for a while, a thoughtful expression on his face, then shrugged and turned back to his work. She's an odd one, he mused, but you can't help but like her, for all her quirks.

Julia threaded her way through the maze that was Old Walls and came to the kitchen.

"Come to help me, have you, miss?" said Mosi.

Julia automatically began to put other ideas into the cook's head, but then hesitated.

"All right," she said reluctantly, "but only after I've had some breakfast."

"Mercy! Have you not eaten yet?" exclaimed Mosi.

As Julia sat, devouring the contents of the various dishes Mosi set before her, Kubiac came in, looking worried.

"Have you seen Ashula?" he asked.

"No, not since last night," replied Mosi. Julia, her mouth full, shook her head.

"I can't find him anywhere." Kubiac glanced around the room as if the wizard might be secreted in a cupboard or up the chimney.

"He'll turn up when he has a mind to," said Mosi cheerfully.

"But I wanted to talk to him *now*," replied Kubiac plaintively.

Julia swallowed and added, "Me too. Let's go and find him."

Kubiac frowned. "I've got to go to the farm."

"Blackwood told me to go to the farm. We can go together."

Julia piled up her plates and, smiling at Mosi, said, "I'll wash these when I get back."

The cook swallowed the lie without rancor, being used to Julia's ways.

"Mind you're back for dinner," she said. "I'm not here just to feed *you* at all hours of the day and night."

Julia was halfway to the door but Kubiac was still uncertain. "Come on," said Julia. "Tam's got something to show us."

Kubiac came out of his reverie. "I know," he said gloomily.

They went out together. Though the day was still clear, the wind was cold and, once in the open, they walked briskly. Kubiac was soon out of breath.

"Don't you ever want to leave Strock?" asked Julia suddenly.

"What?"

She repeated the question, noting his preoccupied air.

"Why?" he replied, slowing his pace.

"Oh, Kubiac! What kind of an answer is that? There's a whole world out there. Mountains. Cities. *People!*"

"There are people here."

"Not many."

"You're here," he said quietly, avoiding her eyes.

"I'd go if I had the chance," she said. "I'm meant for bigger things than this, I know it." Julia quickened her pace, and so did not see the stricken expression that her words had provoked.

They did not speak again until they reached the farm buildings. Catching his breath, Kubiac said, "There aren't any boats."

"I know." The island now boasted only two vessels, neither of these big enough or sufficiently seaworthy to travel the long distance to the nearest landfall. Even if enough wood could be found for the manufacture of a ship, there was nobody left with the knowledge either to build such a craft or to crew it.

"It doesn't matter," said Julia, laughing. "One day, a golden warrior will come in his high-prowed longship and carry me away. I've seen it in my dreams!"

She laughed again and after a moment Kubiac joined in uncertainly. No ship had visited Strock in the twenty-one years of his lifetime.

Tam came out of the barn and beckoned to them. Kubiac's expression changed abruptly, as if he had just remembered something important—and unpleasant. They walked across the yard to the farmer, who was a big man, obviously fond of his food. "Slow and steady" was his motto and Julia felt that it suited all aspects of him perfectly—especially his mind.

The tall barn door stood open and Tam ushered them inside, motioning them to be quiet with a finger to his lips. Despite the open door and the barn's ill-repaired roof, it was dark inside, and when Tam pointed to something at the far end Julia could not make out what it was. As her eyes became accustomed to the light she saw a dark shape on a pile of straw and several smaller shapes moving about it.

"Kittens!" she exclaimed delightedly. As she moved forward there was a fluttering from the rafters, but she took no notice.

"Not too close, missy," warned Tam. "Them's wild."

Julia stopped a few paces away. The mother's green eyes watched her suspiciously but the kittens ignored her presence entirely, continuing with their tumbling games and mock fights. Julia counted six, then saw a seventh, apart from the others. This one was a tabby, like her siblings, but with white patches on chest and forelegs. She watched Julia closely as the girl squatted down and made encouraging noises. After a moment the kitten took a huge bound out of the straw and trotted up to Julia's outstretched hand.

I'll call her Bela, thought Julia impulsively as the kitten put out a tentative paw and patted her hand. Gradually she edged closer until she could rub the kitten's chin and neck. Bela stretched and meowed. Enchanted by her new friend, Julia turned to see if the others were watching. What she saw made her laugh out loud, and sent the startled kitten scampering back to its mother.

Kubiac was staring at the other kittens with manic intensity. His eyes bulged and his face was mottled red as if from great effort, yet he stood quite still.

"What are you doing?"

The spell that held Kubiac was broken by Julia's words, and he stood upright, his taut muscles relaxing and a look of anguish on his face.

"Oh, I *knew* it would be no good!" he cried. "It should have been today." Julia heard the pain in his voice, and going to him, saw the tears in his eyes.

"What is it? What's the matter?"

"I'll never be a w-wizard," Kubiac said, a catch in his voice.

"Why? What are you trying to do?"

"Trying to find my familiar," he replied. "Every true wizard has one."

"Like Ashula's dolphin?"

"Yes. I've tried before but today I really thought . . . Ashula even said . . ." His voice trailed off, dejectedly.

"The kittens?"

"Yes. I tried *so* hard."

"There'll be others," she said kindly, taking both his hands in her own.

"But there are so few animals born on the island now." Kubiac was beginning to sound almost angry.

A raucous cry came suddenly from the rafters and they both looked up. As they did so, something green and smelly fell from above, hitting Kubiac squarely on the forehead and splattering them both.

"Ugh," said Julia, as the odor of rotten fish filled her nostrils. Tam laughed and said, "He's got it in for you, master."

Kubiac began to swear viciously, this last insult being too much to bear, then remembered who was present and shut his mouth. He glanced up at the roof, shaking his fists, almost dancing with rage. He looked so ridiculous that Julia had difficulty in restraining her laughter.

Suddenly Kubiac became still, his arms above his head. His eyes and mouth opened wide and he stared upward in amazement. Julia followed the line of his gaze and saw, on the rafter, a fledgling seagull, its feathers still the speckled colors of immaturity. The bird's beady eyes were set on Kubiac.

"He spoke to me," whispered the would-be wizard.

"What?" asked Julia.

"He spoke to me!" yelled Kubiac, a look of insane glee plastered all over his face. "He's the one!"

"He could have picked a better way of introducing himself." Julia giggled, pleased with Kubiac's obvious delight. "What did he say?"

It was a moment before Kubiac answered.

"His name's Kirt. I can't believe it! It's happened!"

Tam looked on in disbelief, having no idea what was going on. Kirt squawked again, flew down from the rafters, and swooped out of the barn doors. Kubiac capered after him, oblivious to the mess congealing on his forehead. Tam and

Julia exchanged glances, then followed him outside. The seagull was now perched on a gatepost, level with Kubiac's head. Man and bird were obviously deep in conversation. As Julia watched, smiling at their earnest expressions, a small sound made her turn around. Bela came bounding out into the yard, made a beeline for Julia, and, when the girl knelt down to greet her, ran straight up her sleeve and perched on her shoulder. Tiny claws hooked into the wool. Julia stood up slowly. Bela stayed where she was.

"Can you talk to me?" Julia asked hopefully

Bela's meow sounded loud, but meaningless, in her ear.

Chapter 17

$\mathcal{D}$on't stare at me like that. You're making me nervous.

Kirt cocked his head to one side and regarded Kubiac with a glittering eye. *Have you got any fish?* he added hopefully.

No, but I can get you some, replied Kubiac, who felt as if he were floating on air. He had tried so hard and so often, with only Ashula's vague instructions to guide him, only to find that the link with his first partner had been established effortlessly. Communicating this way was far easier than using his voice. It was all he could do to keep from laughing like a madman.

It's all right, replied the bird. *I'll fish for myself.*

Don't go! Not yet, responded Kubiac quickly.

I'm hungry. Kirt sounded just a little petulant. *I've come a long way.*

So you said. Where have *you come from?*

The bird's reply was a mixture of meaningless syllables. Seeing Kubiac's confusion, he added, *Far across the sea.*

How did you find me?

I followed the dream-winds.

Somehow that made perfect sense to Kubiac.

I'm sorry I said what I did back there. I didn't realize it was you, and you surprised me.

Kirt's beak opened and he cried raucously. Kubiac had the distinct impression that the seagull was laughing at him. He didn't care. The bird's next statement sounded rather complacent.

It was a good shot, wasn't it?

You mean . . . ?

I had to get your attention. You were so busy shouting at those silly fur-claws that you couldn't hear me.

Kubiac gaped at Kirt, then burst out laughing, much to the amazement of Julia and Tam, who were watching the otherwise silent exchange with interest. Soon afterward Kirt flew off toward the sea and Kubiac turned to them, his face aglow with pleasure and—something Julia had never seen in him before—pride.

"What were you laughing at?" asked Julia.

"Oh, nothing. We were just discussing our mutual introduction." Kubiac grinned. "After Kirt's . . . message hit me I thought some very rude things about him and of course he heard me."

"You mean he did it deliberately?"

"Yes, and after I swore at him he said, 'That's a fine thing to call someone who's flown across half the oceans just to find you.' And that's when I realized!"

Kubiac's unusually clear-eyed gaze rested on Julia's face but it seemed to the young girl that he hardly saw her. He couldn't keep still, and his arms and hands moved constantly as he spoke. She had never seen him so animated.

"So you're a wizard now?" she said.

Her words brought the young man back to earth, and his expression became serious.

"Only a very minor one," he said quietly. "But it *is* the first step!"

Seeing the hope and longing written so clearly on Kubiac's face, Julia felt a surge of love for her awkward friend, and hugged him fiercely.

"I'm so pleased for you," she said. "It might be just the first step but it's the most important one."

Kubiac, noticing Bela for the first time, nodded and said, "I see you've found a friend of your own."

"Not like yours," she replied, lifting the kitten off her perch, "but she is rather lovely." Bela meowed in agreement. "Where has Kirt gone?"

"To fish. He's hungry. He'll see me back at Old Walls. The 'big rock heap,' he called it."

Julia laughed. "He's an observant bird!"

"Of course," replied Kubiac. "He is the eyes of a wizard now!"

In their excitement, the two young people had forgotten Tam. He spoke now, making them jump.

"I don't rightly know what's going on here but I'm glad for 'ee, Master Kubiac."

"Thank you, Tam," said Kubiac, and surprised the farmer by embracing him briefly. "We must go," he added, glancing up at the sky. "He'll be back soon."

"Can I take the kitten with me?" asked Julia, knowing the answer before Tam replied.

"I doubt the mite would be left behind," he said. "She'd follow you, like as not."

Julia kissed him lightly on the cheek and skipped out of the yard after Kubiac. Tam watched them go, scratching his head. *Like a pair of spring lambs,* he thought.

Kubiac walked quickly, too preoccupied to realize that he should be getting out of breath. His eyes swept the sky continually, following the path of every bird he saw. Julia saw the rapt expression on his face and soon gave up any attempt at conversation. Her happiness for him was tinged with a little resentment. She had been the center of Kubiac's attention for so long, and had taken it for granted. Now she was rival to a seagull and, what was more, she knew the bird had already overtaken her in Kubiac's affections. She consoled herself with a whispered conversation with Bela.

As he strode along, Kubiac's thoughts were racing. Uppermost in his mind was the realization that Ashula had been right all along. It *had* been today, just as the old wizard had hinted! All those hours of study, of listening, learning, and painstaking practice, had proved worthwhile. While his eyes continued to scan the western sky, his thoughts went back through the years to the apparently endless hours spent in Ashula's study, trying desperately to prove worthy of being allowed to use a little of the energy that men call magic.

He learned how to recognize the potential of his own mind, the power that all men have but few could utilize. He learned how to enhance that power by concentration, and to increase it by harnessing the natural resources of various objects and places, even of the earth itself. The ancient sites of power revealed a little of their mysteries to him. Under Ashula's guiding hand, Kubiac sensed the residue of long-past conflicts in the stones of the circle, the barrow, and the tower. Each felt as different to his mind as they did to his fingers.

He saw the patterns in the wheel of the stars, the sun's path, and the movements of wind and tide. He treasured the old stories and learned their hidden messages as best he could. All living things became sources of wonder for him. The lore of herbs and healing were of special interest, for his body was always weak, prone to illnesses and sudden exhaustion.

All this he learned and more, and constantly he longed for the chance to prove himself, to *use* the knowledge he had taken such trouble to acquire.

When that day finally arrived, his career nearly came to an abrupt end.

Ashula placed a stone the size of a walnut on a table and told Kubiac to move it to the opposite side. It seemed such a pointless, not to say trivial, spell that the apprentice had almost protested. After all, he could so easily have just picked it up. But he came to his senses quickly enough. This was *magic*, after all. He knew that he had to start somewhere.

The spell was ready in his mind. He pictured it like a powerful animal ready to spring, awaiting only his words to set it free. The reality turned out to be rather different.

At first he could not focus the power at all, and nothing happened except that his confidence waned. Then, when he finally did channel it correctly, he was appalled by the arduousness of such an apparently simple spell. After what seemed like hours of hard labor he had, at last, caused the stone to flip over and skid a handspan across the wooden surface.

Then Kubiac collapsed and remained unconscious for several hours.

When he awoke and realized what had happened he became deeply depressed. What hope was there for him? The idea that he might become a wizard now appeared ludicrous. But, with Ashula's help, the boy rallied. He had, after all, succeeded in moving the stone and next time, he was assured, it would be easier.

So it proved, though it was a long time before even such simple magic became second nature to the wizard's apprentice. Gradually, he added to his repertoire. Light and fire answered to his command, albeit in limited manner. Searching spells gave him the illusion of soaring aloft, and proved useful in their own right. Many wonderful vistas had opened up before him. But *nothing* had prepared him for the incredi-

ble moment when Kirt had first spoken within his head. It
was the culmination of his life so far, the final justification of
all the years of effort, proof that he really was destined for a
life of wizardry.

As they entered Old Walls, Kirt swooped down out of the
sky and Julia knew that Kubiac was lost to her. She walked
away.

Mosi approved of Bela, claiming that farm-bred cats made
the best mousers. Julia sat on the kitchen floor and watched
as the tiny kitten explored her new environment, so full of
interesting smells and inviting hiding places. By the end of
the afternoon all three were the best of friends.

"It's good to have young things about," said Mosi wistfully.
"I remember when you were little—the tricks you used to
get up to! I never could find it in my heart to scold you, no
matter how naughty you were."

Julia smiled at the cook, but felt a twinge of guilt, remembering how she had diverted the blame for some of her
pranks.

"Your parents, bless them, were no good at that either,"
Mosi went on. "You could do no wrong in their eyes."

Julia studied the floor. Then, hoping to change the subject,
she said, "Mosi, why aren't there any other children on the
island? What happened to them all?"

The cook looked sad. After a few moments she said, "Blackwood and me were the last that could, I suppose, but nothing
ever happened. We're past that time now of course . . ." She
paused. "Bad luck is all I can think, but not as bad as those
who had children only to lose them."

They were silent. Julia had heard tales of young men
drowned and girls taken ill, but until now she hadn't realized
the full scope of the tragedy which had visited Strock.

"The island was dying," said Mosi in a faraway voice, "and
that's no place for children. Perhaps it was a punishment."

"That's too cruel!" cried Julia.

Mosi's eyes came back into focus. "Mercy," she said. "Listen to me rambling on. Besides, when you came, everything
changed."

And after me? thought Julia, but remained silent.

———————————

Neither Ashula nor Kubiac appeared for dinner that night,

a fact which surprised nobody. Mosi had long since become philosophical about catering for wizards and took their empty places in her stride. Julia's parents retired early to bed, as was their habit in the winter months, and the others were busy with tasks of their own, which meant that Julia was alone for much of the evening. She went to her room and found herself reviewing memories of her childhood. Strock had still been interesting to her then, a place large and full of wonders. Ashula had let her sit in on Kubiac's lessons sometimes, and though she understood little of what was said, she found them fascinating. Her favorite times were when the wizard told stories, full of magic and heroes, monsters and beautiful women. They had made a lasting impression on her, and she remembered some of them still.

As she grew older, Julia had begun to appreciate the rudimentary theories of magic, but never considered the possibility that she might make use of this knowledge.

One memory stood out in her mind. It was the time when she realized how incredibly old Ashula was. She was eight, and already knew that the wizard was older than her parents, who seemed ancient to her. Ashula had just finished reading from one of his large leather-bound books, and as he glanced up from the page, Julia looked into his bright blue eyes and felt herself falling into their depths. Down and down she went, all in an instant, seeing the years, the centuries pass by. A rush of places, people, and events so immense that it was impossible to believe it came from one man's memory. She blinked and found Ashula smiling at her. Though the number of years would have meant nothing to her then, she knew, beyond any shadow of a doubt, that the wizard was truly ancient, and the knowledge left her awestruck.

Julia never quite lost that feeling of frightened wonder. She wished now that she could speak to him and try to explain the awful restlessness that was threatening to drive her mad. The fact that Kubiac was so full of purpose at the moment made her feel even more unsettled. And she still had not talked to Ashula about their conversation the night before.

"I wish he was here now," she whispered to Bela, who had curled up beside her on the bedspread.

Then, of course, as was so often the case when she wanted something, Ashula *was* there.

There was a knock on the door, and Julia jumped to let him in.

"Isn't it wonderful about Kubiac!" she exclaimed.

Ashula looked taken aback for a moment, as if he had not considered this as a likely topic of conversation.

"Yes," he said, as he sank slowly into a chair. "He's been waiting long enough. I only hope he gets the thing housebroken before too long."

Julia laughed and said, "He can't be used to being indoors, he's only a baby really."

"All the familiars are at first," the wizard replied. "That's how it works."

"How many have you had?"

"Quite a few."

Julia saw the pain in Ashula's eyes and decided not to pursue that topic. Intuition told her how terrible it must be to lose a familiar. It was already obvious how much Kirt meant to Kubiac, and Ashula must have lived many times the span of most animals' lives.

"What is your dolphin called?"

"The nearest we can get to his name in our language is Csonka."

Julia tried the unfamiliar syllables.

"Is he the one who plays with me?"

Ashula smiled. "Yes. He's very fond of you. He told me once that you would make a good dolphin, which, from Csonka, is high praise indeed. He doesn't think much of humans in general."

Julia glowed with pleasure.

"I dream I'm a dolphin sometimes," she said, and the room grew quiet as they remembered the previous night's conversation. They sat in silence for a while, each wondering how to restart their discussion. Then, as so often happens at times like that, both started talking at once.

"About last night—" began Ashula.

"When you said—" Julia broke off and they laughed self-consciously. Bela chimed in with a high-pitched comment of her own and their laughter became genuine.

"You're special," Ashula went on. "I've always known it and I think you have too." He held up his hands to forestall Julia's protest. "It's not just a matter of your arrival here, or even of your curious talent."

"What then?" she asked, bewildered.

"You've been feeling unsettled lately, haven't you?"

Julia looked at him suspiciously, wondering if he was being sarcastic. She nodded slowly.

"You'll be leaving here soon."

Her eyes went wide. "How do you know?"

"You came here for a reason. Soon you will have to move on. Not because you want to—though I don't doubt that—but because you *need* to. Destiny, it's called."

"And then?" she whispered.

"I cannot see that far ahead."

"How long have you known about this?"

"For a long time."

"And you didn't tell me!"

"What good would it have done? It would just have made the waiting harder." *For all of us*, he added silently.

"When will it be?"

Ashula swallowed his hurt at the eagerness in her voice and said, "I don't know, but there are events brewing in the world that will not wait too long. You are part of them."

After a pause Julia said slowly, "My talent . . . is it magic?"

"Of a sort," replied the wizard, "but like all magic you have to be very cautious in its use." *Careful*, he advised himself. *If I upset the delicate balance now . . .*

"Listen closely, Julia. It is essential that you take note of what I am about to say. Your talent uses the natural power of your mind to link with others. That's fine, provided you only use it to absorb information—that's little more than anyone does when they look at another person's expression."

"But?"

"But you can *influence* people if you want to, and that can be dangerous. Julia, I know it's tempting but, however gentle you try to be, in doing that you *alter* that person. Take it too far and you could hurt them very seriously." *And that's the least of it*, he thought.

"I never—" began Julia.

"I know. You've done no wrong but you have more power than you know. You have a duty both to yourself and to me to use it well."

"I will, I promise." A strange thrill ran through Julia. *Power! In me!*

"I know you will." Ashula smiled. *She's a strange creature,* he thought. *Unique. I hope I know what I'm doing.*

"Why did the moonberries hurt me at first?"

"There was magic in you. It kept you alive but it was not good," said Ashula, his face serious. "I believe you came here because on Strock we could rid you of the bad side of it. The moonberries were part of that process. What I didn't know was how violent it would be to start with."

Julia turned this over in her mind.

"My talent—it comes from the bad magic?"

"Initially, perhaps, but it's changed now. Your life here has seen to that."

"And the dreams?"

"The dreams are all your own. They may tell you of your past, your future; they might be completely meaningless, but if you remember something clearly from a dream, it is usually a sign."

"That's not very helpful," said Julia.

"True," the wizard replied, "but it's the best I can do."

"You know more than you're telling me, don't you? About my future, I mean."

Ashula remained silent, and from his expression, Julia knew she would learn nothing more from him. One thing was certain. She would pay closer attention to her dreams from now on!

Chapter 18

That spring, Julia's seventeenth on Strock, passed more slowly than any she had known. She lived in constant expectation of momentous events and went to bed each night thinking that tomorrow would be *the* day. But as the spring turned to summer and the weather grew milder, she began to wonder if anything would ever happen. Ashula remained infuriatingly vague and she could not discuss her longings with anyone else. Even Kubiac shied away from the subject of her possible departure.

After the initial infatuation with his familiar had abated a little, Kubiac had once more become Julia's most constant companion. Although he had gained a measure of self-confidence, the fledgling wizard was still an awkward specimen of humanity. Julia often watched him and Kirt together and thought them remarkably well matched. The bird's feathers grew lighter and smoother as the year progressed but he retained his ruffled appearance and disreputable habits. One of his legs was shorter than the other and that made his movements when walking as odd as Kubiac's. He was also remarkably large, with a prodigious appetite, and, especially when Kubiac brought him indoors, his cries were ear-splitting. At quieter times, when he put his head on one side and peered at those around him, Kirt could be quite endearing.

When the weather was warm enough for Julia to swim, Kirt flew above or sat on the waves nearby, watching over her where Kubiac could not. The young man was a poor swimmer and remained frightened of the sea and its limitless strength. Though she was never in any danger Julia did not resent their attentions, and was flattered by their concern.

Julia was also the subject of another's devotion. Bela had grown quickly into an energetic and mischievous cat who followed her adopted mistress almost everywhere. She had even walked all the way across the island on several occasions, and added her own commentary to any conversation. Like Kubiac, Bela could not accompany Julia when she went swimming, and at those times patrolled the beach, calling piteously.

Julia loved her new companion but occasionally found her attentions irritating. She was sometimes scared to take another step for fear that Bela would appear under her foot. Contrary to Mosi's prediction, the cat also turned out to be completely useless as a mouser. She would lie in wait at a likely opening, but if a mouse appeared she would shoot, stiff-legged, straight up into the air and then flee to safer ground. On one occasion, in her panic, Bela ran partway up the kitchen chimney. Fortunately the grate was cold, but both cat and Julia, not to mention half the room, were covered in soot before Bela was retrieved.

It was Bela who, one warm afternoon, first sensed Julia's mysterious visitor. Ashula and Kubiac were closeted together and everyone else was either asleep or at work. Julia had gone back to her room after lunch to change into something suitable for swimming, but, knowing that exercise of that kind would be unwise so soon after eating, she had settled down to study a little book. It contained pictures of herbs and flowers, beautifully and delicately painted by Kubiac. He had labeled each illustration in his tiny, spidery writing so that she would be able to recognize the plants they saw on their walks.

Before long, however, Julia's attention was distracted by Bela. The cat suddenly stood stock-still, her fur bristling. Only her ears twitched, though Julia could hear nothing. After a moment Bela went over to the door and sat looking up at the handle as if she wanted to go out. When Julia didn't respond she scratched at the door, then turned to her mistress and meowed. Still Julia did not understand.

"What is it, Bela? There's no one out there."

The cat only repeated her performance until Julia gave in, opened the door, and peered out. As expected, the corridor was empty, but a strange wavering light played on the walls where the passage turned out of sight, and Julia heard a soft, musical humming, like the song of contented bees. Bela set off purposefully in the direction of the light. A tingling sensation ran through Julia's body when she followed her cat.

The light receded before them. As Julia rounded the corner, the source of the golden glow had disappeared around the next. Intrigued and increasingly excited, she quickened her pace. This time as she entered the next stretch of corridor she thought she saw someone, or something, ahead of her. The humming was louder now.

Julia broke into a run and at the next turn caught a brief, dazzling glimpse of her quarry. She gasped and came to an abrupt halt, almost tripping over Bela. She had seen the back view of a man dressed in glittering, golden-colored armor. The light shone from him, rippling and flashing as he moved. He traveled quickly, seeming to float rather than walk, yet his armor made no sound. Only the lovely humming disturbed the afternoon peace of Old Walls.

It was the warrior from her dreams.

Julia realized what Bela had evidently known from the start, that she was meant to follow him. Yet for a few precious moments she stood paralyzed, caught between wonder and fear, need and doubt. Then she was off, running as fast as she could, careering down the twisted passageway. It always seemed that she was just too far behind to see him clearly.

Julia lost her bearings and was surprised when she suddenly found herself outside in the sunlight. She looked around wildly, her heart pounding, and saw the warrior climbing over the first arc of the snake, heading inland. She raced after him and reached the top of the ridge only to see him even farther ahead, still traveling toward the barrow. Julia knew instinctively that that was their destination and she sped off in pursuit, following the flashes of sunlight reflected from his armor.

Julia felt as though she were wading through water, so slowly did her legs seem to move, and an age passed before she found herself at the foot of the longbarrow. The warrior stood on the top, still with his back toward her. She longed to see his face but he made no move to turn around.

Now that she was closer Julia could see that the man was bareheaded. What she had taken to be his helm was in fact straight golden hair, the color of summer corn.

For a few moments they both stood motionless, then Julia

nerved herself and began to climb, only to halt abruptly as the warrior flung his arms wide. Sunlight flashed from the metal of his armor and Julia was seized by a dizzying attack of vertigo. Without warning the island about her disappeared, the humming stopped in an instant, and she found herself in the throne room of a great palace.

All about her was an opulence she had never even dreamt of. Stained-glass windows shed patterns across a marble floor. Banners, tapestries, and shields decorated the walls and beautiful furniture adorned the room's many alcoves. Most amazing of all were the twin thrones at one end of the room, raised above the floor so that their occupants could look down on their courtiers.

If this is an illusion, thought Julia, *it feels more real than any dream*.

The vast apartment was empty but Julia heard footsteps approaching, and shrank back as two men entered. They took no notice of her. The elder of them sat down in the larger of the thrones, while the other remained standing.

"Your Majesty, I merely inquired whether you might be acting a little hastily. The queen has been dead but a few days."

The old man gestured impatiently.

"I will wed!" he exclaimed.

"Of course, sire, but surely in honor of the old queen . . ."

An exquisitely dressed girl entered the room from a doorway behind the screen. Julia gasped at the familiar face, but no one seemed to hear.

"What better honor for the old queen than that the new queen should be crowned?" the girl said in a voice that dripped honey.

The courtier's manner changed immediately.

"Of course, my lady," he said.

"Tomorrow!" said the king. "We wed tomorrow."

The girl smiled as the old man reached out to take her hand.

Julia only had time for the fleeting thought that it was obvious where the power lay in *that* court, when she found herself in an entirely different scene.

This time the room was much smaller and less grand. There were two people in it but they also acted as if Julia were invisible. She quickly recognized the paraphernalia about her as a wizard's accoutrements and found herself studying the man sprawled on a couch at the far side of the room. Kneeling beside him was a girl, facing away from Julia, who fed the wizard with small fruit. They laughed together in a way that made Julia blush.

"Tell me truly, Faramondi. Do you love me?" The girl's voice was eerily familiar.

The wizard nodded energetically.

"Would you do anything for me?"

Again he nodded, comically eager, his mouth open for the next fruit.

"Then prove it," the girl said and lowered her mouth to his. As she straightened up after the lingering kiss, she began to turn toward Julia but her face never came into view, and, once more, the scene changed with disorientating rapidity.

Julia found herself the witness to a tour of inspection of a huge merchant's warehouse. A fat, expensively dressed man was showing a woman around. Her cloak and hat hid most of her features but Julia already knew what she looked like.

"There's no finer store, no greater wealth anywhere on the island," the man boasted. "Not even in the royal treasury in Pevenstone." He spoke easily, confident of his ability to impress, but his guest remained silent. An employee hurried up but, as the woman glanced in his direction, he immediately realized that he had urgent business elsewhere. The merchant did not notice his departure, having eyes only for his female companion.

Before the next scene appeared Julia had a brief glimpse of Strock. The warrior still stood above her, his arms held high. Neither of them had moved.

Why am I being shown all this? she thought. *What does it mean?* There was no time for answers. She suddenly found herself in a most embarrassing situation.

The bedroom was occupied, as was the bed. Mercifully, the couple disporting themselves so energetically—and so noisily—were hidden by a sheet. Even so, Julia tried to look elsewhere, but her attention was dragged back to the bed. She was repelled yet fascinated at the same time.

After a while the erotic tumult subsided.

"Stars!" the man breathed. "No wonder the whole court is talking about you. Go on like this and you'll soon be able to twist the whole island around your little finger."

A young woman's voice replied playfully, "Of course! I shall rule you all with a rod of iron."

"Promises, promises."

Giggling, the girl emerged from beneath the bedclothes. It came as no surprise at all to Julia to find herself looking into her own eyes.

The world fell apart, then reassembled. Julia was once more back on Strock, the warrior still motionless above her. She forced herself to move, feeling her limbs stiff and cramped, as she began to climb.

Surely now there would be some explanation. Surely he would talk to her. If only she could see his face!

A noise sounded behind her, and she turned to see Tam coming across the island toward her; Tam, whose mind was so slow she could read it like a book. It was the last thing she wanted now.

Unthinkingly she reached out with her mind; pushed a little *there*; made a slight adjustment *there*; and snapped the course of the farmer's thoughts.

Tam came to a halt, scratched his head in puzzlement, and then, with a glazed look in his eyes, turned about and headed toward Old Walls.

Julia spun around joyously as the warrior turned to face her, but the look of fearful horror on his face stabbed her like a dagger of ice. His golden eyes were wide and his hands flew up in front of his face as if to ward her off, as if she were some monstrous evil.

The day turned suddenly cold. Gone was the comforting humming, gone the feeling of contentment.

What have I done?

The warrior disappeared, sinking quickly into the barrow beneath him, leaving only the memory of his last agonized expression.

Julia fled.

Chapter 19

*S*he ran headlong, in a blind panic, knowing only that she must get away. Instinctively she made for Old Walls; home and safety.

Julia gained her room without meeting anyone and threw herself on the bed, gasping for breath. Gradually the pain in her tortured lungs lessened, but there was an ache in her chest that would not go away. She began to sob, but dared not close her eyes, knowing that if she did she would see again those stricken golden eyes.

For months she had longed to see the face of her dream warrior, believing him to be the man who would release her from Strock. Yet when the moment had come, he had rejected her in fear and loathing. For Julia, the trauma had been so great, coming as it did after the joy that his presence normally inspired, that she forgot the visions he had shown her.

As she wept, one thought alone pounded through her mind.

How can I face him now when he comes for me?

When a knock came on her door, Julia remained silent, hoping that her visitor would go away, but the door burst open and Kubiac entered, in a state of great excitement.

"There's a ship coming!" he exclaimed. "Kirt's seen it!"

Julia felt as if her heart had stopped beating. Seeing her tears, Kubiac asked softly, "What's the matter? Why are you crying?"

He received no reply but Julia quickly rose from her bed and hugged him to her, hiding her face in his shoulder. Though worried, Kubiac was also pleasantly surprised by her action, and putting his arms around her, he held her tight. Slowly Julia relaxed, but when she drew back a little to look into his face, Kubiac saw fear and supplication in her eyes.

"I can't see them," she whispered. "I can't."

"B-but I thought . . . You always said you wanted a ship to c-call."

Kubiac was hopelessly confused by this latest turn of events. He had lived in dread of any visitors ever since he learned that Julia wanted to leave the island. Yet when Kirt had spied the sail heading their way, he had been swept up by excitement. After all, no ship had called at their tiny isle in his lifetime. Whatever the consequences, it was a momentous occasion for Strock. Julia had in the past made no secret of the fact that she was waiting for a ship, and now . . .

"I can't explain," she said, so quietly that he could hardly hear, then added more loudly, "Oh, why did this have to happen *now?*"

Kubiac's heart ached at the pain in her voice and he asked, "Is there anything I can do?"

Still cradled in his arms, Julia shook her head.

"There must be something," he pleaded.

"No, Kubiac." Even though her words denied him, he was glad to hear her speak more firmly. "There's nothing you can do. I'll explain later, but for now just accept that I don't want the men from the ship to see me."

"But why?"

Julia shook her head again but said nothing. Kubiac gave in.

"All right," he said. "I'm going down to the jetty to guide them in. Ashula wanted you to go to the hall and join the welcome, but . . . I'll see you later," he ended lamely.

Julia nodded, managing a weak smile, and Kubiac left.

Alone again, Julia tried to organize her chaotic thoughts. What could she do? Run away to one of the island's secret places? Hide in the maze of Old Walls? She considered a dozen hiding places but discarded them all. Deep within her she knew that, despite her fear, she would have to see the men from the ship. To refuse this chance would leave her with permanently unanswered questions—and that would be unbearable.

The answer was obviously to find a place from which she could observe the visitors and yet remain unseen herself. But where? The answer came from her childhood memories of games within Old Walls. Beneath the rafters at one end of the hall was a narrow opening, which led into an old storeroom, long unused. From there she could see almost all of the hall and had an especially good view of the main doors, where she presumed the sailors would make their appearance.

If it's him, she thought, *I can hide until he's gone.*

The idea was agony, but she knew that to face the horror and accusation in his eyes again would be even worse.

It took her some time to find her way up to the hiding place, and for a moment she was afraid that the door was locked, but it was only stiff from lack of use. The storeroom was thick with dust and Julia tied a handkerchief over her mouth and nose. An ill-timed sneeze would not be helpful.

The opening was at floor level and she lay down gingerly, peering around the edge. She saw Mireldi, seated at the head of the table, with Reveza beside him, and Ashula at his other hand. There was a noise from beyond the doors and Julia tensed. Footsteps approached, and she heard Mosi's voice. The door opened and the cook and her husband entered.

"They're coming!" Mosi said, unable to hide her excitement.

In the dim light beyond the open door Julia saw figures approaching. She held her breath, her heart thumping. Kubiac stepped into the room.

"May I present Special Ambassador Durc . . ." he announced formally.

Julia did not hear the rest of his introductions; all her senses were focused on the man who stepped out of the shadows into the hall.

She wasn't sure whether to laugh or cry. The newcomer was the complete opposite of the man she had both longed for and dreaded seeing. His tanned, weather-beaten face was framed with ill-cut black hair and a beard streaked with gray. He was tall and lean, and attractive in a rugged sort of way. Though he was clearly well past middle age, he had the look of one who led an active life, and his clothes reinforced that impression. He was clad in dark leather, a long dagger at his belt.

Julia's mind was so busy struggling with this new development and its possible implications that she hardly noticed a second man enter the hall. He was less striking than his companion, younger and more elegantly dressed, but his face also bore the marks of an outdoor life. When Julia's powers of observation returned, she noted that he walked with a slight limp.

Fragments of conversation began to reach her ears. Words of greeting, introduction, and welcome were being exchanged.

"Our daughter, Julia, should also be here to greet you," Reveza was saying. "But we can't find her at present. You know how it is with children." The old woman smiled.

Julia, who no longer considered herself a child, was stung by the reference.

"I shall look forward to meeting her later," Durc replied loudly, having already recognized the elderly couple's partial deafness.

At this point Julia was distracted by a noise behind her and she glanced around quickly. Bela had at last rediscovered her mistress's whereabouts and was now daintily picking her way through the dust toward her. Julia tried to shoo her away silently but the cat took no notice. When she reached the opening, Bela paused, and looked down into the hall with interest. Julia edged forward to try to grab the animal but as she did so Bela meowed piercingly. Julia looked anxiously into the hall and found herself looking directly into Durc's twinkling blue eyes. The special ambassador was smiling broadly.

"I think there are outlaws among us," he said, and the others turned to follow his gaze.

Only then Julia realize that she still had half her face covered with a handkerchief.

After that there was nothing for her to do but to go down and try to hide her embarrassment as best she could. After brushing off as much of the dust as possible and stuffing the handkerchief into the pocket of her breeches, Julia reluctantly entered the hall.

"There you are, my dear," said Reveza, as if nothing had happened. Julia smiled at her thankfully. "Durc, Zunic, this is Julia."

The men bowed gallantly and Julia curtsied awkwardly.

"I am delighted to meet you, Julia," said Durc. As their eyes met, a spark leapt deep within Julia's body.

"And I you," she managed to reply.

Mireldi said, "You'll bring your crew up for dinner then?"

Durc turned to him. "If you are sure—" he began.

"Of course," Mosi interrupted. "It will be a pleasure to cook for so many once again." She was beaming at the idea.

"Some honest cooking would be welcome after months of ship's rations," said Zunic.

"That's settled then," concluded Mireldi. "Two hours from now."

"Thank you," said Durc. He and Zunic bowed to their hosts and withdrew. Blackwood and Kubiac went with them to help with their harborside tasks. Mosi set off toward the kitchen, then hesitated and beckoned to Julia.

"I could use some help," she said. For once Julia jumped at the chance, and gratefully ran out after the cook, leaving her parents and Ashula to ponder over her odd behavior.

"Whatever were you up to, young miss?" Mosi said with a laugh once they were alone. For a few moments Julia did not answer but busied herself with the familiar tasks of preparing a meal.

"I was scared," she finally ventured.

"Why mercy!" cried the cook. "Whatever for? They're gentlemen, that's plain to see. Though they've been through some rough times from the look of their ship."

"You've seen it?"

"Yes. Me and Blackwood went down to see them dock. I don't know when I was that excited. Mind you, I'd say they were lucky to land here."

"Were they lost?"

Mosi shrugged.

"We'll find out at dinner most like." She paused, then chuckled. "You looked a fair sight up there in that hole." More seriously she added, "What were you scared of then?"

"Them. What they might be," Julia replied. "I don't know why."

Mosi considered this for a time. When she spoke again it was obvious that she had decided not to press the matter any further.

"To think, after all this time, a proper banquet to prepare! I hope I can still remember how."

Shortly before the start of the meal, Mosi, who now had Blackwood's help, sent Julia to change. She went gladly, tired from the excitements of the day and her exertions in the oven-hot kitchen.

"Well, I thought nothing ever happened on Strock," she said to Bela. "I can't really complain when *too much* does, can I?"

Now that the immediate danger of meeting the golden warrior had receded, she felt able to consider the extraordinary events of the day. In retrospect it seemed absurd that she had been so sure that the man from her dreams would be on the ship. But who *was* the golden warrior? Was he a ghost? What did the visions he had shown her mean? Had she seen pictures of herself as she might have been? Or of her future?

The questions multiplied inside Julia's brain, each one with no answer. She decided to seek out Ashula as soon as possible. If anyone could help her, he could. For the moment, however, she had other matters to attend to. Unless she hurried, she would be late for dinner with Durc and his crew. After her earlier embarrassment, Julia was determined to make a good impression. She washed, then put on her blue name-day dress, persuading herself that she did so only to show Reveza that she was no longer a child. The little flutter in her heart told her that this was not quite the whole truth.

"I'm nearly a woman now," she said aloud. "I can wear a pretty dress if I want to." Glancing at Bela, who was watching her curiously, she added, "And you can stop looking so skeptical!"

There was a timid knock at the door.

"I'm coming!" she called.

Kubiac was waiting outside.

"You look lovely," he exclaimed, adding in a softer tone, "Are you all right now?"

"Oh, yes." Julia smiled and the young man relaxed visibly. They set off together followed by the omnipresent Bela. Durc and his men had already arrived. A trestle had been added to the end of the dining table and extra chairs and benches brought in. The ship's crew were already seated, and Mosi, with the help of several volunteers, was bringing in numerous bowls and plates. Mireldi sat at the head of the table. On his left were Reveza, Zunic, and Ashula. Durc was at his right hand, talking animatedly. Beside him were two empty seats.

The room grew quiet as Julia entered and she was acutely

aware of—and not displeased—by the fact that every eye in the room turned her way. Durc rose as she approached and the other sailors quickly followed suit. She accepted the offer of the seat next to Durc, and conversation resumed as she and Kubiac sat down.

"You look lovely, Julia," said Durc. She glowed with pleasure at the echo of Kubiac's words from this man of the world.

"Thank you, Ambassador."

"Call me Durc. The title is only an honorary one," he replied, smiling.

Plates were passed around, wine poured out, and the meal progressed. Julia was aware of many appraising glances directed at her from the lower end of the table, but she ignored them, preferring to listen to and talk with Durc and Zunic. Kubiac was quiet, but everyone else around her found much to discuss.

"Durc was just telling us of their journey here," said Mireldi. "An odd business."

"Odd, indeed," agreed Durc. "Zunic and I have done our share of traveling over the years but we've never come across anything as strange as this before."

"What was it?" asked Julia. She expected tales of sea serpents and whirlwinds at the very least, so the reply came as something of a disappointment.

"Fog," said Durc. "Great banks of it, in places it had no right to be."

"There's always fog this far north," said Ashula, watching Durc closely.

"That moves in the opposite direction to the wind?" replied the ambassador.

"With solid gray masses the size of Starhill Castle floating inside it?" added Zunic.

"Icebergs?" asked Mireldi.

"In summer?" Durc replied.

"What else could they be?" said Julia.

"We weren't going to get close enough to find out!"

"We did think about turning back to Rek—we'd just sailed from there—but decided foolishly to stay at sea, hoping the fog would clear and we could go on to Ark."

"Is that your home-isle?" asked Julia.

"Yes," replied Durc. "By rights we should be back there now."

"We're not even sure how to get to Ark from here," said Zunic. "Fine navigators we make."

"That's easy enough," said Ashula. "I have charts."

Julia looked at him in surprise. Was there no end to the wizard's secrets?

"Good," said Durc. "That will help. Though it wasn't exactly our fault that we lost our bearings. We were hit that night by a freak storm, with the strongest winds I've ever come across. We had our work cut out just to stay afloat, so it's not surprising we didn't take much notice of where we were going."

"East, as far as we could judge from the stars," put in Zunic, "but on its own that's not a lot of use."

"When the storm finally blew itself out, we needed to find land quickly. Most of our water had been soiled and we'd not much food left."

"We couldn't make much headway until the rigging was repaired, and in all that time we saw no land at all. We were beginning to worry!" Zunic said ruefully.

"Then yesterday we saw your island on the horizon and thanked whatever star was guiding us. We had never even heard of Strock before," admitted Durc.

"That's hardly surprising," said Mireldi. "Strock is not exactly the largest landmass in the world!"

"Nor is it on the trade routes," added Ashula. "Yours is the first vessel to call here in thirty years."

Durc was astonished. "Thirty years!"

"You can see why your arrival is something of an event for us," said Reveza.

"The weather's been fine here," mused Ashula. "Surely a storm that big would have affected us?"

"You and everyone else for a hundred leagues I'd have thought," said Zunic. "Unless it was meant just for us."

"We may not be perfect," said Durc, "but even we don't deserve that sort of punishment."

Everyone laughed, except Ashula.

Soon after that two of the sailors left their seats and came up to Durc.

"We'll be relieving the watch now, sir," said one. "They'll be half dead from hunger."

"Did no one think to take them anything?" asked Reveza. The men exchanged guilty glances.

"Like me, my lady, they were thinking too much of their own stomachs," said Durc. "Go then, and get the others up here quickly."

"Are you well fed yourselves?" asked Mireldi.

"Yes, my lord. Thank you."

"The best food ever, my lord, and sorely needed."

Mosi, who had appeared with extra dishes, beamed at their words. The men left and were replaced shortly afterward by two others who were soon eating ravenously, intent on catching up with their crewmates. However, they had barely had time to demolish one plateful when their meal was interrupted by the return of one of the new watch. He had evidently been running and his expression was grim. He spoke to Durc but every eye was on him and each person in the room felt the chill in his words.

"There's another ship heading into port, sir," he said. "She's big. Bigger than anything I've ever seen."

"Colors?" asked Durc.

"She's flying none, sir. Just . . . there's a sort of gray light around her, sir. Not natural." The man's self-conscious words halted as a buzz of speculation arose from the other sailors.

How much more can this day contain? thought Julia.

Suddenly, she felt desperately afraid.

Chapter 20

*T*he islanders were thunderstruck. After decades of isolation, the landing of one ship was astonishment, but two in the same day defied belief. Durc was less hesitant. He turned to Mireldi.

"With your permission, my lord, I'll deploy my men. I don't suppose it's a pirate ship, but it can't hurt to take precautions."

Mireldi agreed. Amid the clatter of plates and scraping of chairs the sailors went out, leaving the hall ominously quiet. Blackwood also departed, and after a few moments Kubiac stood up and said, "I'll go too. Perhaps Kirt can tell us something."

Ashula nodded, but his face was pale and drawn. Julia saw his preoccupied air and her premonition of terror grew stronger. She realized that although the wizard had foreseen Durc's arrival, the second ship had come as an unwelcome surprise. That in itself was reason enough for her to be afraid.

Mosi slumped down into Kubiac's empty chair.

"I don't know that my old bones can stand all this excitement," she said, trying for her usual jovial manner. Her voice betrayed her, however, and nobody responded. The tension in the silent room grew to breaking point, then snapped as footsteps were heard approaching. Both Ashula and Julia got quickly to their feet as Durc came in.

"They've anchored in the bay," he reported. "There's no sign of any landing party."

"What does the ship look like?" asked Ashula.

"Can't tell in this light. She's big though. I don't think she could dock here if she wanted to."

Julia felt a measure of relief. At least they couldn't get too close.

"What are the gray lights your lookout spoke of?" she asked nervously.

"Just that," replied Durc. "Faint, gray lights, which don't show us much, and can't be much use for their crew either."

Why should the lights scare me so? Julia wondered.

"They'll come ashore in the morning most like," Durc went on, "but we'll post a watch anyway."

"Thank you," said Ashula.

A sailor appeared in the doorway.

"There's a boat coming in to the jetty, sir," he called. "Three, four men maybe."

"Wrong again," muttered Durc.

"Shall we bring them here?"

Durc glanced at Mireldi, then at Ashula. The wizard nodded reluctantly and Durc relayed the order.

Julia *knew* she must not stay to face the newcomers. Turning on her heels, she ran from the hall, followed after a moment by Bela who, through all the commotion, had sat quite happily underneath the table. Nobody tried to stop them going, though Durc and Ashula exchanged glances.

"Have they docked?" asked Reveza.

"No, my lady," replied Durc loudly, "but there's a landing party on its way. They should be here soon."

Mosi stood up. "I'll get some clean plates," she said and hurried off, feeling glad of an excuse to escape the tense atmosphere. Shortly afterward, Zunic entered, followed by another man.

"Captain Thir," announced Zunic.

The captain bowed slightly but said nothing.

"Welcome," said Mireldi. "Our island is honored by your visit." Thir remained silent, taking stock of those present. His pale face wore a calm but vaguely disapproving expression, as if he found them all rather distasteful. There was a hint of malice in his cold, gray eyes.

Unnerved by Thir's continued silence, Reveza asked, "Will you dine with us, Captain?"

"Some wine perhaps?" Mireldi added.

"No. Thank you." Thir's voice was surprisingly soft. Neither of his hosts heard him and they looked to Ashula to help them out.

"Will you take a seat, Captain?" said the wizard. "If not with food and drink, how may we assist you?"

Thir remained standing, hands clasped behind his back, a frown creasing his face. When he spoke his words were again so quiet that only the sharper ears caught them.

"I am looking for two girls, who were shipwrecked some years ago. It is possible they were washed up here."

"What did he say?" asked Reveza.

"Let me speak," replied Ashula. To Thir he said, "How old would these girls be now?"

"Some seventeen years. They were twins, and have very remarkable violet-colored eyes." He glanced around to see if there was any reaction to his words.

"There are no young people on Strock, Captain. We are an island of old people. What makes you think they might have landed here?"

"It was a small chance only," admitted Thir, "but we have already been to almost all the other islands." He turned to Durc. "You, sir, have you seen anyone of this description?"

"I am only a visitor here, Captain, like yourself," replied Durc evenly, meeting Thir's gaze. The gray eyes switched for a moment to Mireldi and Reveza, then, dismissing them, moved on to Ashula.

"If they are not here, I will impose upon you no longer." So saying, Thir nodded to the company, turned, and strode from the hall.

"But Captain," Reveza began. Ashula put a restraining hand on her arm. At Durc's discreet signal Zunic followed Thir. They waited until the strange man was sure to be out of earshot.

"Stars!" breathed Durc. "I should not like that one to come looking for *me*."

"What did he want?" asked Mireldi. "I couldn't hear a word he said." Ashula explained briefly.

"Where *is* Julia?" Reveza asked worriedly.

"She knew before anyone," said the wizard. "She'll be safely hidden by now." *I hope*, he added silently.

"Do you think he believed us?" asked Durc.

Ashula shrugged. "I don't think he was used to having to ask questions," he said enigmatically. "We seemed to displease him."

"The feeling was mutual."

When Julia fled from the hall, she had no idea where to go;

she only knew that she must get away. Finding herself outside Old Walls in the gathering gloom brought her to her senses, and a moment's thought led her to the conclusion that the most sensible place to head for would be the farmhouse. She was about to set off when a plaintive cry made her pause. Turning, she saw the white markings of Bela's coat as the cat trotted up to her. Julia knelt and scooped up the animal. As she stood up again her gaze fell on the harbor; the eerie gray lights that showed there made her shiver despite the evening's warmth and she quickly set off northward, cradling Bela in her arms.

No lights shone from the farmhouse. Julia realized that Tam and Martin must have heard of the first ship's arrival and made their way to Old Walls. In the half-light she fumbled with the door latch and all but fell into the main room. She collapsed onto a chair, still holding Bela. Sweat beaded her forehead, and her dress clung to her unpleasantly.

Now what? she thought.

The old house creaked about her, and every sound made her jump. She dared not light a lamp. Unable to sit still, she stood, deposited Bela on the floor, and went upstairs to the bedroom. From the window she could see part of Old Walls and a section of the harbor. The gray lights on the ship were still there and, as she watched, another moved away from the shore.

They're leaving! she thought. *Thank goodness.*

She fell back on the bed, sighing with relief. Then, as she lay there looking up at the ceiling the thought nagged at her that it couldn't be that simple. Why *was* she so afraid? Too much had happened this day—she could not take it all in. Julia closed her eyes and listened to the night sounds around her. Minutes passed.

A loud tapping sounded at the window and Julia sat bolt upright, her heart thumping wildly. Wide-eyed she saw a gray-white thing beyond the pane and would have screamed had not a tiny corner of her mind recognized its shape. The tapping was repeated, followed by a loud squawk.

Julia laughed nervously and went to open the window. Kirt strutted in, stretching his neck and clacking his bill. He looked very pleased with himself.

"Where's Kubiac?" asked Julia, then heard someone running toward the house.

"Julia, are you there?" The young wizard sounded terrified. "Julia!" he called again, closer now.

"I'm here! In the farmhouse."

They met at the front door.

"Thank goodness I've found you," Kubiac said, breathing heavily. "You've got to hide. They're coming."

"But they've gone."

"No! I heard them say they would organize a search party. Their captain didn't believe Ashula. He's going back to the ship, but then . . ." Even in the starlight Julia could see that Kubiac's face was aghast. "I saw . . ." he went on. "I saw what they really are!"

"What?" asked Julia, dread rising within her.

"Wraiths," whispered the young wizard. "I saw." He gulped. "After the captain had talked to Ashula and the others, he went back to his boat. Only when he reached the jetty he sort of melted, until he looked like just a wisp of fog, then he didn't walk anymore, he *floated*. They weren't real sailors either, but more like him. Their boat moved off without any sail or oars. That's when I heard them talk about a search."

"For me?"

Kubiac hesitated. It was obvious that he had not even considered the idea that the gray men could be looking for someone else.

"Yes," he said simply in the end, his conviction confirming what Julia already knew. An overpowering terror threatened to envelop her.

"Where can I go?" she asked, her voice little more than a whisper.

"As far from Old Walls as possible," Kubiac replied. "If nothing else, that will give us a little more time to hide. You can't stay here; after the village this will be the first place they'll look."

Kubiac glanced upward. Above them a white shape wheeled among the stars.

"Kirt will keep a lookout and warn us when they move," the young wizard said. "We'd better get started."

They set off inland, Julia cursing the impractical nature of her dress and delicate shoes. They had not gone far when Kubiac looked up, then back in alarm. Silently he pointed. Several soft gray lights were bobbing over the land near the beach. As they watched, more appeared and spread out, ready to comb the island.

"Quick," hissed Kubiac. "We'll find a cave on the eastern shore. It's our best chance."

Kubiac ran on a few paces, then stopped when he realized that Julia was not following. She stood still, her head cocked as if she were listening intently.

"Come on!" whispered Kubiac urgently.

To his amazement, Julia smiled.

"Don't you hear it?" she said.

"Hear what?" asked the bewildered wizard.

"The humming," Julia replied dreamily. "There's the light!" she added, pointing toward the center of the island.

Kubiac followed her gaze.

"I don't see anything," he said.

"There. The golden light." Without hesitation, Julia set off in the direction she had indicated. Kubiac followed, soon realizing that Julia was heading for the barrow.

"There's nowhere to hide here," he pleaded. "It's all open ground. Come away!"

Julia would not be swayed, and marched on, seemingly unhurried, still smiling. Kubiac looked back frantically. The gray wraiths were closer now; he did not need Kirt's clamoring reminder to know that. He wanted to shout at her to come to her senses but dared not for fear that their pursuers would hear. He knew that they had very little time left—and nowhere to hide.

Julia reached the barrow, climbed to the top, and halted. *What is she doing?* Kubiac thought desperately, then his blood ran cold and he gasped in horrified astonishment.

Julia was sinking into the ground below her, into the barrow! Her feet were already invisible and her legs disappeared as he watched.

"Julia!" he screamed, heedless of the noise now, and rushed toward her. Too late. He was just in time to see that she was smiling before her head was swallowed up by the earth and no trace of the girl remained. Kubiac fell to his knees and wept.

He was still kneeling there when, a little while later, a cold gray light touched him and he fell into a deep and dreamless sleep.

Chapter 21

*J*ulia had been in a state composed of equal parts of exhaustion and panic when the gray lights first appeared, and had been more than willing to let Kubiac take charge, to follow where he led. But then the humming sound had reached her ears, bringing with it a wave of tranquillity. When the rippling golden light appeared, she knew immediately that she was meant to follow it. That it led her to the barrow was no surprise, but what happened then certainly was. Sinking through the earth and rock was the queerest sensation she had ever known. It felt a little like swimming in the sea, except that the rock did not part before her but slid *through* her, like water through a sieve. She was aware of the pressure, knew the different textures of soil and granite, but felt no pain. Her feet passed into air again.

The last thing she heard was Kubiac's anguished cry, echoed by Bela as the cat watched her beloved mistress vanish before her eyes.

Then Julia was alone.

She stood on ground that was solid once more. All about her was utterly black, utterly silent. The golden light and the humming that accompanied it were gone.

The realization of where she was and how she had come to be there slowly sank into Julia's mind and her legs trembled. She sat down suddenly on the floor and tried very hard not to think about going mad. A scream rose in her throat but she fought it back and started talking sternly to herself instead.

"He brought me here to save me from the wraiths. They'll never find me here."

Nobody *will find you* here, whispered her fearful mind.

"The light and the humming were good! I know they are. He would not lead me here only to abandon me."

Then where is the light now? And the humming? It's as silent as a grave in here.

"Stop it!" she shouted. "He would not hurt me."

Wouldn't he? Her memory showed her again the warrior's horror-stricken face.

"That was my fault. Because of Tam. He *is* my friend."

Would a friend shut you up inside a tomb?

"To help me. He'll let me out when it is safe."

How?

"I don't know. Leave me alone!"

Her voice was swallowed by the dense and silent blackness. No echoes gave her any indication of how large a space she was in. She deliberately narrowed her thoughts to practicalities. Deprived of sight and hearing, she had to use the senses left to her to examine her situation. The air about her was dry, musty but not unpleasant. She had no difficulty breathing so was not in any immediate danger of suffocation. There was a smell, too, something she could not quite identify. At first she thought it might be candle wax, then caught a metallic tang in the air. *Armor?* she wondered, but shied away from that idea.

Slowly she began to explore about her with her hands. The floor she sat upon was stone, quite smooth and very cold. She could feel nothing else within reach. Gingerly, choosing her direction at random, she began to crawl across the stone on all fours, one hand held out before her blind eyes. As she crept along, the hand on the ground collided with something smooth and cold, which clanked loudly. Almost overbalancing, Julia brought her other hand down quickly—and found it gripped by icy-cold steel fingers!

She screamed and jumped backward, wrenching her hand free of that chill metallic clasp. Silence returned slowly, and Julia regained some measure of composure.

It *was* armor then, she rationalized. She had touched first its arm, then its glove.

Go back and make sure, she commanded herself.

Gradually Julia retraced her path. This time she was ready for the contact and quickly found the glove. It had come away from the armguard, and without thinking, she picked it up. A little dust ran through her fingers from inside the glove. She shuddered. Exploring gently with her fingers she found that the metal was still pure and its joints still movable.

It hasn't rusted at all, she thought in wonder and then realized that the armor was probably gold, not iron. She put the glove down and felt for the armguard. As she did so something dropped from it. Julia picked up what seemed to be an armlet, heavy and intricately wrought. The metal was curiously twisted but it, too, had not decayed.

Acting on impulse, Julia slipped it over her wrist. Her ears rang, as if her very blood were humming. Although no light disturbed the darkness, Julia no longer cared; her whole being was swamped by a warm, contented lethargy.

She lay down beside the long-dead warrior and surrendered herself to sleep.

The island awoke late the next morning. Each person's memories of the previous evening ended abruptly. They had fallen asleep in the oddest of places; some were relatively comfortable in that they were indoors, some were even lucky enough to be in bed, but many sailors were slumped at their defensive posts. They woke stiff and cramped, wondering what could have have happened to them. Many complained of feeling sick and of having had sinister dreams. They soon realized that the gray ship had gone, and connected their speculation concerning the night before with its departure. Many men looked fearfully out to sea, but the horizon was clear.

Mosi came to lying on the kitchen floor. She was bewildered and sore, her head ached and she felt queasy. She stood up gingerly and got a drink of water. As she did so Durc appeared, one hand clasped to his forehead and the other leaning heavily on the doorway.

"I just woke up in the corridor," he croaked. "We didn't have *that* much to drink last night, did we?"

Mosi smiled at his feeble attempt at humor.

"Not drink," she said

"No," he replied, his face becoming serious.

"You look as bad as I feel," she added, handing him some water.

"Thanks."

"What happened?"

"Something gray . . ." They looked at each other.

"Help me find the others," she said with an urgency that denied her sickness.

They found Mireldi and Reveza slumped at their chairs in the dining hall. Both were very cold and breathing shallowly, and were quickly put to bed. Mosi made them hot drinks while Durc contacted his men and began the arduous task of reviving their spirits.

When Ashula emerged from his study, he was white-faced with anger. No one dared approach him after the first attempts met with a string of fearful oaths. He kept muttering to himself, and the terrified Mosi feared that he had finally lost his mind.

It soon became obvious that both Julia and Kubiac were missing. This brought on fresh waves of anxiety, but Durc and Zunic soon organized search parties. Before long, Kubiac was found, wandering aimlessly near the center of the island, laughing wildly and gabbling incoherently. He made even less sense than Ashula, though he was less frightening. The sailors brought him back to Old Walls, though he protested and kept looking back over his shoulder. Once inside, he quieted down, and the two wizards were left together in the hope that they would make sense to each other if to nobody else.

The search for Julia continued without success. Every pace of the island was covered, every beach and cave, every ditch and ruin. Old Walls was virtually taken apart room by room, disturbing decades-old dust. All to no avail. Julia had vanished and her searchers came to the awful conclusion that she must have been abducted by Thir and his gray men.

They kept the news from her parents for as long as they could, but the old couple learned of it eventually, and were distraught. Mosi was afraid for their health, and decided to risk an approach to Ashula. She found him watching over the sleeping Kubiac.

"I've given him a potion," said Ashula calmly as she came in. "He'll sleep the rest of the day."

"Are you all right now?" Mosi asked timidly.

"Yes. I'm sorry about—" He looked up and she waved away his apology.

"Julia?" he asked hopefully.

Mosi shook her head.

"All for nothing," said the wizard bitterly. "Has it all been for nothing?" Mosi had never seen him so dejected.

"Come and see Mireldi," she said. "He's not at all well." Ashula sighed as if to say "What does that matter?" but followed her out.

In the early afternoon Ashula and Durc were sitting in the wizard's study. They had done all they could. Those still suffering ill effects from the previous night were being cared for, the search for Julia had been completed; now they were at a loss.

"I'd go after the ship but . . ." Durc's voice trailed off. The obvious absurdity of this idea was clear to them both. Even if they knew where the gray ship was headed, Durc's vessel could not hope to match it for speed, size, or strength.

There was a fluttering at the open window and Kirt landed on the sill. Ashula was about to shoo the bedraggled bird away in irritation, but saw that the seagull carried a cargo of blue cloth in his beak. Durc saw it too.

"Her dress!" he said, leaping to his feet. Kirt squawked and the fragment drifted to the floor. He flew off and Durc followed, vaulting out of the window and running down the lane after the bird.

Kirt led him inland. Before long Durc needed no guidance as he saw a distant blur of color atop the barrow. He ran on, heedless of his footing, and arrived breathless and dripping with sweat.

Julia lay on her back on top of the barrow, a serene expression on her lovely face. Her eyes were closed and her arms folded over her chest. A lump rose in Durc's throat at the sight of her. *Am I too late?* he wondered.

He knelt and gently took her hand, feeling his heart leap at its warmth. As he lifted her up, her armband nearly slipped off. He pushed it back above her elbow and took her home. She did not wake.

Several people, alerted by Ashula, met them before he reached the village, and Julia was carried inside amid many relieved smiles. Ashula was waiting in Julia's room when Durc laid her on the bed.

"Someone let her parents know," instructed the wizard.

"Mosi's already on her way," replied Durc.

Ashula looked at the sleeping girl.

"She seems fine," said Durc, "just very reluctant to wake up."

"So were we this morning," said Zunic, who was also at the bedside.

"But we're awake now."

"You forget," said Ashula, "That we don't know where Julia has been until now. Her experience cannot be compared to ours." His eyes fell upon the armlet. Though his face betrayed no surprise, the wizard became very still.

"What is it?" asked Durc anxiously.

Ashula did not reply, but gently slid the gold band off Julia's arm and held it up to examine the design. As he did so, Julia's eyelids fluttered and then opened.

"What did you do that for?" she asked accusingly. "I was having such a nice sleep."

"Welcome back," said Ashula enigmatically.

"Are you all right?" asked Durc.

"Of course. Why are you all looking so worried?" Julia sat up and saw the begrimed state of her dress. The others watched her face as the memories came flooding back.

"Is Kubiac here?" she asked.

"He's sleeping," replied Ashula. "He'll be all right by this evening, once he knows you're safe."

Julia started, and looked about her as if something were missing.

"Where's Bela?"

The men looked at each other. No one could recall seeing the cat that day.

"I've got to find her!" said Julia. She swung her legs off the bed and stood up. Durc started forward, thinking to restrain her, but Ashula shook his head.

"Let her go," he said as Julia ran out. "She'll be all right— she's better rested than any of us." He looked again at the armlet, which he still held. The delicate goldwork formed a coiled and twisted serpent, its open jaws looked upon its own tail. Tiny red jewels glittered in its eye sockets. Ashula now knew where Julia had spent the night, and the knowledge both astonished and intrigued him.

Julia was returning to the barrow, the armlet forgotten. All she could think of was the memory of Kubiac's scream and the feline cry that had accompanied it. The rest of her adventure had taken on the aspect of a dream. None of it seemed real.

She saw Bela as soon as she reached the barrow. The cat lay on her side at the base of the mound. Her position was unnatural and her fur was bedraggled, stuck together in clumps as though she had been frozen and then thawed out by the sun. Bela's eyes were open but covered by a gray film, and her white fur was also gray. Looking at her beloved pet, Julia knew exactly how Bela had died and raged inwardly, while tears ran down her face. She felt sick.

"But they were looking for *me*," she groaned aloud. The callous injustice of the innocent animal's fate caused something fierce to grow within her. She made several decisions in that moment, decisions that were to change the course of her life. Drying her tears, she picked up the pathetic bundle that had so recently been so full of life, and set off, stony-faced, back to Old Walls.

Chapter 22

*J*ulia buried Bela next to the tiny grave where the cat's namesake lay.

Later that afternoon she went to seek out Durc and found him at the jetty, organizing the filling of water barrels and the refitting of his ship. She was aware of several curious glances as she approached.

"You're leaving soon, aren't you?" she said without preamble.

"Yes," Durc replied. "We have to. Our homecoming is long overdue, and besides, if trouble's brewing, we should be there."

"Take me with you."

Durc hesitated, aware that several men had stopped their work to listen to his reply.

"This is your home, Julia," he said eventually. "Don't be in such a hurry to leave it."

"A hurry?" she retorted. "I've waited sixteen years!" Before Durc could reply she went on, "Besides, you're a fine one to talk. You've been traveling all your life."

"Not quite," he replied, smiling. "And I always return to my home-isle. You may not be able to."

"I don't think I'm meant to," said Julia. "Ashula said as much. I'm sure that there's meant to be more to my life than hiding here on Strock, and if I don't take this chance, it could be *years* before another ship comes."

"What about the other people here? Your parents?" Durc queried. Julia's face fell, and he knew that he had found the weak spot in her argument. He felt sympathy for the girl, stuck on this isolated isle with no companions of her own age, but Durc was still not willing to grant her wish before insuring that she had thought of all the consequences. At the very least she must discuss it with her family and friends.

Julia mumbled something.

"Pardon?"

"I said they'll understand."

"Have you told them?"

"Not yet." For a moment Julia would not meet his eyes, then she rallied and asked, "You think there's trouble brewing?"

"Yes." Durc was puzzled by the abrupt change of subject. "Why?"

"The strange weather . . . that gray ship . . . what happened here—"

"Don't you see?" she interrupted, her voice almost strident. "They were looking for *me!* That must mean that I'm involved in what's happening, but what can I do *here?*"

"If they were looking for you, then that's all the more reason to *stay* here—and safe," said Durc. "My ship would be no match for theirs in the open sea."

"But eventually they'll come back and I won't be so lucky next time. Please, Durc, this is so important to me."

Durc came to a decision. "Let's go and see Ashula," he said, and set off briskly, leaving Julia no choice but to follow. Behind them a buzz of speculation arose from the *Fontaine's* crew.

They found the wizard seated in his study. From the way that he held himself Julia knew that he was either very tired or sick or both, and felt a pang of guilt. Her parents and Kubiac were ill in bed because of her, and she was plotting to desert them.

Ashula was staring at something on the table before him. With a jolt, Julia recognized the armlet from the barrow. She had forgotten its existence.

The wizard looked up as they approached, and Julia was dismayed to see that, for the first time, his eyes were those of an old man. He waved them into chairs.

"I've almost finished," he said to himself.

"Ashula—" Julia began.

"Of course you must go," the wizard said.

"You know?" asked Durc, unable to hide his surprise.

Ashula nodded.

"You see!" said Julia triumphantly.

The wizard looked at her sadly. "Does it give you so much pleasure to leave us?" he asked quietly.

Julia's jubilation faded rapidly. "No, but—"

"Don't mind me," interrupted Ashula. "I'm very tired now; it will be good to rest."

"Why don't you come too?" said Julia, glancing at Durc.

"There's room for all of you, if you wish," said the ambassador gallantly.

Ashula was obviously not even tempted.

"I'm too old to leave here—and so are the others. This is our home-isle. Julia, it is your destiny to go alone. I will not argue with fate."

"It'll not be an easy trip," said Durc. "My vessel's hardly fitted for luxury, and if the weather gets rough . . ."

Julia looked at him.

"All right, all right," Durc surrendered. "I'll wager you'll make a better sailor than any of us."

"You'll need this," said Ashula, pushing the armlet across the table to Julia. "A word of advice: don't wear it openly. It could be misinterpreted."

She picked it up. "It's very old, isn't it?"

"Yes, even older than me," replied the wizard, the ghost of a smile on his face. "It's powerful too. Magic like that doesn't fade with time. It will protect you if you let it."

"Is that why it made me go to sleep?"

"In a way. It won't do that again."

Julia slid it over her arm. It came to rest just above her elbow. "It feels nice," she said. "Tingly."

"Good," said Ashula and turned to Durc. "How is the refitting going?"

"Very well. We should be finished in a day or two."

"That's it then," said the wizard. To Julia he added, "Your parents shouldn't be disturbed now. Tell them tomorrow."

Julia agreed meekly.

"For now," Ashula went on, "I'm sure Mosi could do with some help in the kitchen. It's not every day she has twenty hungry seamen to feed."

Julia took the hint and went away without demur. The wizard looked at Durc.

"She's important," he said simply.

"I know. I'll take the best care of her I can."

"Of that I have no doubt."

The two men found that they had nothing more to say. As Durc left the study, a noise sounded from the next room. Ashula rose painfully and went to see how Kubiac was faring.

Two days later Durc's ship set sail with Julia on board. Having made her decision she was glad to be leaving. Prolonging the farewells would have only made them more painful.

Her parents had accepted her departure with surprising calm, almost as if, like Ashula, they had known of it in advance. Julia remembered their old, tired faces as she had told them, finding it difficult to say the painful words loud enough for them to hear. They had sat side by side in their large bed, watching her, their expressions unchanging. Julia wondered briefly whether they were quite aware of everything going on about them. Their eyes sometimes seemed out of focus, and they lost the thread of conversation easily. Old age, illness, and Ashula's medication were taking their toll. She hated to leave them in that state, but knew she had no choice. At least they had not tried to dissuade her.

Mosi was quite another matter. Julia had been astonished at the depth of the cook's feelings. When she first learned of Julia's plan, Mosi wept bitterly, lamenting "her baby's" departure, and in her distress, had said things that Julia did not care to recall and which Mosi later regretted. The cook had come close to breaking down completely but, mainly thanks to Blackwood, she recovered and consoled herself in her more usual practical manner. She organized supplies to be taken on board ship, and although she would not help Julia pack her few belongings, she did do some last-minute sewing and mending for her. For his part, Blackwood was sad to see the youngster leave but instinctively understood her need to do so. He was a quiet man, not given to displaying his emotions openly, but several people came to rely on his calm strength during that unsettled time.

Tam and Martin reacted similarly, with a sadness that accepted the inevitability of its cause. The happenings of the last days had bewildered both farmers, and they knew that events beyond their comprehension were taking place.

The one person with whom Julia was unable to talk was Kubiac. The young wizard was up and about the morning after his enforced rest, apparently none the worse for wear. He said little and spent much of his time alone. Julia found it impossible to raise the subject of her impending departure with him and assumed that Ashula had done so.

Ashula himself spent much of his time asleep. He found it difficult to summon any energy, and only roused himself for necessary tasks, such as showing Durc and Zunic his charts and advising them on their use. The wizard felt vaguely that there was something he should tell Julia about before she left, but whatever it was remained elusive, and he forgot about it whenever she was present. There seemed so little for him to do now and sleep became an increasingly attractive alternative to thought or action.

All other necessary arrangements were proceeding well enough. The repairs to the ship were completed satisfactorily and her hold was provisioned. Julia's clothes and special treasures were packed and stowed on board; all that remained was to wait for the most favorable tide.

Now that moment had come. Julie stood on deck with conflicting emotions warring in her heart, as the sailors, with Tam's and Martin's help, cast off the ropes that held the vessel. Her goodbyes had been said and her throat was too choked for more words now, but she returned the waves of the people on the jetty as the ship began to move.

Her parents were still abed but Ashula was there, leaning on a stick. The wizard looked haggard but he was smiling. Mosi and Blackwood stood arm in arm. His face was serious but not stern while Mosi, though she had to keep dabbing at her eyes, was determined to put a brave face on her grief and smiled wanly. The two farmers completed the little group; there was no sign of Kubiac. Julia was very hurt by his absence. However much he loathed the idea of her going she had expected him to put in an appearance now. He had been with her all her life and now she felt that he had deserted her.

What is that, compared to your desertion of all of them? a small part of her asked as the *Fontaine* pulled out of the harbor.

Old Walls was soon lost to sight as they turned to port and sailed around the southern coast of Strock. Then Durc set a southeasterly course, and Julia watched from the stern as the only home she had ever known dwindled into the distance.

Chapter 23

As the ship rounded the headland and passed out of sight, Ashula turned and walked slowly back into Old Walls. Everyone at the jetty was silent. The wizard felt tired but strangely happy. He made for his study, and was about to sit in his favorite comfortable chair, when he stopped short, noticing something amiss on his desk. A quick examination revealed that the secret drawer had been broken into and the parchment within it removed. The trespass had been clumsy, perhaps done in a great hurry, and splinters of wood were strewn far and wide. Amid his puzzlement at the theft, Ashula remembered what he had meant to tell Julia.

Too late now, he thought. *She'll have to work it out for herself.*

"Why is your ship called *Fontaine?*" asked Julia.

"She's named after the queen of Ark," replied Durc. "You'll meet her soon."

Julia considered this. "Did you choose the name?"

"Yes. From the moment we met, the lady and I have shared a special relationship," said Durc, laughing.

"Oh? How did you meet then?"

"I kidnapped her," he replied and laughed again at the expression on Julia's face. Durc went on to tell her of his former career as an outlaw and his subsequent involvement in the affairs of Ark's royal family. His self-deprecating humor and flair for the dramatic made the ex-brigand an excellent storyteller and Julia listened intently. She was confused, and oddly excited, by his account of the magical aspects of the former conflict—something Durc had himself never been entirely clear about—but found the rest of the story enthralling and splendidly romantic. Her regard for the ambassador grew.

"That was a long time ago, of course," he concluded. "Fontaine has children of her own now, not far off your own age."

Julia found this thought comforting.

"I should like a ship to be named after me one day," she said.

"All things are possible," he replied. "You're lovely enough to inspire a dozen sea captains."

She looked at him quickly, thinking he may be laughing at her, but as their eyes met his smile was warm and friendly. They were silent for a time, listening to the slap of the waves against the hull and the whistle of the wind in the rigging. The *Fontaine* had made good time since leaving Strock, helped by clear skies and a steady westerly wind. There was no sign of either storm or fog. Julia had quickly grown used to the pitch and yaw of the ship and found that she was indeed a good sailor. The crew lost their apprehensions about having a woman on board—and Julia in particular—when they saw how quickly she gained her sea legs and that she was anxious to learn about the workings of the vessel. Soon she was helping to trim sails, learning to read the signs of wind and current and even taking a brief turn at the helm. Durc had insisted on vacating his cabin for her and she slept there at night, lulled by the creaking of timbers and the gentle swaying of her bunk.

Two days into their journey they met a school of dolphins, who followed the *Fontaine* for some time, leaping and splashing, intent on putting on a show for the ship's company. Julia was entranced and half thought she recognized her former playmates. The sailors also regarded the dolphins fondly, believing them to be omens of good luck.

It was while watching the dolphins that Julia became aware of the presence of another member of the animal kingdom. Most of the seabirds that had accompanied the *Fontaine*'s departure had followed them for only a short distance. By now the ship was so far from land that few birds were seen, but when Julia heard a raucous cry, she looked around and saw a seagull perched atop the mainsail. Something about the way he stood was familiar, and with a jolt she realized why. The gull's head was cocked to one side and one leg appeared to be shorter than the other.

"Kirt!" she yelled, much to the amazement of those around her. "Is that you?"

The bird answered in his inimitable fashion and one of the sailors had to move quickly to dodge the falling missile.

"A friend of yours, is it?" asked Zunic, grinning at the idea.

"He's Kubiac's familiar."

"I didn't realize the young man was a wizard," said Durc. "Why would he send his bird after us?"

"I've no idea. Those two were hardly ever apart." She paused. "I suppose there's no chance . . . ?"

"Someone would have seen him by now," Zunic said confidently. "I'd swear he's not on board."

"Then you'd be wrong," said a familiar voice. Julia and her companions swung around to face the newcomer as he emerged from the door to the cabins.

"Kubiac!"

"The very same." The young wizard bowed, trying to appear nonchalant. The impression was spoiled by the greenish tint of his face, however, and almost immediately he rushed across the deck and hung over the ship's rail. Julia ran to his side and held him, while the others looked on curiously. When his retching subsided Kubiac turned to face them, the misery that only seasickness can bring showing in his eyes.

"I don't suppose you could keep this boat still for a bit, could you?" he said.

"Not for a while, I'm afraid," Durc replied, smiling sympathetically. "You'll get used to it after a few days."

Kubiac groaned. Kirt alighted on the railing next to his master and squawked loudly.

"How did you get on board?" asked Zunic, still mystified.

Even in his wretched state Kubiac answered with pride in his voice. "A spell of concealment is simple enough. I just walked up the gangplank."

"Concealment?" Julia was impressed. She knew from Ashula that to make such a spell work properly was not nearly as easy as Kubiac was pretending. It was by far the most ambitious magic the young wizard had yet attempted. And to have

fooled the entire crew and remained undetected for two days
was a considerable achievement. She looked at him with
renewed respect, suddenly very glad that he was traveling
with her.

"You could have just asked," said Durc.

"Could I?" Kubiac seemed genuinely surprised.

Durc shrugged. "It might have made things more complicated for you," he said, "but no ship's crew I've known would
ever refuse passage to a wizard."

"I wouldn't be much use for calling up a favorable wind,"
admitted Kubiac. He started to laugh then thought better of
it as the ship rolled heavily. "Or a calm sea."

"We have those already."

"That's a matter of opinion," groaned Kubiac. "It's a good
job my stomach's already empty."

"Stay on deck," advised Zunic. "You'll feel better that way
than cooped up down below. Where have you been all this
time anyway?"

"In your cabin," Kubiac replied. Zunic's expression was so
comical that this time Kubiac had to laugh. Durc and Julia
joined in and eventually Zunic saw the joke as well.

Some time later Julia and Kubiac sat amidships, where the
motion of the waves was minimized. The young wizard was
now feeling considerably better; he was even beginning to
consider the idea that he might eat again—one day.

"I'm glad you're here," Julia said. "My new life will have at
least one link with the old one now."

Kubiac smiled but said nothing.

"What made you decide to come?"

"I haven't analyzed it," he replied slowly. "A lot of things."
He paused, considering his words. "I couldn't face Strock
without you. The island's dying; you know that. Growing old
alone would have driven me mad."

Julia nodded. She understood.

"But that's not all of it. I've never had any great urge to see
the world, as you have, yet I know that your going was
necessary, almost preordained." Kubiac's face was earnest.
"You are going to be a player in one of the great acts of
history—I know it—and I thought . . . I hoped that I could
be of help to you, guide you. Does that sound absurd?"

"No, of course not. I can't imagine a better advisor."

"I can," he said glumly.

"How do you know all this?"

Kubiac looked embarrassed. "I can't explain. It doesn't make sense even to me. From talking with Ashula, books I've read, all the odd happenings recently, involving you, the way you first came to Strock—so many things, but in the end it's just a feeling. I know I'm right."

Julia had the idea that he was not telling her all he knew. *Just like Ashula*, she thought. *Are all wizards habitually secretive?* She decided not to press the issue.

"Well, if we're off to shake the world," she said, "we've made a splendid start. We're in good hands on the *Fontaine*."

"Durc's?"

Julia was surprised by the suspicion in Kubiac's voice.

"Yes, and his crew's."

"He's more than three times your age, you know."

She felt the color rise in her cheeks and hated herself for it.

"What's that got to do with anything?" she retorted.

Kubiac said nothing.

He's jealous! Julia thought suddenly but had the good sense not to say any more.

The fog came on their sixth day at sea. It blanketed the southern horizon in a solid gray mass, stretching for endless leagues in either direction. Everyone watched as they sailed toward the fog bank, and Julia felt the fear of the men around her. As they drew close they could see that the gray mass moved westward, in the opposite direction to the wind. Closer still and they could see that to the west the edge of the fog curved away gradually southward. Durc did some calculations, using his borrowed charts, and reckoned that to follow it in that direction would take them close to the island of Brogar.

"No thanks," said Zunic. "I've heard about that place."

"Agreed," said Durc. "Whatever else we do, we're not going anywhere near there."

"Why not?" asked Julia and was told the story of Mark and Ferragamo's expedition and of the continued isolation of Brogar. It left her feeling chilled, yet strangely fascinated.

"It's almost as if I'd heard the story before," she said to Kubiac later.

By then, Durc had made his decision about their course. He had considered putting it to a vote among his men, but knew in the end that the choice must be his. The crew trusted him, and would follow where he led.

"We're going on," he announced. "I've had enough of waiting around. If we have to go through a bit of fog to get home, then that's what we'll do."

Once their course had been set, the fog seemed to rush upon them. Anxious eyes scanned its surface but no sign of either gray ships or icebergs appeared within its uniformly opaque mass.

The change in conditions as they entered the fog could not have been more dramatic. The sun was instantly blotted out, and within moments its warmth became only a distant memory. The temperature plummeted, and everything was soon covered by a thin film of ice, making both rigging and deck treacherous. Visibility dropped to almost nil. From amidships Julia could only just make out prow and stern; beyond that, all was gray nothingness. The only constant was the wind, which, in defiance of all logic, continued to blow from the west, traveling through the fog without affecting it. Durc was forced to navigate by compass. Everything else was guesswork.

When it became clear that the fog bank was enormously deep as well as wide, various arrangements were put into operation. Only the minimum number of sailors were kept on deck at any one time; everyone not necessary to the running of the vessel was sent below where heat could be preserved. The warmest clothing was divided among those on deck, and the men changed watch frequently. Other than that there was little that could be done except press on and hope for an early end to their ordeal. Durc asked Kubiac if his magical talents could help their plight, but the young wizard was totally in awe of the fearsome cold and knew that such power as he possessed would be useless against it.

After two days of traveling blindly—the nights only distinguishable by a slight deepening of the gloom—they spotted the first iceberg. It loomed up out of the fog, so close and so massive that it defied belief. Only by extraordinary luck was a collision avoided. After that more men were kept on deck as lookouts. Durc was not certain that they could do any good, but he felt that, even in the freezing conditions, it was better for them to be doing something, rather than sitting below waiting for the crash. Several more dark gray shapes were seen but, whether they were icebergs or—as everyone dreaded—gray ships, none came too close. Durc began to believe that the *Fontaine* was leading a charmed life.

It was four days after they had entered the vile bank that the illnesses began. It was at first assumed that the fits of coughing and breathing difficulties that afflicted the crew were the result of chills or colds caused by the freezing conditions. It eventually became clear that it was something more sinister. Several of the men became disoriented and clumsy in their movements, and complained of burning pains behind their eyes and in their throat. One man became delirious and fell to the deck, screaming incoherently, his limbs thrashing.

The worst affected were kept quiet and warm below deck but this put an extra strain on those still working. The time was foreseen when there would be insufficient men to control the ship should any maneuver become necessary.

Julia, who had stayed below, was spared the worst effects for some time, but in the end she began to feel nauseous within her stuffy cabin and was forced to go up on deck. Breathing the cold, damp air, she felt momentarily refreshed, then cried out as a blinding pain filled her head. She collapsed and had to be carried back to her bunk, where she lay writhing and gasping.

It was Kubiac, who had been one of the first to start wheezing and coughing, who found the remedy. He had been searching the stores and medical supplies for anything which might help alleviate the suffering of all on board. His own plight was bad enough but his wizard's sensibilities made him desperate to find a way to help those about him. He had little success until he came across a case of wine bottles in a dusty corner of the hold. The labels on the bottles were blank except for a small faded symbol and the word "Peven." Neither meant anything to Kubiac.

He found a corkscrew and, coughing and breathing harshly with the effort, opened one of the bottles. As he sniffed the contents he felt his lungs clear a little and the numbing pain behind his eyes lessened slightly. He lifted the bottle to his lips and took a sip. The liquid burned his throat, almost making him choke, but then a delicious warmth spread outward from his stomach and his spirits rose accordingly. He was unable to resist taking another mouthful and was amazed at how rapidly he began to feel better. It was the answer to his prayer, and—unlike most medicines—tasted delicious!

Taking the bottle with him he went quickly to find Durc. The ambassador was at the helm, huddled within layers of clothing. He frowned at the scantily clad wizard as he approached, but soon saw the eagerness and pleasure in Kubiac's eyes.

"What's this?" demanded the wizard, holding up the bottle.

Durc squinted at the label. After a moment he said, "I'd forgotten about that. It was a gift from Hoban years ago. It's moonberry wine."

Kubiac was taken aback, and frowned.

"It seems to have done you some good," said Durc, "but if you're going to stay out here at least put a coat on."

The wizard nodded absently then appeared to come to a decision. Handing the bottle to Durc, he said, "Drink some," and watched as the ambassador obeyed. The effect was instant and remarkable and Durc needed little encouragement to distribute the wine among those on deck. Kubiac went back below, opened another bottle, and gave a little to each man, varying the dosage depending on the severity of the illness. Then he carried the case into Julia's cabin where he could keep an eye on it. There was no telling how long they would remain in the malignant fog, and with only ten bottles left, he wanted to control its use.

Julia stirred in her sleep, plucking continually at her left sleeve. Kubiac rolled back the cloth and saw the source of her discomfort. The serpent band was glowing, and was so hot that Julia's skin was red and blistered beneath. She moaned as, using a cloth to protect his own hands, Kubiac slid it off her arm. That done, he tipped some wine into her mouth. She swallowed automatically, then opened her eyes.

"That's good," she croaked.

"Have some more."

"Are you trying to get me drunk?" Julia smiled feebly. "My arm hurts."

Kubiac indicated the armlet.

"I thought Ashula said it would protect me."

"If you let it."

"What do you mean?"

"Nothing. Do you feel any better now?"

"Yes, much. Where did you find this?"

"In the stores. Durc got it ages ago as a present from someone called Hoban."

"He was the Pevenese ambassador," said Julia.

"You're well informed."

"What is it anyway?"

"Moonberry wine."

Julia's eyes went wide. She did not like the inevitable conclusion any more than Kubiac had.

"Then this fog . . . it's magical . . . evil?"

"It could be," replied the wizard, "but we don't know for sure. All that matters is that this stuff acts as an antidote—for whatever reason."

Another three days passed with no sign of the fog lifting or dispersing. Now that the worst of their physical ailments had been alleviated, the travelers began to find psychological pressures building up. Would they ever get out of this fog? If they did, where would they be? What would happen if the wine ran out? The questions went on and on; nobody had the answers.

To make matters worse, the ice in the rigging and all over the ship's surface was gradually getting thicker. Durc began to fear that soon the *Fontaine* would be top-heavy; it would take only one large wave for her to turn turtle, and that would be the end of them all.

Then the miracle happened. As abruptly as it had swallowed the ship, the fog released her, leaving those on deck blinking and shading their eyes at the sudden sunlight. The ice rapidly began to melt and everybody came up on deck. As they got farther from the fog wall, more lungs and minds were freed from its malign influence, and the festival atmosphere increased.

They were now able to travel at full speed, and within a day of their return to the sunlight, they received the best news of all. Kubiac was the first to know, thanks to his familiar.

"Kirt says there's land ahead," he told Zunic.

Shortly afterward the lookout confirmed the seagull's sighting, adding, "It's Ark!"

Amid much cheering, hugging, and backslapping, Durc studied his charts, a serious look on his face.

"Just where I expected us to be," he said, deadpan. "This navigation is easy when you know how."

Julia, whose eyes had been fixed on their island destination, turned to him and smiled.

"Well done!" she said, at which point Durc spoiled his professional demeanor by letting out a great whoop of delight, catching Julia up in his embrace and whirling her around.

"Stop it. You'll make me dizzy," she said, laughing, and he put her down. As Durc turned back to the helm, Julia became aware of Kubiac's eyes upon her. She went to him and hugged him warmly.

"We wouldn't have made it without you," she whispered. Within her arms she gradually felt his body relax. "Isn't it wonderful! We'll soon be there."

From then until dusk all eyes were on the ever-increasing outline of Ark. As the night passed, they traveled along the northern coast of the island and by dawn were within sight of The Shoot, the massive granite gateway to Grayrock Harbor. Both Julia and Kubiac were astounded by the size of the colossal cliffs and all but held their breath as they passed between the fire towers and into the narrow strait. However, that was nothing to their astonishment when the *Fontaine* emerged into the huge natural harbor beyond The Shoot. Neither of them had ever dreamt that so many ships could possibly exist. There were hundreds of them, anchored both in open water and in clusters by the docks on the far side. For the visitors from Strock, it was an overwhelming sight.

Durc and Zunic were also amazed, never having seen the harbor so overpopulated.

"There's a few people got home before us," said Zunic wryly.

"Half the islands must be here!" replied Durc. "What's going on?"

PART THREE

The Eye of the Whirlpool

Chapter 24

For some time before Durc's return, Grayrock had been a hotbed of speculation and rumor. As ship after ship returned to port with tales of the unnatural fog that had barred their way, it had become clear that Ark was now cut off from all islands except Heald, her nearest neighbor. And the noose was tightening. Each day reports were received that the gray bank was getting closer.

Dockside space was soon at a premium and many vessels had to moor in the open water of the harbor and await their turn. Although the authorities tried to give priority to ships carrying perishable cargo, there were inevitable disputes, and these did nothing to help the potentially explosive atmosphere. With hundreds of extra sailors in the town, many of them a long way from home, there was always the chance of trouble. Though the summer was almost over, the weather remained hot, and this, too, brought its problems. Rubbish piled up in the streets and vermin multiplied, bringing with them the threat of disease.

Grayrock was a powder keg; all it needed was a spark.

It was into this strained atmosphere that four ships carrying refugees from Heald sailed. Aboard were over two hundred people, and their arrival in the already beleaguered port caused much consternation. As there were no berths at the docks, the passengers had to be ferried ashore by small boats, which wove in and out of the larger vessels. The newcomers had spent the last few days in cramped conditions, and were heartily glad to get ashore, but their reception was hardly cordial amid the quayside chaos.

An army detachment was helping to keep order in the

town, and when the commanding officer heard of the new arrivals, he knew he had to act quickly. He was dismayed when he learned that the Healdean party included that island's entire royal family, wondering what could have forced them to abandon their home-isle en masse. He refused to panic, however, and decided to defuse the situation by moving the Healdeans out of Grayrock immediately. At the same time he dispatched a messenger with the news to Starhill. He then commandeered horses and carts and went himself to supervise the operation.

There was pandemonium at the docks, but the officer eventually found the Healdean king. About Pabalan milled an enormous variety of people; soldiers, women with babes in arms, street traders intent on selling everything from water to pomegranates, those who had come to see what easy pickings were to be had, and others who were merely curious. Baggage was piled haphazardly and among all this disorder children ran and shouted.

"My lord, I'm sorry you have been faced with this shambles. I am Captain Luca, and my men and I will do all we can to assist you."

"Thank you, Captain," replied Pabalan. "Had we known Grayrock was this busy we would have called at some other port."

"I think it would be best," said Luca, "if you and your party could move on as soon as possible."

"Agreed," said the king. "If only we can find everybody!"

In the confusion of their disembarkation the Healdean party had been split into many small groups; in the unfamiliar setting few of them had known what to do next. However, they were gradually gathered from all corners of the harbor by Luca and his men and were escorted in groups though Grayrock to a hurriedly organized campsite in the countryside beyond the town. The farmer on whose land it stood was not best pleased, especially as he had already suffered at the hands of marauders from the overcrowded port, but he was promised lavish compensation.

The day ended with Luca surveying the makeshift camp, feeling justifiably pleased that the move had gone so well. Serious trouble had been avoided, no one had been lost, and the entire party was now in comfortable, if not luxurious, surroundings. There was food enough for everyone and nobody seemed to have suffered unduly from the effects of their voyage. Luca also knew that there were two wizards among the party who would be quite capable of treating any illness.

Shortly after dusk a rider arrived from Starhill with Mark's promise of aid and transport the following day. Luca took the news to Pabalan. He found the gnarled old king seated on the ground next to one of the campfires.

"Quite like old times, this," he remarked as the captain approached. Luca gave him Mark's message, then asked permission to return to Grayrock with most of his troops.

"Our own men can provide whatever security we need, father," said Ansar.

"I don't think there'll be trouble now in any case," said Pabalan. "Thank you for all your help, Captain. It won't be forgotten. It's good to know that there are still *some* things I can rely on."

"Are there likely to be any more ships arriving from Heald, my lord?"

Father and son glanced at each other.

"No," replied Pabalan flatly.

"It's a good thing I kept my bees in their hive," said Cai. "Let loose in Grayrock they could have caused a riot."

"You nearly did that yourself," replied Moroski. "You should be able to control your temper by now."

"I don't like to see women being taken advantage of," retorted Cai. "Unless it's by me."

The wizards laughed.

"How can you joke at a time like this?" asked Ansar.

The three men were riding together at the head of a long, slow-moving caravan.

"How can I not?" replied Cai, but he fell silent nonetheless.

When, shortly afterward, Ansar saw Starhill Castle, he knew their journey was nearly over.

The arrival of the refugees from Heald was the first aspect of the crisis to have a direct effect upon Ark's capital city. Rumors had been rife, but for most of Starhill's inhabitants, life had gone on much as normal. Arrangements were made to house Pabalan and most of his retinue within the castle, but some had to be quartered elsewhere. Such a large influx of visitors inevitably caused a good deal of toing and froing as accommodations were organized amid a welter of reunions. However, it was not long before some order was restored and the news from Heald could be discussed.

Pabalan and his queen, Adesina, sat in one of the royal apartments, with Mark and Fontaine in attendance. The older couple looked tired, and Mark did not want to press them into talking until they felt ready to do so. Beca had come to greet her grandparents but soon took stock of the situation and departed in search of her newly arrived cousin, Gemma. As she left the room, Ansar came in, having seen his wife and daughter settled. Characteristically, he wasted no time in coming to the point.

"We're in trouble," he said. "Heald's lost and I don't know what we can do about it."

Adesina shuddered. "It was horrible," she said quietly.

Fontaine had never seen her mother so disheartened and went to comfort her. Nobody else seemed keen to continue the conversation, so Ansar went on.

"We could fight an ordinary army—man for man, I'd back our troops anywhere—but we can't fight sorcery."

"You're sure that's what it is?" asked Mark.

"Certain. Ask anyone who was there."

"Where's Moroski?" asked Fontaine.

"He and Cai have gone to look for Ferragamo," replied Ansar.

"I hope they can find him," said Mark. "He's become so reclusive recently that I sometimes wonder if he's here at all." The king's voice was rueful.

"It's magic we're fighting, and the wizards are our main hope," said Ansar.

Pabalan spoke for the first time. "From the expressions on your faces," he said, looking at Mark and Fontaine in turn, "you don't seem to think much of our prospects."

Mark's words were tinged with bitterness. "Ferragamo may have given up already," he said.

"I don't really want to hear what you're going to tell me," said Ferragamo, "but we may as well get it over with."

Moroski and Cai had found their fellow wizard in one of the upper rooms of the tower. They had been shocked at his gaunt appearance and the shadows beneath his eyes. Koria was with him. She looked her usual healthy self but was evidently greatly concerned and stayed close to her lover, as if to protect him.

"How is it *you're* here, Cai?" asked Ferragamo.

"I was visiting," the young wizard replied. "I picked a bad time."

"Or a good one," Ferragamo added. "You don't know how Arlon is faring."

"That's true."

"This . . . *thing* . . . extends beyond Heald, you know."

"What happened?" asked Koria.

"The first we knew of it," said Ansar, "were reports from the south about unusual weather conditions at sea. There were even tales of icebergs unheard of that far south—even in winter."

Pabalan had been watching his son-in-law's face. "Sound familiar?" he queried. Mark nodded.

"Then it started coming inland," Ansar went on, "and before we knew it a dense bank of freezing fog had rolled over Ramsport. That in itself caused alarm—chaos even—but what happened next was even worse. After a few hours' exposure most people fell asleep on their feet. Their eyes glazed over and they didn't hear when you spoke to them."

"Not again!" exclaimed Mark. "It can't be happening again."

"It gets worse," said Ansar. "People from the palace and nearby weren't affected in the same way. We felt sick and cold, but weren't staggering around in a daze."

"There were so many accidents," Adesina put in. "I dread to think what happened to them all."

"It was like waking up in a nightmare," said Pabalan, "and it didn't end there. Soon after we started feeling ill, the invaders came, under cover of the fog."

"They didn't attack anyone who was asleep or wandering aimlessly," said Ansar. "They just came straight for the rest of us. There was no warning—we lost a lot of people before we knew what was happening."

"They were vicious bastards!" said Pabalan through gritted teeth. "They cut down anyone, women and children, armed or defenseless."

"Aye, their swords were real enough," said Ansar, "but *they* weren't."

"What do you mean?"

"Just this," said Ansar. "They couldn't be killed."

Mark and Fontaine looked horrified, not wanting to believe him.

"It's true," Ansar insisted. "The palace guard finally rallied, and we were managing to hold our own, but then I noticed that when one of the enemy went down, after a while his body just wasn't there anymore. I watched one that I'd slain myself—it just shriveled and turned into a wisp of smoke—or fog—and drifted off. Moments later, it re-formed into a soldier who came back against us as good as new."

"So it was only the people who were still awake who were attacked?" asked Luke. The boy had joined the wizards soon after Moroski began his tale and had been listening with horrified fascination.

"Why were they so special?" Luke asked.

"Shall I tell him or will you?" said Ferragamo, his voice grim.

"It took a while for it to sink in," said Moroski, "but we realized that only those who had eaten moonberries regularly, as part of the palace's ceremonial meals, were not stupefied by the fog."

"The wraiths only went after them," added Cai. "They ignored the rest as if they were of no consequence."

"No," said Ferragamo. "Those poor people are important to the enemy, and they need them alive. It's from them that it draws the power to reconstitute the wraiths and continue its advance. So while the moonberry eaters pose a threat to the enemy, the others are a positive asset."

"So the power driving the fog is actually feeding off the unprotected people, off their minds?" Luke could not hide the absolute horror in his voice. "But that's—"

"Yes," said Ferragamo. "We're facing the worst possible corruption of magical talent."

"Again," added Moroski.

"Amarino!" said Luke. "It's the same thing that happened here just before I was born."

"Yes," said Moroski.

"No," contradicted Ferragamo. "Although the nature of the evil is similar, it is now a hundred times more dangerous. Before, we had a target we could aim at. Amarino was the key, and the source of the power we faced. In destroying her, as your father did, we destroyed the menace."

The wizard paused, then took a deep breath, as if fortifying himself to continue speaking the words that were so painful. Koria squeezed his hand in mute support and the others waited until he spoke again.

"What happened on Heald, and possibly elsewhere, is altogether different. The power that drives the invasion is well hidden, literally by the fog and metaphorically by our ignorance. All we can do is strike feebly at its minions who, through their master's powers, are invincible. The enormous scale of it defies belief," he concluded.

His tone silenced the others for a few moments, but then Moroski returned to his tale of the events on Heald.

"Ferragamo's right. The power we faced was huge. Moonberries or not, there was no way we could stand before it for long, even using shielding spells. All we could do was run."

"We could delay the wraiths but not stop them," said Ansar, "so we got as many people out as we could and fled north to Marviel."

"That was the only part of Heald still free of the fog," added Pabalan, "though it won't be now."

"The rest you know," said Ansar. "Our only way of escape was to sail north, and so we ended up at Grayrock—along with half the islands' fleets, by the look of it."

"Only four ships from the whole of Heald?" Fontaine was aghast.

"There may have been others," replied Ansar. "They might have landed at any of the other ports. We don't know."

"You're forgetting that most people would have ceased to care about escaping—or about anything—when the fog arrived." Adesina now spoke with a larger measure of control in her voice. "Even some of the folk in Marviel were reluctant to leave their homes on the basis of our wild tales," she added ironically.

"And now it's too late," said Pabalan. "They're cut off."

"So are we, though in a different way," said Mark. "From all reports, the fog is now all around us. Since it first appeared no ship leaving Ark has been able to get through, though several have tried. And not one vessel has come from the other side of it to reach Ark."

"So we're the last," Pabalan sounded weary.

"Well," said Ansar. "I don't know what else *we* can do. We can't fight fog and we can't fight wraiths. Not with swords at least. This is wizard's work."

"So what do we do now?" Cai asked, when Moroski finished his account.

"Yes," said Koria. "All this talk has been very gloomy, but we can't just sit around and let this happen. We've got to be positive." She looked at Ferragamo hopefully. "You defeated Amarino. There must be a way to win this time."

"Koria's right," said Cai. "Between us we should be able to think of something."

"The stars preserve me from youthful optimism," said Ferragamo, but he smiled wanly as he spoke, and Koria felt the first glimmer of hope. *He's going to fight*, she thought.

"How can we give battle to something when we don't know what—or where—it is?" asked Luke. His face was oddly eager, his eyes bright. It was obvious that he wanted to say more, and eventually Moroski obliged by asking, "Well?"

"We need to force the enemy's hand, make it show itself. Then we'll have something at which to strike."

"That's a good theory," said Moroski, "but how do we go about it?"

"You're the wizards, not me," replied Luke, "but any problem can be solved by learning all the available information and then applying logic."

"Wizards have never seemed very logical to me," said Koria, then smiled at the boyish vehemence of Luke's immediate reply.

"That's where you're wrong. Magic is the supreme logic."

"All right," said Cai. "Let's list what we know. First, the fog is circling around and moving inward slowly, like a spiral."

"Or a whirlpool," said Luke, as if an idea had just occurred to him.

"With Ark at its center," Cai went on. "That must be significant, surely."

"We know that moonberries counteract it to some extent," said Moroski, "though not enough to enable us to turn it back."

"The tree," said Luke. "What happened to the tree when the fog came?"

Cai and Moroski glanced at each other, thinking back to the scenes within Ramsport Palace.

"It was lighter there," Cai said. "Perhaps the fog shied away from it."

"Ansar used it as a rallying point," said Moroski. "Maybe his instincts were correct."

"Well, we know where to make our last stand then." Cai tried to make a joke of it, but nobody laughed.

"What else?" asked Luke.

"We know the fog's cold enough for icebergs in summer," Moroski went on. "It's hundreds, perhaps thousands, of leagues long, but we don't know how deep it is, or how high."

"Atlanta could find that out for us, couldn't she?" asked Cai.

"I suppose so, but I don't see what good it would do us. We can't fly over it."

"Could this all be the doing of one wizard, like it was with Amarino?" Luke asked.

"I don't see how," said Moroski. "It's too vast."

"Brogar?" suggested Cai.

Ferragamo had been listening in silence for some time. He spoke bitterly now.

"Yes! Brogar. Isn't it obvious? It all stems from there. It's just as I said all those years ago, but nobody would listen to me!"

"That's not fair," said Koria, but Ferragamo would not be deflected.

"I suggested then the only solution powerful enough to deal with the problem. Do you want to try the Rite now?" he demanded, but went on without waiting for a response.

"There's no clever little prophecy—however obscure—to

help us *this* time. The stars know I've been searching for something like that for years now, but there's nothing. Nothing!" He paused for breath. "We've got nowhere to run. *This* is the center of the circle." He stabbed a finger toward the floor. "We either sit here and wait for our doom, or we risk everything and summon the Rite of Yzalba." He looked at the stunned faces about him.

"Well?" he asked.

Chapter 25

It soon became obvious that the *Fontaine*'s arrival in Grayrock was causing excited comment from those already in the harbor. Why one more ship in such an armada should be considered so interesting was something that Durc was at a loss to explain. However, it was clear that conditions in the town were not normal, and, as Durc had no wish to be delayed, he left the ship in the capable hands of the first mate and went ashore by boat as inconspicuously as possible. With him went Zunic and the two passengers from Strock, who were still gazing at the maritime city with awe.

"It's not always like this," said Zunic. "There are far more ships here than usual."

The sailors rowed the skiff into a narrow dock which was too small for the sea-going vessels, and thus relatively quiet. The water was dirty; all sorts of debris floated on the stagnant surfaces, and the smell was awful.

"I don't feel well," Julia said quietly.

"Be thankful that the tide is high," said Zunic. "When it's low it *really* stinks."

"It's not that," she replied. "I'm so cold. The fog isn't coming back, is it?"

Durc and Kubiac looked at her anxiously. The weather was fine, but Julia shivered in spite of the sun's heat.

"We'll be on dry land soon," added Durc. "You'll be all right then."

They were glad for the high tide when they reached the steps, for beneath the waterline the stone was slimy and treacherous. As it was, they disembarked without mishap and began to climb. Kubiac insisted on carrying Julia's baggage, then regretted his possessiveness when he saw Durc put his

...round the girl's shoulder to support her as they went up
...steps.

Once on the quay, Durc paused to survey the scene about
them.

"We'll be lucky to find horses here," he said. "Most of
them will probably have been eaten by now if the rest of the
town's as crowded as this."

"Aye, and the ones that *are* left will be at a premium," said
Zunic. "Of course, we could always go back to our old meth-
ods," he added, grinning.

"I'm too old for that," replied Durc. "Besides, in this
atmosphere, they'd probably hang horse thieves without a
second thought."

"Only if they caught them."

"I've never seen a real horse," said Julia. "Only pictures."
She sounded weary yet wistful.

The former outlaws were astounded.

"In that case," said Durc, "we are honor bound to rectify
this omission immediately." To Zunic he added, "Shall we try
Roget?"

"That crook! He'd sell his mother if market forces made it
profitable," replied his friend. "He'd charge over the odds in
normal conditions. In times like these, he'll have cornered
the market and be demanding outrageous prices."

"Exactly," said Durc. "He's the one person we're sure to be
able to do business with. He'll have the best mounts and
we. . ." The ambassador nodded in Kubiac's direction.

"Of course," said Zunic. "Let's go."

They set off, walking slowly between piles of merchandise
and rubbish, avoiding the groups of idle sailors as best they
could and fending off offers of a variety of goods and services
from dockland entrepreneurs. Kubiac did not always understand what he was being offered but his naïveté did not
prevent him from getting the general drift. He grew embarrassed and even more protective toward Julia, who was walking at his side. She was too lost in her own private world of
pain to notice anything. Since coming ashore her body had
been swept by waves of hot and cold, and her chest ached
dreadfully.

"You're not seeing Ark at its best," apologized Durc. "Not
all the island is as depraved as this."

"You seem quite at home," said Kubiac acidly. His concern

for Julia and his own complete reliance on their guides made him unusually aggressive.

"It's just a matter of knowing the unwritten rules," Durc replied. The complacency in his voice needled Kubiac.

"Can't you see she needs to rest?" he asked pointedly.

Durc's face grew sober. "We're nearly there," he said.

By now, they had left the docks and were threading their way through quieter back streets. They emerged onto one of the town's larger thoroughfares, and shortly afterward came to an imposing-looking doorway flanked by two heavyset men who eyed them suspiciously. There were no windows on the ground floor of the three-story building.

"Roget has seen fit to provide himself with a little extra security," said Zunic.

"Don't worry. These lovely lads are just for show," Durc replied. "He's not going to do any business unless the customers get inside."

He knocked loudly on the door. The guards made no attempt to stop him but tensed, as if awaiting some signal.

"What is it?" asked Durc pleasantly. "Once for let them in; twice for throw them out?" The men squinted at him, puzzled. From the other side of the door came the sound of a spyhole being drawn back. Durc smiled broadly at the opening. Three knocks sounded from inside the house, and there was the sound of bolts being pulled back. One of the guards reluctantly reached over and opened the door. Durc ushered the others in ahead of him.

"I'm surprised you can count that high," he remarked to the sentry as he followed his companions inside. They walked into a windowless room, brightly lit by oil lamps. Apart from a desk and a few uncomfortable-looking chairs, the room was bare. A small weasel-faced man sat at the desk. Behind him stood two more muscle men.

"Don't waste my time, Rat. Where's Roget?" said Durc.

The man smiled nastily.

"Roget is a very busy man. Perhaps you would care to wait?" he said, indicating the chairs where Julia, attended by Kubiac, had already sat down. Durc was not put off.

"He may be busy, but he'll see us now."

"I don't think that's possible."

"It had better be. Let me introduce my companion. This is Master Wizard Kubiac from the island of Strock, so unless you fancy spending the rest of your existence as a frog or an ant, say . . ."

Rat looked skeptical but there was a new awareness in his small eyes. Kubiac looked up in surprise from where he knelt by Julia, then stood and faced their inquisitor, trying hard to live up to his billing.

"A bit young for a master wizard, aren't you?" observed Rat.

"A demonstration, perhaps?" Kubiac replied.

"Don't waste your power," said Durc. "Just take us to Roget, Rat."

Rat appeared to be considering, but Durc knew that Roget would not be pleased with his sidekick for delaying a wizard, and Roget was not a man to antagonize. Rat stood up and said, "Come with me."

"Stay with Julia, Zunic," said Durc as he and Kubiac followed Rat into the inner sanctum.

They found Roget in luxurious surroundings that contrasted starkly with the outer room. The corpulent merchant was seated on large cushions on the floor and was making preparations for smoking a complicated water pipe. Rat introduced them and withdrew.

"Durc, my old friend, you *have* gone up in the world, traveling with wizards of such power." His modulated voice was gently mocking. "Do sit down. What may I do for so *eminent* a guest?"

"A simple request," said Durc. "Horses, and good ones, for the journey to Starhill."

"Ah, if only you had asked for anything else," replied Roget. "I would be delighted to aid you." He spread his hands as if to demonstrate his helplessness. "Alas, there are no horses to be had in all Grayrock." He smiled. "But this is foolishness! A wizard would surely have no difficulty acquiring mounts?" Roget eyed Kubiac narrowly. "Would you be so kind?" he then asked politely, indicating the bowl of his pipe.

The young wizard was perplexed for an instant, then saw what was expected of him and quickly produced the necessary enchantment. He nearly overdid it, only remembering at the last moment to control the power so that the leaves smoldered and smoked rather than burst into flame. As he performed the spell, he heard Julia screaming from the other room and glanced around anxiously.

"Thank you," said Roget, ignoring the sound. He took a long pull on the pipe's tube. The water bubbled and he exhaled a thin stream of smoke. "Excellent," he said. "Care to join me?"

Kubiac did not reply. He listened intently for any noise from the outer room, but all was quiet. Durc shook his head.

"You still have your illegal habits, I see."

"One must have one's small pleasures, don't you agree? In any case, smoking is hardly illegal."

Durc sniffed. "Smoking *that* is. I should have you arrested."

Roget laughed complacently.

"About the horses," Durc began.

Less than an hour later the four rode out of Grayrock, Julia and Kubiac perched shakily behind Durc and Zunic. Having never ridden before, they did not feel that this was an auspicious time for their first solo lesson. The mounts were excellent specimens and had only cost three times the normal rate. Once in the open country the group felt free to talk.

"How did you do it?" asked Zunic in open admiration.

"I didn't," said Durc. "Kubiac did."

"Don't you ever do that to me again!" said the wizard fiercely. "Magic is not something to be trifled with."

"You did very well," replied Durc. "Roget never could resist a show of wizardry. I just thought that if I promoted you a bit it would impress them more."

"Well, why didn't you warn me?"

"I'm sorry. I didn't expect Rat to be there."

"And you didn't want me to have the chance to refuse," accused Kubiac. Durc's silence was an admission of guilt, and Julia, who still felt ill, tried to ease the tension.

"How long will it take to get to Starhill?" she asked.

"Most of the day, I'm afraid," Durc answered. "Do you feel up to it?"

"Yes. I'm looking forward to getting there. Starhill is such a lovely name. How did it come to be called that?"

"I've no idea," replied Durc. "Ferragamo might know."

"Who's he?"

"Ark's wizard."

"I'd like to talk to him," said Julia.

I've a few questions for him myself, thought Durc.

Three days after the arrival of the refugees from Heald, the wizards were no nearer to agreeing on a plan of action. Neither Moroski nor Cai would contemplate initiating the Rite of Yzalba except as a desperate last resort. Ferragamo, while understanding their attitude, was intensely annoyed at the lack of any positive action. He was sullen for a time, but Koria soon coaxed him back into helping the others with their attempts to learn all they could. Luke was the driving force in this effort, endlessly questioning and probing the limits of their knowledge. He was convinced that they needed a bait, something to draw their opponent out into the open. What that something should be was still a mystery.

Luke was sitting with the wizards in the tower library when Beca brought some news which gave them all fresh hope.

"Durc's back!" she exclaimed, bursting in on their conference. "He's got through!"

"That's marvelous! Where is he?" asked Luke.

"Gone to find Father." There was a pause.

"All of us?" asked Moroski.

"Yes," replied Ferragamo. "It'll save time. Let's go."

They trooped down the stairs with Beca skipping ahead, delighted to have been the bearer of glad tidings. They found Durc and Mark alone in the king's study. At the door Beca hung back but the others all went in at Mark's invitation.

"You're honored, Durc," the king said. "It is rare these days that we see such a deputation. They are usually much too busy to talk to us."

Cai was stung into replying, "We've told you everything we can!"

"You know that's true, Father," added Luke.

Mark eyed his son thoughtfully. "As you say," he said wearily. "Now you're here you'd better listen to Durc's tale."

So the traveler told his story. It took a long time, with the wizards interrupting and asking questions, but eventually he reached their arrival at Grayrock.

"So you came all the way through the fog?" asked Moroski.

"Yes. Either I'm the luckiest man alive or something more than chance guided us through," replied Durc. "After that first near miss nothing even came close."

"Could it have been the influence of this wizard—what's his name—Kubiac?" suggested Cai.

"I don't think so. He was as much in awe of it as we were."

"Well, you got through. That's the main thing," said Mark. "Do you think you could get out again?"

"I wouldn't want to try. There's only one bottle of wine left!" Durc grinned.

"Where's Kubiac now?" asked Moroski.

"With Julia. The girl took ill again as we came ashore, and had a nasty attack while we were at Roget's. She's better now, but she's gone to bed to rest."

"And you believe Julia's important?" said Luke.

"Ashula seemed to think so—and so did the gray men. I certainly wouldn't want to argue with *them.*"

"Perhaps she's the reason you got through," suggested Luke.

"If so, she knows nothing about it."

"I think we had better see these two," said Ferragamo.

"It's late," replied Durc. "Kubiac won't take kindly to you disturbing her if she's asleep. *He* thinks she's special too."

"So do you, by the sound of it," remarked Cai with a twinkle in his eyes.

"She's a lovely girl," said Durc seriously, refusing to be drawn.

"There's more at stake here than the health of one girl, however *important,*" said Ferragamo angrily. "Every hour brings us closer to disaster."

"All right," said Mark. "Luke, go and find out what the situation is. I'll be along in a minute." Luke went out. "The rest of you stay here for now. If we all crowd in and she collapses, it won't do anybody any good."

The wizards reluctantly obeyed Mark; Ferragamo knew from experience that the king would only allow himself to be pushed so far. As they went back to questioning Durc, Mark followed his son out into the corridor.

———————————

When Luke came to the door of Julia's room he found Beca and Alena hovering outside.

"What are you two doing here?" he demanded loudly, and the two girls jumped. Beca, as usual, recovered more quickly.

"Shhh," she hissed. "You'll disturb her. She's in bed."

"How do you know?"

Beca said nothing.

"Clear off, the pair of you," ordered Luke. Alena appeared ready to obey but Beca hung back as Luke knocked gently on the door. After a moment it was opened by a frail-looking young man.

"Kubiac? I'm Luke. How is Julia?"

"She's asleep. I'd rather you didn't wake her," replied Kubiac.

"May I come in and see her?"

"I suppose so." Kubiac was obviously reluctant, but drew back so that Luke could enter. Beca and Alena immediately appeared in the open doorway, but Luke did not notice them. All his attention was focused on the bed, and on the sleeping, black-haired girl whose head rested on the pillow.

"She's beautiful," he whispered reverently, filled with wonder. He was positively entranced by the visitor.

From the doorway Beca giggled and Alena whispered, as Julia began to wake up. She opened her eyes, then sat bolt upright and gasped, staring straight at the golden man from her dreams.

"The warrior!" she exclaimed.

Luke, still recovering from the impact of the unearthly beauty of her violet eyes, did not hear her. They stared at each other in startled fascination, while Kubiac looked on, disturbed, yet unable to intrude on their private world.

The spell was abruptly broken by a voice from the corridor.

"Why aren't you two in bed?" said Mark sternly. "Off with you!"

There was the sound of scurrying feet and then the king entered the room. The welcoming smile on his face turned to an expression of loathing and shock as soon as he saw Julia. As the others looked at him aghast, he pointed an accusing finger at her and shouted, "Damn you! Why have you come back?"

"What is it? What's the matter?" Luke implored, grabbing Mark's arm.

His father was wide-eyed and shaking. "Don't you see?" he said vehemently. "She has Amarino's eyes. *She* is the enemy!"

Chapter 26

*A*fter her traumatic encounters with Luke and Mark, Julia found it impossible to relax. Kubiac had insisted that she be left alone, practically throwing Ark's king from the room, yet sleep was a long time coming. Her head and chest ached dully and her hands felt stiff and swollen, even though she could see nothing wrong with them. Despite warm bedclothes she felt cold.

Her thoughts kept returning to her ecstatic meeting with Luke, when she had looked into those well-remembered eyes and known that he felt the same way about her. But each time she began to glow with the happiness of that moment, she was thrown into confused misery by Mark's terrible reaction. She could not reconcile the diversity of her feelings for father and son, nor theirs for her.

Late in the night, still sleepless, she remembered the armband and fetched it from her bag. The metal felt cool and smooth in her hands, and hoping her intuition was correct, she slipped it onto her arm and got back into bed. She soon fell asleep but did not find peace even then, for her dreams were plagued by the disembodied voice of a man. He was looking for her, she knew, and, terrified by this thought, made great efforts to elude him. He spoke to her constantly, with mocking, hurtful words that made her want to scream a denial, defy his insinuations—yet her mouth would not open, she could not speak. And still the terrible words droned on.

I've been waiting a long time, but you are within the circle now—I can feel it. You are suffering, and that is foolish. Why fight your true nature? Their magic hurts you. Isn't that proof enough? All this time you have striven to be what these

*feeble men call "good." What is that to such as us? Why
continue to torture yourself when with one decision you could
join us in the glory of the new world? The world that I—that
we—will rule. Your sisters are all waiting for you—except for
the one who is lost. Now our time is drawing near. Soon the
serpent coils will engulf the world. This is your inheritance,
and nothing can stop it. Step forward, Julia, so that I can
help you claim it.*

Julia awoke in a cold sweat, thankful for whatever had
prevented her from speaking. Had she done so, she knew she
would have let the awful searcher hear, and thence see, her.
That, she did not doubt, would have been the last mistake
she ever made. One single thought kept her from complete
despair.

He doesn't know where I am!

———————————

There were others who slept little that night. Mark spent
most of the dark hours pacing the castle battlements, his
mind in turmoil. His thoughts kept returning to Julia's beautiful, ominous eyes and to his betrayal by his own son. On
hearing his father's outraged reaction, Luke had quickly helped
Kubiac remove Mark from Julia's room. He had seen that the
young wizard was badly shaken and possibly on the point of
doing something either dangerous or foolish.

Luke had subsequently sought to reassure his father that
Julia was not his nemesis returned, and had been backed up,
to Mark's dismay, by Ferragamo and Durc.

"Amarino's *dead*," the wizard had said with finality, and,
when challenged, Durc had claimed not to have noticed the
color of Amarino's eyes. "Julia's just a pretty girl," he had
stated.

They had convinced Mark that Julia was safe enough for
the night under the wizards' guard and that they would
question her on the morrow, test her if necessary. After that,
an uneasy peace had descended on the household, but even
Fontaine had been unable to calm Mark's agitated state. She
was almost as disturbed as her husband by the memories
conjured up, but, unlike him, she was happy to leave it in the
wizards' hands.

So Mark paced the castle walls, looking out over the serene, moonlit city. It was only now, when he was so near to losing it that he realized how dear Ark was to him.

I cannot let it happen! he thought. *All this to be destroyed? I must stop her!*

His hand went, almost of its own volition, to the knife hilt at his belt, and, with a cold heart, he turned to descend into the castle's interior. A black and white figure, small but determined, barred his way. Longfur was old now, his fur even more inclined to grow in eccentric directions, but he could still move quickly, and had lost none of his stealth and cunning. Cat and king regarded each other solemnly.

Can we talk?

Not now, Longfur. Yet already Mark felt his murderous determination falter.

I don't like to see you like this, Longfur went on, ignoring Mark's reply.

I'm not enjoying it much myself!

There's always suicide, of course, the cat went on, his tone deliberately lugubrious. *You could just jump off the battlements. That would solve everything—for you, anyway.*

I'll throw you off! Mark retorted.

Longfur leapt nimbly onto the top of the wall, rolled over onto his back, and stuck all four legs into the air.

Do with me as you will, he said mournfully and stared wide-eyed at the night sky, an expression of ultimate humility on his face.

Mark could stand it no longer. *Stop it!* he said, laughing. *How can I be properly desolate with you playing the fool?*

Longfur righted himself and fixed his human with a penetrating stare.

The fool? he queried. *That was my big dramatic role. Have you no appreciation of the finer points of thespian art?*

Overacting is an art?

You should know.

That gave Mark pause for thought.

You think so? he asked eventually.

Why else are you up here?

I'm terrified, Longfur. I don't understand what's going on.

So that's why you decided to sort it all out? the cat replied. *All by yourself, with your dagger?*

Mark closed his eyes and sighed.

How is it that after all these years you can still tie me up in knots? he asked plaintively.

Superior intellect, came the instant reply.

Alena awoke shortly after dawn, and was instantly seized by an urge to look at her "treasure." As soon as the sphere was removed from its protective pouch, its surface rippled and familiar cold eyes stared out at her.

"You are excited," the man said. "Is it at the thought of meeting me in person?" He smiled nastily. "That will happen soon. I hope you continue to please me until then."

Unnerved by the threat implicit in his words, Alena sought for something to tell him, some news that might be of interest.

"We have visitors," she said hopefully. "From a faraway island."

"It's a mistake to lie to me, child."

Alena shuddered,

"I'm not lying," she said as bravely as she could. "A wizard and a girl with violet eyes. She's ill."

The face in the stone became suddenly intent.

"She's in Starhill Castle?"

"Yes."

"You're sure her eyes are violet?"

"Oh, yes. They're lovely."

Alena was confused. Her news had certainly been of interest to the man. He seemed almost eager, but there was another feeling there. Was he angry? Frightened? She could not tell and was given no chance to find out. Abruptly, the face was gone and the stone an innocent white once more.

Mark had eventually fallen into an exhausted sleep shortly before dawn, with Longfur curled in his lap. Fontaine found them an hour later but decided against disturbing them. Needing a down-to-earth friend to talk to, she set off toward Ferragamo's quarters in the hope of finding Koria. However, she was intercepted by Luke, obviously himself in need of someone to talk to.

"Where's Father?" he asked as they settled themselves in Fontaine's drawing room.

"Asleep in the study. I don't think we should disturb him."

Luke looked relieved.

"She's *not* evil," he said, "whatever Father says. I know she isn't."

Fontaine was impressed by the certainty in his voice.

"*How* do you know?" she asked.

Luke looked nonplussed.

"As soon as I saw her . . ." he began, then paused. "Do you believe in love at first sight?"

Fontaine was startled but hid it well.

"I don't know," she said slowly. "It took your father and I quite a while."

"But I've *known* her for much longer," Luke said earnestly. "It's just that she hasn't been here. Now she is."

"What do you mean?" his mother asked.

"I've dreamt about her for years."

"Luke, we all have romantic longings."

"No. I mean I've actually seen her in my dreams. Her! Not some idealized figure."

Fontaine was speechless.

"When I saw Julia it was as if I'd been waiting for her all my life."

"Isn't this a bit *sudden*?" she managed to ask, keeping her tone light. "You only saw her for a few moments, after all. How can you be so sure?"

Luke gestured impatiently. "I don't know, but I *am*. And she feels the same way about me."

This is too absurd, thought Fontaine. *What do I say now?*

"What was she doing in your dreams?" was all she could think of.

"Drowning," replied Luke. "In a whirlpool."

Chapter 27

$\mathcal{F}$ ontaine was not sure whether to allow Luke to attend the wizards' interrogation of Julia, knowing how he felt about her. However, she knew in her heart that any attempt to stop her son would be futile, and contented herself with advising him to leave the talking to Ferragamo.

Although it was still early morning when Luke arrived at Julia's room, he found all four wizards already there. Only Julia took any notice of his quiet entrance. She was out of bed and dressed, with a blanket wrapped around her. Her eyes followed Luke as he shut the door and moved to one side of the room. He smiled at her encouragingly and felt once more the tremor of recognition as she smiled back.

Ferragamo and Moroski sat facing Julia. Kubiac was beside her, looking tense, and Cai stood by the window. Luke found himself next to the young wizard from Arlon, and whispered, "Have I missed anything?"

"Not much," replied Cai. "Listen."

Julia had been distracted by Luke's entry, and Ferragamo repeated his question about the exact date of the twins' arrival on Strock. Her answer prompted an exchange of glances between the two older wizards.

"Just after that time," said Moroski.

"What time?" asked Julia.

"When Amarino was—temporarily—in power here," replied Ferragamo. "I believe Durc told you about it."

"That doesn't prove anything," said Kubiac defensively. "Just because her eyes—"

"Young man," Ferragamo interrupted sternly, "we are quite

capable of deciding what constitutes proof. Moreover, nobody is on trial here. We are merely trying to ascertain all the facts which could have a bearing on our current situation—which you may have noticed is somewhat serious. *When* it is necessary for you to speak, please confine yourself to facts."

Kubiac, stung by the sarcasm in Ferragamo's voice, did not reply, and lapsed into sullen silence. Julia was left to tell her story, from the day her casket was washed up on the beach on Strock, to her arrival in Starhill. The wizards paid particular attention to several aspects of her tale; her reaction to and subsequent eating of moonberries; Ashula's theories concerning her destiny; the arrival of the gray wraiths and her escape from them; and the *Fontaine*'s passage through the fog bank. All these were the subject of exhaustive questioning, and, despite her pain and weariness, Julia answered them as best she could. The only thing she did not tell them of was the golden warrior. Somehow, she could not speak of that with Luke in the room.

Kubiac was called upon to corroborate her words and to add his own knowledge where appropriate, but his replies were monosyllabic. The youngest wizard clearly felt antagonistic, especially toward Ferragamo.

When the talk turned once more to the wraiths, Moroski took his turn in relating events.

"You were lucky. They weren't so lenient on Heald," he said, and went on to give the two visitors a brief account of the bloodshed on his home-isle and the role that moonberries had played in it.

"But *everyone* on Strock eats moonberries," said Julia. "The gray men didn't harm anyone seriously. They were only looking for me."

"The visitors to your isle were not on the same mission," Ferragamo said. "Strock is outside the circle—for now, at least."

"Why were they looking for you?" asked Moroski. Julia had no answer and realized that he expected none. After the pause, Cai spoke to Julia for the first time. There was kindness in his voice, something which had been lacking in the older wizards' questions, and Kubiac looked at him gratefully.

"What do *you* think is causing the fog?" he asked.

Julia looked at him, uncertain now that she had been asked for an opinion.

"I don't know," she replied quietly.

"But?"

"I . . . I think my coming here might have something to do with it." She glanced around, gauging their reactions. "Ashula said it was my destiny to leave Strock. Durc brought me here. Now this is happening. It can't be just coincidence. Can it?"

"I see what you're getting at," said Cai, "but does it mean that the fog is coming because you're here, or. . ."

"You came here because this is where the fog is heading?" completed Luke. His eyes went from Cai to Julia. The others all looked at him, curious at the eagerness in his voice, but Luke was silent again. Julia turned to Ferragamo.

"You said just now that Strock was outside the circle. What did you mean by that?"

"It's outside the fog," replied the wizard.

"It's just that . . . I've heard someone else say something like that," said Julia thoughtfully.

Ferragamo then announced that he had heard enough for the moment, and the three wizards went out. Kubiac obviously wanted to leave, too, for his own reasons, but glanced uncertainly at Luke, then at Julia, who smiled at his anxious face.

"I'm all right, Kubiac," she said reassuringly. "You go and find Kirt. He'll be lost without you."

"But—"

"Luke will look after me. Won't you?" she added, looking at the prince, who nodded dumbly. Kubiac looked skeptical, but gave in when she told him, "Go on!"

As the young man went out, a black and white cat with mudcolored paws entered the room, unnoticed.

Julia and Luke looked at each other. Eventually he spoke.

"I've seen you before. In my dreams."

"And I you," she replied calmly. "Or someone very like you. Oh!" Her face grew pale, her eyes wide. Luke came near, knelt before her, and took her cold hands in his.

"What is it?"

"I've just remembered . . . the voice. It said "You're in the circle now.""

"What voice?"

"In my dreams, last night. He was looking for me. I was terrified."

"Who was he?"

"I don't know, but I didn't want him to find me. I could not, dared not, speak. He said . . . he said I was . . . like him." Her voice trailed off to a whisper. "Evil."

"You are *not* evil," Luke said vehemently.

"How do you know?" she replied, with tears in her eyes. "How do *I* know?"

"He's hunting you because you are *good*," said Luke, "and a threat to him. You can help us defeat him and his vile wraiths." The confidence in his voice began to make an impression on Julia.

"How can *I* do anything?" she asked weakly.

"That's what we have to find out," he replied, "but I'm certain that it wasn't just coincidence that brought you here."

For a while they were silent, gazing into each other's eyes. Then Julia started violently and Luke laughed as the well-known voice sounded in his mind.

You look like a pair of statues, said Muscles. *And you'll get a cramp if you kneel like that much longer.*

"Who was that?" asked the bewildered Julia.

"You heard him?" replied Luke in astonishment.

This is interesting, said Muscles. *You'd better explain quickly or she'll start screaming.* The cat came into view and re-garded them intently.

Shut up! replied Luke. Aloud he said, "This is Muscles. He and I can talk to each other without words. No one else has ever been able to hear him before."

Julia looked at the animal.

I won't scream, she thought tentatively and then jumped at the instant reply.

Good. It's not a very constructive reaction.

Can you hear me? said Luke. Julia did not react.

Of course, replied Muscles. *Did you hear her?*

No. To Julia, Luke said aloud, "Can you speak to Muscles as well as hear him?"

"Yes."

"But not me?"

"No."

Curiouser and curiouser, sounded the cat's voice in both their heads. *Mind-talk between two people would have been something new.*

Luke and Julia were gazing at each other again, still holding hands.

Anyone would think you two were falling in love, came the amused feline comment.

Both humans smiled.

We are, they replied in unison, making Muscles shake his head at the mental echo.

Luke suddenly leapt to his feet. He began hopping about, then fell to the floor, his face a mask of agony.

"What's the matter?" shrieked Julia.

"I've got a cramp," he replied, through gritted teeth.

———————————

The wizards were in Mark's study. The king had listened to them patiently but was clearly far from convinced of Julia's innocence.

"She may have powers," Moroski said, "but she's shown no sign of using them."

"Yet," said Mark.

"But she's been eating moonberries all her life," pleaded Cai.

"We only have her word for that."

"We can test that easily enough," replied Ferragamo. "Will that convince you to trust her?"

Mark was silent.

"Luke trusts her," added Cai. "Doesn't that mean anything?"

"And Luke's instincts are good," said Ferragamo.

The king regarded his old friend, and for a moment, a measure of the warmth that had once bound them together returned. Both knew that it would not last.

"All right," said Mark, suddenly brisk and businesslike. "Where does this leave us? You think she's important. How can she help?"

There was no reply.

Wonderful! thought Mark. *What's the point of having a secret weapon if you don't know how to use it!*

———————————

After Kubiac left Julia's room, he walked quickly to the courtyard, intent on finding Kirt and returning as soon as possible. However, the thoughts he sent out to the bird met with no response, and he was forced to wander about in the afternoon sun in search of his familiar. Entering the tree-yard, he looked up at the dizzying height of the tower and saw a white bird circling about it.

Kirt! he called. *Kirt!*

There was no response and the bird flew off. Kubiac sat down beside the moonberry tree, feeling dejected. He had felt the hostility of the people about him; now even Kirt appeared to have deserted him. And Julia was entranced by Luke for some reason. Although Kubiac was surrounded by more people than he could have ever imagined a short while ago, he felt very alone.

His thoughts went back to the morning's interrogation. He was still smarting from the way he had been treated—as if he were of no account—and from the ordeal which Julia had been made to suffer. He had been tempted many times to enter the discussion, to tell those pompous wizards something that would shake them up a bit, but their attitude had made him hold his tongue.

His hand went to the inside pocket of his jerkin and he slid the parchment out and unfolded it. Reading the enigmatic words again was no help in his effort to decide upon a course of action. Should he tell the wizards? Perhaps they could make sense of it. Should he tell Julia? It was about her, he was sure—that was why he had stolen it before stowing away. But Ashula had not told her of the inscription. Perhaps to do so would jeopardize the prophetic implications. If it was to be used, why had it been hidden away? Kubiac decided to keep it to himself.

But then, what if Ashula had simply forgotten its existence in the emotional turmoil of Julia's departure? Then he *should* reveal it. Perhaps he would say something to Cai. The young wizard would be the most sympathetic, he felt sure.

Kubiac folded the parchment, secreted it once more, then sat quietly, trying to make up his mind. The silence about him was broken by a raucous cry and he saw Kirt perched on the forearm of a huge bald man. Kubiac felt a moment's jealousy until the seagull flew to him and his mind heard the bird say, *This is Jani. He can't speak the noisy way but he hears me sometimes. He gave me fish. I like him.*

Standing up, Kubiac smiled at the giant.

"Hello, Jani," he said. The big man grinned in response.

He's Luke's friend, said Kirt.

That brought Kubiac back to present concerns and he decided to return to Julia.

Come on, he said to Kirt as he set off, waving a farewell to Jani.

With an apologetic squawk to his new friend, the seagull followed his master.

Jani watched them go, a thoughtful expression on his face. After a moment he followed.

The first indication that Kubiac received that not all was well in Julia's room was the piercing yowl of a cat in distress. Kirt called in response, and the junior wizard broke into a run. As he burst into the chamber he saw Luke facing him, his arms stretched upward and his eyes glowing blindly in his upturned face. On his right forearm was Julia's serpent band. He appeared to be in a trance, and behind him Julia sat transfixed, unable to move from her chair.

"W-what . . . ?" stammered Kubiac but Julia motioned him to be silent, and turned to the cat whose cry had first alarmed the wizard. After a few moments Muscles turned and fled from the room in a great hurry. In the silence they heard him calling as he ran along the corridor. Nobody else moved.

Shortly after Muscle's departure, Jani arrived. He stepped into the room quite calmly and, despite his usual appearance, Julia immediately knew that he was a friend. Walking past Kubiac, Jani went up to Luke, took the prince in his arms, and lifted him gently, as though he weighed no more than a baby. As he did so, Luke's body relaxed, his arms fell to his sides, and his head dropped. His eyes remained blank.

Jani, seemingly undisturbed, carried him to the bed and laid him down. Julia and Kubiac came up beside him and regarded the motionless prince.

"What happened?" asked Kubiac quietly.

"We were talking. Luke saw my armband and I asked if he wanted to try it on." Julia looked at the unseeing golden eyes as she spoke. "It *is* his, in a way."

"What?" Kubiac queried, glancing at her, but Julia ignored the interruption.

"When he put it on, his eyes went strange and he lost his voice. He stood up then, like the warrior, and Muscles started complaining about him shouting. Then you came in."

Kubiac could not follow half of what she was saying but one fact emerged clearly.

"Shouldn't we take the armlet off him?" he said, and reached out toward it. His hand was intercepted by Jani's, who smiled reassuringly.

"Who's Muscles?" asked Kubiac then, trying to make some sense of the scene.

"Luke's cat," replied Julia. "He just ran out."

This confused the young wizard even more. After a moment he tried again.

"Luke wasn't shouting," he essayed.

"Not out loud," she replied. "He and Muscles can speak to each other with their thoughts. Like you and Kirt."

"Is Luke a wizard?"

"No. I don't think so." Julia sounded as if the idea had not occurred to her. "Just special. I couldn't hear him but Muscles said that he was yelling and it hurt him. That's why he yowled and why he ran out. He couldn't stand it any longer."

"Muscles *said*?" Kubiac looked at her in amazement.

"Yes. I can talk to him too." For the first time Julia turned to look at Kubiac. Her eyes sparkled. "Isn't that incredible!"

The wizard found himself unable to reply.

"I asked him what was happening to Luke but he said he couldn't tell because of all the noise."

Julia's gaze returned to the prince.

Luke was in another world. As soon as the serpent band had been fitted onto his arm, he had felt a strange, warm sensation all through his body; then the room about him had disappeared, and he found himself soaring into the sky, faster than a bird of prey. Rising, rising, until he was among the stars and looking down upon all the islands. He felt omnipotent, as though he could reach down and, with a flick of his hand, rearrange the sunlit world. Then something in his vision changed, and he felt a chill.

From five of the islands a cold grayness began to leak into the atmosphere. Those isles were soon invisible, as the gray mantle spread. Luke tried to stop it, to reach down and halt the evil plague, but found himself powerless, remote. The fog—for such he knew it to be—began to flow in different directions and appeared to be moving at random. Then a pattern emerged and, in his skyborn aerie, Luke shivered.

The banks of fog were coalescing, moving now with an evident purpose. The gigantic spiral flowed slowly but implacably, always moving around, always inward, until only a small circle remained clear within its serpentine coils. A small circle that would soon be overwhelmed.

At the center of the circle lay Starhill.

Chapter 28

*J*ani says Luke is all right, reported Kirt. *The dream-winds have taken him.*

Kubiac looked at the bird, who was hopping about awkwardly on the bedroom floor, then at Jani, who was now seated in a bedside chair, placidly watching his young charge.

What do you mean?

I can't hear him clearly, replied Kirt, *but I think this has happened before.*

"What should we do?" Julia asked.

"I don't know. Jani obviously thinks he's in no danger." Kubiac paused. "Perhaps I'd better fetch Ferragamo. He's the one who knows Luke best."

Julia nodded, and, after a moment's hesitation, Kubiac left the room. He glanced back, his gangling form framed in the doorway, but Julia's attention was fixed on the prince, and Kubiac went out, with Kirt following.

The wizard's footsteps had hardly echoed away when Luke's eyes lost their awesome golden glow and came into focus. The first thing they saw was Julia's face. Ark's prince smiled and tried to sit up, but his arms gave way beneath him and he flopped down again, a surprised expression on his face.

"Are you all right?" Julia asked anxiously.

"Yes," he replied, his voice little more than a hiss of breath. "But I'm so tired."

"Sleep then."

"No," he said in an urgent whisper. "I can't. There's too much I need to say."

"Kubiac's gone to fetch Ferragamo."

"It's you I need to talk to."

"Me?"

Luke paused, as if struggling to organize his thoughts. "The fog . . ." he said eventually, "it's a huge spiral, covering all the islands. Moving inward, toward us. I saw it from the stars." His voice sounded insubstantial and far away; Julia saw the lines of exhaustion in his face.

"You must rest," she said, taking his hand, but Luke ignored her.

"It started from several islands. Brogar was first but then the others . . ." Luke turned his face to look directly at Julia. "You and Bela were not alone," he said. "Your other sisters—"

"I've seen them!" exclaimed Julia. "The warrior showed them to me. On different islands."

"They've grown up rather differently from you," Luke replied, accepting her statement without surprise.

Julia shuddered. "I could have been one of them. But for Ashula."

"But you're not," Luke whispered fiercely. "You're outside their circle. They form a network, a chain, spread over the isles, and feed power to each other. That's how they can get magic to work over water." His voice trailed off. "It's incredible," he added, so softly that Julia could hardly hear.

"How can we stop them?"

"Brogar is the key. Ferragamo was right all along. It stems from there originally. We have to draw the enemy out into the open." Luke frowned, reviewing the memories of his vision. Something puzzled him. When he realized what it was he struggled successfully to sit up, his face suddenly animated.

"*The spiral isn't perfect!*" he said. "*You're* the missing link. With you and Bela in your destined places, it would have been invincible, but it's not. It's deformed. And *you* can stop it!"

Julia found herself fingering the pendants at her throat.

"How?" she whispered.

But Luke was leagues away, staring into space.

"There isn't much time," he said clearly, then fell back onto the bed, his eyes fast shut.

At the same moment there was a commotion in the doorway. Ferragamo strode into the room, white hair bristling and eyes flashing dangerously. Behind him were Kubiac and Mark, both in a state of agitation.

"What has that witch done to my son?" shouted the king, trying to push past Kubiac, who was ineffectually attempting to bar his way. Ferragamo turned on them both, and with a brief gesture and the single command "Cease!" ended their scuffle. As Kubiac and Mark quieted down, Julia began to feel sick. She staggered and would have fallen but for Jani, who rose quickly to support her.

Ferragamo approached the bed, laid his hand upon Luke's forehead, and closed his eyes in concentration. As the wizard set his power to work, Julia felt a pain begin at the base of her spine. It rose up in her, and grew, filling her body with agonizing heat. She gasped and struggled to breathe. Her pulse raced madly and perspiration sprang from her face. When it felt as though she would explode if the pain grew any worse, she found relief, fainting in Jani's arms.

Ferragamo finished his examination of the prince.

"Luke has come to no harm," he said to Mark. "He is just drained, exhausted. Why, I do not know. But all he needs is sleep." The wizard turned to Julia. "I expect the same can be said of the girl. Perhaps they can explain when they wake."

Jani laid Julia on the bed beside Luke, then with Mark's silent assistance picked up the prince and carried him to his own chamber. Ferragamo followed.

"Call me when she wakes," he said to Kubiac as he left.

The junior wizard nodded meekly and began his vigil.

Luke and Julia lay in their beds and the afternoon turned to evening. Beca was at her brother's bedside and her usual companion, Alena, had returned to her own home, at loose ends. As she approached her parents' room she heard them talking and, from the seriousness of their tone, knew that they would not welcome her intrusion. She crept past to her own bedroom, then sat, trying to work out just what was the matter with Starhill recently. No one smiled anymore, and all the talk was of gloomy things like fog and icebergs. The young girl found it very depressing.

As so often happened when she needed something to lift her spirits, Alena's thoughts turned to her glass sphere, her own special thing. Not even her father knew of it. Even if it was scary sometimes, it was more exciting than all the gloom and despondency.

No sooner had the thought entered her head than Alena felt an irresistible urge to look into the glass. She took the pouch from its hiding place and slipped her hand inside the bag. As her fingers closed on the sphere she cried out, dropping the bag. It hit the floor with a dull thump and the sphere rolled out.

Its surface was frosted and thin white vapors rose from it. Alena rubbed her fingers where they had burned by the terrible cold and watched in awful fascination as the ice crystals fell away.

Within the glass, the man's face appeared, and he wasted no time in giving her explicit instructions. She protested, but the menace in his colorless eyes was so great that she soon fell silent. Needles of pain ran up her arm, emphasizing his dominance.

When the man finished speaking, all Alena could do was nod submissively and try to still the prescient terror that welled up inside her.

That evening, as Luke lay beyond the reach of his family gathered at his bedside, his nightmare returned.

As one part of his mind quailed at the task he faced, another quiet corner watched carefully, knowing that this was much more than a dream.

Luke turned the tiller and his tiny boat swung around to face the gigantic whirlpool, whose thunderous roar filled his ears. As the flimsy vessel picked up speed, he was buffeted by the white-capped waves and soon realized that he was in danger of being swept overboard. He looked around desperately for something with which to secure himself but could see nothing. Still the boat went faster and faster. Luke knew that his only chance to cheat the whirlpool was to defeat it by using its own strength. By sweeping close to the dreadful maw he would gain enough momentum to shoot the boat out the other side. Or so he hoped.

The eye of the whirlpool grew closer; he found himself looking down into the depths of the black spiral, fighting vertigo. For an instant he saw the whirlpool not as a dreadful hole in the sea but as the jaws of a giant snake, a serpent big enough to swallow whole islands at a time. That vision passed in an instant, and again he was nearly thrown from his boat.

Then all thoughts of his own safety disappeared as he saw *her*.

Julia was in the water, struggling to keep afloat within the dreadful current. He knew, without knowing how, that she was the victim of a shipwreck, and that he would have one chance, and one chance only, to save her.

The boat rushed onward, ever closer to the precipitous drop into the depths of the ocean. He would be upon her soon but how was he to rescue her? He could hardly keep himself upright, let alone manage to help her into the boat and still navigate to safety.

Time seemed to slow down. Clinging desperately to the mast, Luke saw her raise an arm and fling something toward him, something that writhed and twisted in the air. His heart turned to lead as he saw it take shape before him.

It was a snake, thin and deadly. Its scales were golden, translucent in the watery light, and its jewellike eyes glittered redly. Its jaws were open and the needle fangs dripped venom. Yet *she* had thrown it. Luke could not believe she would harm him. Still the snake glided slowly through the air toward him.

He stretched out his free arm, unsure yet whether to catch the snake or fend it away. The jaws closed upon his forearm. Luke looked down in shock as the fangs sank into his flesh and blood welled up. Yet he felt no pain. Making a conscious decision, he relinquished his grip on the mast and grasped the snake with his other hand. As he did so, it changed beneath his fingers, becoming a thin but unbreakable chain.

Quickly he bound it about his waist and the mast, securing himself at last, then pulled steadily. She still held the other end of the chain. As the boat sped on she drew closer until, at the deepest, fastest point of his course, she clambered aboard, still pulled by the metal bond.

Time returned to normal. The boat hurtled onward and upward, cresting the whirling waves. At last, the turbulence lessened, and finally they lay together in the bottom of the boat, as it rocked gently on the placid sea. Warm sunlight glanced off the chain that still bound them together.

It was only then that Luke remembered the poison in his veins.

Chapter 29

*L*uke lay still and quiet upon his bed. Only his eyes moved beneath their lids, following the progress of his dream. Ranged about the room were his parents, his sister, Ferragamo, and Jani. His childhood guardian was the only one to appear unconcerned.

Mark had tried to take the serpent band from Luke's arm but had been unable to move it, and Ferragamo had advised him to leave it alone.

"Don't you remember anything?" retorted the king. "Amarino used a dragon image too."

"Not like that one," replied Ferragamo. "It's a very old symbol."

"That little witch has trapped him with it," Mark accused.

"Julia may have brought it here, but the armlet is Luke's. It's part of him; I felt that when I examined him. The band is powerful but not necessarily evil, and in any case, Luke will have to take his chance with it. He's accepted it now and anyone who attempts to remove it from him will suffer for it."

Mark looked doubtful. "Can't *you* shift it?" he asked.

"I won't even try," replied Ferragamo, and the finality in his voice persuaded the king to abandon the argument.

"You can trust Ferragamo's advice in these matters, my love," said Fontaine quietly.

"I trust him. I don't trust *her!*" her husband retorted in exasperation.

Luke's face began to twitch.

Beca suddenly put her hands to her ears, as if to block out an unwelcome noise.

"He's dreaming again," she squealed, on the verge of hysteria. "He's drowning! Wake him up. Wake him up!" She ran to the bedside and shook her brother hard. It had no effect. Beca looked around imploringly. "Wake him up, someone. I can't stand it!"

Getting no immediate response, she tried again—with similar lack of effect—then abruptly turned and ran from the room, tears streaming down her face. Her parents looked at each other and, without a word, Fontaine followed her daughter. Shortly afterward Koria came into the room, going to Luke's bedside.

"They're all right," she said. "Beca calmed down once she got outside."

"What did she say?" asked Ferragamo.

"That Luke's having a nightmare. And she saw part of it. It wasn't very clear, but she thinks Luke is suffering."

"You see," Mark said to the wizard. "Even Beca can recognize the truth *you* are avoiding."

"Nightmares do no lasting harm," Ferragamo replied. "This one may even do some good."

"That's your excuse for doing nothing!" replied Mark bitterly.

Their argument was interrupted by a gasp from Koria. In an instant Mark and Ferragamo were at her side. Wordlessly she pointed at the blood welling from Luke's arm beneath the armlet.

"So it's not necessarily evil?" said Mark furiously, and reached for the serpent band.

"Don't!" said Ferragamo quickly, grabbing his arm. "You don't have the knowledge. Let me try."

Reluctantly the king withdrew and watched impatiently as the wizard composed himself and stretched his hands toward the spreading stain on the sheet.

"Quickly!" urged Mark but Ferragamo ignored him, slowly and deliberately closing his fingers over the metal. As he did so, his face became a ghastly mask of pain and his whole body trembled. Within a few moments, sweat was dripping from his chin and a vein throbbed visibly at his temple. From his stance and expression it was clear that his exertion was enormous, but still the armlet did not move. Slowly, however, the flow of blood lessened, and Luke's clenched fist relaxed a little. Finally the metal slipped and Luke became still as the armlet gradually left his arm.

When Ferragamo at last held the metal serpent his hands

were covered in blood and his eyes were hollow. It was clear
that some of the blood was his own and that he was racked
with pain. Koria moved to support him, locking her arms
about his waist.

"He's safe now," Ferragamo whispered, his throat dry.

The armband fell from the wizard's nerveless fingers and
he staggered, his face for once as white as his hair. Mark
stared at him, unable to speak, his heart in his mouth.

Fontaine returned as Koria led Ferragamo away, and looked
in horror at the retreating wizard.

"What has happened?" she asked quietly, trying not to
panic as she noted her husband's stricken face, and the red
stain on her son's bed.

To her amazement she saw that tears were streaming down
Mark's cheeks, and as she approached him, a sob escaped his
throat. She held him tightly until his weeping subsided,
knowing he would speak when he could. Over his shoulder,
she peered at Luke but her son lay quietly, his eyes still,
breathing normally.

Eventually Mark drew back a little and faced her.

"He did *that* for Luke . . . for me," he said, his voice
breaking with emotion. "Why did I ever doubt him? I've
been so wrong . . . He was always like a father to me . . . and
then to Luke, and I've repaid him with nothing but scorn."
His eyes dropped. "I feel so ashamed," he added in a whisper.

"He never stopped loving you, you know," said Fontaine
gently. "He just lost the ability to show it. As you did."

"I know. I've been so cruel."

"No," she replied. "Just human."

Mark shook his head dejectedly.

"Go to him," urged Fontaine. "I'll stay with Luke."

"It's too late."

"It's never too late. Now go!"

Mark embraced his wife, and, with a last glance at his son,
left the room.

————————————

Later that evening a messenger arrived from Grayrock with
the disturbing news that the fog wall was now visible from
the cliffs—and it was drawing closer. The soldier had some
difficulty finding anyone in authority to whom he could make
his report. Mark was closeted with Ferragamo in the wizard's

quarters and was not to be disturbed. Luke was unconscious, his mother at his bedside. Eventually, the message was delivered to Shill, captain of the Castle Guard. Ansar and Moroski were in attendance, and were appalled at the report.

"So close already!" exclaimed Ansar. "That's terrible!"

"It's moving more rapidly," said Moroski. "At this rate it'll be here in a day or so."

"And we've heard nothing from the south of the island," said Shill. "It must be in the fog by now. Nobody can have escaped or they'd have come to warn us."

―――――――――――

In the deepest hour of the night, when most of the inhabitants of the city were asleep, ignorant of the fate that the morrow would bring, lights still burned in Starhill Castle. Whatever defensive arrangements were possible were being made with all haste, but in his heart Shill knew it to be a pointless exercise, one to ease the thought of their impotence in the face of this unimaginable threat. Endless discussions were held, but no one was able to suggest any possible scheme for their salvation. Of those who knew what was happening, the people of Heald were already deeply downcast by their own recent experiences and the natives of Ark were dejected by the absence of their natural leaders. It was a dark night indeed.

Despite the stillness in the quarters about her room Alena was also awake. She lay, fully clothed, in her bed and yet she was shivering. Her hand still hurt, a constant reminder of her last encounter with the man from the sphere, the man who now controlled her destiny.

When at last Alena was sure that her parents slept, she got out of bed and crept across the room, feeling her way in the darkness. carefully, she opened the door and slipped into Richard and Sophi's bedroom. A dim silvery glow from the moonlit window guided her to her father's clothes, and she silently drew the knife from the sheath on his belt. With one last glance at her sleeping parents, she returned to her own room and thence out into the corridor.

Widely spaced lamps lit the passageway, and Alena moved as quickly as she dared. She heard voices from one room and had to steel herself to pass the door, her heart thumping, but otherwise she saw and heard no one, finally reaching the door of Julia's room. There she stood for several endless moments, trying in vain to delay the inevitable. The dagger shook in her right hand as her left snaked out toward the door handle.

As if in a dream the door opened silently and Alena stepped inside. A lamp burned low beside the bed, clearly outlining Julia's dark head upon the pillow. Alena glanced around nervously but the rest of the room was lost in shadow. Moving with feline softness she crept toward the bed, her eyes fixed on Julia's pale face and exposed neck.

The pendants! She must remember the pendants. The man had stressed that very clearly. But first . . .

Alena raised the knife . . .

Something screamed in her ear and she was surrounded by a frenzied white whirlwind, which shrieked and battered her. Blindly, she lashed out with the knife but her attacker rose above the blow, floating in the air like a ghost.

In the bed Julia moaned and shifted restlessly, but her eyes remained shut. Alena was close to panic and on the point of fleeing from the room when Kubiac rose from the chair where he had been asleep, and appeared before her, looking like a wraith himself. His green eyes blazed with an intensity close to madness and his hands were curled like claws before him.

"Children!" he spat. "He sends a child to do his evil work."

Then the wizard leapt at her, his thin arms lunging for the knife. The two of them collided, crashed into the side of the bed, then toppled to the floor. There was a grunting sound, a hiss of breath; then all was still.

Julia awoke briefly, heard a seagull cry mournfully, and struggled to keep her eyes open, but in the darkness she could see little and the pain dragged her back down into oblivion.

Alena lay on the floor, paralyzed by her own fear, and trapped by the weight of Kubiac, who was sprawled on top of her. She was aware of something warm and sticky spreading over her body and that the wizard was very still, but her brain refused to function rationally.

This isn't happening, she thought. *It can't be real.* It isn't happening!

After what seemed an eternity, she forced herself to move and pushed at the wizard's shoulder. He was surprisingly light and she struggled out from beneath him with little difficulty, leaving Kubiac lying face down upon the floor.

There was a dark wet stain on the front of her dress and the knife was nowhere to be seen. As Alena turned toward the still open door, a man appeared there, carrying a lamp.

Richard stared in shock at the scene before him. The horror of what she had done crashed down upon Alena and she fled to her father's arms.

"Oh, Daddy, I didn't really do it. I didn't mean to," she sobbed. Without thought, Richard comforted her, trying to quiet her tears, still staring aghast at Kubiac's body.

Then he came to a decision.

"Wait here a moment. Don't go away," he instructed, and moved quickly to where Kubiac lay. He rolled the body over and felt a further shock when he saw his own dagger protruding from the wizard's chest. He carefully removed the knife and checked for a pulse. As he expected, there was none. Returning to his daughter, he picked her up and swiftly carried her back to her own room. There he made her remove all her bloodstained clothes and put her to bed. He made her promise not to move, nor speak to anyone. He hid the clothes, determining to burn them later, then cleaned his knife and returned it to its sheath, dressed quickly and went out again.

As he walked back to Julia's room he cursed himself for not acting when he had heard Alena moving about. He had heard her outer door close softly, and waited a while for her return, before finding a lamp and going to investigate. From then on, everything had seemed like a nightmare.

By the time he returned to Julia's room, he had worked out what he was going to do. When questioned, he would say that he had been unable to sleep, and had decided to go to the guardroom to check the latest news when he had heard sounds of a scuffle; on going to investigate he had found Kubiac's body, but no one else in sight.

He peered inside to check that Julia was still asleep, then ran off to find Shill and report his "discovery."

When Julia awoke an hour before dawn, her room was filled with people. She looked around fearfully, confused by all the faces and distracted by the pains in her head and chest.

Several people were kneeling around something on the floor, talking in whispers. Nobody paid her any attention. As one man stood up, Julia saw Kubiac lying on the floor, with blood all over his chest and his face set in a grimace of pain and hate. Julia knew that he was dead but her mind refused to accept the fact. She fainted.

When she woke again the room was empty, and the first rays of the morning sun were coming through the window. Her illness had retreated a little but her head still throbbed as she eased herself into a sitting position.

She caught sight of the stain on the rug beside her bed and memories flooded back, filling her with dread. Where was Kubiac?

The door opened quietly and she looked up hopefully. Luke came in, looking grave and walking slowly as if he were very stiff. He sat down on the bed and took her hands in his.

"I'm glad you're awake," he said gently. "I can't stay long."

"Kubiac?" she asked quietly.

Luke's eyes told her the answer before he spoke.

"He's dead," he said. "I'm sorry."

Julia closed her eyes in anguish. A weight settled on her chest.

"What happened?" she whispered.

"We don't know. It looks as though someone tried to attack you—we've put a soldier outside the door now—and Kubiac tried to stop them. In the struggle—"

"I almost woke up," said Julia. "If only . . ."

"Did you see anything?"

"No. I . . . I couldn't keep my eyes open. Oh, Kubiac, why?"

The tears came then, and Luke moved closer to hold her as she wept, mourning the only person that she had been able to call a real companion for most of her life. After a while she became quiet, and they sat together in silence until a squawk from the windowsill made them jump and look around.

Kirt stood there, his familiar lopsided stance emphasized by the angle of his head. He called again; a small, lost sound in contrast to his usual raucousness, and Julia knew she was not alone in her sadness.

"Goodbye, Kirt," she said, almost choking on the words.

The seagull nodded his head, turned, and launched himself

out of the open window. Luke and Julia watched him swoop away and rise into the empty sky.

For some time neither could speak; the silence was eventually broken by the padded footsteps of Muscles as he entered the room.

You'd better come, the cat said. *They're all there and want to know what's going on.*

"What *is* going on?" Julia asked.

I'll come in a moment, Luke replied to Muscles; to Julia he said, "There's a sort of council of war being held. The fog is very close now and we *must* act. Before I go, I need to ask you something."

"What?"

"That voice in your dreams, the one you were afraid of."

Julia shuddered. "What about it?"

"He's our enemy," replied Luke. "I want you to talk to him, and tell him where you are."

Julia looked at him in horrified disbelief.

"I want you to invite him to come here," added Luke.

Chapter 30

*F*erragamo rarely invited many people to the apartment that he shared with Koria; those rooms were their private retreat. However, in view of his present enfeebled state, the wizard had agreed to Mark's request that they hold their council there. Ferragamo sat now, with Koria beside him, looking at the people around him. All were tired and drawn; this was hardly surprising as most of them had been awake for all or at least part of the night. Even his fellow wizards, Moroski and Cai, with their extra reserves of energy, looked drained.

"The most important council Ark has ever had, and we're all half asleep," he whispered to Koria, smiling feebly.

"You'll soon wake them up," she replied, grateful for any return, no matter how small, of the wizard's usual humor. "Especially if you start shouting like you did in your sleep last night."

Ferragamo raised his eyebrows.

"Complete nonsense it was too," Koria went on. "you sounded almost like Shalli!"

"That's not surprising," he replied. "It was him I was talking to."

Koria looked astonished.

"I'll explain in a minute," Ferragamo said. "Everyone's here now."

"Except Luke."

"Fontaine said he was up and about. He'll be here soon." The wizard looked across at the queen, who sat on a settle between Mark and Shill. She appeared pale but determined. For a moment Ferragamo saw again the rebellious, red-headed girl whose spirited and spiteful tongue had made her so difficult to like when she first arrived on Ark. *She's come a long way since then,* he thought. And Mark too, he added to himself, switching his attention to the king and feeling glad that the events of the night, however costly, had at least brought the two of them closer together than they had been for years. He was glad now that he had removed the serpent band from Luke's arm. It had been the hardest thing he had ever done, and, though he believed that the armlet was not in itself evil, it *had* been on the point of hurting Luke badly. Ferragamo still did not understand how such a link, one which was obviously meant to be, could have such apparently sinister results. Perhaps Luke would explain when he arrived.

"Shouldn't we start?" asked Ansar. The Healdean prince stood between his parents, and was evidently anxious, as eager as ever for action. "Has anyone got any ideas about who killed Kubiac?"

"That is a nasty business," said Ferragamo. "Very odd. But I do think it's a side issue at the moment. We have to decide on a course of action that will determine the fate of Ark and perhaps all the other islands, so I think that the investigation of Kubiac's murder should wait for now."

"You don't think it's significant?" queried Fontaine.

"Comparatively, no."

There was silence for a few moments.

"Before we begin," said Ferragamo, "I'd better tell you about the message I received last night from Shalli."

"What? How did he manage that?" asked Moroski.

"He spoke directly to Owl."

"From the mountains?" Moroski exclaimed. "That's incredible!"

"Shalli never ceases to amaze me," replied Ferragamo. "But even I had no idea he could do this. Owl just relayed the message to me; I couldn't reply, of course. Though I did try," he added, glancing at Koria.

"What did he say?" asked Mark.

"The mountains are covered with fog, and outside the cave it was as though the world had ended. Shalli was very concerned for his animals—but he himself seemed quite unaffected."

"It's closing in fast if it's over the mountains," Shill remarked.

"No wraiths?" asked Ansar.

Ferragamo shook his head. "The only other things he said were 'Go to the source at the center,' and 'Luke is the son.' He repeated both statements several times."

"The tree?" said Mark.

"I suppose so. I can't imagine what else he'd mean."

"We already know it's important," said Cai. "But not how exactly."

"And Luke?" asked Fontaine.

"Your guess is as good as mine," replied Ferragamo, "but Shalli's odd utterances often contain far more wisdom than we can see on the surface. Bear them in mind."

"You sound as though you have a theory," said Adesina.

"I do," replied the wizard, "but I'd like to hear other ideas first."

Moroski and Cai exchanged glances. The younger wizard spoke, addressing his words to Ferragamo.

"We think we should try a warding spell," he said. "Between us we should be able to hold the fog at the city walls."

Moroski took up the idea. "Get as many people inside the city as possible, then if we can keep it at the walls, we deny the enemy its major power source. And we can put all our soldiers at the gates and battlements so that they won't be fighting in the fog but on the edge of it. It might give them an advantage over the wraiths."

"From what I hear," Shill said grimly, "we need all the help we can get."

"The men have been talking," added Ansar. "Our lads don't fancy fighting that lot again, and the castle guard were naturally curious."

"Morale is not exactly sky-high," agreed Shill. "But we might buy some time at least."

"Time for what?" Fontaine asked.

"Exactly!" exclaimed Ferragamo. "All this will do is give us a little longer to contemplate our downfall. How long do you think we could hold a warding against a power so strong that it can swamp entire islands, revive dead armies, and freeze the sea in summer? The sheer scale of the force that we must oppose makes such measures virtually pointless. It would be like attacking an armored warrior with a feather duster."

"What else can we do?" Moroski asked. As soon as the words slipped from his tongue, he knew with a dreadful certainty what Ferragamo's reply would be. But at that moment, Luke arrived, accompanied by Muscles, and it was he, and not the elder wizard, who responded.

"I think I have the answer," he said as he walked in. Everybody turned to look at him, their expressions revealing varying degrees of hope or skepticism. Still moving stiffly, Luke sat down in the only vacant chair in the room.

"Well?" Ansar demanded, unable to contain his curiosity.

"All this time we've been looking for a way to draw the enemy out into the open," said Luke, "so we'd have something to strike at. Well, I think I know how we can do it."

Luke coughed, then grimaced as his body protested at the sudden movement. Fontaine regarded him anxiously.

"Julia is the key," Luke went on. "I'm sure she was sent here to help us defeat this thing. She's the bait we need."

Luke went on to tell of his star-born vision in which he had seen the imperfect spiral spreading over the islands, with its initial source in Brogar. He explained his theory that Julia and her dead sister were the missing links in the chain, the cause of the imperfection, and as such she could now help them triumph. He also related what Julia had told him about the dreams of her other sisters, and of the frightening voice of the man who was searching for her.

"That's him," he said. "The one on Brogar. The real enemy. What we have to do is ask Julia to talk to him, let him know she's here. When he knows that the last obstacle to his perfect power is in Starhill, he won't be able to resist putting in an appearance—and that's our chance."

"Will she do it?" asked Cai quietly when Luke had finished.

"Yes," said Luke. "She's frightened, but if it's our only chance she'll do it if I ask."

"Can she be sure of contacting him?" Moroski asked, but before Luke could answer, his father broke in, unable to contain himself any longer.

"Are you all mad?" Mark exclaimed. "You can't seriously consider this idea. It would be playing right into their hands. She's one of them! Luke just said as much. I could see that from the moment she arrived. Isn't it obvious?"

Luke replied, his face twisted with emotion. "She *was* one

of them, but she isn't now! That's the whole point. Her life
on Strock was the only way she could have been saved, and
was a preparation for her role here."

Several people tried to speak but the king overrode them.
Father and son faced each other, oblivious to anyone else's
presence.

"So she was sent here to save us?" Mark said contemptu-
ously. "How do you know she wasn't sent to guide the
wraiths here? Far from stopping the fog's approach, she could
just as easily be *causing* it!"

"The fog made her ill," retorted Luke. "And she's been
eating moonberries all her life. No evil could have survived
that. She *is* good. I've known that for a long time."

"More *dreams*, I suppose," said Mark witheringly.

"They're more than dreams. You should know that—you
had some yourself once."

Luke stared unflinching into his father's eyes.

"Besides," he went on, "if Julia is evil why did some traitor
try to kill her?"

"Traitor?" Mark yelled. "Why a traitor? It could be someone who knows her for what she really is and decided to put
Ark's safety first!" The king had risen to his feet, his face red
with anger. "Perhaps he was right. We could still rid ourselves of the evil in our midst."

Luke's face had gone rigid and white with rage.

"We haven't all been fooled by a pretty face," Mark added.

Luke leapt to his feet, his stiffness overcome by fury, and
his golden eyes blazing. He was about to speak again when
Ferragamo roared, "Enough!" and the room became suddenly still and quiet. Father and son faced each other across
the room, neither able to understand the other's reasoning.
The others watched them in painful silence.

"This is getting us nowhere," said Ferragamo, in a quiet
voice which could nevertheless have cut stone. "Sit down,
both of you."

Luke and Mark had been the wizard's pupils, and knew
better then to disobey him when he spoke in that tone. They
subsided into their respective chairs.

Nice work, Muscles commented sarcastically in Luke's
mind. *With debating skills like that you'd make a good
brawler.*

What can I do? the prince replied dejectedly. *He won't listen to reason.*

You're right, the cat responded complacently. *Therefore you should be able to convince the others—if not your father. Instead you get into a shouting match.*

I'll try again.

You'd better. This is the only chance and you know it.

Ferragamo was speaking again but didn't get very far before being interrupted by the sound of hurried footsteps approaching the door. Durc came in, followed by Luca. The soldier was streaked with sweat and dirt and his right forearm was wrapped in a ragged and bloody bandage.

"News from Grayrock," said Durc. "I thought you'd better hear it straightaway."

Shill got up to allow the weary captain to sit down. Koria fetched him a drink and he sipped it as he told his tale.

"Grayrock's taken," he began. "There was nothing we could do. We got as many people out as we could, but once their soldiers came, there were so few of us that could stay awake to fight, there was no one left to organize an evacuation. As it was, we lost a lot of good men. It all happened so fast!" He shuddered at the memory.

"Grayrock already," said Shill. "It's moving faster still."

"A spiral would," added Luke quietly. "Near its center."

"We haven't much time," said Ansar.

"No," replied Luca. "It'll be well inland by now. There was no way it could be outrun on foot. And with so few horses available . . ."

There was silence for a while as everyone took in the awful news. Moroski and Ansar asked Luca a few questions and confirmed that his experiences in Grayrock paralleled their own on Heald. The enemy soldiers could be delayed but not destroyed, unprotected men and women became sleepwalkers, and the cold and dark completed the miserable conclusion. If Luca's estimates were correct, Starhill would face the same dreadful prospect within hours.

"Well?" Luke began, preparing himself for another attempt and resolving this time to stay calm. "you've heard how little time we have left. Are we going to sit here and wait to be sacrificed, or do we take the only chance we have?"

"It's got to be worth a try," said Cai slowly, when nobody else responded.

Agreed, said Muscles to Luke. *That's good enough for me.*
The cat stalked out of the room before Luke could reply,
leaving the prince in some confusion. He had no time to
consider his familiar's actions, however, because Moroski was
speaking to him.

"How do you propose that Julia contact our enemy?" the
Healdean wizard asked.

"He's looking for her. All she has to do is stop hiding. She
doesn't need to advertise her presence."

"And then?"

"Then we'll have a target we can strike at. That's what
we've needed all along," explained Luke patiently.

"Wonderful," put in Mark. "As if we didn't have enough to
face. You want to bring the enemy's leader right into our
stronghold!" The king spoke calmly enough now, but the
disbelief in his voice was still evident. "You can't take this
idea seriously."

"I can and I do," replied Luke, striving to keep his tone
reasonable. "Do you think I would contemplate asking her to
do this if I wasn't sure that it was right? Julia will be deliberately exposing herself to the very thing that frightens her
most." He looked around pleadingly. "I love her. I know you
find that difficult to believe, but I do. I wouldn't ask her to
act as bait like this unless I *was* serious."

"Oh, Luke," exclaimed Fontaine. "How can you be so
sure?"

"It's all of Ark you're playing with," said Shill gravely.

"More than that," said Pabalan. "All the islands, perhaps."

"I'm not playing," replied Luke. "I've seen things and I
believe them. I can't explain it any better." *Muscles, where
are you?* he thought. *I need your help.*

Ferragamo reentered the discussion.

"If it works—" he began, forestalling Mark's interruption
with a gesture. "*If* it works, and the enemy does appear,
what do you propose to do then?"

Luke said nothing. He had been intent on a solution to the
first part of the problem, and had taken it for granted that the
wizards would be able to fight their opponent once they
could see him.

"Alzedo is not likely to just lie down and surrender once

he's here," continued Ferragamo. Several of the group looked at the wizard, perplexed at the new name.

"Alzedo?" said Cai.

"Who else could it be?" replied Ferragamo. "Brogar is the key. We all agree about that."

"Of course," said Moroski. "I hadn't thought of him for years."

"He's obviously added to his talents since we saw him last," said Ferragamo. "I don't think you could call him a wizard anymore."

"But he was once?" asked Fontaine.

"Yes."

"Then you must surely know something about him that we can attack," said Luke. "Some weakness."

"Any he had are long gone," replied Ferragamo. "The evidence of that is all around us."

"Literally," said Mark.

"So, even if you are right, inviting him here is to invite defeat," Ferragamo went on. "Only the manner of our end changes."

From the way that the wizard spoke Luke knew that Ferragamo had made up his mind about their course of action a long time ago—and nothing he could say would change his mind. Looking at Moroski and Cai, Luke realized that they, too, knew what was coming.

"We have no choice," said Ferragamo. "We have to summon the Rite of Yzalba."

Muscles stalked resolutely through the corridors of Starhill Castle. *Let the humans talk themselves to a standstill*, he thought. I *am going to act*.

His faith in Luke was absolute, and now that he could also talk to Julia, the cat knew that she had the ability to help them all. That she might also have the power to destroy Ark was something he chose to ignore.

When he reached the girl's chamber, Muscles was surprised to see the door open and unguarded. Quickly, he slipped inside and saw that the sentry was standing just over the threshold, watching a maid who stood beside the bed. Julia was awake and sitting up.

"We found it in his clothing," the maid said. "It's a poem, and we thought you might like to have it."

Julia nodded but the maid hesitated.

"It's . . . not very nice," she said.

"It doesn't matter," replied Julia in a weak voice. "I'd like to see it."

The maid handed her a folded parchment. The blood had turned brown now but the stain was still recognizable. Julia gently pried apart the sheets and read the words within. A variety of expressions played across her face and, as she finished, a tear rolled down her cheek.

"I'm sorry," said the maid anxiously. "Shall I take it away?"

"No," Julia replied softly. "It's for me. Thank you for bringing it."

"Is there anything you want?" asked the maid, smiling awkwardly.

"No, thank you."

The maid withdrew, followed by the guard, who shut the door behind him.

Julia looked at Muscles fondly as he jumped onto her bed.

I thought you were with Luke at the council, she said, the novelty of the process making her mind-voice sound tentative.

I was. They'll be talking for hours.

Have they . . . have they decided yet? The apprehension showed in Julia's eyes.

Yes. Muscles lied with the confidence of a master. *They think it's worth a try.*

"Oh," said Julia aloud.

I'll help you, added Muscles.

Isn't Luke . . . ?

The wizards need him at the moment, replied the cat. *He'll come to see you soon.*

Should I try now?

We could start, but if the voice comes, don't reveal yourself immediately. Timing could be all-important.

How will I know when to act?

I'll find a way to tell you.

When I'm asleep?

Sleep is only a more imaginative form of wakefulness, said Muscles with such solemn profundity that Julia could not help but smile.

What was that the maid gave you? the cat asked curiously. Her smile faded.

A poem. It was Kubiac's. Do you want to read it?

I don't read. With my memory I have no need of such tricks, replied Muscles pompously. *What does it say?*

Julia read it aloud, then asked, *What does it mean?*

I don't know. But it sounds like a verse my father told me about once. He called it a prophecy.

A prophecy? This seems more like a riddle to me.

It certainly doesn't appear to make much sense.

Why did Kubiac have it? Julia wondered, then was lost in thought for a few moments, until Muscles gently nudged her back to more pressing concerns.

May I share your dreams? he asked.

Can you?

I think so.

I'm scared, Muscles.

Good, replied the cat. *That shows you're not stupid. Lie back and I'll sing you a lullaby.*

After a prolonged debate, the council had reached a compromise. In the nature of such things it satisfied nobody completely, but did have the benefit of giving them all something to do.

Ferragamo had insisted that his solution was the only one with any chance of saving them, no matter how drastic it seemed. He had put his case so forcefully that in the end Cai and Moroski—the only ones with any real notion of what he was proposing—had agreed that they should begin preparations for the Rite. For a long time the two had argued that the Rite would have been an incredible risk even had the entire wizard's conclave been present. With just the three of them they considered it nothing short of suicidal. However, Ferragamo responded that the Rite had been initiated by a single wizard in the War and that, if Shalli's words meant anything, Luke might well be able to help them. Besides, they had no choice. Reluctantly, Moroski and Cai had given in. In the meantime their own plan would be put into operation, in part at least.

The wizards would move their center of activity to the

tree-yard beneath Starbright Tower. That would have the double advantage of being the most secure stronghold, and of containing a rich source of power in the moonberry tree. As Ferragamo said—and only he knew whether he was joking or not—if they needed extra magical power all they had to do was eat a handful of the fruit! More convincing reasons for basing themselves there were the experience of the Healdeans and Shalli's enigmatic advice.

From the tree-yard, a warding spell would be set in place around the walls of the city and the battlements manned as best they could. If the ward proved hopelessly ineffective, the wizards would begin the Rite, but if it did hold, they would wait until the last possible moment before resorting to such desperate measures.

Luke had endeavored repeatedly to convince the council to try his idea but had failed. Mark's opposition to the idea remained vitriolic and his attitude made those who wavered entertain fresh doubts. With Ferragamo implacably set on his own course, Luke's task was hopeless. He felt dejected after his optimism of the morning, and the aches and pains in his body asserted themselves anew. Underneath the bandage, his arm throbbed painfully, though he had no idea what had inflicted the wound there. As the council broke up he rose slowly and, at Moroski's invitation, followed the wizard out of the room. Soon, Ferragamo and Koria were left alone.

"You got your way," she said quietly.

"Not my way," he replied. "The *only* way."

"What will happen?"

"I don't know," he replied honestly. "The Earth-mind is there all the time. I can feel it sometimes. But it's asleep. Perhaps the islands are its dreams. What we are going to try to do is wake it up."

"Ark is no dream," she replied firmly.

"Not to you and me, perhaps, but to the earth . . . who knows?"

"And if the dream ends?"

"Something will replace it, as sure as night follows day."

"The next dream?"

"Perhaps."

"Will we live to see it?"

"I don't know." Ferragamo looked into Koria's eyes. He

loved her too much to give her false hope, yet his honesty cost him dear when he saw the fear in her face.

"Come with me to the tree-yard," he said and saw her draw on her last reserves of strength. Her eyes reflected her resolve and she smiled. When she spoke again her voice was back to normal, calm and practical, and he loved her all the more for it.

"Of course," she said. "Whatever is going to happen we'll face it together. As always."

"Always," he replied and kissed her, hoping it would not be for the last time. Then they followed the others toward the center of the castle.

———————

It took Julia and Muscles a considerable time to fall asleep. Despite the cat's bravado, they were both nervous and fidgeted frequently. Julia's illness contributed to her discomfort and, because of the closeness of their contact, Muscles also began to feel some of her symptoms. He had begun by talking to Julia in soft, soothing tones but soon ran out of things to say and started a quiet humming, the mental equivalent of purring. An hour later they were still restless.

This is no good, said Julia. *We'll never do it!*

Keep trying, said the cat.

That's the problem, she said. *I am trying. What I need to do is stop trying—and relax. But how can I do that?*

I could tell you a story, suggested Muscles.

All right. Julia smiled at her companion and shut her eyes again.

You may not know this, Muscles began, *but the world we live in was created by a cat. Oh, he wasn't just any ordinary feline; he was the most wonderfully intelligent, witty, charming, beautifully marked cat there ever was—a bit like me, really. But what was the use of having all those exceptional qualities when there was no one to share them with? So he decided to make a companion for himself, and a world for them to live in, a world where there would always be food, warmth, and loving attention—the things that cats need most. First, he made his lady from one of his own whiskers; she was so beautiful, tender, and affectionate. And then he made the world. His method really was quite amazing. He wasn't sure at first how to go about creating it, but when one*

*day he was playing, chasing his own tail, he knew that that
was the way to do it. He went faster and faster, until his lady
could hardly see him; he was just a blur of color, with sparks
flying from his fur. The sparks joined to form a tiny ball of
energy, and as he carried on whirling and spinning around,
the ball grew—and grew, and grew—until it filled the whole
sky—or what counted for sky then—before it took off on its
own. Our hero by this time was dazed and panting, so he
stopped to have a rest, while the world carried on creating
itself, more or less. It carried on spinning for weeks and
weeks, months and months. Eventually, just as the two first
cats were starting to get a bit bored—for even cats need
excitement in their lives—sometimes—they noticed that things
had started to appear on the huge ball—things like mice, and
fires, and people with laps for sitting in. So they hopped
on—and never looked back.*

When Muscles ended his tale they were both, to all intents
and purposes, fast asleep. Yet the bond between them was so
close that they remained aware of each other at a far deeper
level than that of narrator and listener. Julia had been
caught up in the cat's words and the pictures they evoked.
Glad to have something to take her mind off their real business for a while, she had relaxed, and together they had
slipped into the deeper recesses of their joint consciousness.

It was a curious sensation for them both; neither could tell
where the story ended and the dreams began. These, too,
were disorienting, containing as they did both feline and
human elements. The images were often comforting, occasionally sinister, and almost always startling, but, despite their
vigilance, neither of them could find any trace of the man for
whom they searched, and his voice remained silent.

They had no way of knowing how long they had been
dreaming when the change occurred. The pain was the first
thing to register. Julia's body flinched as it struck and she
groaned aloud. Her mind filled with dark, distressing imag-
ery and Muscles was similarly affected, his limbs twitching
in sympathy. Within Julia's delicate frame a battle was raging, one she could influence but not control. A by-product of
this conflict was the pain that racked them both.

So tightly were they linked that when Julia fell helplessly
into a true state of unconsciousness, Muscles had no choice

but to follow. As he sank he tried in vain to call out to Luke, but no answer came, and the blackness swallowed him.

The tree-yard had become the nerve center of the castle and of the city. The wizards had ensconced themselves there as agreed. With Luke's grudging assistance they set up the boundaries of the warding spell along Starhill's walls, ready to be reinforced, when the time came, with whatever power was necessary. After that, Ferragamo had begun the preparations in earnest. The wizards proceeded slowly, painstakingly, meditating to keep their internal balance between each step and building in as many precautions as possible. Luke soon gave up any hope of winning them over to his idea and helped when and where he could. Despite his distress at the rejection of his plan—and of Julia—he was fascinated by the wizards' actions and found himself drawn more and more into their esoteric world.

Luke also acted as their link with the outside world. There were several people in attendance in the yard at any one time, and the wizards were too intent on their tasks to explain what was going on. When he was not too busy, Luke told Koria what was happening, and she fed the information to Mark, who had set up his command post inside the gateway of the yard, and to other interested parties. People came and went constantly, relaying messages signaled from other parts of the city.

All the soldiers who were to man the walls had recently eaten the traditional moonberry cake, and the wizards had ingested as much as they dared. The only supply still available of the precious essence was the raw berries still on the tree. In a rare quiet moment Luke found himself looking at the thumbnail-sized fruit, recalling the time he had eaten one as a small child. *Could I do it again?* he wondered. *What would happen if I did?*

He shivered and realized that the day had turned cold. Looking up, he was surprised to see the sky was already darkening. Dusk was not far off. He had not felt the passage of time.

Shill had been keeping watch from the tower, and emerged from the door at its base just as Durc entered the tree-yard from outside. Both looked grave and were somewhat out of breath.

"It's in sight," said Shill.

"All around us," added Durc. "It's about a thousand paces from the walls and closing in steadily."

"The cloud is also whirling sideways," said Shill, glancing at Luke.

"Tell them to be ready," Mark commanded his son. "When it reaches the wall, I'll get a signal and they must move quickly."

Luke nodded and broke into the wizards' private circle. They sat, their familiars beside them, about the tree. Although they appeared to be in a trance, Luke saw them acknowledge his message with flickering gestures of eyes and hands.

Jani entered the yard, walked straight up to Luke, and handed him something. The prince took it automatically, and found himself holding a golden serpent armband which he vaguely recognized. Without thinking, he slipped it onto his forearm. As he did so he was aware of Jani smiling but also of somebody—was it his father?—yelling "No!" Then the day's cold disappeared and he felt curiously detached, as if everything about him was unreal. From some faraway place he heard Muscles's voice crying piteously, but could not make out what the cat was saying. He listened intently and caught the faint words *"Help us"* before his attention, like that of everyone in the yard, was commandeered by the sudden and ghastly appearance of a nightmarish phantasm.

Alzedo, the renegade wizard of Brogar, stood at the foot of the tower, looking down on those about him. His face was twisted in an ugly smile and his colorless eyes glittered strangely in the gloom. All about him, his silver and black cloak writhed and twisted. He stood five times the height of a normal man; yet this was not his most terrifying aspect, for Alzedo appeared to be also a snake, a giant serpent, reared up as if to strike. Somehow, the colorless eyes of the man were also the slitted yellow eyes of the reptile, and the light reflected from the cloak became the lustrous sheen of scales.

"Someone has been calling for me," roared the apparition in a voice that was human but which rolled about the tree-yard like a clap of thunder. "I would not like to disappoint them." Alzedo laughed, displaying brown and broken teeth and ice-white fangs. He swept the gathering with his double gaze.

"How pleasant of you all to gather to greet me thus. For the little time you have left, you will provide me with a most amusing spectacle."

All thoughts of resistance fled from the minds of the frozen onlookers. Here was a power so far beyond their comprehension that even to contemplate opposing it was ridiculous. They stared, wizard, king, and soldier alike, in awe and abject terror.

Chapter 31

Mark stood paralyzed, aware that everyone about him was similarly afflicted. His feeling of déjà vu was intense but he knew that this time there would be no escape. He could not even begin to draw forth his sword, the blade which had served so well against Amarino. Even had he been able to do so, he was convinced that Alzedo would merely have laughed at his pretension.

The giant spoke again, his unnerving gaze resting on Ferragamo.

"Ark has long been a thorn in my side. You and your pathetic Servants." He glanced at Mark. "But I have been patient. Your luck has run out."

Within the tree-yard darkness was falling fast, and the apparition's reptilian eyes glowed ever brighter. Hoarfrost began to glitter on the stone walls about them.

"Do you feel the cold, *little ones*?" asked Alzedo, mocking them. "It's closing in. Invincible and unstoppable. Your precious magic tricks won't work this time. Soon you will all be . . ."

His words faltered as something moved within the yard. Longfur emerged from the door of the tower, his fur bristling and his tail erect. Mark saw him and felt a tiny jolt of hope. Longfur had saved them last time. Perhaps . . . The thought faded as soon as it began. I'm clutching at straws, he rebuked himself, and then was shocked by the sight of a second new arrival.

Julia followed Longfur from the tower. She was still dressed in her nightgown, her eyes were tight shut, and she staggered as she entered the yard, betraying her weakness. Muscles walked at her heels.

Luke's petrified gaze was locked upon Julia's wan face. At the sight of her, looking so frail and vulnerable, he felt a painful constriction in his chest. Then he realized that he could hear her thoughts. She was silently reciting a curious refrain, parts of which sounded oddly familiar. As soon as it ended the verse began again, in an endless cycle. At first it appeared meaningless, but as Julia moved slowly forward until she had halted beside the tree, the litany took shape within Luke's mind, embedding itself in his consciousness. He found himself saying it in unison with her and felt the glow of companionship, of shared experience—and something more. He could move!

Somehow, the verse running through their minds was protecting them from Alzedo's paralyzing influence. This revelation caused Luke such excitement that he took no notice of the words themselves, but only of their overall effect. He had been right. Julia *was* important! But how?

As one part of his brain calmly continued reciting Julia's refrain, nonsensical ideas flashed through another.

> *From the sea, peril.*
> *From the sea, safety.*

Of course! he thought. Those were the first lines of Father's prophecy—the one that predicted Amarino's fate. Luke began paying more attention to the words, only to be interrupted by a more familiar voice.

It worked then, remarked Muscles, glancing up at the double image.

Too well! replied Luke. *Shut up now, Muscles. I have to listen to what Julia's saying.*

Then Alzedo spoke. As he did so, Julia's eyes sprang open and she looked at him, pain and shock clear in her expression.

"Welcome, daughter," the phantasm thundered. "Have you come to witness my final victory?"

> *Evil's heir in chains set free*

Luke decided it was time to act; to do something, *anything*. He remembered Muscles's earlier comment about "mind talk between humans" and, knowing that physical proximity would aid the process, decided to go to Julia's side.

Slowly, painfully, he forced his legs to carry him the few necessary paces. It felt as though he were wading through shoulder-high molasses, and every nerve in his body protested at the movement.

Alzedo looked down at him in disbelief, but the monster's astonishment was quickly hidden as his face twisted into a grimace.

"Such a pretty boy," he snarled. "Would you like him for a plaything, my daughter?"

The insulting tone was lost on Luke. He had seen the enemy's momentary hesitation; that was enough. It made him all the more determined to persevere; perhaps there *was* a chance after all . . .

As he reached her side at last Luke felt Julia's recitation falter as the reality of her situation sank in.

I am his daughter, she thought to herself.

Yes you are, but you've overcome it so far, Luke replied vehemently, hoping she would hear.

Julia was obviously confused. *Muscles?*

No. It's me. Luke!

She turned away from Alzedo to face the prince, her eyes wide.

Keep reciting! Luke urged. *It protects us.*

He sensed her obedience and joined in with her. With the free portion of his mind, he went on.

You can't give up now. Too much depends on us. You've beaten him before and you can again. Please try! he urged. *For me. For us! You are a Servant too.*

With those words Luke awoke an echo from his own past and gave Julia the courage to carry on. She took his hand in hers.

"How sweet," mocked Alzedo. "Look above you, little ones!"

His gigantic arms were flung wide, sending silver light flickering over the frozen courtyard. The serpent's coils stretched and shimmered in the unearthly radiance.

All those who were capable of it raised their eyes. Above the wall of the tree-yard there was now a second, far more massive wall. The fog rose above them, above the Wizard's Tower, and up into the sky, leaving only a tunnel of clear air, at the far end of which a small, circular path of evening sky was visible. As they watched, the tunnel grew narrower. Very soon, it would not be there at all; the spiral would be complete and all would be lost. The wizards' warding spell had obviously had no effect, and Luke wondered briefly what had happened to all those men and women in the city that now dwelt within the cold, gray mass. The fog bank was inky black in the failing light, and only the unnatural fluorescence from the evil specter allowed them to see that it was whirling around at an incredible speed.

Silver spiral, black as night.

Luke saw Julia fingering the pendants about her neck. Within the black glass, silver patterns shone brightly, seeming to swirl and revolve, yet remain constant, forcing Luke to look away . . .

Turning ever, ever still.

. . .feeling that he was on the point of being hypnotized, of falling into a trap.

Julia's thoughts were racing, falling over each other in a tangle she could not unravel. She knew now that the prophecy, which she was repeating endlessly, held the clues that might help her solve the riddle, but at the same time nagged at her, emphasizing her self-doubt.

Evil's heir in chains set free

Am I really evil's heir? she wondered. *How can you be set free in chains?*

Shall chain the sun to break the link.

Immediately, Julia's mind was overwhelmed from all sides. Several voices spoke to her simultaneously. Only one was familiar; it was Muscles. Another was similar, but older sounding; another cat? A third was solemn, bringing with it the impression of huge, slow-blinking eyes and silent gliding wings. The next was similarly linked to the idea of flight, but sharper, predatory somehow, seen through eyes of matchless clarity. The last was so unlike anything that Julia had ever experienced that she could not even guess at its origin. This voice was multifaceted, echoing and reverberating until it set her mind abuzz.

And beyond all these, incredibly distant, there was another presence, ancient and magical; and so kind that Julia trusted it immediately.

Although she heard each voice separately, each sent her the same message.

Luke is the sun.

That was all she needed. From that moment, pure instinct took over and her hands moved of their own accord. *Luke is the sun,* she thought, *and my Golden Warrior. I must do this for him.* She released Luke's hand and carefully separated the two necklaces that held the pendants.

"You cannot remove them!" screamed Alzedo. "They are the proof of your real nature, daughter. They bind you to me."

One vast hand stretched out, pointing accusingly. The serpent jaws opened and a long forked tongue flicked out toward her. Julia felt its passage and smelled the snake's fetid breath. She flinched, her hands fumbling at her throat.

"Come, daughter. Enough of this foolishness. Join me." The accusing finger folded back into a hand of welcome.

No! Luke interjected. *He cannot touch you. You can deny him. It is for you to choose.*

Pain rose up in Julia's body as if it, too, were being torn apart by conflicting loyalties. She cried out and nearly fell, but Luke moved to support her and she found herself looking into his golden eyes—so different from the yellow orbs of the snake.

Loving faith...

She made her choice and with it came knowledge. She removed one of the pendants from her neck, releasing the previously unbreakable chain without effort. The silver spiral within the glass shone clearly now. Standing unsupported once more she held out the pendant, offering it to Luke. He was uncertain, and Julia saw the doubt and fear in his face, knowing she could not help him.

"I cannot give it to you," she pleaded aloud. "You have to take it."

Watching her actions, Mark felt a cold dread envelop him. *She will control him*, he thought. *Our last chance is gone. He was the only one who could move—the last Servant. Luke, don't take it!*

"You *must* take it," pleaded Julia.

"You should not take it," said Alzedo. "It will kill you."

Indecision brought beads of sweat to Luke's brow, despite the icy atmosphere.

In Julia's hand he saw the deadly coils of a venomous snake. Well he remembered the golden scales, jewel-red eyes, and the needle-sharp fangs. For a moment he was back within the whirlpool of his dream, its thunder roaring in his ears. He knew what he must do, yet still he hesitated because he also knew the price that he would have to pay.

. . . shall be the test

Luke grasped the snake, flinching as its poisonous fangs sank into his arm. Yet when he opened his fist again a metal chain and pendant lay within, silver gleaming dully within glass. He put it on, slipping it over his head, feeling as he did so the venom spreading within his body, speeding through his veins. Pain flowed with it but Luke was able to set that aside, knowing there were more important battles to be fought.

"Thus your doom is sealed," roared Alzedo, but Luke caught the taint of uncertainty in the massive voice and knew, without needing to look at her, that Julia heard it too. They were both part of the network that had produced the imperfect spiral. They sensed each other within the pattern. Farther away, they felt the presence of Julia's sisters and, at the other end of the spiral, the man who once was a wizard and whose awful image appeared before them now.

Circle's center at its edge,

Luke's nightmare reappeared in his mind. If the snake became a chain then as now, there must surely be other lessons to be learned from the dream. The bond was made between him and Julia—to escape they must now utilize the strength of the whirlpool, of the enemy; turn its power *upon itself* in order to defeat it.

Still the prophetic litany echoed and reechoed within their minds.

> *Serpents's head upon its tail.*

The idea occurred to them both simultaneously and they acted upon it in unison. They drew power from the network, diverting and channeling it into the image of the giant serpent that coexisted with Alzedo. For a while, nothing happened.

Then Alzedo recovered from his bewilderment and laughed. "Thank you, my children," he boomed. "How good of you to aid me thus. My victory will now come all the sooner."

The flow of magical forces within the tree-yard became a palpable process and light flickered intermittently. The serpent glowed ever brighter.

Mark saw what was happening and knew the agony of betrayal. He tried to close his eyes and ears, to shut out the vile scene and Alzedo's victorious words, but he could not even gain that solace. The king was forced to watch as the serpent grew in power and substance, its eyes glowing so brightly that they seemed almost orange. When Mark heard Luke speak aloud for the first time it almost broke his heart.

"Help us," the prince wailed.

Though he did not look their way, each of the wizards felt Luke's appeal was directed at them. Like the others they were unable to move, yet had sensed what Luke and Julia were trying to do. Each of them was now faced with the choice of whether or not to trust the young couple. It would be a complete act of faith for, in their present state, they would be unable to control any power that they chose to release.

Cai was the first to decide. *It's little enough,* he thought, *but if they fail we are lost anyway.*

He opened his mind to them, giving them access to all the magical power he had stored up. In doing so he gave Luke and Julia his life, to do with as they pleased. The swarm approved the decision, rising up and forming a flickering, ever-changing pattern about their wizard and adding one more bizarre element to the outlandish scene.

Cai's contribution was accepted gratefully and utilized swiftly. The snake's eyes were definitely orange now and the reptile was beginning to dominate the double image, at Alzedo's expense.

Within moments Ferragamo and Moroski had come to the same conclusion as their young colleague and their wizardry added fuel to the magical fire, leaving them personally defenseless.

"Are you yielding so soon?" Alzedo taunted them. "I am disappointed. I had expected more fight from you—even in such a hopeless cause." He laughed again, but was clearly bemused by their action, and studied the wizards closely for a moment. He saw Ferragamo's eyes go to Koria, who stood petrified at one side of the yard, and the look that passed between them. Alzedo smiled nastily but was prevented from commenting by another disconcerting event.

The serpent had continued growing, and now appeared almost solid. Its coils began writhing and twisting wildly, causing Alzedo considerable disquiet. To the onlookers the snake was by now clearly the dominant partner in the image, no longer the placid underling that it had at first appeared.

Slowly but surely, its eyes were changing color from orange to blood-red. Their radiance bathed the whole scene in a ghastly hue.

Without warning the snake turned upon its creator. The double image became two distinct entities, and the serpent's fangs were bared in a battle frenzy, its baleful eyes glaring at Alzedo's image.

"You're *mine*," the giant screamed. "You can't attack *me*!"

Together Luke and Julia replied, *It's not yours anymore!*

Transfixed, the humans watched the phantasmagorical struggle, realizing that the snake would not be denied; yet they dared not hope, unsure whether the serpent's victory would improve their fate.

Its terrifying jaws clamped first upon the giant's defensively raised arm. With a vicious twist the serpent tore the limb from its shoulder, the sickening crunch of the separation mingling with Alzedo's screams. At the same time the massive tail swept out, smashing into the sorcerer's hips, deforming them instantly into a bloody and shapeless mass. Another lunge and the terrible creature closed upon Alzedo's neck in a grip that promised certain death.

The vision exploded in a flash of light, painted blood-red by the light of the serpent's hideous orbs, as it now surveyed the tree-yard as its sole master. The berserk blood-lust still shone from the snake's eyes, and those assembled stared at it, wondering who would be its next victim.

But something strange was happening to the serpent; its body was no longer under its own control. Its jaw gaped wide and its sinuous length twisted unnaturally. Luke and Julia knew what was going to happen even before the snake did. The network was feeding upon itself. They were not surprised when the serpent's jaws clamped viciously onto its own tail and it began devouring its own flesh.

The same could not be said for the other spectators, who looked on in astonishment at the uncanny spectacle. The snake was now a circle, continuous and complete. It began to spin. Faster and faster it went, sparks of energy flying outward, so bright that after a few moments nobody could look at it. Soon, all that was left was a ball of dull red light, floating above the tree at the center of the yard. The serpent had vanished. Yet still the human onlookers could not move, and in an instant their newborn hope was cruelly dashed.

Laughter echoed deafeningly all around. Though no longer visible, Alzedo was still with them, and his disembodied voice drummed into every ear.

"So your tricks have killed my pet. That was clever of you, but do not delude yourselves. *I* am not harmed. You will have to do better than destroy a mere image to have any effect on me." He laughed again. "Your world is still doomed. Look about you!"

The fog wall was still there, as dense as before, and whirling ever faster. It was level now with the inner walls of the tree-yard, and still moving inward. Soon those people standing closet to the edge of the yard would be enfolded in its clammy embrace.

Ferragamo glanced desperately at Koria and saw her start to fade into the gloom. *Not this way*, he thought. *It can't end this way!* He wanted to weep, to shout or scream, but none of these things was possible; he could only watch in silent, helpless anguish.

Alzedo spoke again, his huge voice pitched at its most persuasive.

"Come, Julia. Join me. It cannot last long now. Give up this foolishness. Why deny yourself? Why choose pain?"

Luke spoke, or thought he did. Perhaps he only listened while Julia spoke. It did not matter which. The two were now so much part of each other that it was irrelevant, but the words rang in both minds.

He's weakening! The whole network is weakening. We must not give up now.

Yet still the fog closed in. Koria was almost lost, and could hardly be seen.

What can we do?

Muscles provided the answer to their joint question.

He leapt nimbly into the air, plucked one of the fruit from the tree with his teeth—so gently that he did not even break the skin—and brought it to Julia. She stooped and took it from him.

This might come in handy, Muscles remarked.

"That will hurt you—terribly," warned Alzedo in a voice like the crashing of icebergs.

Julia stood facing Luke, holding the berry between them, her forearm pointing upward to the few remaining stars.

"I choose!" she shouted, and clenched her fist, crushing the fruit within.

A searing pain erupted in her hand and arm, and spread rapidly through her whole body, yet, though her face contorted with agony, her eyes smiled. Luke saw and knew the scouring pain that racked her was her cleansing, a final victory over the evil that had been born within her.

Loving faith shall be the test

Luke closed his hand about Julia's small fist, his forearm next to hers, so that the potent juice that squeezed between her fingers ran through his own, and trickled down both their arms. He, too, felt a burning pain but knew its purpose and was glad. The poison that flowed in his veins was being burned away.

Drops of the clear liquid from the moonberry ran down Luke's forearm and reached the serpent band. As they touched it, the metal began to glow softly, and as the liquid ran below the band, its color changed to the crimson hue of blood. The jeweled eyes sparked fire, sending flashes of brilliant red into the dread, incarnadine light that the giant reptile had bequeathed them.

Soon the golden fire on Luke's arm grew so brilliant that the onlookers could hardly see the prince or Julia except as ghostly silhouettes within the pulsating blaze. For Mark this was yet another vision of horror from the past; fire had been his own ordeal of faith.

From ages past, the golden coil

Luke released his grip on Julia's hand and slipped the serpent band from his arm. So incandescent was the metal that he could no longer see it, yet the armband felt cool to his touch and he handled it without pain or fear.

Shall bring to life the quiet star.

Whether he was guided by newfound instinct, by fate, or by an unknown outside power, Luke found that his actions came naturally now, and he rejoiced in this startling certainty after so much doubt and pain.

Holding the fiery band above his head, he sensed the deadly fog wavering, slowing in its ominous progress. For a moment he hesitated, gathering himself. Then in a sudden violent action, boyish in its untamed glee, he flung the armlet high into the air. It collided with the ball of dull red energy that hung above the tree, and the yard immediately exploded into light, light as clear and strong as a midsummer's day. Within their own low and narrow sky, a new star burned.

The cloud walls about them began to draw back, burned away by the fierce new sun which hovered in its midst. Koria reappeared, and Ferragamo, able to move again, staggered to her side. No one else moved far. All were too exhausted, too stunned.

A soldier called from high in the tower, where he had been on watch.

"It's going!" he yelled, unable to hide the joy in his voice. "It's drawing back—and fast!"

"We've won?" asked Durc in disbelief.

"We've won!" exclaimed Shill, practically dancing with happiness as he embraced the bemused ex-outlaw.

Everything was movement then, as they all remembered

loved ones who were elsewhere. Yet, in the midst of all this sudden activity, at the center of the circle, Luke and Julia were still, gazing at each other in an ecstatic communion that owed nothing to the outside world.

As the warmth of the new sun flowed into them, they knew themselves linked together by something more binding than mere strands of metal. No venom coursed within their bodies.

To stand within the whirlpool's eye.

As their joint litany came to its conclusion for the last time, Luke took Julia in his arms. Despite their exhaustion, their first kiss was so urgent that the emotions it aroused were almost more than either could bear. Luke and Julia clung to each other, their tears mingling, but when they finally drew apart, they were laughing.

Chapter 32

*A*s Luke and Julia kissed, the fireball began to rise. Slowly at first and then with increasing speed, it climbed into the sky to take a place among its peers.

Over the next few days it was observed that the new star, unlike its brethren, did not move in the heavens, but shone constantly above the city, so that Starbright Tower always pointed it out to any observer. Although it was wondered whether the wizards of long ago had foreseen this event when building the tower and choosing its name, the truth was never discovered.

On the night of the star's birth, however, nobody had time for such conjecture. Indeed, there was little time for any explanation of the day's extraordinary events. Everyone was too busy making sure that their loved ones were unharmed, and that the people of Starhill had survived their ordeal. With great relief, it soon became clear that there had been no fighting. Although the walls of the city had been quickly overwhelmed by the icy fog, no wraiths had appeared.

"We heard them, though," Ansar reported, for once not sounding disappointed at missing a battle. "They were moaning fit to wake the dead but we never saw them. It was pretty unnerving," he admitted.

"On Heald, they waited for the fog to take its toll before attacking," added Pabalan. "Presumably they were doing the same here."

"And by the time they were ready," said Shill, "their general had other things on his mind."

"So I hear," said Ansar.

"Whatever you've heard, it's not the half of it," replied Shill. "I was there and I still don't believe what I saw."

Among the city's populace, a feeling of confusion held sway. Many had vague memories of wandering about for part of the afternoon in a daze. Others had fallen asleep in the most unlikely and—in some cases—embarrassing places, waking that evening feeling cold and ill. Though they were basically unharmed, there were many who swore never again to touch hard liquor before sundown.

For the residents of Starhill, unlike those of the rest of Ark or the other islands, the ordeal had been mercifully brief. The general reaction was summed up by one denizen of the streets who, on waking up in a tavern doorway, with a vague memory of the icy cold, remarked to nobody in particular, "Terrible weather for this time of year!"

Of those in the tree-yard that night Ferragamo had been the first to react to his newfound mobility. Though he felt as weak as a kitten, he moved as fast as he could to Koria and took her in his arms. She was shivering uncontrollably but her eyes were clear and she managed a weak smile. The wizard's relief was absolute, so great that his strength gave out and together they sank to the floor, sitting side by side with their backs to the wall. They had no need of words but kept very close as they watched the shooting star.

The other two wizards sat up slowly from their prone positions beneath the tree. They looked at each other, as if to reassure themselves that they were not dreaming, that what they thought had happened had really happened. One glance at Luke and Julia, still locked in their fierce embrace, convinced them that it had, and when their eyes met, Cai and Moroski were grinning broadly.

"A fine wizard I feel," Cai said, falling back and staring up at the receding star. "I've just given all my power to a snake so that it could eat itself."

"Be thankful it didn't eat you," replied his friend.

"Are you sure it didn't?" asked Cai. "I distinctly feel as if I've been chewed up and spat out."

"Funny you should say that," said Moroski. "Have you looked at yourself recently?"

"Remind me to insult you when I have the strength," replied Cai, closing his eyes. "For now, just summon up the nubile maiden with a flagon of wine whose services I so urgently require."

It took Mark somewhat longer to regain his equilibrium. As Durc and Shill rejoiced at his side, and then left, the king stood as if still paralyzed, his gaze fixed upon Luke and the girl in his arms. His brain was still reeling from the multiple images of horror that had been thrust upon it, and he was now being forced to adjust his thinking to an enormous degree. He could not cope.

How could I be so wrong? he wondered, his mind fleeing from the implications of his misjudgment. *Even Jani knew*, he thought. *Why not me?*

Unable to face the scene before him any longer Mark turned and ran from the tree-yard, in search of Fontaine and Beca—and peace of mind.

That left Jani, who merely watched over Luke and Julia, waiting until they were ready to move and then seeing that they got safely to their beds. That task accomplished, he relinquished his position as guardian and returned to the tree-yard to assist the enfeebled wizards and Koria. They were all glad of his strength before the night was out. Jani even carried Cai to his bed, not hearing the young wizard's comment that Jani wasn't exactly what he'd had in mind when he'd asked for a nubile maiden.

The next morning dawned bright and clear, much to everyone's relief. Riders left the city at first light for all parts of the island to check on the clearance of the evil fog and to ascertain the aftereffects of the invasion.

Most of those who had been in the tree-yard rose quite late. Luke was the first up, but only because Muscles would give him no peace.

She's calling you, the cat reported, having walked over the length and breadth of Luke's bed.

Did you wake her up too? grumbled the prince, rubbing the sleep from his eyes.

She's not awake, replied Muscles testily. *Can't you hear her? She's nearly deafening me.*

No, said Luke, resigning himself to getting up, and wondering whether he and Julia would ever be mind-linked again.

When Luke reached her room he found Jani sitting placidly outside the door. Memories of his guardian's calm and unselfish contribution to the previous day's events came back to Luke, and as the big man rose to his feet, they embraced.

"Thank you, Jani."

Jani smiled in response, and Muscles remarked that Julia was awake now. As Luke knocked on the door and received an invitation to enter, Jani handed him a stained parchment.

"What's this?"

You'll know, replied Muscles. *Go in now or she'll start up again,* he added in a pained tone.

As Luke entered the room, Julia's eyes lit up. She was sitting in bed, propped up by several pillows.

"I'm glad it's you," she said.

"So am I," he replied softly, sitting on the edge of the bed. "Muscles says you've been calling for me."

"Have I?" Julia looked puzzled. "I was dreaming."

They sat in silence for a few moments.

"Did it really happen?" she asked quietly.

"Yes."

"I feel different."

"You are. You're free now. Forever."

"And you? Are you all right?"

"Me?" Luke thought for a moment. "I'm a little tired. A certain feline wouldn't let me sleep late. Otherwise I'm fine."

There was another pause.

"I love you," said Luke simply.

"I love you too," replied Julia

Excuse me, a third voice added. *I know when I'm not wanted.*

Muscles bounded to the door, which was opened from the outside so that he could complete his exit, leaving Luke and Julia laughing, and momentarily embarrassed.

As their kiss ended, Julia noticed the parchment, and her face fell.

"Poor Kubiac," she whispered.

"He loved you too, didn't he?"

Julia nodded. "He was the best friend I ever had."

"Was this his?" asked Luke, indicating the parchment.

"Yes."

"What is it?"

"It's . . . I think you'd better read it."

Luke unfolded the sheets and glanced at the lines he already knew so well.

"Oh." He didn't know what to say.

"I don't know where he got it," said Julia. "So many things don't make sense. I wish someone could explain it all."

"If anyone can, it's Ferragamo. Let's go and see him."

Julia nodded and Luke joined Muscles outside the room while she dressed. Jani was nowhere to be seen, his duties complete for the moment.

They found Ferragamo and Koria sitting in bed, finishing off what had obviously been a large breakfast.

"I need my strength," said the wizard, noting Luke's eyes scanning the empty trays.

"Would you like some?" asked Koria. "There's plenty more." Without waiting for an answer, she went to the kitchen. Muscles followed her hopefully.

"Well," said Ferragamo. "You two are up bright and early. What can I do for you?" He spoke cheerfully enough, but Luke detected an underlying fatigue and saw the dark rings beneath the wizard's eyes.

"Last night—" Luke began, then changed his mind and, without further words, handed the parchment to his mentor.

Ferragamo read it carefully, his face a mask of concentration.

"Where did this come from?" he asked finally.

"Kubiac had it," Julia replied. "Presumably he brought it from Strock."

"No wonder I couldn't find anything in my library," said the wizard. "I don't recall any mention of your island, and even if there had been, I don't think I'd have connected it with our situation." He was silent for a while, obviously thinking hard, and neither of his visitors wanted to interrupt. Koria soon returned with two more breakfast trays, and Luke and Julia discovered that they were ravenously hungry. That put an end to conversation for a while and gave Ferragamo time to think through the prophecy's implications. They had just finished eating, and Muscles had returned from the kitchen looking smug, when further visitors arrived.

Durc's head appeared around the door.

"Oh, good," he said, looking at Luke. "I thought we might find you here." He came in, and was followed by Fontaine and Mark. The king looked nervous, but came straight to the point.

"I'm sorry for the way I treated you," he said to Julia. "I didn't understand. Can you forgive me?"

Julia had been unaware of the extent of Mark's aversion to her and so was taken aback by the contrition in his voice. She nodded meekly, not really understanding, and the king turned to his son.

"Luke, you were right. I was wrong. I'm truly sorry for the things I said."

"We all owe Luke an apology," Ferragamo broke in. "He knew better than anyone what was happening. Without these two none of us would be in this room now."

"We couldn't have done anything without the help of others," said Luke.

"Whereas I was only a hindrance," Mark added bleakly. He turned to Julia. "Is there anything I can do to make up to you for my behavior?"

Once again, Julia found herself at a loss for words.

"Yes." Luke, answering for her, sounded almost belligerent. "You can agree to our marriage."

It was Mark's turn to find he had lost the use of his tongue. He looked at his wife.

"You couldn't stop it if you tried," Fontaine said. "They've known—and loved—each other for a very long time." She smiled at her son.

Durc's face was a picture of delight. He went up to Julia and kissed her cheek. "If I may . . . I claim the right to give you away," he said to the astonished girl.

Mark recovered his poise at last.

"Of course," he said. "With all my heart."

There followed a round of congratulations and general merriment from which Julia was left confused and happy, and with only two abiding memories. One was of the tender certainty in Luke's eyes; the other was of a comment made to them both by Muscles.

At least you won't have to shout when you're in the same bed, the cat said, making the color rise in the couple's cheeks.

After that, conversation returned to the events of the pre-

vious day. The prophecy was shown to the latecomers, and
Ferragamo explained as much of it as he could, with help
from Luke and Julia. The mention of the silver spiral made
them both immediately touch the pendants that still hung at
their necks.

"Those were the devices by which Alzedo and Julia's former sisters formed the network, and thence the gigantic
spiral," said Ferragamo. "Once Luke wore one, he too was
inside the link, and with a little help—inspiration—from the
past, he was able to find a way of disrupting it from within."

"From the past?" asked Mark.

"A dream," replied Luke. "Like yours about the Mirage
Warrior."

Mark shuddered as Koria asked, "But Julia, how did you
know to give the chain to Luke?"

"I got a message," replied Julia, "from the animals, I think.
It said 'Luke is the sun.' The prophecy says 'shall chain the
sun.' It was obvious then."

"Shalli!" said Ferragamo and Mark simultaneously.

"So *that's* what he meant," Fontaine said.

"And once he got the pendant, Luke became part of the
spiral and could thus help to destroy it," confirmed the
wizard.

"The pattern was already distorted by Julia. I just helped it
to destroy itself," said Luke.

"Your modesty is most becoming," said Durc, "but it looked
to me as if you did rather more than that."

"It just happened," Luke replied lamely.

"From what I've heard," added Fontaine, "quite a lot *just*
happened."

"That's putting it mildly," Durc said, then chuckled ruefully. "At least I didn't *swoon* this time!"

Once the laughter died down, Ferragamo carried on explaining the various lines of the verse to those who did not
see their relevance, and Luke described the "golden coil" to
those who had not seen it.

"Where did it come from?" asked Fontaine.

Ferragamo saved Julia from having to explain by replying
for her.

"From Strock. In many ways that little island was the
center of all this, even if geographically it was on the
periphery."

"Circle's center at its edge," quoted Fontaine.

"That's one interpretation," said the wizard. "The armlet was another artifact from the time of the War of the Wizards. It belonged to one of the original Servants, obviously Luke's forebear. The Golden Warrior as yours was the Mirage Warrior, Mark."

"Then why did it hurt him?" asked Mark.

"What?" said Luke. "It didn't hurt me."

"It did earlier," Ferragamo answered. "My best guess is that although it was meant for you, you received it too early. It recognized you and started to release its power, but had nothing to feed it into. If it hadn't been removed, it would have destroyed you."

"I don't remember any of this," said Luke, looking bemused.

"It doesn't matter. You knew how to use it when you got it at the *right* time," said Ferragamo.

"Thanks to Jani," added Luke.

"And Muscles," Julia said quietly, speaking for the first time in a while.

Why, thank you, sweet lady. One tries to do one's best.

"Yes," Ferragamo continued. "The moonberry provided the final spark—and at the same time destroyed the last vestiges of Alzedo's magic in Julia, and the evil influence that Luke had inherited with the pendant. You don't need those anymore, by the way," he added, indicating the necklaces.

"The chains are unbreakable," said Julia.

"Try it," replied the wizard.

Julia did so and her chain broke easily, several links shattering simultaneously. Luke's proved similarly fragile.

"The network is destroyed—and with it the metal's strength," explained Ferragamo.

Julia tensed suddenly, looking serious.

"Do some magic," she said.

"What?" asked the startled wizard. "Why? I don't honestly think I'm capable of very much at the moment."

"Please! Something small. Anything."

"Let me do it," said Luke.

"No. It has to be Ferragamo."

Koria handed the wizard a taper.

"How about this?" she asked.

Julia nodded, and, though still mystified, Ferragamo used a portion of what little power he had regained to bring a flame to life. Julia watched intently as he did so, her body taut. When the taper had been burning for a few moments, she smiled and relaxed, glancing quickly at Luke.

"All right?" she asked.

"Of course," the prince replied, a puzzled expression on his face.

"It's gone," said Julia happily. "It's really gone!"

Surprisingly, it was Durc, usually somewhat at sea when it came to magical matters, who first realized what she meant.

"Magic used to hurt you, didn't it?" he said. "At Roget's—"

"No wonder you were so ill!" explained Ferragamo. "You were having to fight your infant battle all over again. Your upbringing, and life on Strock, had held it at bay, but the journey through the fog reawoke Alzedo's influence. You had to take that drastic and painful step with the moonberry to silence it for good. Until then, magic only intensified the battle going on within you."

That made perfect sense to Julia but not to several of the others, and Ferragamo was forced to explain at greater length. Julia was the recipient of several sympathetic looks, but was far too happy to notice.

"One thing I don't understand," remarked Durc, some time later, "is how Julia managed to get into the tower from her room without anyone noticing."

"I don't know," said Julia. "When I woke up, I was already in the tree-yard."

"I can tell you that," Mark said unexpectedly. "Longfur had heard Muscles calling for help. He found him, and guided them through the secret passage from the royal apartments to the tower. We used it to escape the other way, a long time ago."

Fontaine shivered as she recalled that dreadful day, and Mark put his arm about her shoulders, pulling her close.

"You can't keep those cats out of anything, can you?" remarked Durc.

Luke and Julia burst out laughing.

"What did I say?" asked Durc.

"It's not what *you* said," replied Julia. "It's what *Muscles* said."

"I don't think we'd better repeat it," Luke added.

While the previous evening's victory was being discussed in Ferragamo's bedroom, his fellow wizards still lay asleep in their adjacent rooms. It was not until much later that Moroski roused himself and went to check on his friend.

"The swarm tells me that the sun is up," said Cai. "They feel I should be up and making honey."

"You're not that sweet," said Moroski, laughing.

"Perhaps not, but picking flowers is about all I feel capable of," Cai replied pathetically. "And then only if they're in a bedside vase."

"You're obviously in need of a competent nurse," said a voice from the doorway. The wizards looked around as Adesina entered. "Might I fit the bill?"

"My lady," replied Cai, "merely the sight of you would enable the lame to walk, the deaf to hear—"

"Really? Then you won't be needing any of this rather special potion," said Adesina, producing a bottle and two glasses from behind her back.

"Well, now you come to mention it . . .", said Cai.

"So much for your outrageous flattery." The queen of Heald smiled.

"I meant every word—on my honor," responded the younger wizard, as he peered at the bottle. "But I *am* very thirsty. What's in it?"

"Don't ask," said Moroski. "Just drink it. You'll be a new man by noon."

"I doubt it," said Adesina. "That was an hour ago."

She poured, and as the wizards drank, a warm glow began to spread through their bodies.

Cai closed his eyes contentedly. "You wouldn't be trying to get me drunk, would you? Because if not, why not?"

Both wizards soon felt much revived, and gave Adesina their version of the confrontation in the tree-yard. The queen had only received secondhand reports until then, but her agile mind soon made sense of the various elements of the story. Cai even found her explaining things to him, and his admiration for the elegant woman rose even higher. *No wonder Moroski thinks the world of her,* he thought.

"Pabalan and Ansar have been very quiet all morning," Adesina said. "Which is not surprising, I suppose. Their skills were completely useless last night and they know it. It's hard for them to take."

"It could have worked out differently," said Cai.

"I'm glad it didn't," she replied. "I've seen enough blood-shed. Besides, sending them off to the battlements got them out of the way. There's no telling what they would have tried to do if they'd been with you." Adesina smiled. "I'd better get back. I'll leave you two invalids the bottle."

"Thank you," said Cai gratefully, as she went out. After a moment he added, "She is a quite remarkable lady. I wonder sometimes if Pabalan realizes just how remarkable. They are an odd couple in some ways."

"Yes," agreed Moroski, still looking at the now empty doorway. "Quite remarkable."

There was a wistfulness in the older wizard's voice that touched Cai's heart and, for once, he felt no desire to make a ribald comment.

The others had gone their various ways, leaving Mark and Ferragamo alone together. They sat in silence for a while, at ease in each other's company for the first time in years. Both felt as if a great burden had been lifted from their shoulders, and they knew that, even though they could never return to the relationship of Mark's youth, they would not be so at odds again. Their reconciliation was complete.

"How are you feeling?" Mark asked eventually.

"Tired, but content," the wizard replied.

"We were both wrong this time," said the king.

"It *can* happen."

"You understand though?"

"I do, but as Julia's going to be your daughter-in-law—and sooner rather than later if I'm any judge—you had better put it behind you."

Mark thought about this for a while, then looked at Ferragamo with a startled expression.

"Stars!" he exclaimed. "If they have children, please don't ever let me be like Pabalan was with Luke."

"I won't be able to stop you," said Ferragamo laughing. "You'll be just the same."

Pabalan was at that time playing with his youngest grand-child. However, because Gemma's parents were also in the room, he was observing a certain measure of decorum. Besides, as he reminded himself, he was getting a bit old for being a horse.

"We should think of returning, Father," said Ansar.

"We are," the king replied shortly.

"Riders have gone out . . ."

"I know. As soon as we get news from Grayrock we'll leave. All we have so far is *visions*. I'm not entrusting the safety of what people I have left to *visions*. I want the evidence of a trustworthy witness."

Gemma looked at the king with wide, innocent eyes.

"Will the fog come back, Grandad?" she asked.

"No, my sparrow," Pabalan replied in far gentler tones. "I don't think so. But it's best to be sure."

"I didn't like the fog."

"Neither did I, Gemma. Neither did I."

Later that afternoon a messenger arrived from Grayrock with the news that the fog had cleared rapidly, leaving the port and disappearing from the sea for as far as could be observed. The town did not seem to have suffered greatly and most of the shipping was undamaged, though the effects of the sudden cold had caused some problems.

"Right," said Pabalan. "We leave first thing in the morning."

As was traditional before a large-scale departure from the court, a communal meal was held in the great dining hall of Starhill Castle, and as many of the visitors from Heald as possible sat down to breakfast with their hosts. It was a noisy, bustling scene, with servants coming and going, and last-minute arrangements for the journey being hurriedly made.

At the round table, conversation had gone back and forth, but it was Fontaine who voiced a question that was preying on many minds.

"How often is this going to happen?" she wondered aloud. "Is every generation going to have to face this evil?"

"No," Ferragamo answered. "We *have* to find a way of stopping it for good. Otherwise Alzedo will rebuild his power and try again. And he gets stronger each time—as we've seen."

"Now that the other islands have suffered from Brogar's

evil," Moroski added, "we should be able to count on their cooperation."

"I hope you're right," said Ferragamo.

"We don't know yet how badly they've been affected," said Pabalan. "There may not be anyone left to cooperate with."

"I'm sure that's not true," Luke said.

"In any case," Mark said decisively, "we'll send ships and envoys to find out just what the situation is elsewhere."

Shill, who had been called away a little earlier, now returned to the hall, looking grave.

"This has been found," he said, handing a letter to Mark. The king read it and passed it without a word to Ferragamo. Mark looked at Shill.

"How long have they been gone?"

"Since nightfall. Shall we go after them?"

Mark glanced at Ferragamo, who shook his head slowly.

"No," Mark said. "Let them be."

Shill nodded and left.

"What is it?" asked Fontaine.

"Richard killed Kubiac," Mark replied, "and has fled, with Sophi and Alena. They'll be at sea by now."

"Richard?" Fontaine was stunned by the news. "But why?"

"He says he can't explain."

"I don't believe it."

"I'm not sure I do either," said Ferragamo. "Something about this letter isn't right, but I don't suppose we'll ever know the whole truth now."

"But he *has* gone?" Julia asked nervously.

"Yes," replied Mark. "He's gone."

Far away, out of sight of any land, Richard stood at the rail of the trading ship—one of the first that had been persuaded to leave Ark—and cursed his fate. He cursed the object in his hands, Sophi for not telling him about it sooner, Alena for being so influenced by it, and most of all he cursed Alzedo, its evil creator.

With all his strength he hurled the pouch containing the vile sphere overboard, and watched as it sank quickly beneath the blue-black water. With it went his hatred, and he slowly turned back to face his wife and child, whom he loved more than anything, and began to think, for the first time, about the new life ahead of them.

As the Healdean party prepared for departure, the scenes in and around Starhill Castle were chaotic, but progress was made eventually, and all that remained was to say their goodbyes. Unsurprisingly, given the size of the party, this also took some considerable time, but at last everything was ready and the horses and wagons left, amid a final volley of farewells.

The castle seemed incredibly quiet after the mass departure, but Mark was soon busy putting other schemes into operation. With Ferragamo's help he began organizing deputations to all the other islands to find out their positions, and requesting help for the battle to come. With that done, his thoughts turned to happier concerns. He called Luke and Julia to his study and, with Fontaine and Durc also present, discussions were held on the arrangements for their forthcoming marriage.

After the tiresome details of guest lists and catering had been discussed, Muscles decided that he felt bored, and thought it time to liven things up.

You'd better have this wedding soon, he remarked to Luke and Julia.

Why? Luke asked.

Because if the way you two look at each other is anything to go by, you'll be breaking His Majesty's record for producing an heir well ahead of time!

Fontaine, puzzled by Julia's sudden and fiery blush, asked, "Why, Julia! Whatever's the matter?"

Luke answered for his betrothed, who found herself quite unable to reply.

"Oh, it's nothing. Just Muscles being rude."

ME, rude! An indignant voice sounded in the prince's head.

When Luke realized that his parents and Durc were still waiting for an explanation, he sighed and went on.

"Well, actually, he was just making a silly comment about . . . the fact that I . . . was born, um, quite soon after you were married. Don't look like that, Father. He said it, not me!"

Mark *did* look rather taken aback, and glanced quickly at

Fontaine to see how his wife had taken it. She was grinning broadly. The king realized from his long years of friendship with Longfur that the cats were quite capable of saying exactly what they wanted, when they wanted.

So he said, with as good a grace as possible, "There *were* rather special circumstances at that time, you know," and managed to sound only very slightly pompous.

Muscles and Longfur exchanged a tolerant glance. As usual, the younger cat had the last word.

That's what they all say!

From the sea, peril.
From the sea, safety.

From the twain, one.
From the one, release.

Silver spiral, black as night,
Turning ever, ever still.
Circle's center at its edge,
Serpent's head upon its tail.

Evil's heir in chains set free
Shall chain the sun to break the link.
From ages past, the golden coil
Shall bring to life the quiet star.
Loving faith shall be the test
To stand within the whirlpool's eye.

Epilogue

*S*ome six months after her first visit to Strock, the *Fontaine* glided once more into the harbor of Old Walls. Aboard, as well as Durc and his crew, were Luke and Julia, now man and wife. They were both eager to see Strock, if for different reasons, and had waited impatiently for spring before they could sail so far north.

The crew had been less enthusiastic about the proposed journey, recalling their experiences from the earlier voyage. However, Durc had convinced them that Julia had in fact been a good-luck charm then, helping them get through the fog, and soon the only misgivings voiced were along the lines of "We've never had a honeymoon couple on board. Hope they can cope with the sway!" or "Is this what they call a royal charter then?"

The third passenger had been welcomed immediately, as no ship's crew is complete without a cat. Muscles had taken to life aboard like a fish to water—or a cat to fish—unlike Luke, who shared his father's propensity for being seasick at the slightest provocation, a fact which caused the crew considerable amusement, and not a little embarrassment to the prince. Thus he was especially glad when the tiny island came into view and the *Fontaine* at last sailed into calmer waters.

Julia knew immediately that something was wrong. The Old Walls she had known had always been extremely dilapidated, but it now appeared more rundown than ever—and very, very still. No one emerged to greet them, no dog barked, no smoke rose from any chimneys.

Julia's unease intensified as they drew close to the jetty and she saw Blackwood's small boat half-filled with water, its tackle left in a sodden tangle. By now Luke and the crew were also affected by the hushed atmosphere.

"It's very quiet," said Durc softly, as the sailors secured the mooring lines.

"Something's happened," Julia said and, without further comment, jumped ashore and ran into the village. Luke went with her, his heart sinking. All about them, the buildings were in ruins. The year's early plant growth was already staking its claim, unchallenged. They came to the largest building in the village and Julia flung open a door and stepped inside. Luke followed more slowly and found his love standing in a damp and dusty chamber. Cobwebs festooned the room, and there were mouse-droppings on the floor.

"This was Mosi's kitchen," Julia whispered.

In a state of shocked disbelief, Julia frantically searched the house from top to bottom. Everywhere was the same, and Luke found it hard to believe that anyone had lived there in recent years. Old Walls was cold and desolate, and yet Luke felt that it was at peace. True, it was the peace of a wild place, one untouched by humanity, but it was none the less profound for that; it felt fulfilled, complete. Julia was clearly unable to accept the fact that her old home was deserted, so he said nothing of this to her. Even when Durc reported that his men had searched the whole village, and found it empty, she refused to give up hope and set off for the farmhouse. There the story was the same, as Luke knew it would be. Even the chickens that used to scratch about in the yard had gone.

The certainty of Strock's abandonment finally registered, and Julia began to cry softly.

"They can't have just disappeared," she said piteously.

Luke took her in his arms.

"Don't you feel it?" he asked gently. "Everything on the island is saying 'We've finished. We've done what we were put here to do.' That's why there's nobody here."

"Islands don't just stop," Julia said, looking at him with tear-filled eyes.

Luke shrugged. "Don't you feel it?" he repeated. "Strock is at peace."

Julia considered. "It is very calm," she admitted, "but for it just to end so suddenly doesn't make sense. Where can they have all gone?"

"Who knows?"

"Oh, Luke, it's so sad."

"For us," replied Luke. "Not for them."

They were silent for a while, listening to the wind and the distant sea.

"Do you really believe that?" Julia asked eventually.

"Yes."

"Then I'm glad for them," she said bravely.

"It's all part of the bigger play," Luke said. "Strock has performed its role and now it's time to rest. There's no point in staying on the stage when your lines are done."

Julia nodded slowly. "Mireldi said something like that once," she said, recalling the past. "He said, 'Before you came I often wondered why we were still alive.'"

Her voice trailed away into silence, her face revealing the shock her memories had aroused. More of Mireldi's words came back to her, unbidden. *If it weren't for you, this island would be the home of ghosts by now. We would all have left—one way or another.*

"You see now?" Luke asked tenderly.

"All for me?"

"You have a leading role in the play," he replied. "And it isn't over yet."

They spent the rest of the day walking over the island, while Julia showed Luke all her favorite haunts; the beaches, the tower, the cliffs.

"The cliffs have started to weaken here," said Luke. "Don't go too close to the edge."

"Some of it's fallen already," she replied. "This winter's storms must have been really bad. It's wearing away much faster than usual."

Luke was particularly interested in the barrow and the spiral earthwork leading to it.

"How odd," he remarked. "The spiral here runs the opposite way to the fog. I wonder if that's significant."

"Who knows?" she replied and they smiled at each other,

knowing that the ancient warrior buried there was now truly at rest.

Returning to Old Walls, their path took them past the spot where the two Belas were buried. Julia noted, without surprise, that there were no new graves beside them. As they paused, both knew, without needing to ask, that the other was recalling the lines from the prophecy:

From the twain, one.
From the one, release.

They sailed again at dusk; not wishing to spend a night on the quiet island. The water in the well at Old Walls had proved to be still fresh and they had sufficient supplies on board for the journey back to Ark.

As the *Fontaine* pulled out of the harbor, Luke and Julia stood at the stern rail watching the village fade into the distance for the last time. In the gathering gloom something white flashed among the broken rooftops and Julia's heart leapt.

"Look!" she exclaimed, pointing. "It's Kirt. It is. I know it is!"

Luke said nothing, squinting in the dim light. In the distance a lopsided seagull cocked its head and watched them go.

The ship sailed on, leaving the bird as the sole guardian of a remote and silent isle.

Announcing Volume Three in

The Servants of Ark Trilogy
by Jonathan Wylie

☐ **THE MAGE-BORN CHILD**
(27270-5 * $3.95)

For two generations, the evil wizard Alzedo has waited to unleash his full power upon the kingdom of Ark. Now he rises to enslave the people with one last paralyzing blow. But the Servants are prepared and Yve comes forward to face him as the prophecy foretold years before.

Don't miss the first two volumes in this exciting saga:

☐ **THE FIRST NAMED** (26953-4 * $3.95/$4.95 in Canada) The powerful wizardess Amarino has usurped the throne of Ark, killing the king and sending his three sons into hiding. An ancient prophecy foretells her defeat by only one prince . . . in a battle that only a true Servant of Ark could win.

☐ **THE CENTER OF THE CIRCLE** (27056-7 * $3.95/$4.95 in Canada) A generation after the first confrontation with the ancient evil seeking dominion over Ark, Prince Luke must face his father's old enemy.

Buy **THE FIRST NAMED, THE CENTER OF THE CIRCLE** and **THE MAGE-BORN CHILD** on sale wherever Bantam Spectra books are sold, or use the handy coupon below for ordering:

Bantam Books, Dept. SF77, 414 East Golf Road, Des Plaines, IL 60016

Please send me the books I have checked above. I am enclosing $_____ (please add $1.50 to cover postage and handling; send check or money order—no cash or C.O.D.s please).

Mr/Ms _____

Address _____

City/State _____ Zip _____

SF77—3/88

Please allow four to six weeks for delivery. This offer expires 9/88. Prices and availability subject to change without notice.